BRUTAL DEFENDER

MAFIA WARS - BOOK EIGHT

MAGGIE COLE

PULSE PRESS

This book is fiction. Any references to historical events, real people, or real places are used fictitiously. All names, characters, plots, and events are products of the author's imagination. Any resemblance to actual events or places or persons, living or dead, is entirely coincidental.

PROLOGUE

Killian O'Malley

Regret is something I try not to let into my life. It can swallow you whole and destroy you, inch by inch, until everything in your future looks dark. I learned that when my father died. It cursed me when Liam went to prison for avenging his killer. When my brother, Sean, got murdered, it almost destroyed me.

At some point, I had to remember I'm a fighter. I take knocks and then I hit back harder. There was nothing I could do about my father or Liam. Circumstances already set their fate in stone. But Sean's death was different. I could wallow in my grief and guilt over not finding out what Sean was involved in or use it to destroy the parties who ended his life. I chose the latter.

Moving forward, I told myself I'd never again regret anything I did. I would make my decisions and live with the consequences. My father always said, "Real men don't make excuses. They step up to the plate."

The problem with my thinking is I never considered my actions would harm one of my brothers. When my brothers, Liam, and I went to rescue Gemma, I'm the one who drove away from Nolan. I also left the house before he did, instead of waiting for him to carry Gemma outside. If I had made a different decision, maybe Nolan wouldn't have been arrested and booked for a double homicide.

So when Tully said all three of us—Declan, Nolan, and I—were on the hook for him solving Nolan's issue, it didn't make sense to me. I spoke my mind and didn't flinch or care when he said I would be the only one to owe him. Neither of my brothers were happy with my decision. They both tried to step in and shift the debt to themselves. But I wasn't going to let that happen. It's one favor then it's over. I'm not about to lose any sleep over it. A deal is a deal.

But Tully's power trip is getting old. It's Nolan's wedding, and I intentionally didn't bring a date. I learned a few years ago there are plenty of hot, horny, starry-eyed lasses who go to weddings looking for a good time to try and forget they aren't the bride. And right now, I'm bored with the women I casually date. I'm ready for some new excitement in my life, even if it's just for the night.

All was good until Tully walked in. And now this argument taking place between him and the O'Malleys is wasting my time. It's one little thing. I do it. It's over. I move on with my life. Nolan stays out of prison. Tully goes back to New York, and everyone is happy.

I toss back more whiskey. I'm ready to party at my brother's wedding, get laid, and move forward. Of course, none of that can happen with Tully around. He starts talking about his alliance with Angelo Marino. Then he brings up Angelo's daughter, Arianna. She got involved in some circles her father isn't happy about, and he wants me to get her out of them.

I roll my eyes. A mafia brat who wants to piss off daddy. Fine. I'll tame her rebel ass. I grumble, "So I have to babysit this woman or something?"

Tully shakes his head. In a stern voice, he states, "No. You're going to marry her."

My brothers, Finn, and Liam go quiet, exchanging shocked glances. I finish my whiskey. "That's funny. Now, what's the job, Tully?" I put my hand on his shoulder and point at a brunette who's been giving me fuck-me-eyes all night. "And stop with the games. You're interrupting my time with that woman."

He sniffs hard. His voice turns hard as nails. "This isn't a game. You will marry her. Next Saturday."

I still think he's screwing with me, but Declan scowls. "What kind of fucked-up arrangement is this? Have one of your sons marry her. Killian isn't—"

"He's joking. Calm down," I state.

Tully's face hardens. "Do you see me smiling?"

My gut suddenly sinks. He's serious. He wants me to marry this mafia princess who made friends with people to make some point to her daddy.

"Absolutely not," I tell him.

"I've promised Angelo, and I don't go back on my word," Tully states.

"You've got four unmarried sons," Nolan points out.

Tully puts his crystal tumbler on the bar. "They live in New York. Angelo wants Arianna as far away as possible."

I motion to the bartender that I need another drink. I fume, "Then send her to Italy. I'm not marrying her. Plus, did you forget I'm an O'Malley? We're Irish. We don't marry Italian brats."

"This is an alliance—"

"Your alliance, not ours," Finn seethes.

Tully tosses back the rest of his whiskey. He slams the glass on the wooden bar and steps closer to me, so we're face-to-face. His sweet, hot breath merges into mine, and his nostrils flare. "The wedding is next Saturday. You show up, and our deal stays intact. You skip out, and it won't only be Nolan who goes down."

"You better watch who you're threatening," Liam snarls.

"This isn't a job, it's a life sentence. Find someone else," Nolan hisses.

Tully spins. "The only one who will be serving a life sentence is you." He steps out of our circle. "Congratulations. Enjoy your bride while you still can." He slaps a wedding envelope with Mr. and Mrs. Nolan O'Malley on the bar then leaves.

The five of us watch him walk away. Upbeat music blares in the other room. I'd normally be dancing right now. Or shagging some girl in a dark corner. Or stepping outside to smoke a joint. Nothing about Tully's demands makes me feel like doing any of that, especially when Gemma walks up to us.

She puts her hand on Nolan's bicep and nervously asks, "Is everything okay?"

Nolan tugs her into him and attempts to cover up his fear, but everyone can see it. Tully doesn't make idle threats. The power he holds can destroy a person in a matter of seconds. He's a heavyweight in the ring with a featherweight. It's an unequal match where everyone knows the winner before the bell rings. If he's on your side, you're safe. If he's not, you're going to be knocked down and not able to get back up.

Nolan kisses the top of Gemma's head. I turn away. I can't look at my sister-in-law in her wedding dress and my brother in his tux and not allow them to have the future they deserve. There is no choice. It's a done deal. What Tully wants, he'll get.

I shout to the bartender, "Six shots of whiskey. Make mine a double."

The bartender sets down the glasses. I toss mine back and pull out my phone. I open my social media and type Arianna Marino in the search bar.

"Gemma, can you give us a few more minutes?" Nolan asks.

"Umm...okay."

"Thanks. I'll meet you for the next dance."

Gemma leaves, and my brothers, Liam, and Finn hover around me.

"Tell me you aren't considering this?" Declan says.

I scowl. "Would you prefer I destroy Nolan's life?"

"We'll figure something else out," Nolan states.

"What?" I ask.

He clenches his jaw.

I glance at the four of them. "Anyone have any ideas how to get Nolan or me out of this?"

Declan grabs the phone. "Let me see her. I'll do it."

I grunt. "Yeah, not having that over my head, either." I snag the cell back and hit the search button. The first account that pops up has over a million followers. I tap on it and am pleasantly surprised.

"At least she's hot," Declan offers.

"Not bad," I mumble, but she could be an Italian runway model. She has golden skin, big brown eyes under long lashes, and high cheekbones women would pay money to attempt to attain. Her pouty lips make me think dirty thoughts. She's not a stick. She's got curves in all the right places and long, shiny black hair.

If I saw her on the street, I'd follow her, strike up a conversation, and ask her out. I've always loved Mediterranean women, but I've never gotten serious about any of them. They're fun for a while, but I'm an O'Malley, meant to keep our Irish bloodline pure.

I hit her video footage, which disappears after twenty-four hours, and my blood starts to boil. She posted it within the last hour. In one slide, she's making out with some thug. In the next, she's dancing on a table while the bastard unbuttons her blouse. She's got a bottle of Cristal in her hand and she takes a long drink.

"Looks like you're going to have your hands full with that one," Declan mutters.

"Shut up," I bark. I grab another shot of whiskey, then walk off to the bathroom. I hit the follow button on the phone.

She immediately follows me back.

My pulse is still racing, and I debate about sending her a message, but one pops up.

Arianna: *Stalking me already?*

Me: *Where are you right now?*

Arianna: *None of your business.*

Me: *I think it is.*

Arianna: *In your dreams.*

Me: *I'd call this a nightmare, not a dream, lass. But if you're going to be my wife, you better get your body parts covered and go home to daddy while you still live with him.*

Arianna: *Body parts? Do you even know what to do with yours?*

Me: *I'm sure you'll have a hard time handling my body parts.*

Arianna: *Right. Sorry to inform you, but I'm used to more than a two-inch tadpole.*

I send her one of the many dick pics I've taken and sent to other women. Several minutes pass without her comments.

Me: *Yeah, I thought so. I better not see any more pictures of that thug's hands on you.*

Arianna: *Don't make empty threats.*

Me: *I'm an implementer. Don't ever forget that. Now, keep your clothes on and go home.*

More time passes. I keep staring at the phone, waiting for something. I don't get a message, but a notification pops up she posted another video.

I click on it, and every angry cell in my body lights on fire. She's on stage, dancing on a pole, and tears her shirt off. The thug who had his hands on her earlier gropes her.

The username for his account pops up. Donato Brambilla. I open up his page. Everything on it screams bad news.

He sends me a message.

Donato: *I had her first. And I'm going to have her tonight.*

My mouth turns dry. I stare at my reflection in the mirror, suddenly wanting to kill someone I've never heard of or met before this moment.

All night, I try to get her out of my mind and focus on my last few nights of freedom, but my blood never stops boiling.

1

Arianna Marino

Several Hours Earlier

My papà's lecture is getting old. It's the same as always. His voice booms, "Arianna, you're out of control. I've told you to stay away from that Brambilla goon. You've done nothing but defy me."

I roll my eyes. I remind him, "I'm almost thirty, Papà. You can't rule my every move."

His dark eyes turn to slits. In a steady, cold tone, he declares, "I won't have you put yourself or this family at risk anymore. I love you, Arianna, and I'll miss you, but your actions leave me no choice."

Men of all shapes and sizes do everything my papà says. I grew up seeing the fear in their eyes. While he tells me nothing about his business, I'm not naive. He's the head of the most prominent Italian crime family in New York. But to me, he's my papà. And I'm not a little girl anymore. I don't have a problem sticking up for myself. Plus, I'm sick of him and my brothers always telling me what I can and can't do. I get no access to any part of the family business, yet my brothers do. My papà won't let me work, insists I stay under his roof guarded until I marry, and tries to control every aspect of my life.

I'm over this song and dance. He's threatened me too many times. I defiantly fume, "You'll miss me? What are you going to do? Lock me up downstairs with your enemies?"

My papà's cheeks turn red with anger. It's something I shouldn't know about but do. Our house has a secret door leading to an underground dungeon. Years ago, I saw my brother, Massimo, open it. He didn't know I was watching, and after a few minutes, I followed him. Men screaming and the smell of decay filled the air. Rats ran everywhere. When my brother turned and saw me, he took me directly to my papà who lectured me on staying away from his business.

Papà rises and goes to the bar in the corner of the room. He pours a glass of scotch then stares out the window into the backyard of his estate. Snow covers the ground, and ice wraps around tree limbs. He takes several sips and lowers his voice. "You're moving to Chicago."

I sarcastically laugh. New York is my home. Papà may have us living in the suburbs, but I love everything about the city and go there almost every day. If it weren't for my papà insisting I stay in his home until I marry, I'd get an apartment in Manhattan. I explode, "When Hell freezes over."

He spins. The expression on his face sends a chill down my spine. It's a look I rarely see. When it appears on his face, he'll do anything to get his way. He's as stubborn as I am. "I've given you lots of options of men to marry. These were good men who would keep you safe and allow you to have Italian babies. You didn't want any of them. Now, they have all found other wives. And instead of choosing them, you run to that Brambilla thug."

"He's not a thug!" I rant. Sure, Donato has a dangerous vibe, but so does every man I've ever grown up around, including my brothers and Papà.

Papà slams his hand on the desk. "You don't know anything about what he's involved in."

"Then why don't you tell me?"

He throws his hands in the air. "I don't need to tell you. I am your papà. My word should be enough."

I shake my head. "I'm so tired of being kept in the dark about everything involving this family. I'm a grown woman. Why can't you treat me as one?"

He studies me and takes a deep breath, then another sip of scotch. "I won't have you destroy your life, Arianna. You've left me no choice. A week from today, you will marry. Your husband-to-be lives in Chicago. Tully assures me he is capable of keeping you safe."

"Tully? What does he have to do with this?" Papà's always had a friendship with the head of the Irish crime family, but lately, they've spent a lot more time together.

He sighs and sits on the couch next to me. He picks up my hand. "If you do not go to Chicago, I'll send you to Italy. Giuseppe Berlusconi's wife passed. He has also agreed to marry you."

The thought of Giuseppe even touching me makes my stomach pitch. Nothing about him is attractive. Years of eating way too much pasta and not taking care of himself is undoubtedly a one-way ticket to a stroke. Every time I've seen him, he's sweating and wiping his face with a handkerchief. Garlic oozes out of his pores, flaring in my nostrils until I feel like I can't breathe. He's also the head of the mafia in Italy and has more security than my papà's house. I'm sure I'd be a prisoner there. I roar, "He's fifty-something with six children! I don't even speak Italian!"

"It's not what I want for you, but it's better than you falling into the hands of a Brambilla," he states.

"You can't make me—"

"Choose, Arianna! It's Killian O'Malley in Chicago or Giuseppe Berlusconi in Italy."

"O'Malley! You want me to marry an Irishman?"

He sets his drink on the table. He puts his hands on my cheeks. "You are almost thirty. It is time you marry. None of the options I presented to you were acceptable in your eyes. There will be no more debate. Come Saturday, you will marry one of them. If you do not choose, I'll pick for you."

Tears well in my eyes. "Mamma would never agree to this."

Grief fills his face. "I have not done a good job. If she were still alive, she would have convinced you to marry by now."

My voice shakes as I reiterate, "She wouldn't have cared."

His thumbs stroke my cheekbones. "You do not know her the way I did. She would never have allowed you to touch a Brambilla or get into any situation where you were even in the same room as one. You would have listened to her when she tried to talk sense into you."

My insides quiver. "Stop talking about Donato without giving me anything to back up your accusations!"

His eyes harden. "I told you he's bad news, Arianna. There is nothing else you need to know. Now, tell me who it will be. Killian or Giuseppe?"

I gape at him, not believing he's giving me an ultimatum.

"You can't force me to marry either," I insist, but it comes out weak.

The calmness in his voice freaks me out further. It's one he uses when he's made a final decision. "You'll marry Giuseppe, then."

"What? No!"

He rises. "It's farther from here. I won't be able to see you as often, but you'll be with our people."

I jump up and grab his arm. "No. Please don't make me leave the States."

"You don't want the Irishman or Chicago. Giuseppe will take—"

"I'll marry Killian. Please. Don't send me to Italy!" I beg.

Papà freezes and arches his eyebrows. "If I agree not to send you to Italy, I don't want to hear another word regarding this situation. You'll spend the next week getting ready for the wedding. Saturday, you'll marry Killian. You won't do anything to embarrass me during the wedding events. You'll be the perfect bride and not dishonor your new husband in any way."

Tears fall down my cheeks. My lips tremble, and I focus on the floor, not believing this is happening.

Papà raises my chin. "Do not test me on this, Arianna. If you do anything to stop the marriage to Killian, I'll put you on the first plane to Italy and have the priest waiting on the runway."

I've always known my papà's a cruel man. We've gone head-to-head about all sorts of things, yet he's never displayed his cruelty toward me. I didn't think he could until now.

Silence fills the air. My papà finally breaks it. "I'm glad you'll be in Chicago. Your brothers and I can visit more frequently. And I believe Killian is a better match for you. He's closer in age and doesn't have kids. You can have a family and all the things a beautiful woman like you should have."

It's not fair. My brothers can roam all over New York, screwing whomever they please, and doing whatever they want. They're older than me and not married. Yet, I get these terms I have to live with for the rest of my life.

"I'll tell Tully to inform Killian you have chosen him. Go get ready for the party tonight," he orders.

My stomach churns. *I've chosen him? Is that what I just did?*

I say nothing and leave the room. I go upstairs toward my bedroom and run into my brother, Tristano.

Concern fills his face. He asks, "Arianna, what's wrong?"

He's the closest in age to me even though he's thirty-five and I'm only twenty-eight. My parents married young. My twin brothers, Dante and Gianni, are forty-two. Massimo is thirty-nine. I was the surprise child. Since my brothers haven't married yet and my father's house is more like a compound, they still live here. Each of them has a separate wing, except Tristano. He and I share one.

I wipe my cheeks. "I'm getting married next Saturday and moving to Chicago."

His eyes widen. He cautiously asks, "To whom?"

"Some man named Killian O'Malley."

"An Irishman?" he questions in shock.

"According to Papà, it's him or Giuseppe Berlusconi."

My brother cringes. "Oh, gross."

"Well, I don't even know what this Killian looks like, or anything about him, so it could be just as bad," I admit.

"Let's look him up." My brother pulls out his phone, and I put my hand on his arm.

"Please. Talk to Papà. Convince him not to make me do this," I plead.

My brother's face falls and he sighs. "Arianna, you've pushed him too far. He told you to stay away from that Brambilla thug."

Anger crashes through every bone in my body. "Stop calling him a thug!"

"He is," my brother seethes.

"Why? Tell me what he's done that's so horrible."

Tristano licks his lips and looks above my head.

"You're all a bunch of hypocrites," I accuse.

His eyes shoot daggers at me. "Don't ever insult us for protecting you. Our business is not something we would ever want you involved in. That includes all the gruesome things we know about, so don't you dare choose that thug over our word."

I angrily point at him. "There it is. The *you have a dick and I don't* philosophy. I'm so tired of it. Just tell me the truth for once. I can handle it."

He crosses his arms. "This is your problem, Arianna. You don't know when to be grateful for all you have and trust the people who love you the most."

"So you aren't going to talk to Papà for me?"

He closes his eyes briefly. "I already have. All four of us tried to find another option for you. He isn't going to budge. I didn't know who he decided to choose for you. I don't know anything about this Killian O'Malley, but if Papà believes it's best for you, then it is."

Anger, fear, and betrayal fill my soul. This is my family, the ones who claim to love me the most, yet they don't allow me to choose who to spend the rest of my life with or love.

I'm not sure if I love Donato. I have deep feelings for him, but I'm not sure if it's love. I've never met a man I fell head over heels for and could see spending forever with, but at times, I think I could with Donato. Several of my boyfriends proposed to me. I turned all of them down, to the dismay of my father. Donato is fun, good-looking, and owns several businesses. While he has a dangerous vibe, he wouldn't ever hurt me. My papà and brothers can't tell me one thing he has done wrong. All it looks like in my eyes is hypocrisy. I don't know much about my father's business, but I know he runs all sorts of illegal operations. He keeps enemies tied up under our house. So what has Donato done that is worse than what my papà or brothers have?

I shove past Tristano. "Thanks for nothing."

"Arianna!"

I ignore him and slam my bedroom door then throw myself face-first onto the bed. For over an hour, I try to figure out how to get out of this without being sent to Italy, but no solutions appear. All I keep seeing is Giuseppe's sweaty, pudgy face. I even smell his garlic odor.

"Ugh," I mutter, then sit up. I pick up my phone and go to my social media. I type in Killian O'Malley. Of course there are tons of them.

Can't even have an original name.

I hit the first account that has hundreds of thousands of followers and says Chicago as the location. I hold my breath and stare at the feed.

I've never attempted to date or even kissed anyone who wasn't Italian. It might as well be a sin in my family for any woman, which makes this entire situation even crazier. It's like my papà lost all his marbles agreeing to let a non-Italian marry me. And I hoped Killian was an improvement over Giuseppe, but holy mother of Mary.

Every inch of him is hard, sculpted flesh, complete with an eight pack and a V. Celtic knot tattoos start under his chin on the left side of his neck and travel down his arm, morphing into other Irish symbols. Four-leaf clovers adorn the left side of his V, trailing into his pants. The initials S and O imprinted over a Celtic cross are inked above his heart. It's the only tattoo on his chest.

Great. I get to stare at another woman's initials for the rest of my life.

While I've never paid much attention to the Irish, I'm suddenly intrigued. His chiseled face is stunning perfection. His green eyes show all sorts of emotions on his page. Sometimes he's broody. At times, he appears to be goofy, like the class clown. Mixed in with all of these are photos of his black eyes, fat lips, and even a broken nose from boxing matches. He has dark hair with a touch of silver and a well-trimmed beard and mustache. His entire feed screams sexy danger with personality. Like my page, he's got tons of comments. Men and women all drool over every photo he has posted, some being more suggestive than others. I wonder how old he is, but assume he might be a decade or so older than me.

My alarm rings and pulls me out of my trance. My papà is having a party tonight. He does it once a month for his closest advisors and their families. In an hour, the house will be full of over a hundred adults and more children running around. One thing my papà loves is kids. He never has an event without them. There's always food they love and entertainment, so they're well-fed and happy. It's one of the things my mamma loved planning. Since she died about ten years ago, I've taken it over.

I turn the alarm off and tear my eyes away from Killian. I get in the shower, thinking about my mamma, and swallow down the grief that never seems to go away. When I get out, a text pops up.

Donato: *We're going to Club D tonight. Can you sneak out? Or do your father and brothers have you on lockdown?*

My pulse increases. It's no secret my family hates Donato. He knows it, claims he doesn't know why but never lets it stop him from pursuing me.

The conversation and threats my papà made swirl in my head.

He said this week and Saturday. He never said anything about tonight.

If this is my last night of freedom, then I'm going to enjoy it.

Me: *I'll see you there.*

I spend time on my hair and makeup then select a black miniskirt and a matching fitted blouse with buttons. I add my jewelry and slide into my thigh-high stiletto boots. The slim credit card holder I use when I go out is in my purse, so I fish it out, then hide it, along with my cell, in my boots.

For two hours, I mingle with the guests, mainly focusing on the kids how I always do. When my papà and brothers are out of sight, I sneak through the house and into my brother, Dante's, wing, then slip out the door. The Uber driver I've gotten to know over the years waits down the street.

When I get to Club D, I go straight to the bouncer and bypass the line. He knows me, kisses me on the cheek, and motions for me to go through. I keep my cell in my boot instead of checking it like I'm supposed to.

Lights flash, and a techno-hip-hop combination pounds into my ears. When I get to the elevator for the VIP suites, the bouncer pecks my cheek.

"Good to see you, Arianna."

"Thanks. Is Donato in his suite?"

"Yep." He pushes the button, and the elevator doors open.

I'm quickly inside the suite. Donato pulls me onto his lap. His dark hair, eyes, and stubble scream everything Italian and what I know. He kisses me, but I don't fall into it like I usually do.

He pulls back. "Arianna, what's wrong?"

I swallow hard and glance out the glass overlooking the packed dance floor. I don't want to tell him, but I have to. "My papà is making me get married next Saturday and move to Chicago."

His eyes turn to slits. "What are you talking about?"

"I-I don't have a choice." A tear slips down my cheek.

"Of course you have a choice. Say no," he orders.

My insides quiver. "If I don't, he'll send me to Italy. I'll have to marry Giuseppe Berlusconi."

"That sweaty, fat, old pig?" he blurts out.

"Yes."

"That's nasty."

I nod. "Which is why I chose the only other option." *There's that word* chose *again, as if I actually wanted this or had a choice.*

"Who is this guy in Chicago?"

I'm unsure why, but my face heats. "I don't know him."

He peers at me closer and demands, "Who is it?"

"A man named Killian O'Malley."

"An Irishman?" Donato snarls.

"Yes. That was my reaction, too. But it has to be better than Giuseppe. At least I won't be in Italy," I state.

He taps on his thigh then says, "Let's elope. We'll go to Vegas tonight."

My insides quiver harder. It's not the first time Donato has said this to me. "My papà and brothers will kill you."

He snorts. "I'm not scared of them."

I may not know what goes on in my father's business, but not a bone in my body doesn't believe they would kill Donato. I shut my eyes, wishing this was a nightmare and I could wake up.

Donato leans closer. "Hey. Have a drink. Let's not worry about this tonight. I'll figure something out before Saturday, okay?"

I open my eyes. "Like what?"

"I don't know, but I'll fix this." He hands me a glass of champagne then kisses me. "Tonight, just relax."

The first glass goes down fast. Donato refills it, and the second one quickly disappears. I only wish I could. Nothing I do makes me escape the ugly conversation I had with my papà earlier. The more the night evolves, the stupider my decisions get.

Club D has a strict rule about no cell phones. I've never broken it, but tonight, I don't think. I pull out my phone, and Donato's buddy Tony takes pictures and videos. I post them on my social media page then have another drink. I go to the restroom and into a stall. I pull out my phone again. The Club D rule isn't something I should take lightly. I'm on good terms with the owner, Derek Derow, and respect him. I don't want to piss him off. I'm not sure if he would kick me out, but I've seen him do it with others.

When I go into my app, a notification pops up.

New follower: Killian O'Malley

My stomach tightens. I follow him back then message him.

Me: *Stalking me already?*

Killian: *Where are you right now?*

Does he think I'm going to just bend over and tell him everything about my life?

Me: *None of your business.*

Killian: *I think it is.*

Asshole.

Me: *In your dreams.*

Killian: *I'd call this a nightmare, not a dream, lass. But if you're going to be my wife, you better get your body parts covered and go home to daddy while you still live with him.*

What a douche bag. He's the one that agreed to marry a woman he's never met before. I doubt either of his parents are pressuring him to marry me. He must be hot but desperate if he agreed to this. Probably a total loser in person, and that's why he isn't married yet.

Me: *Body parts? Do you even know what to do with yours?*

Killian: *I'm sure you'll have a hard time handling my body parts.*

Bet he's all talk and no cock.

Me: *Right. Sorry to inform you, but I'm used to more than a two-inch tadpole.*

A dick pic comes across the screen. I gape at it. *Holy Mother of Mary. Is it even his?*

Yes, it has to be. It's the identical four-leaf clovers on his V I saw on his feed.

Killian: *Yeah, I thought so. I better not see any more pictures of that thug's hands on you.*

Did Papà tell him about Donato?

He had to. Why else would he call him a thug?

Me: *Don't make empty threats.*

Killian: *I'm an implementer. Don't ever forget that. Now keep your clothes on and go home.*

Screw you, Killian O'Malley. I'll show you what I do when someone orders me around.

I leave the restroom, go back into the VIP suite, and down some more alcohol. I give Donato's friend my phone and tell him to video me. Then I step on the stage in the suite and start pole dancing and take off my shirt. I still have my bra on, so who cares. It's more coverage than my swimsuits. Donato gets a bit grabbier than normal, but we're both heavily drinking, so I dismiss it. When I finish, I post the video to my social media and put my blouse back on.

Donato pulls me on his lap so I'm straddling him, and we start making out.

"You have three seconds to get off his lap, or I blow his head off, Arianna!" my brother, Gianni's, voice roars into my ears.

The suite goes quiet, except for the music. I freeze, then glance behind me. My four brothers have their guns pulled. Scowls fill their faces. A chill runs down my spine. It's a contrast to Donato's warm hand stroking my skin under my shirt.

"Why don't you sit down and have a drink," Donato cockily suggests.

Massimo steps forward. "Three. Two."

I jump off Donato's lap and stumble, falling toward Massimo. He catches me and keeps his gun pointed at Donato. "You stay away from my sister. This is your last warning."

I attempt to make my brothers end this hatred I don't understand. "Stop. You're not—"

"We're leaving now," Massimo growls. Dark pools of rage flare in his eyes. I've never seen my brother so angry before.

The alcohol I drank hits me hard, and the room spins. "I think I'm going to get sick." I put my hand over my mouth and swallow hard.

My brothers maneuver me out of the room, into the elevator, and through the club. When I step outside, I throw up all over the sidewalk in front of the line of people.

Shouts fill my ears, and when I finish, tears streak down my face.

Massimo's driver pulls up to the curb. My brother puts me in his car, and my other brothers get in.

"Drink this," Dante orders, handing me a bottle of water.

Tristano picks up a box of tissues and puts them on my lap. "What were you thinking?"

"Give me your phone," Gianni orders.

"Why?"

"Now!" he seethes.

I decide I don't have the energy to fight. I reach into my boot and hand it to him.

"If Papà finds out you left the house, he'll send you to Italy. Is that what you want?" Massimo asks.

"Code," Gianni growls.

"Two-Five-Six-Six-Five-Two," I manage to get out.

"You say you don't want to marry Giuseppe, but you're pushing it, Arianna," Tristano reprimands.

"Shut up. All of you just shut up!" I cry out then start to sob.

Gianni slides my phone back in my boot. In a softer tone, he says, "The evidence is gone. Let's hope Papà didn't see it."

Massimo tugs me into him. "Stop crying. We'll sneak you in the house and say you went to bed."

I wish I could, but I can't. Everything for them is a choice. For me, my only decision is to pick a man who's physically better looking than the other and lives in the United States.

I'm not sure if I'm in love with Donato, but the fact I'll never see him again hurts. And I didn't even get to say goodbye.

2

Killian

A FREIGHT TRAIN SMASHES INTO MY HEAD. LAST NIGHT'S whiskey rots on my breath. A garbage can sits near my bed. Two headache tablets and a full glass of water are on the table.

When I try to sit up, my stomach pitches. I freeze, trying to breathe through it. My tux shirt is still on and my pants are on the floor. I manage to get into a sitting position, take the pills, and get a few mouthfuls of water down.

It takes me a minute to realize I'm in Declan's guest bedroom. The events of the previous night come rolling back to me.

Shit. The last few nights of freedom, and I don't even use it to my advantage.

I can't marry her. I don't even know her.

Nolan's life will be destroyed.

How the hell did I get in this situation?

My mouth. I couldn't shut my mouth.

I stumble to the shower, spend so much time in it the water turns cold, then get out. I throw on a pair of shorts and a T-shirt Declan left on the chair and go out to the kitchen.

"Ah. There you are. Want some breakfast?" Declan asks and flips the bacon.

The smell makes me slightly nauseous. "No, thanks."

"Are you sure you don't mind me taking your driver?" A woman's voice says.

I turn, and my gut drops. It's the woman who was giving me fuck-me eyes all night until Tully told me I was going to marry that mafia brat. After that, I became obsessed with Arianna's social media page and bellied up to the bar.

Declan steps in front of the woman, kisses her on the lips, then cops a feel of her ass. "Not at all. Next time you're in town, give me a call."

"I will. For sure," she chirps.

Declan hands her a brown paper bag and travel mug. "Made you a breakfast sandwich and coffee."

She beams and pats his cheek. "Well, aren't you sweet?"

He winks then walks her to the door and out to the car.

As soon as he comes back, I cross my arms and stare at him.

He smugly licks his lips. "Got something you want to say?"

"You know she wanted me before you."

He grunts. "But she stayed in my bed with me. Guess you shouldn't have cried in your whiskey all night."

"Don't remind me. Who is she anyway?" I grab a seat at the kitchen island.

"One of Gemma's friends who moved to L.A. She's on her way to the airport. She's got two kids and a deadbeat ex, it sounds like. Her mother is watching the children." He sets a plate of food on the counter.

My stomach lurches again. I grumble, "Thanks for the details on your MILF."

He chuckles. "Your face is green. Is it from jealousy or the fifth you drank?"

I groan. "Don't remind me."

"Try to get something in you." He hands me a plate with toast.

I push it away. "No, thanks."

He eats several mouthfuls of food, drinks some coffee, then asks, "Did you look at your account this morning?"

I freeze. "What account?"

He smirks. "The one where the future Mrs. Killian O'Malley was pissing you off all night."

I shut my eyes. *What did I write to her?*

I rise. "Where is my phone?"

Declan shrugs. "My guess is in your suit coat or pants. Check the bedroom."

I leave the room, find my phone in my pants pocket, and go out to the kitchen. "My phone's dead."

He reaches over the counter and hands me the end of the charger.

I plug it in.

"We'll talk to Tully again today. There has to be something else he'll let us do instead of you marrying this girl," Declan states.

I scrub my hands over my face. "Everyone needs to drop it. He's not going to change his mind. You heard him. He made some deal with Angelo. He won't roll over and not deliver."

Declan's voice turns cold. "He's tying us to the Marinos. You know what that means."

I turn in my chair. "At this point, does it even matter?"

"Why would you say that?"

In the last few years, we've created a war between several top crime families in Chicago. We allied with the Ivanovs, and so far, we're all still alive. I tap my fingers on the counter and say, "The Marinos hate the Rossis. So do we. It's more power behind us if we have any new issues. Now that we took a ton of Baileys out, and hit the Petrovs and Zielinskis hard, maybe creating another alliance isn't a bad thing. Perhaps it's to our advantage."

Declan shakes his head. "We're trying to get out of this life. Did you forget why we've been waiting for Jack Christian's company to hit the right stock price?"

Frustration fills me. I sit back in my chair and shake my head. "I've voiced my opinion before, but I'll repeat it. You all are in dreamland. Once we short the stock and make it fall, it isn't going to change the core of who the O'Malleys are."

"We're going to make billions. There will be enough to keep them fed and give them time to adjust to new opportunities."

I grunt. "Get out of la-la land. Too many men in our family aren't going to be able just to switch it over. You don't go from the streets to the boardroom. And what happens when we take our guys out of their territories? It opens it up for the other crime families to take over. I, for one, don't want to see an invasion of new blood in this town."

Declan squints. "What are you saying? You want our clan to stay involved in the drugs and gambling operations Darragh built?"

I sigh. "No. You know I don't. But how do we stop other crime families from coming into Chicago and taking over?"

Declan holds his chin, rubbing his beard. He admits, "I don't know."

"Well, maybe an alliance with the Marinos isn't a bad thing, then," I say, trying to see some good in this crazy arrangement.

"They're in New York."

My phone turns on, and the screen lights up. I tap my security code to unlock it. I confess, "My head hurts too much to think right now."

Declan scoffs. "Since when did you get weak?"

"Shut up." I open my social media app and go directly to my messages with Arianna and reread them. I don't remember much after I told her to put on her clothes and go home to daddy right before her dickhead boyfriend messaged me.

She better not have slept with him.

Of course she did. He was all over her, and she was drunk.

I groan and mutter, "Why didn't someone stop me?"

Declan glances over my shoulder. "What did you write?"

Me: *You better take that video down now.*

She never responded. A half hour later, I sent another message.

Me: *Good. You listen. I hope that means you went home to daddy. I don't want some disease from that thug who's all over you.*

Another message with no response.

Me: *What the hell did you do to piss off your daddy anyway? This seems a bit extreme.*

Still no response.

Me: *Are you ignoring me? Let's set the rules. You don't get to ignore me. If I ask a question, I deserve an answer.*

Arianna: *Are you a complete psycho? Do you have nothing better to do with your night?*

Me: *You better not have banged that goon.*

Arianna: *Jealous?*

Me: *Of him? No. And if he comes anywhere near you next weekend or after, I'll kill him.*

Arianna: *So you ARE a psycho, and you just wrote it so I can report it to the police. Thank you very much!*

Me: *Oh, please. I know what kind of family you're part of. Let's not act like you even like the police.*

She didn't respond, and after five minutes, I wrote a new message.

Me: *You better not be with that dickhead right now.*

Arianna: *Why do you care? You act like I'm going to be sleeping with you.*

Me: *That is what married people do. And I can assure you you'll want to.*

Arianna: *In your dreams. And we'll have an open relationship. You screw who you want, and I'll do the same. And my private life is my business, not yours.*

Me: *Over my dead body. My wife isn't touching anyone else, except me, so get that thought out of your head.*

Arianna: *I wouldn't touch you if it were a choice between sleeping with you or the devil.*

Me: *I am the devil, lass. Whatever he does, I can do it better.*

Arianna: *You know what, I think the guy in Italy my papà wanted me to marry sounds like a better option. You're off the hook.*

Me: *WHAT GUY?*

She didn't respond. After a few minutes, I wrote back.

Me: *I asked a question.*

She never answered.

"Jesus. Since when did you become a needy chaser?" Declan comments.

I turn my phone over and set it on the counter. "I was drunk."

His lips twitch. "You still were chasing her. I thought your motto was to sit back and let them chase you."

"Let's go to the gym. I have an urge to get in the ring and punch the shit out of your face," I grumble.

"I'm not the one who showed all my jealousy cards before I even met a woman."

"No, I didn't. Besides, I was drunk. Anything I said is due to that," I claim, but already know Declan's right, and now Arianna's going to think she's got the upper hand.

"Who's the dude in Italy?" Declan asks.

"How do I know? Did you forget I know absolutely nothing about this woman, except she's a mafia brat?" I state.

Declan arches his eyebrows.

"Why are you staring at me like that?"

"How do you know she's a brat?"

I pick up my phone. I pull up her boyfriend's account. "Of course she is. Her own father wants to send her away because he can't handle her. And look at the douchebag she's with."

Declan studies his feed. "Yep. Total dickhead."

I show him the message he sent me last night.

"You better cut that shit off right away," he advises.

"Wow! Excellent advice," I sarcastically remark. I'm already thinking about how I'll lay down the law. Her communication with that thug is over once she says *I do*. I stand up and take my phone off the charger. "Can you drive me home?"

"Sure."

I gather my tux pieces, slide my feet into the shoes, and get in Declan's SUV. The roads are slippery from the snow, and my driveway has a few inches on it. I make my way into the house then put on a pair of joggers, a T-shirt, and a hoodie. I grab my gym bag and get in my car.

The best thing for me is to get a good workout in. When I get to the gym, a dozen different O'Malley's are training. I go into the locker room, change, then shove my bag inside my locker. I take a quick selfie and post it. I write, *Time to sweat the alcohol out of my system.* #weddingaftermath

By the time I get to the stretching mat, comments are already coming in. Only one notification on the screen interests me.

Arianna Marino: *#ragingjealousalcoholic*

I cringe inside. I'm never going to hear the end of this. I shouldn't respond. Ignoring her is the best thing I can do. But I can't help myself. Instead, I dive right in.

Killian O'Malley: *#takesonetoknowone*

A private message pops up.

Arianna: *Do you have an alcohol problem I should know about?*

Me: *Says the girl who was stripping with a bottle of Cristal. Why are you talking to me? Don't you need to fly off to Italy for your wedding?*

My insides flip. The thought of her doing that bugs me. I'm not sure why. I don't know this woman, nor do I probably have anything in common with her. So far, she's proven she's only going to be a pain in my ass. Her going to Italy would get me off the hook with Tully and be a blessing.

Several minutes pass. I stretch and stare at the screen, waiting and wondering if she's going to turn silent on me again.

Arianna: *Are you backing out? Don't have the balls to go through with it?*

Me: *Listen to me, lass. I have bigger balls than anyone else you'll ever meet.*

Arianna: *Do you think about anything besides your dick?*

Me: *I didn't say anything about my cock. Sorry if you're obsessing over it.*

"Killian! I've got twenty minutes before my next session if you want to get some training in," my uncle Patrick shouts.

I toss my phone on the table and go over to him. But no matter how many punches I get in, I can't get the face of Arianna's dickhead boyfriend off my mind or stop wondering who this guy in Italy is. And I wonder if she's serious about having an open relationship. If she is, she's got another thing coming. No wife of mine is touching another man, whether she likes me or not.

3

Arianna

All week, my papà has the best of the best meet with the two of us to plan the wedding. It only makes me sad. A couple in love should plan their wedding, not a father and his daughter. Whenever I don't give my opinion, Papà reminds me I made a deal with him and need to engage. The threat of having to go to Italy and live with Giuseppe and his children is enough to make me participate.

The seamstresses sew my handmade, lace-stitched dress in record time. It's beautiful and everything I would ever want. Every time I have a fitting, Donato's words fly into my head. *"Let's elope. We'll go to Vegas tonight."* During several weak moments, I almost call him and tell him to come get me. In each instance I consider it, my brothers or Papà appear as if they know what I'm thinking.

The only time I'm able to talk to him is at night. He only calls at three or four a.m., when he gets home from partying. The pictures on his social media feed show him doing the same thing as always. He's at different clubs, and there are always girls around. I wonder if he's already replaced me. Then he'll call, slurring his words, telling me I'm not marrying Killian.

The morning of the rehearsal dinner comes, and I haven't heard from him. All night, I wait up, wanting to hear his voice. Instead, I scroll my social media feed. Some girl took a selfie of her kissing Donato at the club. She tagged him and wrote, #takinghimhometonight.

A lump grows in my throat. *Would he really do that to me so soon? Did we technically even break up?*

Another post pops up. Some girl on Killian's social media feed named Molly posts a picture of him and a bunch of other men. It's after three in the morning. It appears like they're in a bar and wasted. Two blondes, a girl with magenta hair, several with darker hair, and a redhead all circle him. He has his arm around the redhead's waist, and she's leaning into his ear, smiling, with her hand in his hair.

The caption in the photo reads: *Bachelor party out of control. Some people need to go to bed.*

I'm going to kill him.

Papà insisted I had enough wild nights out and said the only bachelorette party I could have would be with his bodyguards surrounding me and at a restaurant. Instead of going through the motions, I passed. If I couldn't go out and have a good time, what was the point? All it would do is remind me how screwed up my life is.

Seeing Killian living it up, with the sexy redhead fawning all over him, makes my blood boil. I assume she's Irish and probably everything he's attracted to. I message him.

Me: *I hope your slutty redhead is clean.*

He doesn't answer. I pace my room, fuming. About an hour later, I get a reply.

Killian: *You better watch your mouth.*

Me: *I think you're the one who needs to worry about his mouth. I'm sure she's a gyno's dream for treatment. Go ahead and enjoy it though. I hope she gives you chlamydia and you get erectile dysfunction.*

Killian: *Rule number one. You don't ever talk about her.*

Jealousy flares in my belly so intensely, I see red. I furiously pound my phone screen.

Me: *Enjoy sticking it in her tonight. It'll be the last time you see her.*

Killian: *I'm bringing her to the wedding. And the rehearsal dinner.*

Rage annihilates me. If he thinks he's going to flaunt his floozy in front of me, he better think again.

Me: *Try it. If she steps foot in New York, I'll have my brothers take care of you.*

Killian: *You think I'm scared of your brothers? Newsflash, daddy's brat. I'll tear your brothers to shreds, and they'll still be alive begging for their lives.*

Me: *I'll add this to my documentation for the police. And I don't know why you call me a daddy's brat, but I can assure you I'm not.*

Killian: Sure, you are. I've already spoken with your father and know exactly why he's shipping you off for me to tame your ass.

My heart races. *He talked to my father?*

Another thing I don't get to know that concerns me.

What did Papà tell him that would give him the idea I'm a brat?

Killian: *I'd say go to sleep, and it'll be nice to meet you tomorrow night, but somehow, I don't think nice and you go together.*

Me: Have fun with your slut.

Killian: You're going to regret saying that.

Me: *Another empty statement. Enjoy your new STD. Add it to the rest of the list of diseases I'm sure you have.*

I return to pacing my mostly empty room. My personal items got packed yesterday while I was at a dress fitting. Papà had everything shipped to Chicago. The only remaining contents are a few outfits, my toiletries, my luggage, and the furniture.

What am I doing? I can't marry this monster. Why am I doing what my papà wants? I should tell Donato I'll elope with him and suffer the consequences.

Papà will probably disown me, but at least I won't have to move or live my life with a cheating scumbag.

I close my app and call Donato, ready to tell him, let's go to Vegas and elope. It rings twice, and a woman's voice answers. Her giddy voice makes everything worse. She giggles. "Call back later. He's busy." There's a sound as if the phone fell.

My stomach quivers. I almost hang up then freeze.

"Oh God! Yes, baby! Right there! Don't stop! I...oh!" she screams.

"Fuck, your pussy tastes good," Donato's deep voice hits my ear.

My hands tremble so hard, I drop the phone. *She tastes good? That's what he tells me.*

I put my hand over my face, trying to fight the emotions tugging at my heart, but I can't stop the tears from falling. He replaced me already. How did I ever mean anything to him if he's already with another woman? It hasn't even been a week.

Every call we've had since I left him at Club D on Saturday night were just lies. He always tells me I'm the only woman for him, and he wants to marry me. But none of it is true.

I bury my face in my pillow, no longer able to control all the hurt I feel about issues surrounding my life. Everything I know is changing. As much as I'm angry at my brothers for not helping me persuade my papà, I still love them. They've always kept their eye on me. While it's annoying at times, like when they showed up at Club D last Saturday, it's something I love about them. Where I'm going, no one cares about me. For the first time in my life, I'm going to have no one to protect me.

The house I've spent all twenty-eight years of my life in, the one my mother took her last breath in, I won't even be able to visit without hopping on a plane. And as mad as I am at my father, he isn't a spring chicken. My mother's death taught me anything can happen at any time. Since she died, I make sure he eats well, gets massages to destress, and works out. I'll no longer be able to see him and make sure he's okay.

At some point, I fall asleep, exhausted from barely any rest over the last week and the reality of my situation. When I open my eyes, sunlight streams through my window. My papà sits on my bed.

"Papà, what are you doing in here?" I ask and push myself up to a seated position.

He smiles. "It's almost three in the afternoon. I figured you must have needed the rest, but it's time to get ready. Killian will be here in a few hours."

New tears well in my eyes, and I turn away from him.

He turns my chin back toward him. "Don't cry, my bambina. Today is a good day. It's the start of your future."

My papà hasn't called me his bambina in years. When I was a little girl, it was his term of endearment for me. My tears fall. I point out, "You're shipping me away to some man you don't even know. He could be worse than anyone I meet around here."

He embraces me. "He's not. Tully has vouched for him, and I have spoken to him. He understands you come first, or I'll rain down the worst kind of hell upon him."

I sniffle and glance up. All the things I've been scared to voice come out. "What if I hate him? What if you're sending me to someone who I'll never have any feelings for and can't even stand?"

He strokes my cheek and smiles. "I understand your fear. Your mamma and I had an arranged marriage. Neither of us wanted the other. But over time, we didn't just learn to love each other. We became each other's soul."

I stare at him in shock. "You didn't know mamma before you married her?"

He shakes his head. "Not until she walked down the aisle. I had never seen her and didn't even know what color her eyes or hair were. But that is why I want you to meet Killian before tomorrow. It will make things easier if you've at least met and spent some time together."

"Why didn't you ever tell us about you and mamma?" I question.

He shrugs. "It never seemed important before right now. I wish she were here to help you through this."

Grief replaces my fear. "I miss her so much."

Papà clenches his jaw and nods. He pulls me back into his arms, and it only makes me sob, hard. "Shhh. I promise you everything will be okay. I've scheduled a trip to Chicago a week after you return from your honeymoon."

"My honeymoon?"

"Yes. Of course."

My stomach flips. "Where am I going?"

He chuckles. "It's not my place to tell you. I'll let Killian be the one to surprise you."

The thought of going on a honeymoon with Killian makes me anxious. I try another tactic. "If I don't know where I'm going, how do I know what to pack?"

Amusement twinkles in his eyes. "Don't worry, bambina. I've already taken care of it. Your suitcase will arrive at your destination."

I stay silent and wipe my face. There's no getting out of this. My papà has thought of everything.

He kisses the top of my head. "I'll miss you around here, but I'm confident your new life will be good for you. And this will always be your home."

"That I can't visit unless I get on a plane," I grumble.

"Or drive, but it's easier to fly." He winks. "I put a present in your closet and on your dresser for you. I'll let you get ready."

I watch him leave the room and sigh. I go to my closet and pull out the chocolate-brown, satin designer cocktail dress he had flown in from Italy, along with a pair of matching stilettos. They're beautiful. One side has a long sleeve. The other is sleeveless. The waist is ruched and will show off my curves. The shoes have four-inch heels and look like pure gold.

I go to my dresser and open the box. A wide, hammered, hinged-cuff bracelet with a satin finish rests inside. Engraved on the inside of the cuff is *"You'll always have my heart, no matter where you are, my bambina. Ti amo, your papà."*

New emotion swells in my chest. I set the bracelet down and decide it's best to take a shower and put on my big girl pants.

Nerves flutter in my gut, thinking about having to meet Killian and leaving my home. I spend over an hour getting ready, taking time to straighten then curl my hair. I carefully add makeup to my face. I step into my dress, slip on my shoes, and add my jewelry. Then I spray perfume on my wrists and dab my neck. When I finish, I study myself in the full-length mirror, looking for any signs of imperfection or that I was crying.

Content I don't see anything, I stroll through my wing and go down the stairs. Voices, including Russian and Tully's Irish accent, hit my ears. I pause. Why are there Russian people in the house? Did I get it wrong, and Killian is some sort of Irish wanna-be who's really Russian? Am I going crazy?

I get to the bottom of the steps and turn the corner to go inside the living room. I bump into a hard chest, go flying backward, and a strong arm circles around my waist. He pulls me close to him, and a loin-curling aphrodisiac flares in my nostrils. I'm pretty sure it's mint, orange blossom, and bourbon vanilla. I don't think I've ever smelled anything so intoxicating. His deep voice sends a delicious chill down my spine. "Whoa, lass."

I glance up, and green flames lick my skin, creating the most intense set of tingles I've ever experienced. Suddenly, it's hard to breathe against his hard flesh.

A cocky expression appears. I want to smack it off him even though I'm sure I have wet panties from it. "Arianna Marino. We finally meet."

My face turns hot, and he licks his lips as his smug expression grows. His eyes wander to my chest then back to my face. His large palm slips to my ass, and damn if it doesn't feel like it belongs there.

His hot breath merges into mine and he states, "You look nice."

My nerves annihilate me. "You want to remove your hands from me?"

He smirks. "I don't know. Are you sure you want me to?"

My insides scream no. The beating of my heart is so hard, I wonder if he can hear it. My skin continues to crackle, as if he's hitting me with a stun gun.

When I don't respond, he leans into my ear and grips my body tighter to his. "I think it would be easier if we got along, don't you?"

My knees buckle, and his arm and palm hold me as close to him as possible. I take a deep breath. He's right. "Yes."

He puts his face in front of mine and stares at my lips. "Good. Let's tell your father and brothers everything is fine between us so they can stop giving me the stare down like they want to cut off my balls."

A laugh escapes my mouth. I taunt, "I thought you weren't scared of them?"

"I'm not. Still doesn't make me enjoy their threats," he admits.

Fair enough. Maybe he isn't so bad after all. I consent, "Okay. I'll agree."

"The bathroom is down here," my brother, Massimo, says.

"Thanks!" a woman's voice replies.

I glance over at the doorway, and my blood boils so hot, I wish I had a knife in my hand. The same gorgeous redhead who was fawning all over Killian smiles up at my brother. She's even sexier in person. I glare at Killian and shout, "You brought that whore into my father's house?"

Anger flares in his expression. He seethes, "Watch your mouth!"

I reach back and slap him as hard as I can. His face jars toward the wall and he releases me. I lunge toward the woman.

My brother grabs me around the waist. "Whoa! What are you doing?"

The woman's eyes widen when I reach for her. She takes a step back.

I scream, "Get that STD-infested slut out of my house!"

4

Killian

Nora's face turns as red as her hair. She gapes at Arianna whose limbs are flailing as her brother holds her back.

"Arianna! Stop this!" Massimo orders.

"Get her out of here!" Arianna roars, her face so inflamed with rage, I think she might actually kill Nora if Massimo didn't have her.

Boris steps out of the room and pulls Nora into him at the same time I move between them. His Russian accent is thicker than normal, and he asks, "Why are you threatening my wife?"

"Your wife?" Arianna shoots me more daggers. I wince inside, knowing the shit is about to hit the fan. She explodes, "Your wife and Killian are sleeping together!"

Massimo scrunches his face and glances between Nora and me. "Is this a joke?"

"Get that whore out of my sight!" Arianna yells and tries to get out of Massimo's hold.

Boris tugs Nora behind him. "You've got some messed up notions, and I assure you that you're wrong."

"Why would Arianna think this if it isn't true?" Massimo questions.

"Do you realize what you just asked?" Boris asks in disgust.

Nora scolds, "Killian! What did you do?"

My gut sinks.

"Why is she still here?" Arianna rants.

Angelo and Tully come out in the hallway. Angelo glares at me and asks, "What is going on?"

I ignore him and inform Arianna, "Nora is my sister."

"I don't care what lie you—" She gapes at me. An entirely new wave of anger surfaces on her face.

Great.

"Killian!" Nora seethes.

I spin and hold my hands in the air. "Don't look at me. I'm not the one who went all crazy and wanted to kill you."

Nora steps out from behind Boris. She jabs me in the chest. "What did you do?"

One by one, everyone moves from out of the living room and into the foyer. Angelo steps next to Nora. "Answer the question. My daughter doesn't try to attack people in our house for no reason."

"She saw a photo I was tagged in and jumped to conclusions about my sister and me," I state.

He scowls at me and turns to Arianna. "Is this true?"

Arianna's eyes glisten. She blinks hard, pins her hurt gaze on me, and I want to die on the spot. I expect her to throw me under the bus, but she doesn't. She refocuses on Angelo. She clears her throat. "Yeah. That's true. It's my fault."

Declan crosses his arms and steps next to Arianna. He scowls at me. "Let me guess. Killian didn't set you straight about who Nora is?"

I don't wait for her to answer. I firmly state, "No. I didn't."

"Why was she calling Nora an STD-infested slut?" Declan demands, and I want to punch him for digging me into a deeper hole.

"I'm... Oh God! I'm so sorry," Arianna says to Nora and puts her hand over her mouth in shame.

Nora steps forward and slings her arm around Arianna's shoulder. She continues to give me a look of death. She assures Arianna, "It's fine. I'm sure my brother isn't an innocent party in all this."

Gemma holds out her phone in front of Arianna. "Is it this photo that caused all this?"

Arianna glances at it then around the room. Everyone in the picture is now standing in front of her. She winces. "Yes. I'm sorry. Really, I am," she says to Nora.

"Of course it would be Molly," Gemma comments under her breath.

Arianna looks around. "Which one of you is Molly?"

Gemma shakes her head. "None of us. She's a server at Nora's pub. She seems to have a knack for stirring up trouble on her social media page."

"That was innocent," Liam points out. "It's not Molly's fault Arianna thought what she did."

So much for my family sticking up for me.

"Why didn't you set her straight?" Finn asks, and I officially want to slap the shit out of my brothers and cousins.

I blurt out, "Well, I didn't know she was going to attack Nora."

Tully steps in front of me. His hardened expression meets mine. "I expect more from you than this."

Arianna interjects, "It's not only Killian's fault."

Shocked again that she's taking the blame for this, I glance at her, but she only focuses on Tully.

"Honestly, Tully. We're both at fault."

Tully looks like he wants to shoot me, and I'm not sure why she's stepping in to take the hit. He gives me another scowl then steps back.

The room turns to silence. My entire family and all my friends are giving me dirty looks. Arianna's family is glancing between her and me. Her brothers and father look like they want to slice me in two.

A server opens a door and says, "Mr. Marino, your other guests have begun arriving."

Angelo turns toward her. "Thank you. I'll be in shortly." He steps in front of Arianna and studies her. Then he says, "Arianna, can you show the women to the ballroom? I have some things to discuss with your future husband."

She nervously glances at me then looks back at her father. She scrunches her face and opens her mouth.

He cuts her off. "Please. Do what I ask."

"Come. Show us the rest of your house on the way there," Nora says and smiles.

The women slowly leave the room. Angelo motions for me to go into the other room. My brothers and the Ivanovs all trail behind me.

Angelo refills his glass of scotch and Tully's. He walks around, topping off everyone's glasses.

My brothers and the Ivanovs stand by my side, across from Arianna's brothers, who never stop scowling.

Tully shakes his head in slight movements.

"Can we get this over with? I fucked up. I'm sorry. I won't do it again," I state.

Angelo takes a long drink of his scotch. He studies me then says, "When we spoke on the phone earlier this week, I thought I made myself clear. You are to show respect to my daughter at all times."

"I'll tell you what I told you on the phone. I don't disrespect women," I claim.

"What would you call what you did to her? You think leading her to believe you're screwing another woman is respectful?" he growls.

I cross my arms. His daughter isn't an innocent bystander. She played her part in our exchange. Since I'm a man, I'm not going to throw her on the fire. But I'm also not going to be intimidated by Angelo. "I said I made a mistake and won't do it again. You have my word."

He points to my brothers and the Ivanovs. He warns, "You have everyone around you who has always been in your life. She's leaving everyone and everything she knows. Do not make me regret allowing you to marry her."

Allowing me. As if I even have a choice in this matter. I open my mouth, but Declan steps forward. "My brother made a mistake and sees the error of his ways. He won't do it again, and we will all watch out for your daughter. You have my word on this as well."

"And the vow of the Ivanovs, too," Maksim promises.

Angelo assesses Declan and Maksim then turns his dark orbs of death on me. "This isn't solidified yet. I'm taking a risk on you. And maybe the better solution is for her to go to Italy."

My chest tightens. "And marry that other guy? No."

Angelo's eyes turn to slits. "What do you know about it?"

I admit, "Not a lot. But she doesn't want to go." Arianna never stated this to me, but my gut says if she wanted to be in Italy with this guy, then she would. I continue, "And I think I have a right to know who this man is that you're trying to marry her off to."

After a few seconds, Angelo nods. "Fine. I'll tell you. It's Giuseppe Berlusconi."

The head of the mob in all of Italy? No wonder she chose me. I'm unsure why I'm fighting to stay in the game on this. It's my chance to get out of marrying her and being tied to the Marinos for life, but thinking about Arianna with that disgusting, old pig makes me cringe inside. I blurt out, "I assure you, I'm a much better match for your daughter than him."

Angelo takes another drink then turns to his sons. "Please take our guests to the ballroom. Killian will stay here. Ask Arianna to come back." He nods at Tully. "You go, too."

Tully and her brothers give me another heated look then do as Angelo orders.

When everyone is gone, I say, "I'm sorry I didn't put my best foot forward. From now on, I promise you I will."

"We'll see about that."

My stomach tightens. "What does that mean?"

He doesn't reply.

"Fine. Stay quiet. I'll just wait until you decide to speak again."

He shakes his head. "You need to learn to control your mouth, son."

I scoff and clench my jaw.

Arianna enters the room. She nervously says, "Papà, Dante said you wanted to see me?"

"Yes, come here, please."

She stands in front of him, and he puts his hands on her shoulders. "This is your life, and I want you to make the decision. It is not too late to change your mind. Giuseppe will still be thrilled to marry you. Would you rather do that?"

Is he serious? He thinks that slob can make his daughter happy?

Of course he'd be thrilled to marry her. She's a hundred on a scale of ten, and she's half his age.

Arianna spins. Anger and hurt flare in her eyes. Her lips tremble. "Are you trying to back out?"

I pin my gaze on hers. "No. I told him I'd make you a lot happier than that disgusting pig."

"Do not talk about Giuseppe with anything but respect!" Angelo barks.

I'm over this entire conversation. I chastise, "Come on. Can we get real for a minute? He's at least twenty years older than Arianna. His children are closer in age to her than him. And take a look at the guy. You want to force her into his bed?"

"Don't speak of my daughter—"

"What do you think is going to happen?" I belt out.

The room turns silent.

I step closer to Arianna and lock eyes with her. "I'm only going to ask you this once. Who do you want to marry? Me or Giuseppe?"

She furrows her brows, and her lips tremble harder. Fear fills her eyes.

I press harder. "I need an answer. Are you choosing me or him?"

She swallows hard. "You."

"Good." I turn to her father. "This conversation is over." I slide my arm around her waist then lead her out of the room and through the house. We say nothing, our fate sealed.

I could have gotten out of it. I'm unsure why I fought not to, other than the thought of any other man touching her is creating a rage inside me I'm not sure what to do with.

5

Arianna

Killian leads me down the hall as if he intrinsically knows my father's mansion inside and out. When we get to the ballroom entrance, he glances behind us, then spins me into him. "Hey."

I arch my eyebrow, afraid of uttering any sounds. My insides are still quivering at the thought of my father sending me to Italy. And my pride hates I had to admit to Killian I was choosing him over someone else.

He leads me around the corner and moves me against the wall. His smoldering green eyes make me wonder how I ever thought any other man's were hot. The aroma of mint, orange blossom, and bourbon vanilla hits me and almost makes me dizzy. He apologizes, "I'm sorry. I shouldn't have let you believe that about Nora."

It throws me for a loop. I didn't expect to hear an apology. So I decide there's no point in rehashing it all or holding a grudge. I'm going to be with this guy for the rest of my life, so I tell him, "It's okay."

His lips twitch. "You've got quite the fight in you. I was impressed how you gave it a good go. If your brother hadn't stopped you, we might have had to call an ambulance to resuscitate Nora."

I'm not sure if I should laugh or continue to be embarrassed. I finally reply, "Thank you for not going back on your word. I-I don't want to go to Italy."

His face falls, and he snorts. "Not sure what your father is thinking on that choice."

Uncomfortable silence fills the air as he studies me. "The wedding isn't until tomorrow evening. Do you want to get out of here after dinner?"

I shake my head. "My father won't let me go. He has me on lockdown."

Arrogance fills Killian's expression. "I'll handle him. Do you want to go?"

Flutters intensify in my gut. "Okay. If you think you can get him to change his mind."

"Watch me." He glances at my lips then steps back, assessing me. "I lied when I said you look nice."

My gut falls. I bite on my lip to try and cover up the sting of his words.

He drags his finger down my bare arm. "You're a smoking-hot lass in this dress."

I release a relieved breath then smile. "Thanks."

"Come on. Let's deal with all the boring stuff then get out of here." He tugs me back into his body, and I do my best not to let my knees go weak as he steers me to our table. I'm not sure why he's having this effect on me, but I didn't prepare myself for it. He pulls the chair out for me next to a woman named Selena. I sit, and he takes the seat next to mine.

Tristano is on the other side of Killian and leans over the table so he can see me. "Arianna, are you okay?"

"Yeah. I'm fine." I smile so my brother will drop it.

He studies Killian.

Killian doesn't flinch. "Got something you want to say?"

My brother scowls at Killian.

"Tristano!" I warn.

Killian ignores him and puts his arm around me. "Arianna and I are going out later. Whoever wants to go can come with us." He leans in front of my face. "Where are we going?"

"Ummm..." I say the first thing that comes to my mind. "Club D?"

He smiles. "Good choice. We have one in Chicago."

"You do?"

"Yep."

"We should see if Derek has any empty suites," a Russian guy who I think is named Maksim says and pulls out his phone.

"You know Derek?" I ask, shocked again.

"Yeah. We did the construction on his club," Maksim states.

"Wow!"

Maksim sends a text to Derek, and Papà comes into the room. He sits at the head of the table, not far from me.

"After dinner, I'm taking Arianna out," Killian states.

Papà's eyes turn to slits. "She doesn't need to go out."

"Papà—" I start, but Killian puts his hand on my thigh. Zings fly straight to my core.

He challenges, "I can't take my fiancée out for a date before we walk down the aisle?"

Papà continues to assess us.

"We'll go with them," Tristano assures.

"We're all going," Maksim adds. His phone buzzes, and he glances at it. "Derek has a suite for us."

"Not us. Skylar's too pregnant," another Russian says.

"I don't want to take Kora into a nightclub, either," another man I think might be brothers with the other Russians states.

I ask the woman sitting next to him, "Are you pregnant, too?"

She smiles. "I am. Only a few months. We just started telling people."

"Congratulations."

"Thanks. By the way, I'm Kora, and this is Sergey," she responds.

"Nice to meet you."

My papà glances around the room. Most of the guests are all his age or older. He sighs. "Okay. You can go. But, Arianna, if you try—"

"I won't let her out of my sight," Killian states.

My papà finally concedes. He points to Killian and me. "Okay. But you two better not be sick from drinking too much tomorrow."

Killian tugs me closer to him. A smug grin fills his face, and he pins his intense gaze on my lips again, then meets my eyes. "We won't. Will we?"

Heat races to my face. "No."

The server comes over and fills my glass with Barolo. She tries to fill Killian's glass, and he puts his hand over it. "I'm good, thank you."

I question, "You don't drink wine?"

He chuckles. "You make that sound like a sin."

"It is," I insist.

"I stick with whiskey and Guinness."

I raise my eyebrows. I've never met a man before who doesn't drink wine. In my house, it's at every dinner.

Selena laughs, and I tear my eyes away from Killian. She has a beautiful Greek accent. "You can't get any more Irish than the O'Malleys."

"Are you from Greece?" I ask.

She nods. Her eyes light up. "Yes. I moved to Chicago when I was barely in my twenties. If you want, I'll take you around and show you the city when you have a chance?"

"Sure. That would be really nice."

"Have you been there before?" she asks.

"No."

Killian dramatically gasps. "You've never been to Chicago?"

"Now you're acting like that's a sin," I tease.

"Anna moved from New York, too," another Russian man across the table states.

The woman next to him smiles. She says, "It's like a smaller New York but with its own charm. I'm sure you'll love it."

Her husband beams and says, "Since you're all here, we should tell you. Anna's pregnant, too, so we'll be staying in tonight."

The room erupts in congratulations.

"Do you like yoga?" Selena asks.

"Yes."

"Great. Us girls meet up for yoga and do brunch afterward on Saturdays. You should come."

"I'd love to," I reply, grateful I'll have something to look forward to with some other women. I've never really had girlfriends. The private school Papà sent me to was full of backstabbing snobs. When I got older, several I was close to got mad at me for their boyfriends hitting on me. I didn't even like their scumbag beaus. My best friend wanted Massimo. When he turned her down, she stopped calling me. One by one, all my friendships disintegrated. I decided it was too hard to meet genuine women and stopped trying. My wedding party consists of my cousins who are younger than me and I'm not even close to. I opted to meet them at the church and not even let them help me get ready.

Will things be different in Chicago? Is it possible to have a group of girlfriends?

Nora picks up the bottle of wine and takes a photo of it with her phone. "Is this what you like to drink, Arianna?"

"For dinner, yes."

She smiles. "I'll order some cases for the pub, then."

"Thanks," I say, feeling a bit overwhelmed at how nice they all seem, and especially Nora, when I accused her of sleeping with Killian and having STDs.

Nora looks at her husband. "It's a good thing Svetlana convinced us to leave Shannon with her. It looks like we get a night out."

I question, "Do you have a daughter?"

Nora nods, then pulls up a picture on her phone. "This is Shannon."

A baby girl with hair as red as Nora's fills the screen. I say, "She's beautiful."

Boris interjects, "Looks just like her mother."

The conversation continues. Everyone seems nice, and it makes me feel less nervous about moving. We eat dinner, and a few hours later, Killian leans into my ear. "See. You have nothing to worry about. You'll fit right in."

I'm not sure how he knew I was worried, but it's another thing that makes me feel better about this entire situation. "Thanks."

"Can we get out of here now?"

I softly laugh. "Sure. I need to get my ID out of my bedroom."

The group of us going to Club D rise. My papà warns us again about drinking too much, and my brothers assure him they'll keep an eye on all of us.

Killian steers me out of the room. "How long have you been on lockdown?"

Guilt and embarrassment fill me when I think about the video of me drunk and dancing on a pole with my shirt off. I start walking up the staircase and quietly say, "Since Saturday."

"I see. And you've been locked up in this mansion like Rapunzel since then?"

I laugh. "I wouldn't exactly say that."

"But pretty much?"

I nod. "Yeah."

"So what did you do all week?" he asks.

I sigh. "Spent hour after hour planning the wedding."

"Why don't you look happy about that?"

I shrug and open my bedroom door. "Not exactly every bride's dream to plan her wedding with her papà threatening to send her overseas."

"It's not?" he teases.

I roll my eyes. "Nope."

His face falls. "Sorry you had to do it all on your own."

My chest tightens, but I decide to ask him what I've wanted to know since I learned my papà made an arrangement with him to marry me. And now that I've met him, I still don't understand it. "Can I ask you something?"

"Sure."

"Why did you agree to marry me?"

Uncomfortable silence fills the air. He replies, "I didn't think it was fair for your father to send you to Italy to get groped by that dirty old man."

"I'm not talking about that. Why did you agree before you ever met me or knew about him?"

He doesn't move, intensely gazing at me. I wait for him to speak, needing to know. He finally reveals, "Tully did a favor for my family. I had to repay my debt."

I gape at him. I'm a debt repayment. I'm not naive. This is a strange situation, but learning I'm a repayment for his debt hurts. In my mind, I convinced myself he was a social outcast or hard-core asshole and couldn't get anyone to marry him. Now that I've met him, I know it's untrue. The real truth feels so much worse. I manage to point out, "This is a little bit bigger than a favor, don't you think?"

He grunts. "It is what it is."

His lack of giving me the details only upsets me further. "What does Tully have to do with me getting married?" Tully's always been my papà's friend, but why does he have any part in this?

Killian goes quiet, and it's a smack in my face.

I lower my voice, trying to stay calm. "Are you going to be like my papà and keep me in the dark about things?"

"I don't know all the details," he claims.

"You're lying," I accuse.

He crosses his arms. "No, I'm not. I don't know all of Tully and your father's business."

"But you know something you aren't telling me?"

His eyes turn to slits. "That's not true, Arianna. All I know is they're friends, and Tully gave his word to your father to help him out."

"Okay, then tell me what you did that you owed Tully," I say.

His face hardens. "No. That's my and my brothers' business."

Everything becomes clear. All I'm doing is moving from one person who won't tell me anything to another. And I might as well be a check he's handing over to Tully. My voice shakes. "I'm so sick of this."

"Sick of what?" he asks, genuinely looking confused.

I only give him half the truth. "Of being the person who gets left in the dark."

"Don't push your daddy issues on me. Whatever is between you two is exactly that—between you two, not me. And you can't expect me to tell you O'Malley business," he claims.

Anger fills me. "Okay, so you owed Tully. My papà gave you an out today. Why didn't you take it?"

"I already told you. And I seem to remember you choosing me over that fat prick," he declares.

I shake my head and grab my evening purse. I stick my phone and slim wallet in it. I head for the door.

He puts his hand on it so I can't open it.

I roar, "What are you doing?"

"Arianna, why are you pissed off at me right now?"

My insides shake. "You're just like my papà and brothers. That's why."

He snorts. "I'm nothing of the sort."

"Yes, you are."

He runs his hand through his hair. "Can we go back to where we were before you started prying into my business?"

"Yeah, sure. Whatever. Now move," I command.

"Way to be mature," he comments.

"Seriously? You let me think you screwed your sister, and you want to lecture me on maturity?" I seethe.

He clenches his jaw then opens the door. "Glad to see you can only stay in the nice zone for a few hours before returning to your normal self."

I brush past him. "Have fun tonight. I'll be with my brothers. Just stay away from me and give me my final night of freedom without you breathing down my neck."

He grabs my arm, yanks me back into the room, and pushes me up against the door.

My pulse shoots through the roof. He cages his body over mine and presses his forearms against the wood. He steps so close, his warm, hard flesh pulses against me. His scent permeates all my cells, sending heat straight to my core.

"Wh-what are you doing?" I meekly ask, wishing I could push him off me but only wanting to wrap my arms around him. It all confuses me more. How can I feel anything but hatred toward this man who is marrying me to pay off a debt? Plus, he's just as trapped as me. Maybe I had some deep-down grand notion he wanted to get married and chose me, but it's not the case.

His hot breath hits my ear, and when his lips brush against my skin, I shudder and my body pulses. "You seem to have a misconception about me breathing down your neck. To be clear, *this* is me breathing down your neck."

I try to turn off the zings flying all over my skin, but it's pointless. Killian O'Malley is sexier than he appeared online, is everything I've never experienced before, and my body doesn't want to be anywhere but against his.

His breath trails over my jaw until his lips are inches from mine. His eyes glow like a wild animal in the dark. "Rule number one. You're going to be my wife. Not your father's, and not your brothers'. Mine. So you'll go into the club with me, and you'll come back out with me. And I'm not sure what you think you're going to do for your final night of freedom, but it sure as hell isn't anything unless I'm a part of it. Do I make myself clear?"

I glare at him, not trusting what might come out of my mouth and cursing myself. His lips are so close, I can taste the whiskey on his breath. Against my will, I lean closer.

He sees it and his arrogant expression appears. He pulls away, takes my hand, and opens the door. "We're leaving, and don't test me, Arianna."

6

Killian

ARIANNA POUTS THE ENTIRE WAY TO THE CLUB, IGNORING ME and acting like the brat I've always assumed she would be. If she thinks she's going to behave like this in Chicago, she's got another thing coming. I'm not putting up with her attitude for the rest of my life. To keep the peace and get through this weekend, I'm letting her have her little fit.

Her brothers, Massimo and Dante, are in the car with us. Everyone else separated into several other vehicles. I concentrate on my conversation with them and keep my arm around Arianna the entire ride into the city. It's pissing her off. She's keeping her body stiff next to mine, and frankly, I'm enjoying getting under her skin if she's going to sulk.

"Your brothers said you're a boxer?" Massimo asks.

"Yeah. My family has a gym. Most of my cousins fight, too."

Dante whistles. "Is that getting harder on your body, now that you're almost forty?"

I chuckle and admit, "Recovery takes a bit longer than it used to."

"Dante used to fight," Massimo informs me.

"Really? Why did you stop?"

He taps his head. "Bad concussion."

"Ah. Nolan had that happen. Declan had to have his nose reconstructed after it got broken too many times. His sinuses got so bad, he could hardly breathe. Both of my brothers only do boxing workouts and avoid matches."

Dante nods. "You ever consider hanging up the gloves?"

I snort. "Not unless I'm dead. It's who I am."

"That's what I used to think."

"Don't you miss it?"

Dante crosses his arms and sits farther back in the seat. Darkness fills his eyes. He gives me a knowing look. "Sometimes. But I get my aggression out in other ways."

I don't need to ask what that means. I'm sure the Marino brothers get plenty of punches in. Nothing about them screams weakness. All four of them are tall and built. To the average person, they would seem intimidating. But I'm used to men like them.

Arianna huffs then mutters, "Would that be in the dungeon?"

Dante and Massimo's eyes turn to slits. Massimo barks out, "Watch your mouth."

"Oops. Sorry." She crosses her arms and throws daggers at her brothers.

I want to ask what the dungeon is, but I get the feeling now isn't the time. I highly doubt Dante or Massimo will tell me. I make a mental note to interrogate Arianna later.

Dante scowls. "What's up your ass right now?"

"Don't talk to your sister like that," I warn.

Dante jerks his head back. "Don't tell me what I can or can't say to my sister."

I don't flinch. "Your sister is going to be my wife. I'm only going to tell you one more time not to talk to her like that again."

Arianna gasps. It's quiet, and I'm sure I'm the only one who hears it. The car goes silent. Neither Dante nor I blink. He may be her brother, but come tomorrow, she's no longer theirs. She's mine—an O'Malley. And I won't have anyone talking down to her.

Massimo cuts the tension. "Arianna, what's wrong? Do you not want to go out?"

Her body relaxes, and she softens her voice. "Of course I do."

"Then why the attitude?"

"Nothing anyone in this car will help me solve," she fires back.

"What does that mean?"

"She's upset she's marrying me and not Giuseppe," I tease to try and break the tension.

Arianna tilts her head and smirks, but her lips twitch.

"Thank God. We all told my papà that was a bad idea," Dante admits.

I roll my head toward Arianna. "See, lass. You have so much to be grateful for that it's me you're marrying."

She rolls her eyes. "Can you get any more full of yourself?"

The driver parks in front of Club D. I reply, "You'll have to tell me what you think once you're stuck with me." I wink and step out of the car then reach in to help her out.

Massimo takes the lead. I follow him to the front of the line. Dante stays behind us. The other vehicles with my family and friends pull up and join us.

We get inside and check our phones. Arianna opens her purse to show the girl it's empty. She motions for us to go through, and I lean into Arianna's ear. "Where's your phone?"

"I don't have it."

I freeze and let the others pass.

Arianna's eyes widen. "Why are we stopping?"

"Rule number two. Don't lie to me, lass."

She glares at me. "I'm not sure who you think you are, but I'm not your child. You don't have a right to declare rules like I'm going to bend over and obey you."

Uneasy tension crawls through my body, going faster until it's racing through my veins. "Want to make a bet?"

She tries to shrug out of my grasp. "You're on planet delusional. Time to jump off it."

I step closer to her and put my arms around her waist then fist her hair. I tug her head back and dip over her face.

Golden-brown flames singe me, turning me on so much, I have to remind myself I'm trying to make a point. My dick twitches against her stomach, and she smirks. "You can tell your cock to simmer down, too."

I slide my palm to her ass and squeeze it, which only makes me grow harder. She's got everything in the right places. If I'm stuck with her for the rest of my life, at least she's someone I'm going to enjoy making mine. I stare at her lips and threaten, "You won't lie to me. If you do, there'll be consequences."

She reaches down and slides her hand between us, dragging her finger over my erection. "Yeah? What are you going to do to me? Tie me up? Chain me to your bed? Make me do things to you against my will?"

The humming in my blood grows. "I won't ever have to make you do things. You'll do them voluntarily and enjoy every second."

"Hmm. Not much of a punishment, is it? So what does that mean? Are you going to beat me?" she challenges.

"Don't ask dumb questions. You aren't a stupid woman," I reply.

She shimmies her hand down my pants and grips my dick while stroking my balls with two fingers.

I hold in a groan but can't stop my erection from hardening.

She brushes her lips against mine as she talks. "Since you seem to like rules, let me give you some. Rule number one. Don't make threats you aren't going to make good on."

I resist kissing her and slide my finger over the slit of her ass. "Yeah? What's rule number two?"

She takes her hand out of my pants, glides it up my chest, and locks her fingers in my hair. She rises on her tippy-toes. Her hard nipples press into my pecs. I almost get dizzy when her hot breath hits my ear. She grazes my lobe with her tongue. "Rule number two. Don't underestimate me. I'll cut off your balls when you're sleeping."

She tries to take a step back, but I tighten my arms around her and kiss the curve of her neck. She trembles in my arms. I reveal, "I saw you put your phone in your purse. And I can feel it hidden between your tits. The next time you lie to me, I'll give you a pat-down for everyone to see." I lower my hand so it's on the back of her thigh then move it under her dress.

She squirms.

I curl my finger under her panties then trace the hole of her sex. I taunt, "Why are you wet, lass? Has this tight little pussy of yours been dying to know what a real man feels like?"

A gasp flies out of her lush mouth. It hits my ear and sends heat racing down my spine. Her heart beats hard against my chest.

"Killian? Are you with Maksim's crew tonight?"

I release Arianna and turn to the side. Derek Derow, the owner of Club D, has a huge grin on his face. He's a former professional basketball player and towers over us. His personality is always as big as he is.

I shake his hand, grateful I just used my left hand to taunt Arianna. "D! How are you doing?"

"I'm good, man. Arianna." He picks her up into a hug and kisses her cheek. When he sets her down, he asks, "Didn't know you two knew each other."

"Oh...umm..." Arianna fumbles.

I tug her close to me. "We're getting married tomorrow."

He raises his eyebrows and chuckles. "No shit?"

"Yep."

"Well, congratulations." His face turns stern, and he focuses on Arianna. "A little birdie told me a rumor, but I'm sure it's gotta be just that."

Arianna's face turns beet red. "What's that?" She bites her lip.

He studies her for a moment, letting her squirm. "Someone said you had videos posted on your social media page, and it looked like you were in one of my suites."

She winces. "Derek, I'm sorry. I was really drunk, and they weren't up long."

"You know it's a strict rule."

"Yes. I know. I'm-I'm really sorry. I promise it will never happen again. Please don't kick me out," she begs.

"D, can you give her a pass? She's been under a lot of stress with the wedding and not making good decisions. Her father has her on lockdown. I practically had to sell my soul to get him to agree to let her out tonight. I personally guarantee you she won't do it again," I inform him.

He hesitates then sighs. "I'll give you a warning. If it happens again, you'll be banned. It includes the club in Chicago."

"I won't! I promise. Thank you," she states.

His grin appears again. "Okay. Congrats again, and you two have fun. Will I see you in Chicago? Or will you live in New York?"

"Chicago," I state.

He pats me on the back. "All right. See you there." He takes off.

Arianna spins on me. "Seriously?"

Confused, I ask, "What?"

She puts her hand on her hip. "I'm not making good decisions? I've been on lockdown?"

"All true."

"You're an asshole." She angrily shakes her head and bolts toward the elevators. When she gets there, the security guard eyes her over then hugs her and kisses her on the cheek.

I step next to her, not happy with him checking my woman out or putting his grimy hands on her. I bark, "Ivanov suite."

A smug expression meets mine. If he weren't D's bouncer, I'd knock him senseless. He pushes the button. "Arianna, you should know there have been some rumors going around about you. D found out."

She puts her hand on his biceps. "I know. I begged for dear life, and he put me on a warning."

The elevator opens, and I steer her inside, not waiting for him to respond. I hit the close door button then growl, "Rule number three. Do not touch other men." I press the button for our floor.

"Rule number three. Stop making rules!"

"When you learn how to behave, I won't," I declare.

The elevator opens. We step out, and I glance in both directions. I ask the bouncer, "What suite is the Ivanov one?"

"Four A. Have you been here before?" he asks.

"Long time ago. I know the one in Chicago well."

"Cubs or White Sox?"

I snort. "Cubs, of course."

He holds his fist out.

I bump it and ask, "Are you a fan?"

He nods. "I grew up in Illinois."

"Really? What part?"

He reveals, "Down south. A town called Decatur."

"Been there. How long have you lived in New York?"

"Only a few years."

"You like it?"

He grins. "Best place on earth."

I chuckle. "I'll have to disagree with you on that one. Nothing beats Chicago. Nice meeting you. Have a great night."

"You, too."

I spin and look for Arianna. My blood pounds between my ears when I don't see her at first. I finally find her grasping the railing and staring at the dance floor. When I get to her, her lips are shaking and her knuckles are white.

I step behind her, circling my arm around her waist. "What's wrong?"

She shuts her eyes briefly then shakes her head. "Nothing. Let's go."

"Arianna—"

She pushes me away from her and spins. "What suite is ours?"

She's lying to me again, but something tells me to give her a break. "Four A."

She rushes to the suite, grabs a glass of champagne off the server's tray, and downs half of it.

"Slow down, lass."

She ignores me, beelines it to the couch Aspen and Hailee are sitting on, and plops down between them.

Obrecht's lips twitch. His Russian accent fills my ears. "Did you piss her off again?"

"Obrecht!" Selena reprimands but stifles a giggle.

"What? I'm just asking what everyone will want to know."

"Who knows with that woman," I mutter. I pull the server to the side and ask, "Can I get a double Jameson single malt, neat?"

She smiles. "Sure."

Selena pats my arm. "I'm going to go talk to your fiancée."

"Have at it. Careful of her bite," I warn.

Arianna's brothers circle me. Gianni hands me a drink. "Grabbed this from the bartender for you."

"Thanks." I swallow a mouthful. It slides down my throat in a smooth burn. I glance over at Arianna, making a mental note to cut her off in a while. She's already on another glass of champagne. I'm not sure how many it takes for her to be over her limit. Plus, she already had wine at dinner.

My brothers, cousins, and the Ivanovs soon form a larger circle. Sports comes up. Boris and I get into a heated debate with Arianna's brothers about different teams. Boris has a knack for betting, and I've learned to follow him. So far, he hasn't steered me wrong.

Nolan hands me another tumbler of whiskey. The subject turns to the wedding. I remind myself I need to cut Arianna off and spin.

The blood drains from my face until I feel as if there's nothing left but empty veins. Arianna, Selena, and Gemma are missing.

I growl, "Where did Arianna go?"

The conversation goes dead. Everyone turns to the couches.

I fly across the room. "Nora! Where's Arianna?"

Her eyes widen. "Calm down. They went to the restroom."

"You let her leave by herself?" I bark.

Nora rises. She firmly replies, "No. Selena and Gemma are with her. I didn't realize they had to have a leash on them."

I point at her. "I expected more from you."

"Killian—"

I don't wait to hear the rest. I trail Arianna's brothers, Nolan, and Obrecht, who are already out the door. Her brothers split in both directions. I race toward the neon bathroom sign hanging from the ceiling.

She better be in there.

When I get to the bathroom, I don't hesitate. I storm through the door.

"Sir! This is the women's room," a bathroom attendant reprimands.

"Arianna!" I shout.

Gemma steps out of a stall. "Killian! What are you doing? Get out of here!"

"Where is Arianna?" I growl.

The toilet flushes, and Selena steps out. I start opening stalls and yelling, "Arianna."

When it's clear she isn't here, I explode, "Where is she?"

Selena holds her hands in the air. "Maybe she already went back?"

Frustrated, I leave the bathroom and start searching VIP suites. She's nowhere. I grip the railing and peer out over the dance floor.

It's dark, far away, and crowded, but I think I see the top of her head. A tall, dark-haired man is guiding her toward the exit sign.

I take the stairs two at a time. Rage eats through my bones. The only thing I can think is, I'm going to kill him.

7

Arianna

Ten Minutes Earlier

The club is full, and I study the dance floor, wondering if I'll be locked in the suite all night or if Killian can even dance.

He probably can't and only knows the Irish jig, whatever that is.

The freedom everyone else has that I don't seems like a cruel slap in the face. Killian can take his rules and shove them up his ass. We aren't even married yet, and he's bossing me around. His ego is so big, he acts like he's a porn star I won't be able to get enough of.

I almost turn toward Killian when my heart nearly stops. Donato walks in and glances up. Our eyes lock, and I blink hard, trying to stop the emotion growing in my chest.

He lied to me. Said he wanted to marry me then screwed another woman. I don't understand how he could forget about me before I even said my vows. He promised he would find a solution to get me out of this mess, but all he did was keep suggesting we elope.

Killian puts his arm around my waist. My body buzzes against his, but I remind myself he's a controlling asshole. "What's wrong?"

"Nothing. Let's go."

"Arianna—"

I push him away from me and spin. "What suite is ours?"

He pauses then states, "Four A."

I rush to the suite, grab a glass of champagne off the server's tray, and down half of it.

Killian orders, "Slow down, lass."

Fuck off, Killian O'Malley!

Instead of telling him my thoughts, I ignore him, find the farthest spot away from him, and plop between Aspen and Hailee. "Hi!"

Hailee smiles. "Are you doing okay?"

I chug the rest of my champagne. "Yep." I pick up another glass.

Nora sits down. "Is my brother bothering you?"

"Is he always so bossy?"

She winces. "Yeah. All my brothers are. They mean well though."

"It's an O'Malley trait," Hailee adds.

"Well, the Ivanovs aren't any different," Aspen chimes in.

"Ugh. I hoped I was going into a different situation. Between my brothers and Killian, I think I might never be able to make another decision again," I grumble.

Hailee leans closer to me. She smirks. "You have to set your boundaries. Liam and I have a deal. He gets to wear the pants if it regards my security. If it isn't about that, then it's fair game."

Gemma and Selena join us.

"Did Killian tell you where he's taking you for your honeymoon?" Nora asks.

My gut twists. *An entire...week? Month? Who knows how long I'll have no way to escape Mr. Bossy.* I reply, "No. Do you know?"

Nora's face brightens. "Yep. But he'll kill me if I tell you."

I almost complain but then remember what I heard at dinner. I say to Gemma, "Hey, I'm sorry our wedding made you postpone your honeymoon."

She shrugs. "It's fine. We'll leave from here. Plus, we got to come to New York!"

I inquire, "Where are you going for your honeymoon?"

Her eyes light up. "Ireland for two weeks."

My cheeks heat. "I feel bad saying this, but I don't know much about Ireland."

Hailee gasps then teases, "How could you? You're marrying an O'Malley!"

I cringe but ask, "Do you think that's where Killian is taking me?"

Nora pretends to zip her lip and toss the key. "Sorry. It's in the vault."

"Is this my revenge for calling you an STD-infested slut?"

The women all laugh.

"At least we'll always remember our introduction," Nora claims.

I cover my face and peek through my fingers. "I'm so sorry!"

"All good. Killian should never have let that happen."

I finish my champagne and reach for the bottle. Something catches the corner of my eye, and I freeze. My heart pounds in my chest. All the feelings I had earlier rear their ugly heads. Donato leans against the railing, staring at me. He breaks our gaze, does something on his phone, and my phone vibrates in my cleavage.

I need to get out of here before I lose it.

I put the bottle down and my hand on my stomach. "I'm going to the restroom."

Selena rises. "I'll go with you."

Gemma follows. "Me, too."

We slip past the men—well, I sneak, since I'm pretty sure neither Killian nor my brothers would let me leave the room without one of them. They're all in a heated conversation.

As soon as I get into a stall, I pull my phone out.

Donato: *Meet me in the stairwell. We need to talk.*

My insides quiver. I debate but not very long. I'm sick of men claiming to have my best interest at heart but never telling me anything or lying to me. I decide I'm going to give Donato a piece of my mind, if for nothing else but closure.

I leave the bathroom, relieved Selena and Gemma aren't out of their stalls, then continue down the hall to the staircase. I open the door.

Donato puts his arm around my waist and guides me down a flight of stairs. He's so much stronger than me, I don't have a choice except to move my feet.

"Stop! What are you doing?" I cry out.

"We can't talk here." He turns me on the landing.

"I'm not going with you. You're a cheating, lying—"

He spins me into the wall. His dark eyes sear into mine. The body I know too well, the one I've always melted against, pins me to the brick. His hand slides on my cheek. "I got drunk last night and fucked up. All I thought about was you."

My insides quiver. I'm too afraid to speak. Betrayal, maybe love, and confusion about how he could love me and be with another woman threaten to explode.

"We need to talk," he claims again. Before I know what's happening, he returns to maneuvering me down the stairs.

I find my voice and command, "Stop!"

He doesn't listen. I'm too weak to physically stop him. He leads us through the club and toward the door then outside.

"Donato!"

His car pulls up. He opens the door and demands, "Get in."

"No!"

His eyes turn darker than I've ever seen them before. Through gritted teeth, he orders, "Get in, or I'll make you."

Goose bumps break out on my skin. For the first time ever, I'm scared of him. I attempt to back away, but he tightens his arm around me.

My voice trembles. "I'm not getting in your car!"

"You want to play hardball? Fine," he growls. He grabs my hips, forces them backward, so my knees bend and my butt falls on the car seat. "Slide over or—"

Donato's eyes widen in surprise, and his body spins. Killian punches him in the face, and blood spurts everywhere. Donato quickly recovers and the two men go at each other.

I scream, "Stop!" but it falls on deaf ears.

Declan reaches into the car and yanks me out. My papà's car parks next to the curb, and he pushes me in it, then shuts the door. The driver locks the vehicle so I can't get out. I stare in horror as Donato's crew races outside, trailed by my brothers, O'Malleys, and the Ivanovs.

An all-out brawl occurs. Police sirens ring through the air. Guests waiting to get inside the club all shout. Several bouncers and Derek fly into the street and try to pull Donato's guys off ours.

Four cop cars and a police van arrive. The police pull their guns and shout on the bullhorn, "Get on the ground." No one listens. I'm scared they'll all get shot.

The policemen remove taser guns and, one by one, begin shooting each man with them. Like dominos, they all fall to the ground and are soon lying on the wet, snowy cement.

My hands tremble. Not sure what else to do, I pull my cell out of my bra. I hit the button for my papà.

"Arianna, are you okay?" he answers.

I sob, "No! Everyone is getting arrested."

"What? Where are you?"

"Outside Club D. There...there was a fight...they've all been tasered."

"Stay in the club—"

"I'm in the car. Aberto has me locked in. The-the other women are inside still."

My papà's voice turns colder. "Do not attempt to get out of the car, Arianna."

"I-what about the others?"

"I'll send men. Give the phone to Aberto," he instructs.

I put the divider window down and hold my phone out. "My papà wants to talk to you."

He puts the phone to his ear. "Boss."

I block out their conversation. The police begin reading each man their rights and handcuffing them. Killian gets ripped off the ground then Donato. Blood covers their faces. Donato's nose is on the left side of his cheek. The vehicle's windows are tinted, but both of them stare at me, eyes hardened, swollen jaws clenched.

The car moves, and I ask, "Where are you going?"

"Your father said to take you home."

"The other women are inside."

"He will take care of it." He reaches through the window to hand me my phone.

A message pops up from my papà.

Papà: *It was that Brambilla thug, wasn't it?*

I close my eyes and lean back into the headrest. More tears fall.

Papà: *I want an answer, Arianna!*

Me: *Yes.*

He doesn't text anything else. When I get home, the guests are gone, as well as Tully, my papà, and the other Ivanov men who stayed with their pregnant wives. Papà's bodyguard rises when I come into the room. He states, "Your father said to go to bed and not to leave your room. He will come in when he returns."

I gape at him. The women aren't even back. And I'm not going to get a moment's rest until the men are, either.

His eyes turn to slits. "Now, or I'll carry you."

It's pointless to argue. I have no doubt he'll follow through on his threat. I obey and go into my room. I pull out my phone and stare at the screen, waiting for something, anything, to pop up letting me know everyone is okay.

An hour passes before the women come home. Hailee, Gemma, Nora, Selena, and Aspen step into my room and sit on the bed.

"Are you okay?" Selena asks.

I lose control of my emotions and break down.

Selena pulls me into her arms. "Shh. It'll be okay."

"It won't. I-I didn't want to go. I-I couldn't fight him," I shriek.

She tightens her arms around me. "Everything will be okay."

"How? How do you know?"

"I just do."

But I don't know if anything will ever be okay again. My entire world is falling apart. My brothers and the others might go to jail, and I'm sure my papà will send me to Italy now.

More time passes. Sergey knocks on the door. "Everyone is back."

"Oh, thank God!" Nora blurts out.

My room slowly clears out. I don't move, waiting for my papà. Except he never comes. The only person who does is Killian.

Loathing leaps from his eyes, surrounded by his swollen, bruised face. New tears drip off my chin, and my stomach quivers so hard I hold it, feeling like I may get sick. He lunges across the room.

"I-I didn't want to go with him. I swear!"

His expression never changes. He swipes my phone off my bed and growls, "Code. Now."

"What?"

"I said give me your code. Do not make me repeat myself," he snaps.

"Two-Five-Six-Six-Five-Two." My gut drops, knowing what he's going to see. I scold myself for not erasing Donato's text.

He reads it, sniffs hard, then tosses the phone at me. The scowl on his face grows. I've never felt so much hatred toward me. Ice drips from his voice. "How long did it take you to run to him in the staircase, Arianna?"

"I-I—"

"Don't lie to me! Don't you dare after everything that happened tonight," he barks.

"I was going to tell him off, that's all," I admit, but it comes out weak.

Disgust grows on Killian's face. "You don't know when not to push your luck, do you?"

I think he's referring to me wanting to give Donato a piece of my mind. I blurt out, "He-he cheated on me last night. I called him and heard it!"

Killian stares at the ceiling and takes a deep breath. When he finally looks at me, his calmness scares me. He quietly says,

"You had him last Saturday. I assumed you got that thug out of your system. But I was wrong, wasn't I? Your plan to screw whoever you want once we're married wasn't you just blurting out a bunch of shit, was it?"

I gape at him, shocked he thinks I would ever want that in any relationship I'm in.

He crosses his arms, giving me a look filled with so much abhorrence, I want to die on the spot.

My lack of words only digs me in the hole deeper. Any chance I had of making this right no longer exists.

He firmly states, "I'm not a man who sits in the back seat, letting other men drive my women around. You've made it clear who you are and what you're about. Find someone else to marry." He spins and walks toward the door.

I jump off the bed and grab his arm. "Killian!"

"Too late. I'm not going to be your fool."

"My papà will send me to Italy! Please! Let me explain what happened. You have this wrong!" I beg.

"That's not my problem. Have a nice life, lass." He shrugs out of my hold and slams the door on his way out.

Paralyzed, I stare at the door. My heart seizes and tears drip on my floor. The most confusing part is, I'm unsure if I'm more upset my papà will send me to Italy or that Killian no longer wants me.

8

Killian

"Whoa! Easy!" Boris states.

I pour another finger of whiskey in the crystal tumbler. At least if I have to stay another night in this house, Arianna's father has top-shelf liquor. I snort and take three mouthfuls. I set it down, pick up a glass, and fill it with vodka. I hand it to Boris.

He clinks my glass, drinks some, and I follow suit. We sit in the den in leather chairs. Tully told me ten minutes, and it's already past fifteen. If he doesn't come out of Angelo's study soon, I'm going to barge in.

Boris's face looks as bad as mine. He winces when his back hits the seat.

"Those tasers are no joke," I mutter.

"Tell me about it. I think they got me right on my spine," he declares.

I let another mouthful of whiskey slide down my throat and tap my fingers on my thigh. No matter how much time passes, I can't seem to calm myself down. Reading the text her thug boyfriend sent her has me ready to find out where he lives and show up unannounced.

"Nora said she was only trying to tell him off," Boris offers.

I grunt, chug some more alcohol, and scoff. "Isn't that convenient."

"What if it's true?" he asks.

"I don't care what she claims. I'm out. Tully can find someone else to cover his ass with Angelo."

"No, I won't," Tully's Irish accent hits my ears.

I groan inside, don't acknowledge him, and add more whiskey to my already-flooded bloodstream.

Tully pours a drink and takes the seat across from me.

"I don't want to hear your bullshit," I mutter.

He turns to Boris. "Give us a minute."

Boris raises his eyebrows then rises. He finishes his drink and pats me on the shoulder. "I'll see you tomorrow."

"Yep. On the first flight out of this place."

Tully gives me an exasperated stare.

"Did you forget you don't intimidate me?" I point out.

His lips twitch. "Always the straight shooter."

"Except I'm not laughing this time. I'm on the first flight out of here when the sun comes up. Have Angelo send his brat to Italy. Let that fat fucker do whatever he wants with her," I bark but wince inside saying it. The thought of Arianna with Giuseppe or any other man still angers me, but I'm not signing my life away to a woman who would run to another man the first chance she gets.

"What did you expect, Killian? Did you think this would be all sunshine and leprechauns?" Tully questions.

I blurt out, "I didn't think I was marrying a liar and cheater." I finish the rest of my whiskey.

"She did no such thing," he states.

Bitterness grows. The thought I was in the club, and she was about to leave with him, isn't something I'm just going to get over. I took this commitment seriously. No matter how we got here, I wouldn't do it without one-hundred-percent effort. Arianna thinks it's a game. "Yeah. I stopped him from getting into the car with her. Otherwise, I'm sure she'd have had her little rendezvous." The vision of that scumbag touching her enrages me again, and I rise.

Tully stands. "You will show up to the church tomorrow. If you don't, when Nolan and Gemma get on their plane to Ireland, Gemma will be the only one coming back to Chicago."

I step in front of him, eye to eye, seething. "Your threats are getting old."

"I don't make threats without execution. Don't test me, Killian." He downs the rest of his drink then sets it on the table. "I'll see you at the church tomorrow."

No amount of deep breathing can calm me. I'm not marrying her. She made her choice tonight.

I glance at my watch. It's two in the morning. There are fifteen hours until I'm supposed to walk down the aisle. Somehow, I need to figure out how to get Nolan out of the shit he's in.

I climb the stairs and go to my room. I pace while every thought possible goes through my head.

I could kill Tully.

How would I get past his security?

Maybe I'll shoot him at the church.

No. Too many people. Someone else could get hurt.

I give up and jump in the shower. Grime covers my palms and body, which permeated my clothes when I laid on the slush-filled street. My back has a sore from the taser prong, and I breathe hard through my nose when the water hits it. Then I take a washcloth, soak it, and hold it to my face.

The stinging sensation is nothing compared to what Arianna did. I saw Donato Brambilla as a thug on social media. My encounter with him tonight only confirmed my thoughts.

She still wants him.

"Fuck!" I mumble then turn off the water. I don't know why I'm allowing this to bother me. She's a spoiled little brat and did nothing except prove my theory tonight. All it took was one text, and she ran to him. If she's telling the truth, he didn't take more than five minutes to sleep with someone else. She still chose him over me.

I dry off and climb in bed, but all I do is toss and turn. I'm lying on my side, trying to get comfortable, but there are wounds no matter what position I choose.

The door creaks. I open my eyes, but there is only blackness. I smell Arianna before I see or feel her. Her perfume slices through the air, flaring in my nostrils, stirring everything I felt for her since the moment I laid eyes on her.

The mattress dips down. Her hand trembles on my back.

A war rages inside me. I want to flip her over and fuck her, but my ego won't allow me. The rage I felt earlier reignites. All I can see is her in Donato's arms and running to the staircase the first chance she had to ditch me.

"I'm sorry," she whispers. A tear drips on my side, rolling into the taser wound and creating a new sting.

But I'd rather have physical pain than mental. I'm used to beatings, wounds, and getting back up. Women not throwing themselves on me isn't something I ever experience. And I'm definitely not used to them running into other men's arms. I order, "Go to bed, lass. You made your decision."

"You have it wrong."

"You got caught red-handed. It's over," I say, but it doesn't come out very strong. Everything about Arianna makes my body react. I hate myself for not having enough control to turn my attraction to her off completely.

"I-I just wanted to tell him off! I swear! Please! I won't ever talk to him again. I promise," she begs.

"Yeah, until your other men come out of the woodwork," I mumble.

"What are you talking about? I was only with Donato."

"Don't say his name ever again," I growl, unable to control the rage burning within me.

Her hand shakes harder. The room turns silent, except for her sniffles. My racing thoughts try to figure out how to get her to go and not fall for her lies. All I smell is her and the forbidden fruit she represents.

She reaches for me and runs her hand on the side of my head. My mind tells me to remove it, but my mouth won't form the words, nor will my arms move. She states, "I'm sorry you got hurt."

I grunt. "That bastard's a pussy. He's lucky the cops showed up and stopped me from killing him."

"I think you broke his nose. It was on the side of his face," she blurts out.

Her statement gives me some satisfaction. At least she caught a glimpse of how I can tear him up.

"Do you want me to get you some ice?" she offers.

I should say yes. An ice bath would be appropriate. Instead, I reply, "No."

Her nails graze my scalp, and her other hand slides under the covers, touching my thigh. It's all too much. I can't be next to her without feeling a buzz. It mixes with my determination and her scent that I can't seem to get enough of, until I'm dizzy on everything that's her.

I grasp her wrist and move her hand off my head. I release it and order, "Go to sleep, Arianna."

A moment passes. She finally rises, and I think she's leaving. I close my eyes, resisting the urge to tell her to come back.

There's a soft thud, and the bed sinks. I open my eyes and turn to the opposite side. She's so close to me, her energy zaps me. I swallow the lump in my throat and try to keep my erection from turning harder, but it's impossible.

Her hands hold my head, and she presses her trembling lips to mine. I don't return her affection. I mumble, "I said to go to sleep."

"I am. With you."

"Why? So you can pretend I'm him?"

She freezes. It's a low blow, and I instantly feel guilty. I don't doubt the scumbag screwed someone else last night. Part of me believes she went to tell him off. It's totally her style. She's not a doormat and speaks her mind. It's something I like about her, even if she's a pain in the ass sometimes.

She still met up with him as soon as he texted her, I remind myself.

"Go to your room," I hurl.

In a hurt voice, she says, "If you tell me to leave one more time, I will."

Her challenge hangs in the air. She slides closer, so her hard nipples touch my chest. The heat of her pussy swirls around my cock, making it impossible to push her away. I call her out on her threat. "No, you won't."

She takes a shaky breath and quietly asks, "What do you want from me, Killian? I'm trying. I'm-I'm not ready for everything in my world to be upside down."

"You mean you aren't ready to leave him behind," I snarl, my pulse creeping too high again.

"No!" She moves closer so her body presses against my flesh. Her lips brush mine. "Stop talking about him. I don't want to talk about him ever again."

"That's convenient," I mumble, trying my hardest to let my ego win over my dick.

She picks up my arm and positions it so my palm is on her bare ass. Her smooth skin is a contrast to my rough, calloused palms.

Breathing becomes more difficult. She kisses me again, and this time, I let her explore my mouth with her delicious tongue that officially makes her the devil in disguise. I refuse to fall into the temptation. Still hanging on to my pride, I only give her a little effort, but damn, if she's not the best kisser I've ever experienced.

I finally crack and begin to really kiss her back. She pulls away and murmurs, "Please don't make me go to Italy."

I freeze.

She's not here for me. She's here for herself. She wants me to save her from Giuseppe and all he represents. I push her away. "Get out of my bed."

"What?" she breathes, confused.

"You heard me. Get out."

"Killian!"

"You want to stay, fine. I'll leave." I get up and turn on the light. It hits me like a hurricane, and I blink a few times to adjust. And I wish I would have kept the lights off. Everything about Arianna Marino's flushed cheeks, hurt brown eyes, and perfect naked body is going to stay with me until the day I die.

I tear my eyes off her, pull shorts and a T-shirt out of my bag, then put them on.

"Killian! Please! You're taking everything the wrong way!"

I cross my arms, as if I can somehow protect myself against her. "Then look me in the eyes and tell me you didn't come in here to convince me to marry you so you didn't have to go to Italy."

Her eyes well with tears. "I don't want to go to Italy. But that isn't—"

I clap. "There it is. You don't need to say anything else. The first sentence is the only bit of truth you need to disclose. The rest is a bunch of nonsense I don't want to hear."

She sits up and pulls the sheet over her breasts. She whispers, "Why are you so cruel?"

I scoff. "Did you think I wasn't? Did you have this big misconception that your daddy, or brothers, or even that thug you prefer over me, have something I don't?"

She bites on her lip, staring at me.

"Of course you did. Well, guess what? I can assure you, my wrath is ten times worse."

Her voice grows stronger. "Stop putting words in my mouth!"

"I'm sure it's better than the other things you've had in it," I hurl at her.

Jesus. Why did I say that?

She opens her mouth to speak, shuts it, then swallows hard. She avoids my eyes and reaches to the floor, picks up her nightgown, then tugs it over her head.

Regret instantly digs at me. I take some deep breaths, knowing I just crossed a line that was extremely hurtful and not necessary.

She spins. Her eyes are full of tears. "You're off the hook." She opens the door and steps out of the room.

I follow her and call out, "Arianna! Wait!"

"You've spoken loud and clear," she claims, trotting down the hall.

Tristano steps into the hall. He yawns. "What's going on?"

"Nothing. Mind your own business." I continue toward Arianna's room.

He follows me. "Arianna! What's wrong?"

She gets to her bedroom and opens the door. Standing straighter, she spins and tells Tristano, "Tell Papà to call Giuseppe and book the flights."

My stomach flips.

"Have you lost your mind?" Tristano accuses.

She says nothing, goes into her room, then shuts the door. The sound of the lock clicking hits my ears.

"What did you do to my sister?" Tristano angrily asks.

"Nothing," I say, but it's a lie. I know what I did, and now I'm afraid of the irreversible damage it's going to cause.

Tristano steps forward. The black eye he got from Club D is so swollen, it's barely a slit. "You did something for my sister to say that."

He needs to get out of my face so I can make things right with Arianna. I raise my voice. "I told you to stay out of my business."

Declan comes out of his room holding a bag of ice to his face. "What's going on?"

"Nothing," Tristano and I both yell at the same time then return to scowling at each other.

Declan shakes his head and sighs. "Would you mind taking your nothing fight and moving it to a different wing?"

Nora opens the door and steps out. She ties her robe. "What's all the shouting about?"

"Nothing," the three of us say.

She arches her eyebrows, shakes her head, then grabs my biceps. "Let's go."

"Where?"

"The kitchen. You need ice. Your face looks like raw meat. Arianna isn't going to have every girl's dream wedding photos," she comments.

"They aren't getting married. Arianna just told me to tell my father to send her to Italy to marry Giuseppe," Tristano seethes.

Nora gapes at me then her eyes turn to slits. "Killian, what did you do?"

"Nothing," I lie again.

Her cheeks turn red with anger. She tugs on my arm, and I let her lead me down the hallway, exhausted from this entire night.

We go through the mansion and get to the kitchen. She finds a plastic bag and fills it with ice then grabs a towel. She points to the chair. "Sit."

I do as she says, sick of fighting. She hands me the ice pack, and I try not to wince when I put it on my face.

Nora sits next to me. In a low voice, she says, "Tell me what happened."

"You know what happened. You were at the club."

Her voice turns stern. "No, tell me what happened that was so bad Arianna agreed to go to Italy."

I bounce my leg under the table, wishing I could take it back. I admit, "I said something I shouldn't have."

"What did you say?"

"I'm not repeating it."

Nora taps her fingers on the table. She says, "You always do this."

"Do what?"

"Let your arrogance create so much anger inside you that you say stupid things."

I snort. "That about sums me up."

"Are you really going to let Arianna go to Italy and marry that old man? He sounds horrible," Nora adds.

The air in my lungs curls, clawing at me until I feel like I can't breathe. Visions of Arianna with Giuseppe's hands all over her make me nauseous.

"I don't know what Tully has over you that you committed to marrying her, but I like her. I think if anyone is in a bad situation, it's her, not you."

"You don't know what you're talking about," I interject.

Nora puts the butt of her palms on her eyes and shakes her head.

I scoff. "Whatever you want to say, get it over with."

Nora turns more in her seat. "Okay, I will. She's losing everything she knows. Her family, her friends—"

"Her thug boyfriend."

"That's not fair. And she said she was going to tell him off."

"She ran to him the first chance she had."

Nora groans. "Jesus, Killian. Wake up. Her father told her a week ago she had to marry you or be shipped off to Italy. Her entire life is changing. What's changing for you?"

I snort. "All my freedom."

"Yeah, well, you still have everything you know. The only person I see losing their freedom in this is Arianna."

I remove the ice pack. "I thought you were supposed to be on my side."

Nora smiles. "I am on your side. Always. I'm also okay telling you when you're a complete dickhead. Whatever deal you made with Tully, you aren't getting out of. My assumption is your mouth got you into it."

"You know me well," I mutter.

"Yeah, well, you agreed to it. And marriage is hard, so stop thinking it's going to be four-leaf clovers."

"What's with you and Tully and the Irish references?"

Nora ignores my question. She rises and pats my shoulder. "I'm going to bed. Keep the ice on your face. It looks like you lost."

"Gee, thanks."

She pauses and studies me for a moment. "Have you asked Arianna one thing about her life?"

"What do you mean?"

"Dinner was all about Chicago and you. I didn't hear you ask her anything about her."

I sigh. "Anything else you want to point out I've done wrong?"

Nora smirks. "Only whatever you said to her, you need to make right. She doesn't deserve to be shipped off to marry that guy. No matter how much she pissed you off, whatever you did to drive her to agree to Italy is ten times worse."

I grumble, "You can go to bed now."

She doesn't say anything else and leaves.

I don't sleep. I rotate ice on my face, wondering what the solution to everything is. But I don't see one.

9

Arianna

LOUD KNOCKS WAKE ME UP. AT SOME POINT, I CRIED MYSELF to sleep. Sunlight streams through my window since I forgot to pull the shades. I slowly sit up, and the events of last night hit me like a brick.

He thinks I'm a slut is the first thought that hits. But then I cringe with anxiety and regret. *I told my brother to tell my papà I would marry Giuseppe. Ugh!*

Another knock hits my ears and the doorknob rattles, but it's still locked. All I want to do is pull the sheets over my head and never get up, but I don't. I'm sure it's my papà telling me he booked the flight and everything will be fine.

I reach for my robe, put it on, then unlock and open my door. All of the women who arrived with Killian stand before me. Excited smiles light up their faces. Each holds something in their hands, and they sing in unison, "Happy Wedding Day!"

Selena holds out a tray. "Carmella said this is your favorite breakfast. Where should I put it?"

Nora holds another tray. "Mimosas for everyone not preggers! That includes me this time!"

"Ummm... I ummm..." Their chipper elation is throwing me for a loop. Did no one tell them the wedding with Killian is off?

Kora shakes a small box. "As soon as you let us in, you get to open this."

I step back, open my mouth again, but I'm not sure what to say. They barrel through the doorway until my room is full of women and a stack of presents sits on my bed. I blurt out, "I'm sorry. Did no one tell you the wedding is off? I'm sure my papà has booked the flight and I'll be leaving for Italy soon."

Gemma scrunches her face. "Eww. No. Killian might be an arrogant jerk sometimes, but you are not marrying that old, gross guy."

"You don't know anything about him," I point out.

"I know enough."

Kora holds a small box in the palm of her hand. "You should open this."

"And this," Hailee chimes in, shoving an envelope close to my face.

"What is it?" I ask.

"You have to open it to find out. Here, read first." Hailee pushes the paper closer to me.

I gingerly reach for it, not sure what's happening. I sit on the bed and open the envelope. A plain white card is in it.

Arianna,

As soon as I said what I did, I regretted it. I'm sorry. I didn't mean it, and it wasn't fair. If you haven't noticed, sometimes my mouth gets me in trouble...

Don't go to Italy.

Killian

P.S. - I would have told you this in person, but there are too many nosy, bossy women in this house.

P.P.S. - I hope you like your gift. I realized I made another pretty big mistake.

Four times I reread the note. I'm unsure what to think and slightly uncomfortable with eight women's eyes on me.

Kora puts the box on my lap. "Open it."

My insides quiver. I pull the white satin bow and open the lid. Time seems to stop. The room is quiet, and I can't seem to inhale any oxygen.

A perfect, round diamond gleams at me. Smaller round and pear-shaped diamonds float on compass points around it, separated by tiny yellow gold pieces. They match the shiny band, which also has delicate beading lining the bridge and inner band.

I gape at it then grasp the box and note. "I have to go to the bathroom." I rush to the door and close it before anyone can stop me.

I sit on my vanity stool and put the note and box on the counter. Then, I pick the ring up and slide it on my finger, blinking back tears.

It's perfect. It's as if he knew I only wear gold. All of my ex-boyfriends who proposed to me bought platinum rings. While I love them on other women, it would never feel right on me.

Did my papà or brothers tell him?

No, they couldn't have. I've never told them my feelings on platinum.

My phone buzzes. I must have left it on the counter by accident. A notification pops up I have a message in my social media inbox.

Killian: *Did you get my note and gift?*

My heart races, and I take a deep breath, debating what to say.

Me: *Yes. It's beautiful.*

Killian: *You like it?*

Me: *I love it.*

Killian: *I thought it would match the cuff bracelet you wore last night. Plus, I noticed you only wear yellow gold in your photos.*

I smile at his admission.

Me: *Stalker.*

Killian: *Possibly.*

I wait for more, not sure what to write.

Killian: *I meant what I wrote. I'm sorry for my mouth. I didn't mean it.*

Me: *Thank you. And I'm sorry for last night. I only went into the stairwell to tell him off.*

Several minutes pass, and anxiety tightens in my chest, wondering if I said the wrong thing by bringing it up again.

Killian: *I hated seeing him touch you. If he comes near you again, I will destroy him.*

I bite my lip, not sure if I want Donato dead but not opposed to the thought, either. Aside from the fact he slept with another woman so soon, he scared me last night. He crossed the line when he manhandled me through the club and physically forced me to get in his car.

Me: *Should I put this with the rest of my police files?*

Killian: *Ha ha.*

More time passes, and I stare at the ring on my finger.

Killian: *Does this mean you don't want to go to Italy?*

My pulse increases.

Me: *You know I don't want to go.*

Killian: *Okay then. I'll see you at the church?*

Me: *Okay.*

Killian: *You aren't going to stand me up, right?*

A tearful laugh escapes me.

Me: *I'll see how I'm feeling later in the day.*

He sends me a crying emoji.

I laugh again and close my app. Relief fills me, but it's short-lived.

Oh, crap. Tristano.

I text him.

Me: *Did you tell Papà to send me to Italy?*

Tristano: *Nope. I was hoping you would come to your senses. I don't think Killian is good enough for you, but he's a step up from Giuseppe.*

I smile.

Me: *Thanks. I'll see you at the church.*

Tristano: *Thank God.*

I put my phone down and study my reflection in the mirror then cringe. All the crying I did last night made my eyes puffy and red.

There's a knock on the door. Nora's voice calls out, "Arianna, your hair and makeup artists are here."

My gut sinks, and I wince. I open the door. "I'm a mess and haven't even showered yet."

Piero, my hairstylist, steps into view. He gasps. "Girl! Have you been crying all night?"

I wince. "Yeah."

He snaps his fingers. "Well, get in the shower. Come on. We've got a lot of work to do."

Vannie, one of the top makeup artists in New York and Piero's boyfriend, pushes past Nora. He dramatically puts his hand over his mouth. "Oh my!"

"Thanks for making me feel better."

He claps his hands. "Shower! Now!" He steps in front of the tub and turns on the water.

"Don't wash your hair!" Piero hands me a claw clip.

They leave. I shower, brush my teeth, then put my robe back on. When I step back into my bedroom, it's a party atmosphere. I get whisked to the couch. Nora passes out mimosas, except for the pregnant women, who only get orange juice. Selena sets a plate of avocado toast on the coffee table. Vannie places a bottle of eye drops in my hand. "Two drops in each. Should get the red out."

I put the eye drops in.

"Eat! We don't want you passing out when you walk down the aisle," Piero orders.

I obey and reach for the toast.

Selena grabs my hand. "OMG.! Your ring is beautiful!"

The room erupts in more enthusiasm, and heat flares in my cheeks from all the attention.

I finally get a few bites of avocado toast in when Selena hands me a box. She glances at my ring and beams. "I think I picked the right thing."

I open the box and pull out a delicate lingerie set. White and gold embroidery embellish sheer white tulle and satin, creating a peek-a-boo tattoo effect. A matching garter belt is with it and has an ice-blue sapphire in the middle. I've never seen anything like it, and it makes the white set my wedding planner dropped off look cheap. "Wow."

"Look out, Killian," Kora booms, and heat floods my cheeks.

"Girl! That's going to look so good on you!" Piero gushes.

Hailee asks, "Where did you get that? It's gorgeous!"

I glance at Selena. "Yes, where? This is beyond beautiful."

Her smile widens. "Obrecht told me last Sunday about the wedding. I tracked you down on social media then had it flown in from the U.K. There's a designer I get a lot of stuff from, and when I saw it, I thought you'd look hot in it."

"Your boobs and ass are going to look fantastic in this," Vannie bubbles.

"It's perfect for your Italian skin! Girl!" Piero tsks. "I hope Killian knows what he's doing!"

I cover my face, trying to hide my flaming cheeks.

"Yuck! That's my brother," Nora moans.

Vannie's signature clap echoes in the room. "Time to get you in the chair. Ladies, keep the mimosas coming."

I get swept into the bathroom. Piero leans into my ear. "You got everything waxed, correct? That little number isn't going to look good with little dark hairs peeking out."

I reveal, "All good. Had it done a few days ago."

"Phew! There's nothing worse than a hairy woman."

"Except a hairy man," Vannie sings.

"True!" Piero winks, and I roll my eyes. I can only imagine all the manscaping they do.

The next few hours I spend at my vanity. My hair and makeup get styled to perfection. Vannie and Piero keep me laughing like they always do. The girls rotate in and out of the bathroom.

When Vannie and Piero finish, the women shower me with more gifts. Nora gives me a white silk robe that has Ms. O'Malley embroidered with gold bling on the back and a roll of duct tape.

Confused, I hold it up. "What's this for?"

Her green eyes sparkle with mischief. "I went and got it this morning. I thought you might need it to tape Killian's mouth shut at some point."

The room erupts in laughs, and more gifts get handed to me.

When I finish opening all the presents, my bedroom represents a high-end sex shop. Handcuffs, vibrators, cock rings, nipple rings, dildos, oils, lotions, scented candles, and more lingerie cover my bed.

"Oh! Don't forget our gift!" Vannie hands me another package.

I tear off the white paper and open the black box. Rows of shiny, stainless steel form the shape of a dick, along with another thick ring but bigger. A gold padded lock and keys lay inside. I glance at the men. "What is it?"

Piero gasps. "It's a cock cage."

"Ummm...what does it do?" I ask, and my cheeks once again burn with fire.

"Think of it as a chastity belt but for him," Vannie informs.

"Why would she need that?" Skylar asks.

"Yeah. Why would she want to deny herself the O Train?" Kora asks.

Piero huffs. "To show him who's in charge, of course."

"Or punish him," Vannie adds.

Aspen picks it up and studies it. "Does it hurt?"

"Ummm..." Piero glances at Vannie.

He smirks. "Think of it like this, ladies. Your man wants...no, needs to get an erection. But he can't fully let it loose. He can't masturbate or orgasm, and only you can unlock the cage and give him the gift."

Skylar tilts her head and scrunches her face. "So it does hurt?"

"Sounds like it," Anna mutters.

Piero steps behind Vannie and puts his hands on his shoulders. "Look at it this way. I want Vannie aroused but not too much."

Vannie wiggles his eyebrows at Piero. "You also want to show me you're the boss."

Piero bats his eyes then cups Vannie's crotch. "So, I put the cock cage on him, lock it up, then do all sorts of things to him that would normally get him off."

"But I can't! And I get to do all sorts of things to please him to earn my way out." Vannie naughtily purses his lips.

"So it does hurt?" Skylar repeats.

An exasperated sigh comes out of Vannie. He shakes his head. "Raise your hand if your man has ever gotten you nice and hot—I mean right on the edge. You were about to come, but he makes you beg for it instead of completing the job. And the more you beg, the longer he makes you wait, but then when you do come, it's so intense, you think you're going to lose your mind."

All the hands in the room slowly go up but mine. I raise mine so I'm not the lone wolf in the room, but I've never had a man deny me an orgasm. Some of them couldn't get me there, but no one has restricted it. I didn't even know this was a thing.

Gemma takes it from Aspen and studies it. "So it's like role reversal?"

Hailee raises her eyebrows. "Are you going to put Nolan in one?"

Gemma tosses back, "Maybe you should try it first with Liam."

Nora covers her ears. "Don't make me think about it."

Kora picks up the cage and waves it in front of Nora's face. "Well, this is meant for Killian."

"Ugh!" Nora winces.

I grab it and put it back in the box. "Thanks. It was very sweet of you. All of your gifts were. Really, thank you." I rise and kiss Piero and Vannie on the cheek.

There's a knock on my door. Anna opens it. The team of seamstresses my papà hired flood into the room. They spend the next hour fussing over me and doing last-minute alterations. The closer it gets to the wedding, the more my stomach flutters with nerves.

When my lingerie, dress, and shoes are on, I add my new cuff bracelet and a pair of Italian-made gold teardrop earrings my mother wore on her wedding day. I swallow down the grief building in my chest.

Hailee says, "Do you have anything borrowed?"

I shake my head.

She reaches into her pocket and pulls out a stunning gold necklace. It's a trinity knot with emeralds and diamonds. "This was Liam's grandmother's. She gave it to his father before she died to give to his wife. It was to welcome me into the family. I never knew her, but I'm sure if she were here, she would want to welcome you, too. No pressure, but would you like to wear it today?"

Something about the sentimental value of the necklace and how genuinely nice everyone has been to me brings tears to my eyes.

Nora says, "Hailee's right. She would love for you to wear it."

I take a deep breath and fan my eyes so my makeup doesn't smear. "Okay. Thank you."

"Girl, don't make me fix your eyes!" Vannie whines.

I laugh, and Hailee clasps the necklace around me.

"Ladies, would you mind giving me a moment alone with Arianna?" my papà says, stepping into the room.

Everyone leaves, and he shuts the door. His eyes glisten, and he steps in front of me. The custom tux he had made fits him perfectly. He says, "Wow. You look stunning, my bambina."

I stay silent. My nerves grow at how real this moment is. I'm about to leave him and everything I've ever known. I scrunch my face and try to stop myself from crying.

Papà circles his arms around me and kisses the top of my head.

"Why didn't you come see me last night or this morning?" I ask.

He steps back. "There was too much emotion. I needed to calm down, as did you, so neither of us said something or made a choice we would regret."

"I didn't willingly go with him, Papà."

His eyes turn dark. "Yes. That is what I heard. I am grateful Killian was there to stop him. But do not worry about that thug anymore. Your brothers and I will take care of him. He is your past, not your future."

I take a deep, shaky breath, not sure what he will do to Donato. However, I can't worry about that right now. My entire life is about to change drastically, and anxiety is beginning to build.

"If your mamma were here, she would be so proud of the beautiful woman you are," he states.

It makes me tear up further.

He puts his hand on my cheek. "I'll miss you, my bambina. Nothing will be the same without you here."

"I don't have to do this," I blurt out.

For a brief instant, I think he might tell me I don't have to. But then his face hardens. "This is the right thing for you."

My insides quiver harder. I turn away from him, staring out into the snow-filled yard I've looked at every day for the last twenty-eight years.

He moves my chin so I can't avoid him. "I am your papà. I would never do anything that wasn't in your best interest."

"It doesn't feel like it," I quietly admit.

He nods. "Yes, I understand. When you return from your honeymoon, I'll be there to check up on you."

It should bring me some comfort, but it doesn't.

He smiles and takes my hand. "Come, my bambina. It's time to get to the church."

10

Killian

SHOTS OF WHISKEY GET DISTRIBUTED. MY NERVES ONLY GROW, the closer it gets to wedding time. I kept to myself most of the day. Before the rest of the house was up, I used the gym in the Marino estate, still clueless about how to make things right with Arianna. In the middle of my workout, I realized I hadn't even given her a ring.

I showered, had a driver take me into the city, and looked at rings for hours. Nothing seemed right. Everything felt like all the other rings I see on women's hands. When I found it, I was at the third store. I would have given it to her when I got back, but Nora and the other women stopped me.

After that, I tried staying away from everyone else. An hour ago, Declan came into my room and told me it was time to leave.

And now I'm in a room on the side of the church. Airflow seems nonexistent. Arianna's brothers, the O'Malleys, and the Ivanovs are all here with me. No one appears to be overheated, except me.

I take off my tux jacket and remove my bowtie. "Can they turn the heat off in here?"

Declan arches his eyebrows. "It's not hot. I assumed the heater was broken."

"Maybe I'm getting sick," I state.

"Or you're shitting your pants from nerves?" Finn mutters so no one else can hear.

"Shut up. I don't get nervous," I grumble.

"First time for everything," Nolan quips.

Liam hands me a shot. "Maybe this will settle your nerves."

"I'm not nervous," I insist again. I've boxed my entire life. I don't even get pre-match jitters. Nerves are a result of insecurity. I've learned how to shove any inkling of it out of my head.

"Everyone shut up a minute!" Declan shouts.

The room goes silent, and my gut pitches.

Jesus. What the fuck is happening to me?

He holds his glass in the air. "I never thought I'd see it happen, but, Killian, in twenty minutes, you'll no longer be a free man."

My stomach rumbles. My chest feels as if someone is squeezing all the air out of it.

Declan's eyes twinkle. "You've had a good run, lad! I promise to represent for you with the single lasses!"

The room erupts in shouts.

"May you make Mrs. Killian O'Malley happy for the rest of her life and yours. Slàinte!"

"Slàinte!" the men all shout and knock back their drinks.

I swallow the bile coming up in my throat and manage to wash it down with the whiskey. My brothers pat me on the back.

The priest enters the room. "Killian. It's time for your confession."

Heckles fill the air. I ignore them all and follow Father Ercole. The tiny booth is an outdated confessional where he sits across from me and a dark screen separates us. It seems pointless since he already knows it's me, and something about it adds to my discomfort.

A bead of sweat rolls down my face. "Fuck this," I mutter and unbutton my shirt.

"Excuse me?" Father Ercole says in a shocked tone.

"Is your heat on full blast?" I ask.

"No. Most of our parishioners wear several layers and claim they are always cold," he states.

"Yeah, well, excuse me while I get naked so I don't stain my clothes with sweat," I mumble then remove my shirt.

"Nervous?" he asks.

"Nope."

"Lots of grooms are."

"I'm not," I firmly state.

"It helps—"

"No offense, Father, but can we get to the part where I tell you my sins and you forgive me?"

He chuckles. "It is not I who forgives you but God."

"Right. So how does this start again?"

"Bless me, Father—"

"Ah, right. Bless me, Father, for I have sinned. It has been..." I stop in the middle of making the cross. "I'm not sure how long it's been."

"Just estimate then."

I was in high school. I do the math in my head. "I believe it's been twenty-five years." I grab a tissue and wipe the sweat off my forehead. "Jesus. Do I have to tell you everything I've done since then? We might be here all day."

"No. Let's try not to take the Lord's name in vain while in the confessional," he advises.

"Sure. I'll save that for outside it."

"I wasn't suggesting that."

I shift in my seat. "Are you sure the heat isn't on full blast?"

"No, Killian, it's not."

I sigh. I need to get out of here before I burn up.

"Is there anything heavy on your heart you want to ask God for forgiveness for?" he asks.

I rack my brain. *Have I done anything I want forgiveness for?*

Father Ercole suggests, "There is a list of the ten commandments on the ledge. Since it's been a while, maybe you should focus on what you've broken."

"Sure. Good idea." I pick up the laminated sheet and go through each one. "I've never broken the first one. There's only one big guy in my eyes."

Amusement fills his voice. "That's good."

"Well, you heard me already break the second one when I took the Lord's name in vain."

"And are you seeking forgiveness for this?"

"Nope. I don't see the big deal. If someone wanted to curse with my name, I'd be honored. Like instead of saying Jesus Christ, they would shriek, Killian O'Malley! I think Jesus secretly likes it."

He stays quiet.

I return to the list. "I don't go to church anymore on Sundays. I broke the third one."

"And are you seeking God's forgiveness for this?"

"No. I think the big guy still loves me. I'm good."

The priest clears his throat.

"Hmmm...four is out. Both my parents are dead." I swallow the lump in my throat.

"Oh, I'm sorry to hear that. Hopefully, they're in the Kingdom of Heaven."

I don't reply and move past the subject. "Okay, let's break the rest of the list down. Six through ten are out. I've never broken those."

"But you've broken commandment number five, thou shall not kill?"

My mouth goes dry. I've never admitted it out loud. "Yes."

"And this is the sin you wish to seek forgiveness for?" he asks.

I slide my feet out of my shoes then rise. I unbuckle my pants and take them off. *Why is it so hot in here?* I reply, "Would that mean I don't regret killing them?"

"If you are seeking forgiveness, then yes."

"Then no. I'm not seeking forgiveness. I would do it again."

Deafening silence fills the box again.

I fan myself with the laminated card, wondering why I'm sweating like a pig. "Do you have a shower in this church?"

"In church? No. But the priest quarters next door has one," he informs me.

"Great. I need to use it when we finish here," I state, thinking I'm going to be resembling Giuseppe Berlusconi if I don't get this off me.

"Son, is there anything you regret that you'd like God's forgiveness for?" he asks.

I continue fanning myself. I blurt out, "What if I already said I was sorry to the person I offended, but I'm not sure if it falls into the commandments?"

The screen turns darker, which makes me believe he's leaning closer to it. "Tell me about this event."

I wince recalling it. "I said something horrible to Arianna last night."

"What did you say?"

"I don't want to repeat it. Do I have to tell you?" I ask.

"No. But you are sorry for this and seeking God's forgiveness?" he asks.

"Does God need to forgive me? Isn't it only Arianna who does?" I ask.

Father Ercole firmly states, "Genesis 1:26–27 says we are all created in God's image. If you have offended her, you have offended him."

I scratch my neck. "I'm seeking his forgiveness, then."

Silence fills the booth.

"Did you leave or die of heat exhaustion?" I quip as my stomach somersaults again.

"No. I'm saying a few extra prayers for your soul and listening to what God wants you to do for penance," he replies.

"Don't you tell me to say some Hail Mary's?"

He chuckles. "Not for this one. Just give me a moment, please."

More sweat breaks out. I debate about removing my boxers that are sticking to my ass.

"Are you ready for your penance?"

"Give it to me straight up, Father." I tap my fingers on my thighs then use my other hand to fan myself with the ten commandments sheet again.

"Since this is possibly the most important day of your life, and this sin involves your wife, your penance will be to love her and show her how much you cherish her above all others," he says.

I drop the ten commandments. It echoes in the tiny booth. I blurt out, "Love her? I hardly know her."

He takes a deep breath then slowly releases it. "You have a lifetime to work on your penance."

"When do I get forgiven? It's an O'Malley tradition to marry without any sins hanging over our heads," I state. I may not go to church, but this isn't something I take lightly.

"I'll absolve you, but you'll need to complete your penance. Is there anything else that is heavy on your heart?"

I think for a moment. "No. Nothing else comes to mind."

He completes several rituals then gives me a blessing. I slide into my shoes, grab my clothes, and leave the confessional.

Father Ercole steps out and gapes at me.

"Shower?" I ask.

He regains his composure. "Yes. Come with me." He leads me through an exit door. The cold snow hits me, and nothing has ever felt more refreshing. It's only a hundred yards to the priest's quarters, but I finally feel like I can breathe again.

Father Ercole shows me where the shower is, and I close the door. I put my clothes on a chair and decide my boxers aren't going back on my body. I peel them off and toss them in the trash.

I turn the water on cold, rinse off, then step out. My reflection fills the mirror. I stare at my battered face, hearing Father Ercole's voice.

"Love her and show her how much you cherish her above all others." It's like a broken record taunting me.

Love. I groan then put on my clothes. I don't do love. I have fun with women and show them a good time. That emotional stuff just isn't me. I'll be faithful to Arianna, but marriage isn't going to change the core of who I am.

There's a knock on the door. Father Ercole shouts, "The ceremony needs to begin. Are you almost ready?"

I open the door and he hands me my bow tie and jacket. I put them on and we trot across the parking lot. This time, the cold wind whips into my face, and I shiver from the bitter air.

When I get inside the church, I go directly to the front of the altar. My brothers, Liam, Finn, and Boris, are lined up in a row. The church is full of people I don't know, except for a few rows of pews on the front right side.

Music begins to play and several bridesmaids in matching black dresses stroll up the aisle. It hits me I don't know their names or if they are Arianna's friends or relatives. The thought alone makes my chest tighten. I don't know anything about this woman. I'm about to commit to her for the rest of my life.

I clench my fists at my sides, suddenly wanting to run. My feet take a step forward. Arianna appears, and I freeze. My mouth turns dry, and my heart pounds hard against my chest cavity.

She's an apparition of beauty and grace. Her long hair hangs in curls. Delicate off-white lace hugs her body, showcasing her hourglass figure. A thin veil covers her face, but I can still see it. I lock eyes with her, mesmerized and wondering how a woman can appear so angelic.

Her father stops and turns Arianna toward him. He lifts her veil, says something in her ear, then kisses her cheek. He gives her a final embrace then spins her in front of me. Instead of leaving, he leans into my ear. "If you don't make my bambina happy, I'll hunt you down, fillet you into millions of pieces, and feed you to the pigeons."

I clench my jaw, then pat him on the back. I quietly reply, "Noted, Daddy."

He grunts, smiles for the crowd, and takes his seat.

I turn back to Arianna. Her lips are quivering and her eyes are glassy. She's breathing in shallow breaths. I grab her hands and lean into her ear. "Beautiful doesn't describe how stunning you look, lass. Thanks for not playing runaway bride. It would have killed my ego."

A soft, nervous laugh escapes her.

"Breathe. You're the sexiest woman here," I remind her, but it's also a lie. She's officially stepped into the sexiest woman on earth.

Her smile widens, and her face flushes a deeper maroon. I take a step back, and a lump forms in my throat.

How did she get my nana's necklace?

Hailee must have let her wear it.

This is happening. She's going to be an O'Malley.

The priest starts the ceremony. It's a long, traditional Catholic mass. I don't let go of Arianna's hand the entire time. She starts to relax, but then it comes time for our vows.

Her hands tremble in mine. Anxiety plagues her face. I squeeze her hand tighter, and she offers a small smile.

The priest says, "Repeat after me. I, Killian Gallagher O'Malley, take you, Arianna Dolche Marino, to be my lawfully wedded wife."

My chest tightens. This gorgeous creature is about to make a vow to me, and I didn't even know her middle name.

Her eyebrows pinch together, and she bites her lip.

I realize she's waiting for me to speak. Instead of going step by step after the priest, I bypass him. One thing I always do before a match is come prepared to win. I figured this was just as important. After I found her ring, I spent part of the morning memorizing the vows.

"I, Killian Gallagher O'Malley, take you, Arianna Dolche Marino, to be my lawfully wedded wife, to have and to hold, from this day forward, for better, for worse, for richer, for poorer, in sickness and in health, until death do us part."

She gapes at me, and I wink.

Father Ercole chuckles. "Arianna, please repeat after me. I, Arianna Dolche Marino, take you, Killian Gallagher O'Malley, to be my lawful husband."

She squeezes my hands harder. I stroke the back of her hands with my thumbs. Her voice shakes. "I, Arianna Dolche Marino, take you, Killian Gallagher O'Malley, to be my lawful husband."

"To have and to hold, from this day forward, for better, for worse," Father Ercole recites.

Arianna takes a deep breath and stands straighter. "To have and to hold, from this day forward, for better, for worse, for richer, for poorer, in sickness and in health, until death do us part."

Pride swells in my chest. She came prepared. Even though she's nervous, she nailed it. To me, it says a lot about who she is as a person.

My wife is a winner, crosses my mind.

The priest says some other things, but I don't hear a word. Arianna's eyes pin mine. Nerves begin to fill her expression again, and I hear Father Ercole say, "I now pronounce you husband and wife. You may kiss your bride."

Arianna takes another anxious breath. Her brown eyes widen. Uncertainty, a bit of fear, and the desire I saw at certain points last night fill them.

The memory of her lips on mine and how I didn't embrace them and make her mine flashes in my head. I step forward, hold her cheeks, and tilt her head up. I dip over her, studying her entire face, including her goddamn plump lips that I've wanted on me since I first saw her on social media.

She holds her breath.

I'm unsure why I do it, but I kiss her forehead, her cheekbones, then finally, her sinful, red mouth. The moment our lips touch, she parts hers. Our tongues collide, hot, wet, so greedy, I slide my hand down her back, palm her ass, then pull her closer to me.

Her knees buckle as my erection digs into her stomach. She softly whimpers. So much heat soars through my veins, I forget I'm in church. Our kiss turns carnal. I fuck her with my tongue, wishing my cock was inside her and not against her.

Father Ercole clears his throat and says, "Mr. and Mrs. Killian O'Malley."

I'm still kissing her when the guests begin to cheer and the organ begins to play. When I pull back from our kiss, we're both breathless. A smoldering fire lights her eyes, glowing above her flushed cheeks.

I put my arm around her waist, lead her down the aisle as quickly as possible, and ignore the wedding planner who tells me to stop outside the door of the church. The cold air hits me, barely cooling the blood boiling in my veins.

Our driver gets out and opens the door. Arianna gets in, and I tell the driver, "Ritz Carlton."

11

Arianna

Tingles burst all over my skin, replacing the wedding flutters with lust-filled ones. Killian gets in the car, slides me onto his lap, and resumes kissing me.

"The people?" I murmur into his mouth.

"What people?" He slides his tongue against mine again, and I think I might combust. It's nothing like our kisses the night before. Every cell in my body aches to get closer to his. Filthy thoughts fill my mind, remembering the few moments I spent skin to skin with him last night.

He tugs my hair, and his hot breath hits my neck.

I breathe, "My papà...the guests..."

His lips brush my collarbone. He drags his finger along my cleavage. "Fuck 'em." He slides his finger under my dress and onto my breast.

"Mmm...but... Oh God!" I moan when he pinches my nipple.

He licks the back of my ear and bites on my lobe. "Everyone can wait. You're my wife, and I'll bring you to the party when I'm good and ready. Besides, I have my penance to do." He deeply inhales and runs his tongue up the front of my neck. "This dress needs to come off."

I shudder and squeak out, "Penance?"

"Mmhmm." He glides his tongue back in my mouth, and my insides pulse so hard, I squirm on his lap.

His hand reaches for the door, and he opens it. I didn't notice the car stopped. He slides out of the SUV while carrying me.

I tighten my arms around him. "Are you going to let me walk?"

"Nope." He gives me another loin-burning kiss, goes through the lobby, and fumbles in his pocket. His green eyes scan my face then my chest. The door opens to the elevator. He steps into it, slides his key in, and hits the buttons.

The rest of the journey to our suite becomes a blur. Hands, tongues, and lips become magnets, unable to resist the other. When I come up for air, we're in the room, and Killian kicks the door shut behind him.

He sets me on the ground, spins me, and moves my hair over one shoulder. His fingers glide above the zipper as he pulls it down, creating an eruption of tingles along my spine. My dress falls to the floor, along with the top of my lingerie.

Warm palms cover my ass. His breath hits the back of my ear. "Christ, Arianna."

I glance behind me, and his mouth connects with mine as if he hasn't kissed me a hundred times since the church. I attempt to spin into him, but he holds me against his body, drops his hand in my panties, and slides two fingers through my slit.

He groans. His arrogant eyes lock on mine. "No hair. Good lass. I'm going to eat your pussy even longer now as a reward." His fingers slip inside me, and he presses his thumb against my clit.

I gasp and clench his digits, closing my eyes, already slightly dizzy from the buzz he evokes.

"Open your eyes, Arianna," he demands forcefully. I obey, and he asserts, "Rule number four. I'm in charge of your tight little pussy. When you come, you look at me."

I gape at him, panting hard. No man has ever made me look at him while being intimate. I usually have sex in the dark.

His fingers manipulate me further, and my knees buckle. I don't fall farther than an inch before he tightens his forearm against my stomach. He kisses my neck, licks my jaw, then says, "Rule number five. Anything any other man has done to you, forget about. Your pussy's going to crave me at all hours of the day. When you least expect it, you're going to be jonesing for me like an addict without a needle." He presses his thumb harder and circles faster.

Heat and adrenaline wash through me like a riptide crashing into the shore. I cry out, "Killian."

"Eyes on me," he bellows, his green orbs burning like a crazed animal.

I concentrate on him until the dizziness overpowers me, I'm a rag doll pressed against his body, and my eyes roll.

He sucks on my bottom lip and slides his hand between us. The sound of his belt buckle hitting the wood floor echoes in the room. An erection so hard it could be steel digs into my back. He murmurs, "Your pussy is my dessert, lass."

I don't have time to comprehend it. He spins me so fast I see stars, then he pushes me onto the bed. His fingers work quickly, unbuttoning his shirt while he scans every inch of my body. I imagine it's what he looks like in the ring. While I don't think he'll hurt me, his gaze is so intense, there's no question whatever he wants, he'll get.

I crawl backward on my hands toward the bedframe. The white tux shirt falls to the floor, revealing the most stunning specimen of a man I've ever seen. My eyes drift over all of him, taking in his tattoos, getting distracted by the four-leaf clovers on his V traveling straight to the biggest cock I've ever seen. Flutters take off in my belly, and I tear my gaze away but then fixate on the only tattoo on his chest, the S.O. initials.

My gut drops, but I can't dwell on whoever the woman is. He lunges over me, as if I'm prey he'll devour. Warm flesh hovers over my breasts, and I reach, ready to explore everything I've been dying to touch since I saw him online.

His hand slides in my hair, fisting it. He puts his face in front of mine. "It's time to show you what a real man's like." He pushes my thigh up and sinks into me.

"Oh God!" I scream, seeing stars.

His thumb caresses my cheek. "Shh."

"I...oh... Killian... what the..." I attempt to breathe, but I can't. Everything is pulsing. My body's on sensory overload, fuller than ever before. Then he starts thrusting.

"There's more, lass. Relax."

I look at him like he's crazy. "I... I can't..."

"Hold on to me." His lips shut me up. His tongue flicks in my mouth, torturing me. I grip his shoulders, digging my nails in his back, as my body slowly accepts all of him.

A gravelly rumble fills his chest. His cock shimmies against my walls, creating a sea of endorphins buzzing against him. I move my hips with his, frantically wanting every inch of the glorious friction of our bodies against the other.

"Jesus, your pussy is tight," he mumbles, studying me.

I can't speak, only whimper.

He gives me a chaste kiss then gazes at my mouth. "I'm going to fuck you everywhere. These goddamn lips of yours..." His hand trails down my thigh and onto my ass cheek. "And this perfect little ass of yours... Jesus."

I gasp. I've never let any guy do that to me before, but I don't argue since I tremble harder from the force of his body pounding into mine.

Smugness fills his expression. "Ah. No one's taken you like that before." He leans into my ear. "I told you I was going to show you what a real man's like."

I close my eyes, unsure how that would feel or how he wouldn't split me in two.

His hand moves to the side of my breast, and he circles his finger on it. New zings ignite. He claims, "I don't know if I'll enjoy sucking or fucking your tits more."

I've had men say dirty things to me before, but not like this. Not while they were in me, not missing a beat, creating sensations so toe-curling, I can barely breathe. And something about his cocky definitiveness, like there's no questioning I'll do everything he wants, turns me on more.

His thrusts become harder, and when he slides back in me, it's like he hits an on button inside me. It's unexpected, and I completely unravel.

"Oh...what the...oh God, Killian!" I scream, gripping him for dear life as my body spasms and trembles like never before.

"Fuuuuck, lass," he groans, and his cock pumps so ferociously in me, another hit of adrenaline causes me to dig my nails deep into his back.

He collapses into the curve of my neck, trying to catch his breath. Our chests heave against one another, and he licks my ear and mumbles, "Dessert time."

"Wh-what?" I pant.

He licks his lips arrogantly then drags his tongue down the middle of my torso until his face is in my pussy. He slides his arms under my thighs until my legs are draped over his shoulders. His tongue lazily glides over my clit.

My mouth hangs open, and my pulse creeps back up. No man has ever gone down on me after penetration. I love everything about oral sex, but everything is already sensitive from what he's already done to me. It makes me feel like an ignorant virgin again.

Jesus. My husband is filthy.

My husband. Oh my God. This man is my husband.

His hand slides up and teases my nipple. I moan, and he asks, "Feel good, lass?"

"Mmhmm. So good," I admit and put my hands on his head.

Amusement enters his voice. "Does Mrs. O'Malley want this?" He flicks his tongue faster.

"Oh! Yes!" I squeeze my thighs against his cheeks. My hands grip his hair, desperate for his face to be as close to me as possible.

"Or this?" He blows on my pussy then sucks me so hard, I arch off the bed. His fingers slide inside me, and he pulls them out, then shoves them in my mouth, taunting, "It's only fair you taste me."

The salty thickness of his cum mixed with my arousal hits me like a drug. I suck on them, eagerly wanting more.

His green orbs meet mine. "Maybe I should show you how I really eat pussy."

More flutters erupt in my stomach. He removes his hand from my mouth and places a palm on my stomach, stroking my mound with his thumb. His lips, tongue, and teeth annihilate me. Every time I arch up, his palm keeps me in place.

An earthquake of chaos starts in my toes, growing stronger as it races up my body. I lose control of everything, screaming out his name and profanities.

When he finishes, he cages his body over mine. "We're going to our party now. And while I love your lingerie, your panties will stay here."

I arch my eyebrows, still breathing hard.

"All night, when you feel my hand on your ass, you better clench your tight little pussy."

"Why?"

He slides his hand over my thigh and outlines the garter belt I forgot I had on. "When it's time for me to remove this, if there's a drop of juice anywhere, I'll be licking it off."

"In front of everyone? You wouldn't!"

He dips to my ear. "Don't ever underestimate me, my dear wife. Now that you're mine, I'll lick you, suck you, kiss you, or bite you wherever and whenever I want. If I want to fuck you in a room full of people, I'll find a way. The only rules that exist in my world are the ones I create."

Excitement, and a tiny amount of worry, fills me. I ask, "Have you always been this cocky?"

He chuckles. "Only about things I'm sure about." He rolls off me then scoops me off the bed.

I yelp.

He pecks me on the lips, sets me on the floor, then pats my ass. "We need to get clothes on."

"I'll need help with my dress." I grab the bustier Selena gifted me and attempt to put it on.

He comes up behind me. "Let me help." Within a minute, he has it on and spins me. His eyes travel over my body then back to my eyes. "You're beautiful. You know that?"

It doesn't matter all the things I just did with this man, who may be my husband but is still a stranger. My cheeks burn.

He drags a knuckle over my cheek then traces his grandmother's necklace. "Did Hailee let you borrow this?"

I nod. "Yes."

Something passes in his eyes. I'm not sure what it is, but it quickly disappears. "I'm glad you wore it. I think she would have liked you. Well, besides the fact you aren't Irish."

I softly laugh. Maybe some people would be offended, but before this week, I never thought I would be with any man who wasn't Italian. "Yeah, my grandmother would probably roll over in her grave that I married a non-Italian."

He takes a deep breath then picks up my dress. "Let's get you back in this."

Once I'm in my dress, he goes to put on his pants. I ask, "Are you not wearing any underwear, either?"

"Mine are in the trash can in the priest's quarters."

Confused, I tilt my head. "Why would they be there?"

"That church was an inferno. I had to take another shower and peel my underwear off my ass after confession."

"Confession?"

He pulls his trousers over his hips and zips them. "Yeah. Every O'Malley goes to confession before they get married. Then they're free of sin before they say their vows."

I've been Catholic my entire life, but I wouldn't call myself a super religious person. It strikes me as odd Killian would go to confession. "Do you go to confession a lot?"

"No. I hadn't gone since high school."

"Huh. Well, did you confess anything good?"

He slides his arms into his shirt. "That's between the big guy and me."

"Fair enough." I grab his bow tie and step in front of him. I lace it through his collar and tie it. When I finish, I go to step back, but he puts his hand on my ass.

"Hey."

I glance up. "Yeah?"

"I'm glad you didn't go to Italy and marry that fat, old guy."

I bite on my smile. I admit, "Me, too. Is my hair or makeup messed up? Do I need to call my people in for an emergency session?"

He puts his fingertips on the top of my head then smooths down my hair. "All good. As stunning as always."

My heart skips a beat. "Thanks."

He slings his tux jacket over his shoulder and puts his arm around my waist. "Should we go grace everyone with our presence before we leave for the airport?"

"We aren't staying here tonight?"

"Nope."

"Then how did you have this room?"

His sexy smolder fills his face and my pussy pulses again. "I booked it after I chose your ring."

My lips twitch. "So you had this planned?"

"Nope. But I always prepare to win."

A laugh escapes my mouth. "So this was a win?"

His smug expression makes me squirm. "I'm pretty sure it was a win for both of us, wouldn't you say?"

I admit, "Yeah. So where are you taking me?"

"I'm not telling you."

"Come on!" I whine.

He chuckles. "Nope. Now let's go." He leads me out of the room, through the building, and out to the car. We get in, and he slides his arm around me. I melt into him, wondering why I thought this would be so bad. Maybe my papà was right, and there was nothing for me to worry about. Maybe everything between Killian and me will be easy.

Of course, I'm wrong.

12

Killian

Angelo meets us at the door. "Where have you been? You left everyone at the church. The wedding planner said she told you to stop. You didn't even get your pictures taken."

"Papà, I'm sorry...umm..." Arianna frets.

I tug her closer to me. "I was spending time with my wife. You have a problem with that?"

Arianna softly gasps. I'm sure no one speaks to Angelo with any defiance. He may be my father-in-law, but he's not going to rule my or Arianna's life.

Angelo's dark eyes meet mine. "In our family, you show respect at events."

"Papà—"

I step closer to Angelo and cut off Arianna. "A wedding is

about the bride and groom, not the guests. We are here. Look around. No one is upset over this but you. Do not stress my wife out today."

Angelo and I intensely stare the other down until Tully breaks our gaze. "Angelo, something has come up we need to discuss."

Angelo waits several seconds then steps back and addresses Tully. "What's going on?"

"In private."

Angelo orders, "Go interact with our guests."

"This isn't how this is going to work. You don't get to order my wife or me around," I proclaim. If Angelo thinks I'm going to bend over and do whatever he says for the rest of my life, he's wrong.

Surprise, then anger, fills Angelo's face.

"Watch your mouth," Tully warns.

I turn to him. "The same goes for you. I did what you wanted and fulfilled our deal. My debt no longer exists. Every time you see my wife on my arm, you can look at my payment and refresh your memory. From this point forward, we're even again." I turn back to Angelo. "And no one is making decisions for Arianna but me."

Her body stiffens against mine. I guide her past Angelo and Tully. When we get far enough away from them, she demands, "Stop."

I freeze and glance at her. "What's wrong?"

"I'm your payment?" she says in a hurt voice.

"We've already talked about how I owed Tully. Why do you act surprised?"

Her face is red. She doesn't answer me. "And you can't speak to my papà like that."

I snort. "I can, and I will. He doesn't own me."

"That was disrespectful."

I cross my arms. "No, it wasn't. I was laying the ground rules."

She jerks her head back and glares at me. "Ground rules?"

"Yeah. He's no longer in charge of you. I am."

Darts fly out of her eyes. "In charge of me? I'm not your child you get to control. I'm a grown woman."

"Who's going to follow my rules."

She throws her hands in the air. "Here we go again with your delusional rules."

"You didn't seem to mind my rules an hour ago. In fact, I seem to recall you screaming out my name and almost drawing blood on my shoulders," I arrogantly state.

Her face turns red. "You're such an ass."

"Don't be a brat," I fire back.

Her eyes widen, and she shakes her head. "Go to hell, Killian." She spins and storms off.

"Piss your bride off already?" Declan steps in front of me and hands me a drink.

I grab it and take a mouthful of whiskey, enjoying the smooth burn, which only matches my current mood. I mutter, "I'll tame her rebel ass. Lass has a rude awakening coming to her."

"What did you say?"

"Drop it," I demand.

Declan glances behind him at Arianna. When he turns back, his blue eyes turn dark. "We've got an issue."

The hairs on my neck rise. "What?"

He pulls out his phone, taps the screen, then hands it to me.

My stomach drops as I read it. A major news outlet has an article on Jack Christian.

Where is Jack Christian?

The cybersecurity tech guru Jack Christian, whose company, Christian Cybersecurity, went public only a few months ago, seems to be nowhere. Anonymous employees for the firm report they haven't seen him since before the listing on the stock exchange. Mr. Christian was not in New York to ring the bell. He sent a statement to the press saying he was taking care of a close friend who was sick. While he would like to be at the exchange, his team of colleagues would represent him.

Over the last few months, numerous memos and statements have trickled in from Jack, but our reporters haven't spoken to one person who can testify they've seen him. It's like he has disappeared into thin air, a very unusual move for the head of a company that just went public.

If Jack isn't running Christian Cybersecurity, then who is? And does it remain a good investment?

My blood runs cold. I meet Declan's eyes. "Shit."

"Yeah. I already called Gianluca and told him to wake up his brother in Switzerland. Liam spoke with the other bankers. We've instructed them to place the short positions."

"We were so close to the price we wanted. When the exchange opens Monday, this could be drastically lower before our short positions start to take effect," I point out.

Declan shifts on his feet. "The futures are already moving down. At this point, whatever price we can get the short orders in so we make money on the downfall is our best bet. Once we know all our positions are secure, we need to put everything else in motion to make sure this drops to zero quickly."

Obrecht joins us as if he knows what we're discussing. He scowls, "As soon as Monday hits, Jack is mine."

Declan takes a big swig of whiskey and shakes his head. "The end is near, but we need our positions secured."

Obrecht snorts then growls, "Monday. Jack Christian is going to see my wrath then. You're out of time. No one is stopping me from taking him out."

"Obrecht," Selena snaps from behind us.

He spins.

Her lips tremble. "We had a deal."

He reaches for her cheek, but she steps back. His face falls and he states, "I have waited long enough. Your nightmares are getting more frequent."

She swallows hard. "This is my decision. Liam has not told me he is no longer useful to him."

Obrecht sniffs hard. "It is time you stopped waiting for Liam to permit me to end him. What he did to you—"

"Gives me the power to decide this, not you!" She jabs him in the chest.

He clenches his jaw.

Her voice is cold, which I've never heard before. She's always warm and sweet. "You already broke part of the deal we made when I told you that you weren't to see him until I said you could kill him."

"He's in our garage. I explained why I couldn't hold to that part."

Tears well in her eyes. "If I cannot put my trust in you regarding this issue, then you won't have it going forward on anything else." She spins and beelines toward the hallway.

"Fuck!" Obrecht hands his drink to me and follows her.

Finn joins us, and I groan inside. He looks just as pissed off as Obrecht, and I already know why. He snarls, "It's time to pick up Judge Peterson. Jack Christian still needs to be alive. And you all better keep Obrecht away."

"Just chill. Selena is still waiting for Liam's go-ahead," I inform him.

Declan grunts. "If Obrecht doesn't convince her otherwise."

For real? What a stupid thing to say in front of Finn. Selena was married to Jack. She divorced him, married Obrecht, then Jack kidnapped her. He did a ton of vile things to her during their marriage, and when Obrecht stormed in to rescue her, he had her in a cage. If anyone is staying in control of this decision, it's her. I glower at Declan and firmly state, "He won't."

Finn steps closer. "Those two know Brenna's location. I've waited long enough to pick up that bastard. As soon as we get in town, I'm picking him up. Nothing is showing up on the wiretaps between him and his son. Everything I've done to attempt to bait them into a conversation is failing. All I'm doing is wasting time."

"Maybe I should cancel my trip," I suggest.

"No. It's your honeymoon. Go," Declan commands.

"Nolan will be gone, too. Plus, little Ms. Daddy's Brat doesn't deserve the nice trip I booked for us," I grumble.

"Jesus, you're an idiot," Finn scolds.

"And why is that?" I angrily question.

He taps my head with his finger. "Wake up, Killian. You have a beautiful wife who you get in your bed every night."

"Don't act like she's my soul mate. I'm only here so Nolan doesn't spend his life in prison. And I've never had an issue getting women in my bed. Now my freedom is gone, and I'm stuck with Ms. Defiant," I claim.

Disgust fills Finn's expression. "Are you ever going to grow up and realize what you have?"

I toss back the rest of my whiskey. "Lecture someone else." I walk away from them and head toward the bar but catch sight of Arianna out of the corner of my eye. I watch her for a moment, going from table to table and talking to guests.

Feeling guilty, I figure I better go over to her, help her out, and try to get back on her good side. I step behind her and put my hand on her hip.

She stiffens and glances at me. Her eyes are glistening, and I'm not sure why. She turns away from me.

"It's just so sad your mamma isn't here. She loved weddings. Remember when your cousin, Amato, got married and she spent most of the night dancing with you? Oh, you were so adorable. It's amazing how much you look like her," some old lady claims.

Why isn't her mamma here? How is it I didn't even notice her mother was missing?

Arianna's body trembles. It's faint, but I feel it. I slide my palm around her stomach and put my other hand in front of her. "I'm Killian. Arianna, who is this beautiful woman?"

The woman blushes, and her smile lines deepen. "Oh, aren't you the charmer?" She takes my hand and shakes it.

Arianna sniffles. "This is my great-aunt Greta."

I lean down and kiss her hot cheek. "Greta. Sexy name." I wink and move Arianna to the next guest. It's another older woman, but she appears to be a generation younger than Greta. "And who is this?"

She smiles. Her eyes remind me of Arianna's.

"This is my aunt Aurora. She is my mamma's sister," Arianna states.

I keep the conversation light, continuing to move Arianna from person to person. When we get past the last table, I lead her to the bar. "Let's get a drink, lass."

A man's voice cuts through the air. "Please take your seats for dinner."

"What do you want?" I ask Arianna.

"I'll have wine at dinner."

"Double Jameson single malt, neat," I tell the bartender. I refocus on Arianna and gently ask, "Why isn't your mom here?"

She scrunches her face and looks away. A grief-stricken voice hits my ears. "She died a few years ago."

My heart stammers. I swallow the lump in my throat. "I'm sorry."

She wipes her face and shrugs. "Can't do anything about it." She faces me. "I'm..." She closes her eyes briefly. "Why didn't I ask you this before? Sorry. There are so many new people, and I didn't even realize..."

"Realize what?"

"Why aren't your parents here?"

Emotions I try not to engage in surface in my chest. I push them back down. "They're dead as well."

She gapes at me, speechless.

The bartender puts a crystal tumbler down. I pick it up, steer her over to the front of the room, and pull out her chair.

We sit. Declan takes the chair next to me. I pick up the bottle of red wine and fill Arianna's glass. She smiles and once again mesmerizes me. She's too beautiful for her own good. I'm not sure if she realizes it or if I even want her to. I know she's not innocent. But there's something I can't put my finger on about her—almost a naivety.

Declan jumps on his chair and clinks his fork on his glass. The room soon echoes of the clanging sound. Arianna's face turns red. Golden heat grows in her eyes, making my dick twitch.

I fist her hair, tug it back, and part her lips with my tongue. She gasps, and I flick into her mouth like a snake tasting the air. Her sexy moan causes my pants to become tighter. The pads of her fingers press into my inner thigh. I deepen our kiss, drowning out all the cheers filling the room until my cells are like lava, overflowing with an insatiable hunger.

Determined to get dinner over with, then find a dark corner to remind her who she belongs to and release the tension in my pants, I end our kiss. It's the wrong move. The heavy longing in her eyes and flush in her cheeks only create more tension in my body.

The MC's voice blares on the microphone. "Get a room."

The ballroom erupts in laughter.

"It's speech time! Let me introduce the best man, Declan O'Malley."

More applause fills the air. I wrap my arm around Arianna's shoulders then sit back and take a swig of whiskey. Nolan was Sean's best man. I was Nolan's a week ago. I cringe inside, not knowing what Declan will say and remembering parts of Nolan's and my speeches. Plus, we're O'Malleys. There's always some sort of a roast.

Declan snatches the microphone from the MC and, with a mischievous expression, glances at us. He tsks then says, "Arianna, do you know what you signed up for, marrying my brother?"

She smiles and shakes her head. "Nope."

He wiggles his eyebrows. "Want me to tell you?"

"Please," she chirps and smirks at me.

"It'll all be lies, lass," I mutter.

She strokes her pinky finger so it grazes my cock. I'm going to change her taunting, haughty little smile into an O as soon as possible. She practically sings, "Doubt it."

Declan puts his hand on my shoulder. "Here's all the things you need to know about Killian."

"Easy. I know where you live," I warn under my breath.

He continues, "Keep steaks in your freezer. As you can see, he takes a lot of punches before he knocks his opponent down."

I breathe deeply and take another drink. If he's going right into insulting my boxing skills, this can only get worse.

"He loves looking at himself, but you probably already know this from his social media page."

Is that all he has? Maybe this won't be so bad.

Declan turns toward my family. "Should I tell Arianna about his followers?"

Oh shit. He's not going to go there.

Of course my brother, Liam, and Finn all tell him to go for it.

Declan's face turns serious. He focuses on Arianna. "Several polls were conducted by social media sites. Your husband took number one in..." Declan smirks at me, and I scowl. Heat crawls up my face. I don't have any issues with gay guys. My motto is "to each their own." One of the toughest fighters I train with is my younger cousin, Aidan. I hang out with him and his boyfriend Cain all the time. Maybe it's why the dudes who message me online don't bother me. It's just social media, and I don't control what happens. Plus, you can't help who you're attracted to. I take their attention as a compliment. But I'm only into women. Usually, I don't care about my brothers' and cousins' jokes. And Aidan and Cain say the same shit to me my brothers, Liam, and Finn do. But this is a roomful of people I don't know and my new wife's family.

Declan's arrogant expression grows, and he studies Arianna. "Well, let's say an array of wish lists. The social media sites were Out of the Closet, Backdoor Pleasure, Make Me Out You, Be My Banging Daddy, Your Holy—"

"That's enough!" Angelo growls and tears the microphone out of Declan's hand. For the first time since meeting him, I'm grateful for Angelo.

Declan pins his eyebrows. "I wasn't finished."

"Yes, you are." Angelo shoots daggers at him.

"Fine. Ruin the fun," Declan mutters and plops in his seat.

I ignore the smug expression on my family's faces and glance at Arianna, but it only makes my blood boil more. She's covering her mouth and stifling laughs. I mutter, "It isn't funny."

She arches her eyebrows.

Angelo stands behind us. His voice booms, "First, thank you all for coming tonight. The day a father gives his daughter away is a special moment. While I'll miss my bambina terribly, I have confidence her new husband will make her very happy." He grips my shoulder so hard, I struggle not to flinch.

"Arianna, I wish your mamma could see what a beautiful woman and stunning bride you are. I know she would be proud of the woman you have become."

Arianna's eyes turn teary.

Angelo continues to keep his death grip on me. "Please raise your glasses in honor of Arianna and her new husband, Killian. May they have a lifetime of happiness, good health, and love."

There's that word again. Is everyone in denial about how this was a shotgun, arranged wedding?

The crowd raises their glasses. Angelo digs his claws deeper into me until his knuckles turn white. "Never forget, Arianna. I am your papà and will always be here if you need me. Salute!"

The room shouts, "Salute!" and downs their drinks.

Angelo keeps a smile on his face and leans into my ear. "You've been given a gift. So far, you've shown me you're unworthy of her. Don't you ever show disrespect to my family or me again. If I find out you hurt my daughter in any way, you'll wish you took Tully's punishment over mine." He releases me, bends down, and embraces Arianna.

His threats are getting old, and I haven't even been married twenty-four hours. Declan mutters, "Daddy needs to relax a bit."

I snort. "Tell me about it."

The servers arrive with food. My stomach growls, and I realize I haven't eaten all day. Platters of Caprese Crostini, Parmesan Risotto Cakes, Pan Seared Striped Bass, Chicken Marsala, Cacciatore Vegetables, and Four Cheese Spinach Lasagna fill the table. I lean into Arianna. "Did you pick the menu?"

Worry fills her expression. "Why? You don't like it?"

"No, it smells awesome. Did you decide on the family-style platters versus the dinky plate that never fills anyone up?"

Relief replaces her anxiety, and her face lights up. "Yeah. My family does this at a lot of events."

I give her a chaste kiss. "Good decision." I pick up her plate. "What do you want first?"

"Vegetables and risotto cakes, please. Oh, and a crostini."

I add everything but put an extra crostini on her plate. "Have two. They're small."

"Yeah, but there's a lot of other stuff I want to eat."

"So? Eat it. I wouldn't want you to lose any weight."

She arches her eyebrow. Doubt fills her voice. "Really?"

"Yeah. Why would you question that?"

She tilts her head and squints. "You wouldn't want me to take a few pounds off my ass? Or maybe my thighs?"

I scoff. "Hell no."

"What about my stomach?"

"You have a flat stomach. How is this even a topic right now?" I add the same things I put on her plate to mine and stick a crostini in my mouth.

"Hmm." She puts a mushroom on her fork then pops it in her mouth.

"What's the hmm about?" I ask then try a risotto cake.

"Nothing."

"It had to have meant something."

"Nope."

I groan. "Please tell me you don't have some low self-esteem issue about your body."

She straightens up and sticks her chin out. "No. I feel fine about my body."

I study her then get angry. "Some dickhead said something to you?"

"It's not important. Anyway, you should try this with wine. It's way better," she claims.

"I don't do wine. I tried it when I was in high school. Never had the desire to put it in my mouth again," I admit, trying to forget about some loser putting ideas in her head that her curvy body is anything but perfect.

She huffs. "I can assure you this tastes better than anything you tried in high school."

"Fine." I wipe my mouth on my napkin, pick up her glass, and take a sip. It's not as bad as I remember, but it still isn't something I'd choose to drink. "I'll stick with whiskey."

She laughs. "Fair enough."

"Maybe you should drink whiskey."

She cringes. "Eww. Yuck. No way."

A sudden urge to pour whiskey all over her and lick it off gets my dick all riled up again.

She nervously asks, "Why are you staring at me?"

I lean into her. "Make sure you eat a lot. When we leave here, you're going to need all the energy you can get, Mrs. O'Malley."

13

Arianna

My papà hugs me and kisses my head. "I'll see you next week when you get to Chicago. Call me if you need anything."

I blink back my tears, suddenly freaking out about leaving him, my brothers, and New York. I sniffle. "Promise me you'll eat right and work out. And get your massages."

He tightens his arms. "Don't you worry about me. I promise I'll stick to everything."

"Stop keeping her all to yourself, Papà," Massimo orders.

My papà releases me and, one by one, I hug each of my brothers, not able to control my tears.

Killian puts his arm around me. "Ready to go?"

I put my hand over my eyes, and a new surge of waterworks

floods my cheeks. He tugs me closer to him. "All right, lass. Everything will be okay. You'll see them in a week."

I straighten up and nod.

He leads me outside and helps me into the SUV. We changed before we left. Whoever Papà had pack my belongings did an excellent job. I'm in yoga pants, a tank top, and an oversized tunic. It's comfy and perfect for traveling. Killian's in grey joggers and a black hoodie.

When he gets in, he slides me onto his lap, then dabs my face with his tux handkerchief he must have put in his pocket. "Always wondered if these ever came in handy."

I let out an emotional laugh. "Sorry. My makeup is probably everywhere."

He swipes under each eye. "Nope. All perfect again." His green eyes assess me. "You look tired."

"I didn't sleep a lot."

He nods and pushes my head to his chest. "It's been a long day. Take a breather."

Mint, orange blossom, and bourbon vanilla permeate all my cells. It calms me, and I drag my finger along his Celtic knot tattoos. "Are you taking me somewhere warm?"

"Yep."

"Will you tell me?"

"Will it make you feel better?" he asks.

I tilt my head. My lips twitch. "Yep."

"Okay then. We're going to the Riviera Maya, Mexico."

I sit up. "Complete with cabanas, fruity drinks, and beach-front massages?"

He grins. "If that's what you want, I'll make all of it happen."

I clap. "Yay! I haven't been there, but it's on my travel list!"

"You have a travel list?"

"Sure. Don't you?"

He shakes his head. "No. What places are on yours?"

"Tons of cool spots."

"Where?"

Excitement fills me, thinking about all the places on my list. "I want to do a tour of all the Hawaiian Islands. New Zealand, Australia, ohh! If you're going there, you also have to go to Bora Bora and Fiji since you're already so close. They have those awesome huts over the water."

His green eyes sparkle. "I think we'd need a few months to experience all those places."

"At least. But you also have Europe. I wanted to backpack around it when I graduated. My friends went and stayed in youth hostels, but my papà shot that down," I admit, the disappointment still stinging.

Killian purses his lips.

"What?"

"Doubt I'll agree with your father a lot, but pretty sure he made the right decision on that one," he claims.

Anger climbs up my gut. "And why is that?"

He chuckles. "Don't get your Italian temper all riled up."

"My Italian temper?"

My attitude doesn't faze him. It only seems to encourage him more. He tugs my hair back slightly so I can still see him but barely. My pulse increases, and he drags a finger from my chin down to my cleavage. "A woman like you shouldn't be in a dirty hostel, sleeping with a bunch of horny dudes next to you."

I squirm on his lap, and my breath picks up. I claim the same things I told my papà, "I can take care of myself."

"Is that what you think?" He leans forward and kisses the middle of my neck. "You may speak your mind, but you wouldn't stand a chance against most men overpowering you."

Donato, manhandling me through the club while I was powerless to stop him, flashes in my mind. Embarrassment fills me, and I turn toward the window.

Killian's lips brush against my ear. "It's nothing to be ashamed of, lass. You're a woman. Men are supposed to be stronger. You shouldn't assume anything else or feel bad about it."

"That's super sexist," I accuse.

His teeth scrape my neck, and I shudder. He mumbles, "Yeah? I'm pretty sure you want me to be stronger than you."

"Not true," I breathe, wondering if I'm going to stain my pants. My papà decided we weren't doing a garter toss at the wedding after Killian pissed him off. It upset me, but Killian told me to let it go. I'm still unsure if he was serious about licking me in front of everyone, but I haven't felt dry down there all night. And there wasn't a pair of underwear in my travel bag. Every time we danced, he kissed me, or put his large palm on my ass, my insides pulsed.

"Now you're lying, lass." He slides his hand up my shirt and circles my nipple.

I whimper, trying not to react to him, but it's impossible. Everything he does sends me into sensory overload.

He nibbles on my lobe. "I can overpower you, and you love it. If I couldn't, you wouldn't be attracted to me. Like right now. I'm holding you exactly how I want you. Your brain's telling you to run, but your pussy wishes you could sit on my cock." He pinches my nipple and flicks his tongue behind my ear.

I close my eyes and decide not to deny it. I whisper, "But you want it, too."

"Yeah, Arianna. I want your tight little cunt over my swollen cock and your round ass in my palms." His lips slowly travel across my jaw.

I swallow hard. "Is that all?"

"No. I want your tits bouncing in my face and your pussy juice dripping on my thighs." His hot breath hits my lips. I part them and try to put my tongue in his mouth, but he only grazes it, then kisses my chin.

"You're so dirty," I try to reprimand, still shocked at how he talks to me, but it comes out weak.

He moves his hand off my breast, slides it around my back, then drags his fingers up and down my spine while I shudder. "I'd ask if you want me to be prim and proper, but I already know you don't."

"What if you're wrong, and I do?" I reply, just to hear his reaction.

He puts his face in front of mine, so we're eye to eye. Smugness fills his glowing green orbs. He challenges, "No, you don't."

"How do you know?"

He licks his lips. "The heat from your pussy. The way your body melts into mine every time I speak. Your breasts rising and falling faster while your nipples harden without me even touching them. But most of all, your eyes give everything away."

I stay quiet, not sure if I like him being able to read me so well.

The car stops, and he glances out the window. He pecks me on the lips. "We're here."

I stare at the small aircraft. "We have a private plane?"

"Not exactly."

"No?"

"Kind of. Think of it as a charter."

Confused and wondering if he invited his friends on our honeymoon, I ask, "Oh. Do you know the other people?"

"Nope. My cousin is a travel agent. I asked him where a good place for a honeymoon was, and he raved about the resort. I let him book it all. He said his buddy in New York had two available seats. I figured it would be better than commercial."

Relief and a bit of panic fill me. It shouldn't. A week alone with Killian and no one else is a bit intimidating, but the other side of me wants him without any distractions. "Okay."

"Don't look so apprehensive," he mutters.

"I'm not," I lie.

He snorts.

"What's the name of the resort?" I ask, hoping to avoid another fight.

He shrugs. "No idea. He asked me about my requirements. I said five stars, full amenities, on the beach, and adult-only."

"If you don't know where we're staying, how will we get there?" I ask.

He grins and moves me off his lap. He opens the door. "Don't worry, lass. I've got everything covered. A driver will be waiting for us. He knows where to go."

I smile. "Well, that's good."

He reaches in and helps me out of the car. "You should trust me."

I glance up at him. I blurt out, "I just met you."

His lips twitch. "You made a lifelong vow to me. Remember?"

Nerves fly in my chest. I tilt my head. "Does that mean you trust me?"

His face falls.

"Wow," I mutter, looking away. The sting of his truth bites me. I wish I never asked. He seems to forget he made the same vow to me.

"Arianna—"

"All good. Let's get on the plane." I try to brush past him, but he steps in front of me and puts both hands on my cheeks. My lips tremble with hurt and anger.

"You didn't let me answer your question."

I fire back, "You aren't the only one who's readable, Killian."

He takes a deep breath. "Okay. Let's make a rule."

I roll my eyes. "Here we go again. More rules for Arianna but none for you."

He clenches his jaw and stares at me. "Rule number six. From this moment on, you trust me, and I trust you."

My pulse beats hard in my neck.

He arches his eyebrows. "That work for you?"

I quietly agree. "Okay."

He spins me and leads me toward the plane. "Good. We're going to have an awesome time. My cousin assured me there's no better place in the Riviera Maya."

A flight attendant near the steps asks for our passports. Killian pulls them out of his pocket. She scans them and motions for us to go inside.

I climb up the steps and go to the only seats left. Killian throws the duffle bag with a few of our other items inside the overhead bin. He plops down, and the plane soon takes off.

I state, "I hope our clothes get to wherever we're going."

He licks his lips and checks me out until my cheeks are burning. "You won't need a lot of clothes, lass. I plan to keep you naked all week." He leans back against the headrest.

Flutters take off. I nervously laugh. "Do you think about anything besides sex?"

He rolls his head toward mine. "Do you want me to look at you and not think about sex?"

My blood pounds harder in my veins. I attempt to decipher what he said. My brain tells me the answer should be yes, that he should think about something else. The problem is, I can't think of what else I would prefer him to think about regarding me.

He says, "Good answer."

I scoff. "I didn't say anything."

His eyes twinkle. "Because you can't deny it. Also, I'm good with you looking at me and thinking about sex." He winks, puts the armrest up, and demands, "Put your seat back."

I obey.

He does the same then slides his arm around my shoulders. "I'll be your pillow. Take a nap if you want. We've got close to six hours."

I tease, "What? No bathroom sex?"

He grunts. "Not in this small plane. Don't worry, lass. I'll make sure you can barely walk by the time we get home."

I softly laugh and curl into him.

He kisses the top of my head. "Go to sleep."

"Stop being so bossy," I mumble, but I already have my eyes closed. I don't understand it, but Killian is strangely comfortable to be around. I thought it would be awkward and take me a long time even to let him touch me. I've never had a one-night stand or even casual sex. I've always been in a relationship. Everything about being in his arms makes me feel cared for and safe.

I fall asleep and don't wake up until he's stroking my cheek. "Lass, time to open your eyes."

"Hmm?" I take a deep breath and snuggle deeper into him.

He chuckles. His warm hand slides into my pants, and his finger slides between my ass cheeks.

I fling my eyes open and sit up in my seat.

"You're too predictable," he taunts and moves his hand off my body. He rises. "Everyone is already off. Time for sunshine."

I glance outside the plane, but it's still dark. "What time is it?"

"Five thirty."

I stretch my arms and yawn.

Killian opens the overhead bin, slings our bags over his shoulder, then holds his hand out. "Come on. Up and at 'em."

I take his hand, and we exit the plane. A man is holding a sign with O'Malley on it.

Killian steers me toward him. He holds out his hand. "Killian O'Malley. This is my wife, Arianna."

The man says something in Spanish. The only word I recognize is hello.

Killian cocks an eyebrow and glances at me.

"He said hello and something else," I offer.

"Don't you know Spanish?" Killian asks.

"No. Why would I?"

He shrugs. "Didn't you go to a fancy private school?"

"And that means I would know Spanish?"

Confusion fills his face. "Doesn't it?"

I slap his biceps. "No. I took French."

"Not Italian?"

I cover my face and groan. Partly because my papà and I fought over me not taking Italian, and I regret it. The other half of me just can't believe he's making these assumptions.

"No Español?" the driver asks.

"No," we both state.

"Hmmm." He taps the sign then points at Killian. "Tu?"

"That means you," I say.

Killian jerks his head toward me. "I thought you didn't know Spanish?"

"I don't!" I point to him and tell the driver. "O'Malley."

The driver smiles, motions for us to get in the van, then picks up our suitcases that seemed to have magically appeared by the car. He tosses them in the trunk.

We get in the vehicle. I mumble, "I hope this guy isn't an ax murderer. Or one of those rebels who kidnap tourists and cut off their fingers for their jewelry."

Killian pins his eyebrows together and grabs my hand. "We better hide this."

My heart races. "Seriously?"

He bursts out laughing. "No. Chill out. My cousin would never steer me wrong."

By the time we get to the resort, the sun is close to rising. A man stands at a check-in desk outside the building. "Hola. I'm Ricardo. Can I get your name and passports, please?"

"O'Malley," Killian states.

Ricardo types something on his keyboard, glances between the passports and us, then wiggles his eyebrows. "Honeymooners."

My face flushes. Something about the way he says it feels a bit dirty, but I'm sure I'm paranoid.

Killian tightens his arm around my waist. "Yep."

Ricardo whistles and throws his hand in the air. A driver in a golf cart appears. Ricardo hands us each a fruity drink. "Matteo will take you to your suite. The beach is private. We have three outdoor swimming pools, six restaurants, and our Tease Me nightclub. Our spa has a full menu including couples' massages, and you'll also want to check out our Scandalous Menu."

I have no idea what that means, but Killian motions for me to get on the golf cart. The suitcases get added, and we take off down a paved path. It weaves through lush green lawns, beautiful floral gardens, and a view of the ocean.

Excitement fills me. The sparkling turquoise water and stretch of white sand are just like the pictures I've seen online.

"I did good, didn't I?" Killian boasts.

"You did. You—" My mouth hangs open. I can't help but turn my head as we pass a couple running.

They wave and sing out, "Good morning!" Neither are wearing clothes, except for a pair of running shoes.

Killian mutters, "What the..."

The golf cart turns the corner, and an outdoor restaurant is half full. Some of the patrons are eating food. A few have women sitting on the table in front of them and are eating them out. Several are watching while masturbating and drinking their coffee. Another man has a woman bent over the railing and is thrusting into her. No one is clothed.

Killian turns his head as we pass, continuing to gawk at the restaurant. I elbow him. He jerks his head back. His eyes are wide, and for the first time since I met him, he seems to be speechless.

I blurt out, "What kind of place did you bring me to?"

14

Killian

ARIANNA PACES THE LIVING ROOM. THE SCANDALOUS MENU IS in her hand. "All your wildest dreams can come true during your stay. Please reserve services forty-eight hours in advance to guarantee an available time slot. A waitlist is available for same-day cancellations." She looks at me with a straight face. "At least we know we can get on a waitlist for today and tomorrow."

"Maybe if anyone gets food poisoning from pubic hairs in their food," I mutter. I'm going to kill my cousin. I didn't say to send us to a hedonism club. I'm not interested in eating off a table stained with someone else's pussy juice.

Arianna continues, "Professional sex tape session." She smirks. "Editing is included."

I don't reply. I'm never going to hear the end of this.

"Orgy on the beach. Maybe we should sign up for that one?" She gives me a challenging stare.

"Don't even think about it," I warn.

"Stripper fantasy. One male or female stripper. Add a second for only another $150 USD. Be teased and pleased. Can we get two guys instead of a girl?"

"Not funny," I growl.

Her eyes widen. "Why? You didn't bring me here not to partake in the fun, did you?"

"I told you, my cousin—"

"Foursome erotic massage. Two couples. One jacuzzi cabin room. Ohh. You get a sparkling bottle of wine with this one! I'll have yours since you don't drink it." She smiles.

"Anything else?" I sarcastically ask.

She glances at the menu. "Bondage A through Z. Leave no possibility hidden. That sounds fun."

"You done now?"

She puts the menu on the table. "Yep. That's all they offer. But there's a stripper pole in the nightclub. I can show you my skills later tonight."

"Over my dead body," I threaten.

She scoffs. "Please. Let's not act super prudish. It's just a stripper pole."

My chest tightens. "You're not doing anything in this place where anyone can see any part of you they shouldn't."

"Your social media page has pictures of you pretty much naked all over it. Don't be a hypocrite," she accuses then opens her suitcase.

"I don't have any pictures of my cock online."

She snorts. "No, but it's as close as possible without showing it. One photo even has you holding your cock with two hands."

"I'm a dude."

She rifles through her suitcase. "And here's my husband, the sexist. You even have your ass all over your page with hundreds of thousands of followers kissing it."

"You should talk. You've got over a million people following you. And I've seen your cleavage shots and your tight, barely-there dresses," I admit.

She glares at me. "My cleavage shots?"

"Yeah. Your selfies."

She crosses her arms. "So let me get this right. You think photos of me wearing dresses where I have a little bit of cleavage sticking out, and I'm wearing a club dress, but all my private parts are covered, is the same thing as you flaunting your naked self, minus your hands over your cock?"

My normal brain-to-mouth filter shows up. It's not the first time I wished I could keep my mouth shut, but I don't think before I say, "Yes."

"Really?"

"And you have photos of you in your bikini on there, too," I add.

She tilts her head. In a calm voice, she questions, "So my bikini is the same as you covering up your cock or showing your ass?"

Blood pounds between my ears. I have this notion she's trapping me, but I can't stop myself. "It's exactly the same. You're a woman."

She removes her shirt and bra. "Yeah, you're still losing me on this 'I'm a woman you're a man' thing. How is you showing your ass online the same as me in my bikini bottom, which isn't even a thong?"

I stare at her round, full breasts, watching her nipples harden.

"Eyes up here and answer the question," she orders.

I tear my gaze off her chest. "Okay. I will. It's the same. You're a woman. Men get aroused by looking at women with clothes on or off. Women don't have the same visual stimulation as men."

She holds up her bikini bottom. "So this bathing suit doesn't make a difference? I might as well post my naked bottom?"

"Exactly," I confirm.

She picks up her bikini top. "And this is useless, too? It's the same as me going bare?"

"Yep. Now you're starting to understand."

"Hmmm." She steps forward and pats me on the cheek. "Thanks for explaining things to me. Get changed so we can go to the beach."

I put my arm around her. "No problem. Glad we got that cleared up."

She sweetly replies, "Yep."

"I'm sorry about this place. I'm going to kill my cousin when we get home."

She shrugs. "I'm fine with it. We have a beach, three pools, and sunshine."

"That's a good attitude," I say, relieved she isn't pissed.

"Don't stress so much. Like you just said, we're pretty much naked online. Let everyone do what they want, and we'll do what we want," she suggests.

I kiss her. "Agreed."

She beams. "Good. Get changed. I want to grab a cabana before they get full."

I release her, and we both put our suits on. When I spin, she's in her swimsuit and sandals. "Aren't you wearing a cover-up?"

She tilts her head. "No. I'll have more clothes on than anyone else here."

I take a deep breath. Every man in this place will look at her whether she has a cover-up on or not. But I probably need to chill a bit. "That's true."

She picks up a small beach bag and looks inside it. "Cool. Whoever packed for me put sunscreen in here. I'm ready to go. Are you?"

"Sure." I lead her through the suite, out of the building, and through the resort. I try to stay calm about the other dudes checking her out, but it makes my blood boil. I scowl at all of them.

We arrive at the beach, get our towels, and choose our cabana. I pull the sunscreen out of her bag and wiggle my eyebrows. "Time for a rubdown."

"Great. Will you make sure you get it under my suit, too? This sun is strong, and I don't want to get burned."

I've never worried about getting burned through my clothes before, but I'm not going to argue. I cover her entire body. Since no one's around, I slide my hand down her bikini bottoms and play with her clit. I kiss her to keep her quiet until she's sweating, moaning in my mouth, and her entire body is trembling.

Other couples start to come on the beach. Some wear clothes. Some don't. The ones that do start stripping. I ignore them, pull my hand out of Arianna's pants, and kiss her again.

She drags her nails on the side of my head. Her lips twitch. "Let me get your lotion on so you don't get burned."

"Why do you look naughty right now?"

She smirks.

I chuckle and lie on my back. She gives me a massage as she rubs in the lotion. I add another thing to the list about what I really enjoy about her. She straddles me. "You need to roll over."

"I can't do that if your sexy little body is on me, now can I?" I shove my hands under her suit.

She giggles. "Get your hands out of my bottoms, and I'll get off you."

I groan and release my hands. "Fine."

She pecks me on the lips, rolls off me, and I flip over. She orders, "Close your eyes and relax."

I do it, and she starts with my feet, giving me a foot massage I'd pay big money for, before traveling up my leg. She slides her hands in my pants, rubbing knots out of my ass. Then she straddles me and does the same with my back.

"You're a keeper," I mutter, feeling the most relaxed I have in a long time. *Maybe this having a wife thing won't be so bad after all.*

She leans down, licks the back of my ear, and her hard nipples graze my skin.

She's so hard for me, I can feel it through her suit, I haughtily think.

"You know how you said you wanted to fuck my mouth?" she mumbles in my ear, her hot breath sending tingles down my spine.

"Don't tease me," I reply. The waves crash against the sand, and birds squawk as they fly overhead. The smell of salt, sunscreen, and Arianna flares in my nostrils.

She softly laughs and lies on top of me. "It's not against the rules. Or you could turn over, drop your pants, and I could ride you for a while."

I smile, continuing to keep my eyes shut. "You'd like that, wouldn't you?"

"Mmhmm. Remember what you said in the car? My tight little cunt over your swollen cock. Your palms on my ass."

"Jesus, you're the devil's temptress," I happily remark.

"I just want to be a good little wife for you."

"Keep this up, and you'll be top of the list, lass."

She shifts her hips then puts them back on me. "Do you still want my tits bouncing in your face and my pussy juice all over your thighs?"

"Christ. You're making me hard."

She slides her finger under my face and smears her arousal on my lips.

"Oh, you naughty little lass."

She pushes her digit in my mouth.

I suck on it. Loving everything about how she tastes and her dirty talk. I reach behind me and place my palms on her ass. "I love how smooth your body is."

"I love your hands on me."

"Mmm. I'm glad you admitted it. See, we're making progress. This husband-wife thing isn't hard after all, is it?"

She blows on my ear, and my erection twitches. She arches back and forth over my spine so her nipples graze my skin. She moans, "Ohhhh...no, it's not hard, baby. But you'd make me so happy if you just flipped over and let me ride you. I'm so wet. Feel me." She moves her knee and pushes her ass up. Wet heat slides on my lower back.

"Fuuuuck, Arianna." I'm so tempted. She's quickly becoming my dream woman. I could turn, remove her bottoms, and put a towel over us. I stroke her ass cheek again and freeze. My eyes fly open and I flip over so fast, she falls on the bed.

My sexy, voluptuous wife spreads her legs. She puts one hand on her naked pussy and the other on her bare breast. She begins stroking herself, and I almost blow my wad.

Almost.

From the corner of my eye, the guy next to us is sitting up. He looks straight at us with his feet on the sand and plays with himself.

I toss my towel over Arianna and lunge over the cabana. I grab the guy by the throat and lift him until he's on his toes. The woman next to him screams.

"Killian! Let him down!" Arianna shouts.

His face turns red.

I bark, "You know what I do to men who disrespect my wife?"

He gasps for air, his arms flail, and the woman gets on her knees while screaming, "Help!"

"Killian! He can't breathe!" Arianna cries out.

I lift him higher so his toes leave the sand. "You motherfucker. That's my wife. Mine. Not yours to look at and jack off to!"

He turns purple. His brown eyes morph into red. He grasps at my hands, but I'm stronger than him.

"Killian!" Arianna pulls on my arm.

"Step back, Arianna!" I demand.

"No! Let him go!"

The woman continues to shriek, and the man's eyes roll.

Fuck, he's going to die.

I toss him on the bed and spin to Arianna. She's standing naked, shaking, and more rage flies through me. I wrap a towel around her, grab her suit, and stuff it in the bag.

The man continues to hack, and the woman is crying. She has her hand on his back, trying to soothe him.

Arianna's eyes swirl with fear. I should calm down, but I can't. I throw her over my shoulder and ignore all the resort guests gawking at me.

"Killian! Let me down!" she belts out then smacks me on the ass.

"How dare you!" I fume.

"Killian!" She smacks me again and tries to kick me, but I have her thighs and calves secured.

Rage burns so hot, I can barely see straight to get to the room. The moment I get inside our suite, I set her on the bed. I warn, "Don't you dare move."

Tears stream down her face. "You're a psychopath."

I pull out my phone and hit the call button.

Declan's chipper voice answers, "Killian. Miss me already?"

"I need two plane tickets out of here."

"What's going on?"

"Now, Declan!"

He lowers his voice. "Text me photos of your passports and what hotel you're at."

I hang up and do what he asked. Arianna sniffles. "You're such a hypocrite."

I send off the text and spin, roaring, "I'm a hypocrite?"

She angrily points. "You got me off on the beach! You said being naked and having my bathing suit on are the same thing!"

"So you baited me?"

She looks away and closes her eyes. She sobs. "A hypocrite who can't look at anything besides his own viewpoint."

"Fine. I'm a hypocrite. Get your clothes on. We're going home," I fume.

She gets up and searches inside her suitcase.

Chaos continues to churn my stomach. The vision of that man getting off while watching my wife burns me like I've never been before. I bark, "What are you looking for? I said to get your clothes on."

She sticks her chin out. "Where's my phone?"

Her cell is in my overnight bag. Her father gave it to me when she was changing. "What do you need a phone for?"

Her voice cracks. "None of your business."

More anger dives so deep within me, I have to put my fists at my sides to steady myself. "That's where you're wrong again. Rule number seven. Everything you do is my business."

Her golden-brown eyes glisten as teardrops fall at an increasing rate. She repeats in a shaky voice, "Where is my phone?"

"You must have left it in New York," I lie.

She shuts her eyes.

I study her, wanting to pull her to me and make this entire thing go away. But I don't. She crossed a line, and she's going to learn this is never happening again.

She reaches for me. "Give me your phone."

"Why?"

She shuts her eyes, and her face crumples. She sniffles hard, stands straighter, then defiantly glares at me. "Give me your phone."

"Why? So you can call daddy?" I badger.

Her hand trembles, and she puts it over her stomach. She whispers, "Please give me your phone."

I pick up the outfit she wore on the plane and hold it out to her. "I said to get dressed. There's no calling daddy. I told you this before, and I'm never repeating it, so get it through your head. He's no longer in charge of you. I am. And you will follow my rules."

Through her tears, all I see is hatred. It cuts at my heart, making me feel like I can't breathe. But I still take it a step further, reminding her what her new reality is.

"Put your clothes on. We're going home to Chicago."

15

Arianna

It's a full commercial flight. I'm between Killian and some other man. I'm too scared to even look at him or reply when he greets me. I spend the journey with my eyes closed, trying to stop the tears from rolling down my cheeks, thinking how ironic life is. I'm trapped on this plane, just like my marriage.

The pilot comes on and says, "Looks like another windy day in Chicago. We'll be landing soon."

My gut flips, and my chest tightens so much, I think I'm having a heart attack. I grasp at my heart, panting. All I can think is I need to get back to New York, but I don't know how. I didn't think before I left about my purse with my credit cards or where my phone went. I was a stupid, delusional bride, trusting this psychotic monster I married. I bend forward, trying to get some stale air in my lungs.

Killian's hand goes to my back as the plane makes a bumpy landing, and the brakes screech on the pavement. "Arianna, are you okay?"

I try to shrug out of his hold on me, but I can't. There's nowhere to go.

"Ma'am, are you having a heart attack?" the man next to me asks.

Killian moves his hand up and down my spine, and I manage to order between short breathes, "Get your hand off me!"

"Maybe the flight attendant should call the paramedics," the man states.

"I'll handle my wife. Keep your nose out of it," Killian barks.

I jump, and more heart pains stab me. I put my head between my knees and manage to take a few deeper breaths.

Killian's entire arm slides down the side of my body, and he hovers over me. His hot breath hits my ear. "Lass, do you need me to call a doctor?"

"Don't touch me," I whisper.

"Arianna, you're freaking me—"

"Don't touch me!" I shriek, finding the strength to sit up and force him off me. My eyes fling open and I meet his widening gaze.

I close my eyes again, trying to regulate my breathing and stop the trembling in my hands. A ding sounds and the shuffling of people rising and opening overhead bins echoes in the aircraft. I feel Killian move away from me and hear the latch above us unlock.

He says, "Arianna, we need to get off the plane."

I open my eyes and keep them on the floor, avoiding his face. I follow the others in front of me. The cold air feels good in my lungs when I exit the aircraft. My heartbeat slows, and the pains weaken. I wipe my face.

Halfway through the jet bridge, he puts his hand on my waist. I loudly snap, "I said don't touch me!"

His face hardens, and in a low voice, he warns, "Don't make a scene."

"Then don't touch me," I wildly repeat.

I walk faster, and when we step out into the terminal, I look for the baggage sign. He must have gotten the message. For the rest of the way, he only stays close to me. At the bottom of the escalator, he says, "Why don't I take you outside and you can wait in the car with my driver. I'll get the luggage."

Getting away from him, even if it's only for a few moments, sounds like a good plan. I don't answer and move toward the doors. A gust of snowy wind slaps my face the moment I step outside. It's hard to see anything. Killian puts his arm around my waist, and I allow him to lead me to the car.

When I get in the back seat, I stare at the white blanket of passing cars. I've never missed New York or my papà and brothers. They've always been a constant in my life. I don't know who to talk to or how to get out of this situation. The gravity of being married to this stranger, this man who has a set of rules for himself but different ones for me, is worse than the sexist traits my papà and brothers have. It seems so much more personal.

Killian gets in the car, and a gust of freezing air floods the space. I move closer to the door, not wanting his presence anywhere near me.

Silence fills the air, but I can feel his intense gaze on me. The driver pulls out of the airport when Killian quietly asks, "Are you feeling okay?"

An emotion-filled, sarcastic laugh escapes my lips. It mixes with new tears.

"Arianna—"

"Leave me alone, Killian!" I cover my face with my shaking hand. My stomach somersaults.

A loud, exasperated sigh fills the vehicle. The remainder of the car ride is silent. When we stop, the snow is so thick I can't see anything. Killian clicks something. The driver pulls the vehicle into a garage.

"We're here," Killian says.

I take a deep breath, open the door, and get out. The driver takes the suitcases out of the trunk, and Killian opens the door leading into the house. I step inside, get to the end of the hallway, and stand off to the side, not knowing where to go.

Everything about it is unlike my papà's house. The kitchen and living space are connected. Everything is modern, as if recently renovated. The color theme is gray, silver, and black. There are no other colors anywhere, except a green four-leaf clover hanging above the mantel with "O'Malley" under it. It's a reminder I don't belong here and have nothing in common with Killian. And everything feels sterile compared to the rich mahogany, gold, reds, and blues I've lived my entire life around. I swallow the lump in my throat and can't help compare how it's just like him—cold.

The sound of suitcases rolling on the dark wood floor sends new dread throughout me. I glance at the window but only see ice and a blizzard of white.

Killian's teasing voice states, "Home sweet home."

I squeeze my eyes shut. This isn't home. It will never be. It might as well be a prison.

Tension fills the air. I don't move, afraid I'm going to fall apart entirely and never get put back together. My insides quiver so hard, I feel sick.

He clears his throat. "Do you want me to show you around?"

I wipe my face and spin, still avoiding his eyes. I manage to nod.

He puts his hand on my lower back, and I step away from it. He demands, "Arianna, how long are you going to pout?"

I finally look at him. My voice shakes. "I've told you not to touch me. Don't ever touch me again."

His eyes harden. He seethes, "You're my wife. I'll touch you if I want to."

"So you'll force yourself on me?" More tears I wish I could stop gush down my face.

His jaw clenches. Green flames ignite in his orbs. Time seems to stand still as he takes deep breaths, assessing me, as if debating how to answer my question. He finally speaks and repeats, "You're my wife."

I stand as tall as possible and stick my chin out. "You can cut off access to my family, my personal items, and create all the rules you want. The only way you'll ever touch me again is against my will. And I won't enjoy it because you're stronger than me."

He swallows hard, takes a step forward while reaching for me, and I retreat until I'm against the window. The cold of the glass permeates into my spine.

His eyes widen, and he stops several feet in front of me. He shakes his head, spins, then grabs keys off the side table. He leaves the house, and I hear the garage door open and a vehicle start.

I turn and faintly make out a black SUV pulling out of the driveway and hear the garage door close.

After several minutes, I cautiously step farther into the house, then go room to room. There's a master suite and a guest bedroom with a Jack and Jill bathroom connected to an office. The office has a desk and love seat in it. A half bath is near the kitchen. Every room has the same color scheme.

I take my suitcase and roll it into the guest bedroom. I unpack and then go out and get the duffle bag. I dump everything out on the bed to see what is mine. I freeze.

That lying bastard!

My phone, charger, and purse are all on the bedspread. I try to turn on my cell, but it's dead. I plug the charger into the wall socket and connect it to my phone.

I stuff all his belongings into the duffle bag and put it back next to his suitcase. When I return to my phone, it's lit up. A notification says I have five missed texts.

Papà: *I miss you already, my bambina, but I hope you're having a blast on your honeymoon. Something has come up, and I have to go to Italy. I may need to delay my trip to Chicago by a week. The cell phone service will be iffy where I'm at, but I'll try to find a spot to call when you return.*

I shut my eyes, cringing.

Massimo: *Pick me up a bottle of real tequila with the worm in it. See you in Chicago.*

Great. Should be a fun explanation why I didn't deliver on that request.

Dante: *I ran into Orlando. Told him you got hitched. I think he wanted to cry.*

Orlando was one of my ex-boyfriends who proposed. Now, I wonder why I turned him down.

Gianni: *Bought you VIP tickets for the summer fashion show. I'm assuming you'll want to come back for it?*

I smile. Every year, I go to all the shows during the different fashion weeks.

Tristano: *The wing is too quiet without you. Miss you. See you in a few weeks.*

My heart hurts more, and home seems farther away. The temptation to call my brothers and tell them to come get me or use my credit card for a one-way plane ticket is high. For some reason, though, I don't.

I click on my social media app and scroll through my messages. My heart pounds in my chest.

Donato: *We still need to talk. I miss and love you. No matter what your father forced you into, I'll get you out of it.*

I reread the message several times. *Do I want Donato to rescue me from Killian?* I debate in my head but finally decide it isn't a better situation than the one I'm in now. Donato can say whatever he wants, but if he loved me, he wouldn't have slept with that other woman. And I can't forget how he shoved me into the car.

I leave my messages and scroll my feed when my gut drops again.

A photo of Killian's broody expression fills the screen. His ripped abs and pecs are covered in sweat. He's wearing a black boxing glove. The tattooed S.O. initials mock me. The caption reads: *Sometimes, no matter how many punches you get in, it doesn't alleviate your anger.*

It already has over ten thousand hearts and a few thousand comments. Women and men both kiss his ass. They tell him how amazing he looks, what they want to do to his sweaty body, and ask him if he's okay. He engages with tons of them, which only burns me further.

He's such a hypocrite. He can't even go twenty-four hours without flaunting himself all over the internet after our fight.

Darkness fills the house. I pace, not sure what to do or when he'll return. There isn't any doubt he'll know I took my personal items. I'm assuming he'll try to take them back. So I look for places to hide my phone, charger, and wallet, but everywhere I think of seems too obvious.

After several trips around the house, I finally put my wallet in the heating vent in his office. My phone shows it's fully charged. I ransack Killian's kitchen drawers and find a roll of duct tape.

Should have used the one Nora gave me and taped his mouth shut as soon as he said "I do."

I turn the phone off, drop it and the charger in a plastic bag, then seal it. The black leather sofa is heavy, but I manage to lift it, tape the bag to the bottom, then put it back, so it looks untouched.

The garage door opens as I'm shoving my purse in the duffle bag. I close it, run to my bedroom, and shut the door. My ears ring from the blood pounding in my skull.

"Arianna!" Killian shouts.

I shut my eyes, not sure what I'm going to say to him and praying for a miracle he'll leave me alone.

My door flies open, and the light turns on. He seethes, "What are you doing in here?"

"Trying to sleep, leave me alone," I fire back, keeping my eyes shut.

A moment passes, and I think he might leave, but then I hear drawers opening.

I sit up. "What are you doing?"

He says nothing and leaves with a handful of my clothes.

I jump out of bed and follow him. "Killian! Give me my things back!"

He tosses them on his bed then shoves past me. I try to gather them, but he's next to me, throwing another pile down quicker than I can scoop my things up.

"Killian! Don't ignore me!"

Green darts fly at me. He growls, "Rule number eight. You sleep in my bed. With me. Your husband, who you made a vow to for life. Your things stay in my room, next to mine. Are we clear?"

So many emotions swirl in my veins, but one is more potent than the others. I whisper, "I hate you."

Hurt passes in his expression, but it doesn't stay long. "That's your choice." He leaves and continues making trips until all my things are in his room or bathroom.

I stare at the heap on the bed. He disappears into the closet then comes out with a bunch of hangers. I glare at him as he hangs up my shirts.

He nods to the dresser. In a calm voice, he says, "The top two drawers are for you. I cleaned them out before I left for New York."

"Do you want a medal?" I snap.

He ignores me, takes a handful of hangers back to the closet, then comes back and picks up my underwear. He opens a dresser drawer and drops them inside.

I continue watching him until all my items are no longer in sight, except for a sexy nightgown.

"Get ready for bed," he orders.

"I'm not wearing that."

He crosses his arms. "Then what one do you want to wear?"

Nothing here is anything except risqué. Whoever packed my suitcase wanted me to get laid every night.

When I don't respond, he gives me a challenging stare. "It's this or you can be naked. I'm fine with either."

I pull the cover back and go to slide in, and he grabs me by the hips and yanks me back.

"No! You aren't wearing daytime clothes. Choose, Arianna. Nightgown or nothing."

I look up at him, and every ounce of anything I have left seeps out of me.

His intense gaze pins me. It's the one he wore when we took our vows. And it shoots right through my heart and destroys me further. Mint, orange blossom, and bourbon vanilla permeate all my cells, stirring up feelings for him I hate myself for and don't know how to terminate. He wipes a tear off my cheek. "It doesn't have to be like this."

"You mean as long as I do everything you say without question and become your 'yes wife,'" I accuse.

His eyes close briefly. He sighs. "That's not true, lass."

I sniffle. "Yes, it is. You want to do everything you've always done and have me be your new puppy dog on a leash, begging for your attention and obeying your every command."

Shock fills his face. "Arianna—"

No longer able to be this close to him or smell his intoxicating scent, I push away. I grab the nightgown, go into the bathroom, and shut the door.

My reflection in the mirror mocks me. It's worse than the morning of my wedding. Too many days of crying, lack of sleep, and fighting about one decision after another have taken their toll. I cringe then wash my face, brush my teeth, and change into the gold satin nightgown. It hugs every curve of my body and barely covers my ass. The satin dips so low, it hits the top of my areolas.

My plan to run to the bed and get under the covers doesn't work. I step out of the bathroom as Killian emerges from the closet, naked. We lock eyes, but then his drift down my body. My flutters take off, and I curse myself. More rage ignites when his S.O. tattoo glares at me. It's enough to make me move my feet and hide in the bed.

Killian lifts the covers. "Slide over, lass."

Of course I would choose his side, and lord knows he's not changing. I move as far away as I can.

He gets in, turns the light off, then tugs me to him. "I didn't say go to a deserted island."

I let out an emotion-filled laugh and loathe myself even more for giving him any satisfaction. But also because I should try to get out of his grasp and can't seem to push away from his warm, hard body.

His lips brush my forehead. "Isn't this better than my lonely guest room?"

I stay silent, wishing the humming in my skin would go away. So much confusion ignites inside me. How can I allow him to hold me like this after everything that's happened?

He flips me on my back then cages his ripped frame over mine. I gasp. Heat smolders so fiercely off our bodies, the room could be on fire.

His green eyes glow like a depraved animal who will stop at nothing to get what he wants. Tantalizing breath makes my mouth water. His fingers stroke my cheek, making me dizzy. "All I see is that man watching you. No matter what I do, nothing takes it away. And I don't understand it."

"Understand what?" I whisper.

"Why I care so much. I could say it's because you're my wife, but it's not only that. And I just..." He exhales. His heart beats into my chest.

"Just?" I push.

"I don't do this with women."

"Do what?" I ask, still not understanding what he's saying.

"Care." He lowers his head and slides his tongue in my mouth, intensifying all the sensations I swore I'd never allow him to give me ever again.

My body relaxes, and I wrap my arms around him, unable to stop myself. However, I'm not sure what he means. He doesn't care about anyone he's with? How is that possible?

He pulls back. "I don't care who talks to them." He slides his tongue back into my mouth.

This time, I greedily open my mouth wider. I arch my chest into his.

He mumbles, "Or who looks at them." He returns to kissing me until I'm whimpering and my thighs drip with my arousal.

As soon as he retreats, I blurt out, "I didn't know he was looking. I-I—"

"Shh. I know." He runs his knuckles over the side of my breast, grazing my nipple. My knees bend. His smooth erection presses against my clit, and he shifts his hips.

"Oh God," I whisper, lifting my pelvis to get more friction.

His wet tongue flicks my lobe, and he works my clit harder with his cock. "Let me do my penance, lass."

I shudder and breathe, "Penance?" This is the second time he's said this, but surely the priest didn't tell him to have sex for his penance?

"Mmhmm." He kisses the curve of my neck. "Before everything went bad, do you know how hard you made me?"

Sweat pops out on my skin. I whimper from the adrenaline growing in my cells, ready to combust.

He moves the strap of my nightgown down and kisses my shoulder. "As hard as it is right now, rubbing against your pussy." His lips return to mine. He gives me several controlled kisses, pulling back every time I moan. Then he comes at me again with more intensity, as if he could fuck me with his mouth and erase all our problems.

Every time his green orbs meet mine, the air between us burns hotter. My skin crackles from his every touch. I thrust my hips faster under him and shut my eyes. Wishing this was the only way we could be.

"Open your eyes, lass," he demands.

I obey, but it's only seconds before they roll back, and I'm trembling beneath his rigid flesh, calling out his name.

He shimmies down my body, and tremors erupt all over. His lips and tongue take ownership of my endorphins, as if there's a dial he's able to slow down or speed up.

"Killian!" I cry out, tugging his hair, not sure how much more I can take.

"Admit you want me, Arianna," he growls.

I freeze.

He sucks me so hard, I orgasm again.

"Admit it!" he orders then shoves his tongue inside me, flicking it like a snake.

My body spasms against him. White light seems to blink in the room. My voice becomes hoarse from crying out.

He lunges over me then flips over in a seated position. He tugs me over him in a straddle position.

I don't wait and slide on him the moment I'm able, moaning into the darkness.

He declares, "You know what I want, Arianna."

"No, I don't," I admit, confused about too many things.

He holds my cheeks in front of his face. "This, Arianna. Us. Like this. You're tight little cunt over my swollen cock."

"Your palms on my ass," I breathe.

He nods and moves them there then sets the pace of my hips circling on him. "Yeah, lass. What else do you want?"

"My tits in your face," I confess.

He lowers my other strap and pushes the satin until it's below my breasts. He dips down and sucks on them, squeezing his warm palms on my ass cheeks.

Everything about Killian O'Malley when we're like this feels right. It's perfection in ways I didn't know existed. Every move he makes, he does with precision, as if he doesn't even have to debate about how to touch me. His body in mine and his mouth and hands all over me is like dry wood on a fire. It's as if I was only burning a wet log before him. Then he came along and showed me how I should really burn.

He positions his face in front of mine. In a stern, no-room-to-argue voice, he says, "Your pussy juice all over my thighs."

"Yes," I cry out.

His lips and tongue once again claim me. And there seems to be no more him or me. I don't know how it's possible, but I can't tell where he ends and I begin.

He presses his forehead against mine. "You're mine, Arianna. My wife. No other man gets to look at your body. And I'm the only one who gets to touch you, eat you, and fuck you. Do you understand?"

A tear falls down my cheek. I hold on to him tighter. "Yes."

He kisses it then thrusts me harder over him. Beads of sweat roll down his face. "Tell me it's what you want, too, Arianna. That you want me and only me."

"I don't want anyone else," I admit, surprised by how quickly the truth comes out. But I don't. And as much as he has hurt me, I do want him.

Satisfaction and something else I can't decipher appear on his face. He thrusts his hips up, and I spasm so hard, I bury my head into his neck as my body convulses.

"Fuuuuck, Arianna!" He detonates in me, and one of his arms slides up my back until he's palming my head.

Our chests heave, trying to find air. He tugs my hair and pins his gaze on me. "We made a vow, Arianna. I'll kill anyone who comes between us."

16

Killian

WHEN I WAKE UP, ARIANNA ISN'T IN THE ROOM. PANIC consumes me. I jump out of bed then look in the closet and bathroom. She's nowhere.

"Arianna!" I shout, toss on boxers, then rush into the main room. "Arianna!"

"No need to yell," she reprimands.

I turn toward the kitchen and freeze. Her dark, curly hair looks disheveled. Probably from sleeping on it. Pink flushes her cheeks. Her pouty red lips appear slightly swollen. Golden-brown eyes peek out under long lashes. She's wearing her nightgown and the only apron I own. Nora had them made for all of us. It's green and says "O'Malley's" in gold.

My morning wood gets so stiff looking at her, I debate if I should get the lube and give her a new experience or bend her over and slide into her pretty little cunt.

She bats her eyelashes. "Morning."

A stupid grin forms on my face that I couldn't stop if I wanted to. "Morning. What are you doing up so early?"

"Mmm, you know it's after ten, right?"

"Is it?"

"Yep," she says, popping the p.

"Must have needed my rest after a sexy lass kept me up all night."

She beams and holds a knife in the air. "You mean your sexy wife."

I chuckle and step around the counter. "Turn."

She obeys.

I step behind her and press my aching cock in her back, inhaling her muted perfume. "You look hot as fuck in this outfit."

She glances up, and the pink in her cheeks turns red. I give her a peck on the lips. "How long have you been up?"

She shrugs. "Maybe a few hours. I'm making you breakfast."

"That's a good lass! Get right into those wifely duties," I tease.

She elbows me. "Don't be annoying, or I won't do it again."

I steal another kiss, pat her ass, then glance at the counter. One bowl has yolks, and another has the egg whites. A handful of spinach and tomatoes is in a small skillet. "What are you making?"

"Well, you're kind of low on food, but I figured it out."

"Okay. What is it?"

"Spinach and tomato egg white omelet and toast."

"Egg white?"

"It's healthier. And you're almost forty, so you need to watch your cholesterol and heart health," she states.

"You're joking, right?"

She shakes her head. Her voice is solemn. "No."

I point to the yolks. "What are you going to do with those?"

"Toss them down the sink."

"I have a better idea." I open the drawer and pick up a fork. Then I lean over her and grab the yolk bowl. I scramble them and dump them in with the egg whites.

"Killian!" she reprimands.

"What?"

"That's all the eggs you have!"

"Even better. I'm hungry, and it'll be more food," I claim.

She stares at the bowl and furrows her eyebrows. Her lashes flutter quickly.

The feeling I just did something terrible again reappears. "Lass, why are you looking so upset over eggs?"

She takes a deep breath and slowly looks up. "Do you know how much cholesterol is in egg yolks?"

"Cholesterol is necessary to make hormones, including testosterone. It gets a bad rap. And there's nothing wrong with egg yolks," I insist.

Anger flares in her face. "Cholesterol can create fatty deposits in your blood vessels, which can block blood from getting to your arteries. The deposits can also break off and form a clot that causes strokes or heart attacks."

I pound my heart. "Nothing wrong with me, lass. I'm fit as a fiddle."

She glares at my chest for a moment then redirects her laser stare on mine. "How do you know?"

I grunt. "Don't ask crazy questions you already know the answers to. I'm the walking epitome of health."

She puts her hand on her hip. "So you've had bloodwork done?"

"Sure." I step past her and open the fridge. The bag of shredded cheese is in the drawer. I pump a victory fist in the air.

"When did you have it done last?" she asks.

I open the bag of cheddar and throw a handful in the egg bowl. "I don't know. Not long ago."

"What were your numbers?"

"My numbers?"

"HDL. LDL. You know, your lipid panel."

"Are you a nurse or something and I don't know about it? If so, I'm down with some role play. Actually, you'd look superhot in one of those candy stripper outfits."

"You mean striper. You said stripper."

I study every part of her body until she squirms. "No, I meant candy stripper." I fold the eggs and cheese together and hand it to her. "Now this is ready."

She gapes at the bowl, saying nothing, as anger grows on her face.

I set the bowl on the counter. "I think you're analyzing these egg whites a bit too much."

She picks up the skillet with the vegetables and sets it on the stove. "Where's your cooking spray?"

I grab a bar of Irish butter out of the fridge. I hold it out to her. "Use this. It makes everything better."

She takes it from me and reads it. She spins. "Eight grams of saturated fat per serving. My guess is you're going to use way more than just one. That's horrible for your heart, Killian."

Okay, this woman must have a severe body image issue, and I'm going to need to set her straight.

I tug her into me so her face is staring at my heart. I tap on it. "This heart is in mint condition. My cardio workouts for boxing are more than what most people do in a week. I also lift and burn so many calories a day, I don't need to worry about what goes in my body."

She stares at my chest, and her breathing gets shorter. Maroon fills her cheeks.

I put my hands under her armpits and pick her up. I set her on the counter then place both my hands next to her hips. "You're gorgeous. Everything about you is perfect. You have the right amount of fat on every part of your body. Now, if you want to work out, that's fine. I'm all for it. But whatever this starvation diet thing is you have going on this morning, it's ending today. And I'm not sure what asshole told you to watch your weight, but I'm telling you to get it out of your head."

Her mouth hangs open. She turns away from me, and I figure she's embarrassed, so I kiss her cheek, then step back. "Want any help cooking this?"

She avoids looking at me and jumps off the counter. She quietly says, "No."

"Okay. I guess I'll sit back and watch you in action."

"You do that," she mutters.

I assume she's still embarrassed, so I decide to give her some space. I leave the kitchen, grab my phone, then sit on a barstool. I scroll through my social media feed and add my opinion on a few things the people I follow posted. I also respond to some comments my followers made on my posts. A text pops up.

Declan: *We need to talk with Liam and Finn. Today.*

Me: *What time?*

Declan: *Later at the pub? Meet up for dinner? I'll have Liam bring Hailee to keep Arianna company.*

Me: *Sure.*

Arianna comes around the counter and sets a plate down with dry toast.

I reach across the counter and grab the butter. "Are we splitting this?"

"Nope. All yours." She hands me a fork.

"This looks nice, but you need to eat."

She doesn't respond and asks, "When will my things arrive from New York?"

I cut the corner of the omelet off. "Your father said today. Declan was originally going to come by. The movers were going to notify him when they were an hour out." The cheese oozes when I try to separate the bite. I twirl it around my fork while continuing to pull it. I finally stuff it in my mouth.

Arianna watches me.

I chew and swallow. "This is perfect, lass. Thank you." I shove another bite in my mouth.

She steps behind me and slides her fingers along my scalp. Then she massages it.

I groan. "You're the best wife ever."

She leans over and kisses my cheek. "Would it be okay for me to call my papà and see if he found my phone anywhere? Or my purse? It's just so strange no one gave it to us!"

Guilt fills me. *Should I tell her I have it?*

No. She'll know I lied. Better to keep the peace right now. Maybe I can plant it in one of the boxes that arrives today.

I put my fork down and spin in my chair. I pull her onto my lap. "Tell you what. Why don't I call your father to tell him we had an issue with the hotel and came back early. I'll handle all the hard questions and then you won't get grilled."

Something passes quickly in her expression. But then she tilts her head and smiles. "Aww. Would you mind? You know how he is."

"Not at all."

"Thanks. You're the best." She pecks me on the lips then says, "Eat before it gets cold. I'm going to shower so I'm ready for when the movers get here. I can't wait to unpack all my things."

I squeeze her ass. "Sure you don't want any food? I don't want anything happening to this."

"No. And don't worry, I had toast earlier. No crazy starvation issues here. Promise!" she chirps.

"You did eat?" I double-check.

"Yep." She pats my cheek and steps back. She takes two steps then pauses. "Hey, Killian?"

"Yeah?"

Her eyes seer into mine. "I'm really glad we made rule number six."

More guilt crashes through me. *Rule number six. You trust me, and I trust you.*

I need to figure out this phone mess then only be honest from here on out.

"I am, too," I tell her. And I am. I only wish we made the rule after she got her belongings back.

Once the shower is on, I sneak over to the front door and dig into my duffle bag. Her phone, charger, and purse are in it. There is also a T-shirt, pair of shorts, and dress I thought I saw on the bed last night. I tell myself it must be my paranoia. I was too enraged to know for sure. Plus, I saw what was in the bag when we got to Mexico.

I stick the cell phone and charger in the purse. Then I hide it under the kitchen cabinet. I zip the duffle bag back up, and the doorbell rings.

A delivery man has a large box. I sign for it then take it into the kitchen. It's addressed to Arianna and has her father's return address on it.

It hits me that this is the perfect opportunity. I get her purse out, slit the box open, then take a handful of the filler paper out. I slide her contents inside and put the paper back on top then go into the bathroom.

Arianna has a towel wrapped around her hair. She's in a robe and is sitting at the vanity.

I lean down and say, "Good news."

She spins. "Oh?"

Another white lie comes out of my mouth. "A box came from New York. I slit the tape off so you can go through it. Hope it's okay. I didn't look inside."

She smiles again, and I'm glad I figured out how to get past this one last bad situation between us. From this point forward, it's all honesty. She waves her hands between us. "Thanks, but you don't have to ever worry about that. We've got rule number six, remember?"

"That's right, lass," I say, feeling another bolt of guilt.

"I'll go open it now." She rises and walks out to the kitchen.

"Wonder what it is," I say, happy this situation will soon be over.

She lifts the flaps and pulls out the brown paper. She dramatically gasps then pulls out her purse. "Oh, I'm so happy this is here."

"Does it happen to have your phone in it?" I ask.

She unzips it and pulls the charger, phone, and her wallet out. "Well, this is a relief."

"Yeah, bet you felt a bit naked without them," I add.

"Oh, you have no idea." She tosses everything back in her purse, glances in the box, then shuts the flaps. "Will you bring this into the bedroom? It's the gifts the girls got me."

"Sure." I do as she asks and put it on the bed. "Want some help unpacking it?" My phone vibrates, and I pull it out.

Declan: *Movers are ten minutes away. Sorry, they just sent a message now.*

"Your stuff will be here in ten minutes. I'm going to hop in the shower."

She motions to the bathroom. "Go. I'll take care of this box."

I take a shower, happy with myself that I solved all our issues and Arianna and I are in a good place. From this point forward, I vow it's going to be nothing but smooth sailing for us.

17

Arianna

THE NIGHTSTAND ON MY SIDE OF THE BED HAS THREE DRAWERS. Nothing has ever been in them or Killian scrubbed it clear of any evidence. I toss the numerous sex toys in the drawer, fuming.

That lying piece of shit! What else is he lying to me about?

After we made up last night, I thought it was best to put all the things that were in the duffle bag back in. Surely, he wouldn't try to keep my phone and wallet away from me now that we worked things out.

I even tried making him a healthy breakfast, but apparently, he thinks he's invincible. Plus, he now believes I fat shame myself.

I toss another box in the drawer and mutter, "Asshole."

He had the opportunity to come clean and didn't. Even after I reminded him about rule number six. It only goes to show his true colors. But if he thinks I'm going to have a set of rules about trust and he doesn't have to stick to them, he's back on planet delusional.

I toss several outfits on the bed and get to the bottom of the carton. The long black box Piero and Vannie gave me is the last item. I glance behind me to make sure Killian isn't around and peek inside.

I should put this on him while I sit on his face and make him suffer.

Like I could even get him to put it on. I doubt Killian is into wearing cock cages.

I toss the box in the top drawer and shut it. Killian comes into the room in a towel. "Forgot to tell you, lass. I'm taking you to Nora's pub tonight. The guys and Hailee will be there, too."

"Okay. That sounds fun."

"It will be." He walks into the closet and shouts, "Hey, there's something I should ask you."

"What's that?"

He comes out in joggers and puts his T-shirt over his head. "I know I was joking about you being a nurse—well, not about the candy stripper. You can always be a candy stripper, and I won't have any issues with it."

My face heats, and I roll my eyes. "I think you're the horniest man I know."

"Didn't hear you complaining all night, lass."

I toss a pillow at him. He catches it and chuckles. "Okay. Serious question. Are you ready for it?"

"Yep."

"This is another one of those questions we should have asked each other before we got hitched, but better late than never, right?"

My stomach flips. Things we should have asked and never did is probably too long of a list to write out. "What's the question?"

"What do you do? For work? I've got a lot of connections in Chicago. I might know someone who can get you hooked up with a new job. It'll make the application process easier."

I turn away from him. So much heat flies to my face, I think I might break out in a sweat. My papà and I went round and round about me working, and he always forbade me. I quietly admit, "I don't work."

The room goes silent.

Killian carefully asks, "Do you mean you recently quit your job, or you never had one?"

I twist my fingers in my lap. "My papà didn't want me to work. He said it wasn't necessary and added another layer of danger to my life."

His voice is full of doubt. "So you've never had a job before?"

More shame appears. "No."

He sits on the bed next to me. "Okay. So what do you do all day?"

The doorbell rings, and I jump. "That'll be my stuff."

He opens his mouth, but I leave the room, relieved to avoid further interrogations about how I spend my boring days. He follows me, and we're soon in a sea of boxes.

All day, we unpack my items, rearrange things in his closet, and try to figure out where my stuff will fit.

Overwhelmed, I stare at the bed covered in clothes. "I think I need the guest room closet, too."

"Why do you have so much stuff? Maybe we should start a donation pile," he suggests.

"What? I'm not giving my clothes away!"

He picks up a dress. "When's the last time you wore this?"

I gasp. "There were only fifty of those dresses made. I got it during Fashion Week two years ago."

He arches his eyebrow. "Have you worn it?"

"Of course I've worn it."

"How many times?"

I grab the dress from him. "I'm not getting rid of it."

He selects another dress. "What about this one?"

I put my hand on my hip. "Do you not like my clothes?"

He assesses the stack. "No. But if you aren't going to wear it, I think you should donate it."

"What are you going to donate?" I ask.

He scrunches his face. "Nothing. I don't have an excessive amount of stuff."

I huff and go into the closet. I grab the pile of pants my arms can barely fit around then throw them on the bed. "Does anyone need..." I count each pair. "Fourteen pairs of joggers?"

He smirks. "Fifteen. I'm wearing a pair."

"Why do you need that many?"

"They're joggers," he states, as if I asked him a stupid question.

I point to the pile. "Eleven of the fifteen are gray."

Smugness fills his face. "A few of them were sent to me by the designers. They wanted someone who could represent to wear them and post." He winks.

I try not to laugh. I know all about his joggers posts, and I can't deny he has the perfect everything to wear them. "You could get rid of several, and you wouldn't miss them."

"Says the woman who has thirty black dresses."

"Okay, fine." I go back into the closet and grab another large handful of shirts. I add those to the bed. "Why do you need this many O'Malley's shirts."

"Don't be dissing those. That's sacrilegious."

I groan. "You're impossible."

"Just honest."

Without analyzing it, I blurt out, "I'm not giving my clothes away. You have everything you've always had in your life. All I have are my clothes."

He tugs me into him. "Yeah, but you have me now."

I push his chest, but he holds me close to him. "You're so arrogant."

His lips twitch. "Don't worry, lass. Everything inside my joggers comes with me."

I stifle my laugh and tilt my head.

He kisses me and squeezes my ass. "Okay. You win. But I think you're going to need the closet in the guest room and my office."

"Lead the way!" I exclaim, happy the debate about my clothes is over.

We spend another hour putting everything away. When we finish, Killian proclaims, "Just in time. We need to leave for the pub."

I take a dress out of his office closet. "This should be in our bedroom one."

"Another black dress! However will you choose?" he quips.

I ignore him and go into our joint closet. He follows me. I ask, "What should I wear?"

"It's a pub."

I bite on my lip, staring at my clothes. Anxiety tightens in my chest. This is Chicago. Is it different than New York?

"Arianna, why do you look stressed out?"

"I'm not," I quickly state then pull a pair of pants off the shelf. "Jeans okay?"

"Perfect. I'm wearing what I have on."

I glance at his joggers and O'Malley T-shirt, realizing how unfair it is that guys can wear sweatpants and it looks hot, but women have to fix themselves up.

"Don't stress. It's a pub." Killian steps out of the closet.

I debate what to pair with the jeans and finally settle on a chocolate-brown mesh top and matching ankle boots. I put on makeup and fix my hair, then add a spritz of perfume. When I sling my purse over my shoulder, my anger over Killian lying to me this morning resurfaces.

I wonder what other lies he'll tell me.

I push my worries aside. It's not the time to get into a fight. Plus, I'm looking forward to seeing Hailee. Maybe I can start going to their yoga class this weekend.

When I get to the main room, Killian holds my coat out. I slide into it, and he leads me out the main door. A car is waiting in the driveway. I also notice several other similar vehicles in the street near his house.

"You aren't driving?" I ask.

"Try not to when I'm drinking."

"Oh. That's smart," I say. He opens the door, and I get in. He follows, and I ask, "Why are there several of the same vehicles in front of your house?"

His eyes darken. "They're O'Malley's guarding the house."

My stomach flips. It makes no sense. My papà had too many bodyguards to count. The only time I wasn't with one was when I would sneak out. "Why do you need them?"

His frame stiffens. He shifts uncomfortably then turns. "Lass, I know you aren't innocent. You do understand what kind of family you come from, correct?"

The reality is, I know very little about what goes on in my papà's world. I defensively snap, "Of course I do!"

He holds his hands in the air. "Calm down. I just meant that you didn't think your father would allow you to marry anyone not in a similar type of family, did you?"

"What does that mean, exactly?" I ask, hoping to get more from him than my papà gives me.

He arches his eyebrow. "I have to spell it out?"

Embarrassed I know so little, flames flood my cheeks. "Can you be straight up with me instead of going around the question?"

"Had you not heard of my family?"

"No. Why would I?"

His eyes widen in shock. "We're the O'Malleys of Chicago."

I shrug. "So?"

"I can't believe you haven't heard of the O'Malleys," he says, insulted.

Annoyed, I snap, "Can you get past it and answer my questions? Plus, what exactly do you do besides box and flaunt your body on social media? I'm sure the latest jogger designer isn't paying the bills."

"Says the woman who's never worked a day in her life."

I stare out the window, his words creating a shameful sting. I quietly say, "Who are the O'Malleys?"

"We're a crime family, just like the Marinos."

I'm not sure why I feel any surprise. He's right. Why would my papà marry me off to anyone who wasn't in a crime family? I ask, "Who's the head?"

"Liam."

Shocked, I spin toward him. "Liam? He's...is he younger than you?"

In an offended tone, he says, "No. He is not younger than me. He's a year older."

"Ohh. A whole year!" I mock.

"If you must know, his father, my uncle Darragh, just passed," Killian adds.

I instantly feel bad. "I'm sorry."

"And so you aren't worried about being fed, I do a lot of things that you don't need to know about. But we're also in the middle of starting a tech firm."

Same excuse my papà always has. I push my annoyed feelings aside. "What kind of tech firm?"

"Cybersecurity."

"Are you a tech guru?" I ask.

"No. Declan and Nolan are. But don't look so shocked. I have brains, too," he states.

I chirp, "Really? That makes me excited to know since I'm married to you."

"I see you have your sense of humor tonight," he mutters.

The car stops in front of a building, and Killian opens the door. He gets out, reaches in for me, then leads me toward the pub.

My nights out in New York were mostly at clubs or high-end restaurants. I haven't even been to a pub before. I don't have any expectations, but I freeze when I step inside.

"Lass, what's wrong?" Killian asks.

"This is beautiful. It looks brand new." Creamy white wallpaper has tiny slivers of Kelly green running through it. Stone tiles in different sizes are arranged in a pattern and trim the edge of the bar and the rich wood floor. There's another room with games in it and has the same stone tile pattern. The booths and tables look high-end and new.

Pride sweeps Killian's face. "Nora just remodeled it. She worked with Anna, who's one of Chicago's top designers. My brothers and I did a lot of the work."

I playfully squeeze his biceps. "So these do more than flex and beat people up?"

He grunts. "My brothers and I had a construction firm for years. We can do anything."

"Wow. Did you update your house?"

He nods. "Yep. You should probably start calling it our house now, though, don't you think?"

I blurt out, "But it's not mine. It's nothing like mine."

Killian's eyes turn to slits. "Sorry. Forgot you're probably having withdrawals from daddy's mansion and feel like you're in a shoebox."

I jerk my head back. "That's not what I meant."

"Isn't it?"

"No! It's—"

"Arianna! Killian! Why aren't you in Mexico?" Hailee asks.

I spin then stare at Killian, not knowing what to say. He puts his arm around my shoulder. "The resort sucked."

Liam pulls me into a hug and kisses my cheek. "You doing okay, lass?"

I force a smile, still upset over Killian's assumption. "Yeah."

Finn and Declan come in. After more greetings, we settle into a corner booth. It's round and seats ten. A server hands out menus. "Are you Killian's new wife?"

"Molly, this is Arianna. Arianna, meet Molly."

So that's the girl who took the photo. She looks nice enough.

I hold my hand out, and she takes it and says, "Nice to meet you."

"You, too."

"You're from New York?"

"Yes."

"So why aren't you on your honeymoon? I thought you were going to Mexico?" Molly asks.

Heat flares in my cheeks.

"Hey, Molly, we're starving and dying of thirst. Do you mind getting us a round of Guinness and whatever the lasses want?" Declan chimes in.

She straightens up. "Sure. Hailee, Arianna, what do you want?"

"I'll have a cucumber basil gimlet," Hailee states.

"Do you have a Barolo?" I ask.

Molly's forehead wrinkles. "Is that a brand of liquor?"

How do you not know what Barolo is? That's a sin.

I nicely reply, "No. It's red wine."

"Sorry, we don't."

"Do you like Pinot Noir? Nora stocks Meomi," Hailee informs.

"Sure. I'll take a glass of that then."

Molly nods and leaves.

I study the menu, trying to find the healthiest thing I can.

Killian says, "You should try the fish and chips. People drive from all over to order it."

I don't tell him I avoid fried food like the plague or lecture him on how horrible it is for your heart. I settle on the Salmon of Knowledge Salad and shut my menu.

Molly comes back with the drinks. Everyone places their order. She turns to me. "What can I get you, Arianna?"

"I'll have the Salmon of Knowledge Salad without the eggs, please."

Killian groans. "Lass, I thought we discussed this."

"You don't like eggs?" Molly asks.

My face heats again. I shouldn't have to explain my food choices to anyone, but I say, "I don't eat egg yolks."

"Ever? That's the best part," she claims.

"Thank you, Molly!" Killian takes a sip of his Guinness.

She tilts her head. "So what's wrong with the yolks?"

"They're bad for your cholesterol," I reply.

Killian turns to me with annoyance in his expression. "Do we need to have another talk?"

Exasperated by his assumption that I have a fat complex, I hand my menu to Molly. "No. You were very clear."

Liam's phone rings. He glances at it then says to the men, "Let's take this in Nora's office." He rises and answers, "Gianluca."

The men follow, and Hailee holds up her drink. "Cheers."

I toast her. "Saluti."

I take a sip of the Pinot Noir, missing the Barolo I've drunk almost every night since I was sixteen. I set it down and ask, "Are you all going to yoga Saturday?"

"Yes." She takes out her phone. "Let's exchange numbers. I'll add you to our group text."

"Thanks." We enter each other's info into our phones.

Hailee leans closer. "Okay. What's the real scoop on why you aren't in Mexico?"

My stomach flips. I glance behind me to make sure no one is nearby. "The resort was...well, Killian's cousin never told him what kind of place he was booking for us."

Hailee bites a smile. "What kind of place was it?"

I double-check we're still alone. "It was a hedonism resort." I take a sip of wine.

Hailee's mouth drops.

"Yep. That's what Killian's face looked like when we drove by the *eat whoever you want* breakfast buffet."

She covers her mouth and laughs. "No!"

I nod.

Surprise replaces her amusement. "And Killian wasn't into it?"

"Nope."

"Huh." She takes a sip of her gimlet.

"Why do you sound surprised?"

She shrugs. "Liam wouldn't be down at all for that. He'd kill anyone if they even looked at me. I guess I just assumed Killian would be cool with it."

I wince and admit, "Yeah, well, Killian almost did kill a guy. I'm surprised he's not in Mexican jail right now."

"Wow! That's so not like him. He's usually super laid back. Honestly, the girls I've seen him with get hit on in here sometimes, and he doesn't even flinch."

Killian's words last night that he normally doesn't care tug at my heart.

Hailee adds, "I guess I shouldn't be surprised after how crazy he went when he couldn't find you in Club D."

"Hailee! Girl, where have you been? I haven't seen you in here in a few weeks." A woman slides into our booth. Her straight, dark hair is flawless, her brown eyes scream confidence and fun, and bright-red lipstick colors her mouth. Her floral perfume is a bit overwhelming, making me think it's cheap or she bathed in it. Her tight top showcases her well-endowed chest and cleavage.

Hailee stiffens. "Hi, Becky."

She grabs Hailee's gimlet and drinks a quarter of it. "Whew! I needed that after the day I've had." She sticks her hand in my face. "Hi! I'm Becky! Who are you?"

I move my head back and take her hand. "I'm Arianna."

She glances between Hailee and me. "Do you two work together?"

More embarrassment about my lack of a career seers my cheeks.

Hailee clears her throat. "Arianna is Killian's wife."

Becky freezes. Her eyes dart quickly between us then she bursts out laughing. "Very funny, Hailee."

"I'm not joking," Hailee states.

"Please. Like Killian would ever do anything that serious. He can't commit to anything beyond casual. Trust me. We had it out again the other weekend with all his bells and whistles. Nice try though."

My gut churns. *She was with Killian. And what does she mean bells and whistles?*

Uncomfortable silence fills the air.

Hailee quietly says, "Becky..."

Becky's face falls. "You're serious?"

"Yes. They got married Saturday," Hailee confirms.

Becky slowly locks eyes with me. A tight smile forms on her lips. "One thing I know about Killian O'Malley is he gets bored easily. I give you less than a month. Enjoy him while you can." She downs the rest of Hailee's drink then saunters over to the bar. She glances over her shoulder and gives me a look like she knows a dirty secret I don't.

The thing I hate more than the fact it's about my husband is, I don't doubt her words are valid. And I'm not sure how I'm interesting enough to give Killian enough stimulation to stay into me for the long haul.

18

Killian

"CLAUDIO CONFIRMED ALL SHORT ORDERS WERE PLACED AND filled," Gianluca, our stateside contact for our Swiss financial accounts, vouches over the phone.

"How much did we lose from the dip before we got in?" Liam asks.

"An estimated fifty million," he replies.

Liam looks at Finn and angrily shakes his head.

"Your positions are already up, if it makes you feel any better. And after this is over, I'll find new investments for you to make it back," Gianluca states.

"No. After this, we're out of the market. The money is to get funneled how we discussed. Don't attempt to play us on this, Gianluca," Declan firmly warns.

I glance at him in question, unsure why Declan is suddenly worried about him screwing us.

Gianluca states, "It's a lot of money to do nothing with."

"You don't deviate from our initial instructions," Declan barks.

"Easy. Everything will happen how we discussed, as long as you do your part," Gianluca iterates.

Declan crosses his arms and takes a deep breath. He spins and stares out the window.

I'm unsure what's riling him up, but I also have a feeling like this sounds too easy. I ask, "So after we set everything in motion, we just sit back, let it fall, then collect our checks?"

"Yes. You'll profit from the company's downfall. Stop worrying, gentlemen. This is what you planned for and how all the hedge funds make their money. Now, get the next part done and consider it a done deal," Gianluca advises.

There's a moment of silence. Liam picks up his phone. "Okay. Keep us posted."

"Will do," Gianluca states.

Liam hangs up. He mutters, "Fifty million."

Finn pulls a chair out and sits. "It could have been worse."

I glance at my brother's tense shoulders and ask, "What's going on, Declan?"

He turns. "I'm not sure. Something feels off to me regarding Gianluca."

The hairs on my arms rise. "What's he done?"

"Hopefully nothing."

"But?" Finn asks.

"I have this gut feeling. It started a few days ago. It might just be jitters since we're so close."

"Jitters? Since when do you get jitters?" I blurt out.

Declan locks eyes with me, and my pulse increases. The last time Declan got jitters, Sean got murdered.

Finn seethes, "If that bastard fucks us—"

"I'm going to hack into his and Claudio's personal and work communications, as well as the bank's server. If they're up to anything but what we've agreed upon, I'll find out," Declan states.

I scratch the back of my neck. "Once you're in their server, pull the information from our accounts. I'll go through it to make sure the numbers all add up or find any discrepancies."

Liam scrubs his face. "There better not be any."

"How long will it take you to hack in?" Finn asks.

Declan shrugs. "Not sure. My guess is the bank will take longer."

I rise and pat Declan on the back. "Well, you have fun with that." I take a step toward the door.

"This meeting isn't over," Finn states.

I spin. "What else is there to talk about?"

His eyes harden. "Jack Christian and the judge."

Declan puts his hands on the desk. "Liam, Jack isn't going to stay alive much longer under the conditions we have him in. It's time to pick up the judge, let Finn do what he needs, then let Obrecht end Jack."

"I agree. You need to talk to Selena and have her give Obrecht the go-ahead. If Jack dies before Obrecht gets to him, there are going to be issues with the Ivanovs," I warn.

Liam assesses all of us then looks at Finn. "Pick up the judge. I'll give you forty-eight hours before I allow Obrecht in. Let me talk with Maksim to make sure he stays away. But whatever you do, you don't touch Jack."

Finn orders, "Invite Obrecht. He can participate in the first forty-eight hours."

"Don't trust yourself?" I ask.

Finn scowls at me.

"Easy there, big boy. Save it for your enemies," I tease, and my phone rings.

I groan. "Gee, this should be fun." I answer, "Massimo, what's going on?"

His voice booms through the line. "Is Arianna next to you?"

My pulse increases. "She's in the other room. Why?" I get up and leave the office. I walk down the hall and see she's still at the table with Hailee. I shouldn't even question it. Boris took over the pub security from Nora, and it's always a combination of O'Malley and Ivanov men who would fillet someone in a moment's notice.

My relief is short-lived. Massimo informs, "We can't find that thug. He got released and disappeared."

"What do you mean, disappeared? Your father insisted I allow you to take care of him," I seethe.

"Donato has gone underground. I don't trust he won't make his way toward Chicago. My father is in Italy, but I'll send security for Arianna."

"Keep your security. I know how to protect my wife," I growl.

"This is my sister—"

"She's my wife. I'll take care of it. No one is going to guard her except men I choose, whom I trust. So get it through your head, or I'll put it there," I threaten.

"Do not—"

"I am an O'Malley. Arianna is now an O'Malley. This is no longer your decision."

He sniffs hard. "This is not something for us to battle over. We need to work together."

I stare at the back of Arianna's head, trying to calm the rage building inside me. Massimo is right, but I'll be the one calling the shots. I snarl, "I hope he comes to Chicago. I guarantee you he won't leave."

"Arianna—"

"Will have the highest level of security on her at all times. You're right, we must work together, but I'll determine who guards her." I turn to go back to the office.

Silence fills the phone. Declan, Liam, and Finn give me questioning looks.

"Your father knows I'm capable of this, or he wouldn't have had me marry her," I remind Massimo.

He heavily exhales. "Fine. But if you need reinforcements—"

"Then I'll call you. But I won't need help. If he pops up anywhere, let me know."

"Of course."

"Your father is in Italy?"

"Yes. He had an emergency situation come up. We may not be able to come to Chicago as planned. It might be the following week," Massimo states.

"Fine. Keep me informed." I hang up and address my brother and cousins. "That thug from New York is missing. The Marinos can't find him anywhere. Massimo thinks he may come to Chicago. I'm adding additional security on Arianna."

"I'll bring two more guys back from Indiana. Now that most of the Baileys are dead, that territory hasn't had any threats in over two months," Liam says.

"Thanks."

There's a knock on the door. Molly pokes her head inside. "Your food is going to get cold."

"Thanks, lass," Liam says, and we return to the table.

I slide into the booth next to Arianna. She stiffens then takes a sip of her wine, avoiding me.

"Did I miss something?" I ask.

Hailee nervously glances at me then Liam.

Arianna turns and smiles, but it feels forced. "Nope."

"You sure?"

"Yep. I'm hungry. Let's eat." She picks up her fork and takes a bite of her salmon.

We eat, and she participates in the conversation, but I can't shake the feeling something is wrong. By the time dinner is over, she seems back to her normal, chipper self, so I tell myself I was just paranoid.

Molly removes our empty plates from the table, and I ask Arianna, "Do you know how to play pool?"

She tilts her head. "Are you asking me since I'm a woman?"

I chuckle and hold my hands up. "No."

"So you would ask a man if he knew how to play pool?"

I shrug. "Not sure. I've never thought about it."

"Ha! Caught you! You've never thought about it because you've never asked one before. You assume they know how to play."

I put my face in front of hers. "Are you a crazy feminist, and I need to be worried about everything I say?"

She grins. "Never was, but I think I might become one married to you."

"Does that mean you know how to play?" I ask.

"How much do you want to bet I'll win?"

"I'll feel bad taking my wife's money." I grew up in this pub and playing on that table. There's no way she's beating me.

"Thousand dollars," she offers.

"A thousand dollars? Do you have a gambling problem I need to be aware of?"

She raises her eyebrows. "Scared?"

I snort. "Nope. Fine. Thousand bucks it is. But when you have to pay me, don't say I didn't warn you."

She slides out of the booth. "Alrighty then. Show me what you got."

We all make our way to the game room. I rack the balls and tell Arianna, "Ladies first."

"You're so predictable." She rubs chalk on her stick, blows it, then bats her eyes at me. She breaks the balls, and four stripes go into the pockets.

"Bravo!" Hailee cheers.

Declan grunts. "You're in trouble."

Arianna smirks then moves to the other side of the table. "Ten ball middle pocket." She sinks the ball.

"Yep, you're in deep shit," Finn proclaims then motions for Molly to bring more drinks.

Arianna studies the table. "Fifteen, right corner." She bends over, pins her eyebrows together, and taps the ball. It bounces off the left side then rolls into the right pocket."

"Wow! She's going to clean up. You're toast, Killian," Hailee badgers.

"Nah. That's an almost impossible shot. As soon as she fumbles, I'll clean up the table," I boast.

Arianna gives me a challenging stare and says, "Twelve ball." She taps the pocket in front of her.

"No way."

She rolls her eyes. Then, she purses her lips, leans down, and shoots the cue ball. It hits the purple stripe, ricochets off both sides of the table, and falls into the pocket.

Holy shit. My wife is a pool shark.

Declan chuckles. "You shouldn't make bets you can't win, Killian."

"Shut up!"

Arianna points. "Eight ball, left corner." She shoots, and it flawlessly rolls in. The room erupts in claps, and she holds out her hand. "Thousand dollars, please."

"Hold on. I get a chance to clear the table."

She snorts. "Good luck."

Molly arrives with more drinks and Irish Car Bombs. "Darcey said to give you these."

"What's in it?" Arianna asks.

Molly looks at her like she's crazy. "You don't know what an Irish Car Bomb is, and you're married to Killian?"

Arianna's face turns red. "No."

"She's Italian. Give her a break," I order and put my arm around Arianna.

Molly says, "Some people call it an Irish Slammer. It's Baileys Irish Cream, whiskey, and Guinness."

Arianna scrunches her face.

"Oh, come on now, lass. You've gotta try it before you judge it. Just don't sip it," I order.

"Why?"

"The cream will curdle. Get it down fast."

"It isn't bad, but he's right. Don't sip it," Hailee offers.

We all pick a shot up, and I say, "Sláinte." Then everyone downs it.

Arianna blinks hard. She puts the back of her hand over her mouth and the other on her stomach.

"You don't like it?" I ask in shock.

She winces. "It's interesting."

"Is that your polite way of saying you don't like it?"

She nods. "Sorry. Maybe we can do sambuca next time?"

I kiss her forehead. "Sure. I'll even light it on fire for you."

She laughs. "Now we're talking!"

"Molly, tell Darcey sambuca for Arianna from now on."

Molly furrows her brows and leaves.

I pick up my pool cue. "Now, stand back, lass, and watch me clear the table." Declan lifts the rack, and I shoot the cue ball at the others. They break. Three stripes and a solid roll in the holes, and my gut sinks. I grumble, "You're kidding me."

The room erupts in mocking cheers, and I spin. Arianna holds out her hand, biting on her smile.

I pull my wallet out and hand her two hundred dollars. "I'll give you the rest at home."

She stuffs it in her pocket. "Maybe I'll buy a black dress."

"Very funny. I forbid you!" I set down the pool cue. "I'm going to the men's room." I stroll through the restaurant and do my business in the bathroom. When I step outside, Becky, a woman I've had a casual relationship with over the last few years, stands against the brick.

She's always wanted more. We had a pattern. We'd have sex and hang out. For a while, things would be great. Then she'd start getting clingy and want more. I'd remind her of the rules, have to cut her off, then she'd come begging for me to hang out with her again. It always came with a promise she'd stick to the rules regarding our casual status and what that meant. The last time I spoke with her was the weekend before Nolan's wedding. When I left her, she was sobbing like every other time I'd cut her off. I felt terrible, but I also hate the drama. It was another reminder of why I didn't want anything serious with her.

She leaps at me so quickly, she takes me by surprise. She's also drunk and almost falls.

I catch her and hold her up. "How much have you had to drink, lass?"

She reaches for my face and puts her hand on my cheek. In a hurt voice, she asks, "You got married?"

My heart pounds in my chest. I don't want to hurt her, but I'm not going to lie to her. "Yes."

She moves her hand over my cock. "Maybe we should go into the bathroom, and I can remind you what you love about me most."

I try to remove her hand, but she falls, so I grab under her armpit. "Becky—"

She laughs and fondles me again. "My mouth on your cock. I know exactly what you like, don't I?" She slips her hand inside my joggers.

I move my hand to her waist and attempt to steady her so I can get her hand out of my pants. I bark, "Becky—"

"I bet she doesn't suck you off how I can. See, you're even getting hard. You miss me." She shimmies her hand over my shaft, and I hate myself.

My dick hardens further. I seethe, "Get your hand out of my pants."

She sticks her tongue out, and I turn my head to avoid it. "Becky—"

Dammnit!

Arianna is staring at me, with her face beet red and her lips trembling.

I shove Becky off me, no longer caring if she falls. She can break her neck for all I care at this point. Arianna turns and takes off through the restaurant.

I catch up to her and spin her into me. "It's not what you think."

Golden flames leap from her eyes. She raises her chin. "We're leaving. Now."

19

Arianna

"Arianna, I swear—"

"I don't want to hear your excuses! You're such a hypocrite!" I accuse, glaring at Killian.

He reaches for me.

"Don't touch me!" I scream and move closer to the door.

He puts his hands in front of him. "Okay. But she doesn't mean anything to me. I tried—"

"Yes, Killian! We all know women mean nothing to you, and you get bored easily. I guess I'm the one to blame for thinking my husband could stay interested in me for more than a few days," I snap as I climb into the car.

The vehicle turns silent. Blood pounds in my ears, and I fight tears. I won't give anymore to him. I saw and heard the entire thing. When I went to go to the restroom and saw Becky standing outside the men's room, I knew she was waiting for him. She might have thrown herself on him, but he didn't shove her off.

He's such a hypocrite. A guy looks at me, and he almost murders him. Becky gives him a hand job in the pub's hallway, and he thinks I should just smile and forget about it?

He firmly says, "I'm only interested in you."

"Save it for someone who believes your lies."

"Arianna—"

I jerk my head toward him and bellow, "Are you still hard? Did she get any of your pre-cum on her hand?"

"That's not fair—"

"Not fair? How delusional are you right now? She touched you. No one touched me, and you choked a man on the beach. We didn't even start our honeymoon before it was over, yet you want to sit here and tell me about fair?"

He closes his eyes briefly. "She was drunk and falling over. I—"

"My mouth on your cock? Is that the same as my palms on your ass? Did you tell her all the things you told me?"

He sniffs hard. "I didn't say to her what I said to you."

"I don't believe you."

"I didn't."

"You're just one lie after another, aren't you?" I accuse.

"I just told you, I never said what I said to you to her, or anyone else for that matter," he insists.

I sarcastically laugh. "Yeah, and my purse magically arrived with my phone and charger in that box today."

His eyes widen.

"Yeah. I know. I hid them before you came home. But then I thought we were going to be okay. So I put them back. I even gave you an opportunity to come clean. But you didn't, did you? Nope. You had to create more lies."

He swallows hard. "Arianna, I didn't want you mad at me again. I thought—"

"That you would lie some more! For once, can you just keep your mouth shut?" I bellow.

He licks his lips and focuses on the ceiling.

The driver pulls into his garage. I fling open my door then stomp into the house. I pick up Killian's pillow and go to the hall closet. I grab a blanket and throw it on the couch.

"You aren't sleeping on the couch," Killian states.

I laugh and put my hand on my hip. "Yeah, you're right. I'm not. You are!"

His face turns red. "I'm not sleeping on the couch. We're married. We sleep together."

"You should have thought about that before you let another woman put her hand down your pants!" I shout then retreat to the bedroom and slam the door.

I go into the bathroom and wash my face.

Killian comes in.

"What are you doing in here?" I fume.

He turns on the water. "Showering."

"Good idea. Scrub her nasty cheap perfume off you while you're at it."

He strips and stands behind me. "Arianna—"

"Get away from me right now, Killian. Don't you dare touch me," I warn. My insides shake, and the emotions I've been fighting back threaten to pop up. But I won't cry in front of him.

"I didn't do anything," he claims.

I spin. "You didn't do anything? Your dick sure has another story."

His face hardens. "If some guy stuck his hands down your pants—"

I jab him in the chest. "He wouldn't be alive! You would have killed him by now! Then you would have made some new rule for me to follow. But since I'm a weak little female, you think you can do whatever you please without any consequences."

"I didn't—"

"You didn't push her away the moment she threw herself on you. Then you still didn't when she grabbed your crotch. But that wasn't enough, was it, Killian? Nope! You had to let her molest you. How far would you have let her go if you hadn't seen me watching you? Huh?"

He stares above my head and takes a deep breath. "You aren't listening to me. I didn't want her to fall—"

I push away from him. "Take your shower. Her nasty perfume is making me more nauseous." I go into the closet, put on a silk nightgown I know will drive him crazy if he sees me in it, then return to the bathroom and brush my teeth.

I peek at him in the mirror and see him staring at me through the shower glass. I take an extra few minutes to brush my teeth. He can stare at me and see everything he's going to miss. I'm not putting up with this kind of behavior, especially when I get reprimanded for anything I do wrong.

He turns off the water, and I go into the bedroom. His pillow is back on the bed. I toss it on the floor then slide under the covers.

The moment he gets into bed, he tugs my backside into his hard flesh.

"Killian—"

He puts his hand over my mouth. "Just listen to me for a minute."

I still. There's no point fighting him. I might as well let him speak then kick him out again.

He removes his hand and puts it on my chest. "I don't want her and haven't been with her in a long time. She knows this. I would never touch her or any woman now. I made my vow to you."

I laugh. "A week is a long time for you? Wow! She was right. You do get bored easily."

"What are you talking about?"

"She said you had it out the other weekend."

He flips me on my back. "The last time I spoke with her was the weekend before Nolan's wedding. And I haven't done anything with her for at least a month before that."

I shouldn't be relieved. Anything he did with anyone before our marriage isn't wrong. But it makes me feel better he wasn't with her the weekend he first messaged me.

"When did you talk to her?" he asks.

"When you were in the office."

"Why didn't you tell me?"

I huff. "So you could look for her and be ready for her to seduce you in a dark corner?"

He puts his hand on my cheek. "The only one I want to seduce me in a dark corner is you." He kisses the curve of my neck, and damn him, because it creates a surge of flutters in me.

"You can't kiss your way out of this, Killian!" I say stronger than my melting insides.

He softly laughs. "We should test your theory out." He presses his lips to mine, parting them with his tongue and igniting a fire in my veins. His erection hardens against my thigh. "See how much you turn me on, lass? I can't even kiss you without getting hard."

His words snap me back into reality. He also couldn't have Becky's hands on him without getting hard. Well, it's time Killian O'Malley learned how to control his erection.

I wrap my arms around him and kiss him back. It's way easier than resisting. As angry as I am, I could fall right into everything that is Killian. But he needs to learn a lesson. I'm not dealing with women falling all over him for the rest of my life. And maybe I've become just as crazy as he is from being around him only a few days.

He pulls me on top of him and slides his palms to my ass. "This is better. You. Me. Us."

It tugs at my heart. I only want us, but he's broken my trust too many times today. I murmur in his ear, "I think I know why this happened."

"What do you mean?" he asks.

I flick my tongue behind his ear, and he groans, then squeezes my ass, trying to push me over his cock. I slide over him, slowly circle my hips a few times, then say, "Now that you're covered in me, I think it's time I showed you how much better my mouth on your cock is than hers."

He freezes.

Hook, line, and sinker, sucker!

I lick his lips. When he comes toward me, I retreat, pinning my gaze to his hot green eyes. "Tell me you want my mouth on your cock."

His lips twitch. I can almost see him salivating. He strokes my hair. "Yeah, lass. I want your mouth on my cock."

I circle my hips a few more times and deeply kiss him, then order, "Put your hands on the headboard so I can cuff you."

He arches his eyebrows. "Cuff me? Were you going through my drawers?"

I try not to show him my disgust. Whatever is in his drawers is getting tossed in the trash tomorrow unless it's in a box with plastic wrap over it. "No, baby. My stuff."

He grins. "What do you have? I don't remember unpacking anything."

"No? It was in the box you put my purse in. It's the gifts from the girls."

Guilt crosses his face. "I didn't go through your things."

I ruffle his hair and bat my eyelashes. "Are you going to be a good boy and put your hands on the headboard so I can show you my skills?"

He licks his lips and grasps the wrought iron. "Bring it!"

I slide off him and open the drawer, grateful he keeps the room slightly dark. I take out the metal handcuffs Kora gave me, saying a silent prayer of thanks she gave me expensive, high-quality ones. I attach them to his wrists.

"What else do you have in there?" he asks.

I drag my finger down his pecs, avoiding the cross and S.O. initials I hate so much. "I've got drawers of goodies. In fact, I think you need a massage, too. Hold on, baby." I peck his eager, smug expression, then take out the box with the cock cage. I slide down his body and take a few long licks.

"Yes!" he hisses, and the sound of the metal cuffs clanging against the headboard fills the room. "Jesus, lass."

I remove the cock cage then realize I'm not going to be able to put it on with his erection. I panic for a moment, then say, "I'll be right back."

"What? Where are you going?"

I chirp, "Be right back. There's something else I need to get for you."

"What?"

"You'll see." I race to the kitchen and take out a dishcloth. I hold it under cold water then stick it in the freezer's ice chest for five minutes.

"Arianna! What are you doing? Get your sexy ass back here," Killian orders.

"Just a minute," I call out then take the cloth out of the freezer. I return to the bedroom and straddle Killian's thighs. "Did you miss me, baby?"

"Yep. Now, I think your mouth was—What the fuck is that, Arianna!" he shouts and practically lurches off the bed.

I hold the cloth to his cock until I feel it shrivel. I innocently say, "I heard men love this. Is this not the case?"

"Only if you want me to have my dick in my pelvis!"

I remove the cloth. "Oh, I'm sorry. I thought you'd like it!"

"No. Don't ever do that again unless I'm old, took a pill, and can't get my erection to go down after screwing you for forty-eight hours."

I toss it on the floor then lay on top of him. I deeply kiss him until he groans. "Sorry, baby. Should I make it up to you?"

"Yes," he murmurs.

"Okay. Let me take care of you." I slide down him and warm him back up a bit, but not so he's fully erect. Then, I put the cock cage on him.

"What is that?" he asks.

I secure the tiny padlock then put the key on the nightstand.

"Arianna!"

I shimmy on top of him and drag my finger down his cheek. "We have a problem we need to solve. You can't seem to keep your dick under control. So we're going to work on this tonight."

"What are you talking about?" he growls.

"Shhhh," I taunt, then give him a peck on the lips. "Rule number nine. The only woman who touches you is me. The only woman who makes you hard is me. All others get flaccid Killian."

"Get this thing off me!" he barks and attempts to move his hands, but they stop an inch away from the headboard. "Arianna! What the fuck is this?"

"It's a cock cage. You're staying in it until you earn your way out! And you're going to get very clear on *my* rules!"

20

Killian

"Arianna!" I growl and sway my hips side to side, but all it does is slam the metal cage into my thigh.

"Stop moving!" she commands and scurries onto my torso.

I obey, not used to listening to anyone but also not looking to break my most favorite body part.

"Unlock me now," I demand.

Gold fire leaps from her eyes. "No. You're going to see what it's like to be me under your reign. And until you learn your lesson, you aren't being released."

I'm not a man who scares easily, but something about this situation has me a bit petrified—of my wife. I open my mouth.

"Threatening me will only make things worse. So think before you speak, Killian," she warns.

I shut my mouth, breathing hard and feeling like I'm about to break out in a sweat. I swallow the lump in my throat and study her, wondering what's going on in her mind.

She scoots higher over my chest until her knees are under my arms and her pussy is a few inches from my face. The heat and scent of her smacks into me, and a feeling I've never had before annihilates me. Something about Arianna's body is like an entirely new experience. She's a glass of top-shelf whiskey compared to a cheap bottle. I resist sticking my tongue out and seeing if I can get to her. My erection fights the cage, but it can't rise to the occasion how it wants to. And I'm not used to that.

She trails her finger down my cheek then over my jaw. "Remember how you told me I like you overpowering me?"

My stomach sinks. Once again, my mouth has gotten me in trouble. I try to stay calm and state, "I didn't mean it offensively."

She pats my cheek and cheerfully says, "No offense taken, baby. I wanted to ask if you like me having more power than you?"

Saying nothing, I clench my jaw. I'm not liking this one bit. I don't ever let women handcuff me. *I* restrain *them*. But since we were in a fight and she wanted to, I thought it was best to let her have her way. All I could think about was her lush mouth I've been dying to have on me. But I won't make that mistake again.

"I get your point, lass. You had your fun, now let me out," I order.

"Tsk, tsk, tsk. Did you miss the part where I said you had to earn your way out?" She tilts her lower body closer to my face.

Unable to resist, I move my head toward her, but she pushes my forehead back on the pillow. In her sweet voice, she reprimands, "Did I say you could sample my goodies?"

My punishment is a mini scalp massage. I close my eyes, already on sensory overload but unable to not enjoy the way her fingers feel.

"Does that feel good, baby?" she coos.

My dick twitches in the cage, and the uncomfortable feeling seems to oscillate in all my cells. "Yeah. Let me out of this so I can show you how good you make me feel."

She releases one hand and stretches behind her. She cups my balls.

I groan. "Fuuuck, Arianna." Sweat pops out on my forehead.

"What are you going to do the next time some floozy tries to throw herself on you? Hmm?" she innocently asks.

"Your point is made. I'm sorry I didn't push her off me. You're right. I was wrong. Now let me out," I try again.

She massages me once more then says, "What do you think about my nightgown?"

"You know what I think."

"Do I?" She tilts her head.

I grasp the bar of the headboard, feeling like my skin is crawling from not being able to touch her. "You're hot as sin in those little pieces of silk. If this prison cell weren't around my dick, I'd be hard as fuck and stripping you bare."

Her eyes widen, as if she's an innocent woman. "Hmm. So does that mean you prefer me wearing this to bed, or would you rather have me naked?"

I don't need to think about that answer. "Naked. Is that even a question?"

She drags her fingers down my nose and says, "Okay, baby. Is this better?" She takes the little nightgown off, and my body fights against the metal again.

"No. It would be better if you moved a little closer and sat on my face," I tell her, knowing I'm going to torture myself more but not able to stop my glands from salivating.

She comes closer. I stick my tongue out and manage to get a taste of her. She inhales sharply, and her full breasts rise and fall. It only tortures me further. I'm suddenly craving to see her tits bounce all over the place while I eat her out.

Chaos reigns in my lower body. I lift my hips and torso, trying to move her even closer. I order, "Put your hands on mine and let me show you how sorry I am."

"Do you think I'm going to be one of those wives who allow you to screw other women, then come home and have sex with me, so I look the other way?"

"No, and I wouldn't ever do that to you," I firmly state and mean it.

She crosses her arms. "Hmm. I don't think I believe you. That woman had her hand down your pants, and we've only been married four days. Four! What's going to happen when you get bored? What are you going to let women do to you then?"

"Why are you assuming I'll get bored with you?" I ask.

"Kind of your M.O., isn't it?"

This entire conversation is starting to really piss me off. But I remind myself to stay calm and lower my voice. "Whatever I did before I married you doesn't have anything to do with you."

She throws her hands in the air. "Wrong! Not when your past has her hand down your pants!"

"I already explained that!" I growl. "And I think you have a lot of nerve talking to me about my past relationships when you dated Mr. Thug. At least I never slept with anyone after I committed to marrying you."

She jerks her head back and goes quiet.

"Yeah. I get to think about you with him for the rest of my life. But you don't see me putting a chastity belt on you."

"I didn't sleep with him after my papà told me I had to marry you," she claims.

I grunt. "Nice try. He was all over you in your videos. I may have been drunk at Nolan's wedding, but the image is clear as daylight in my brain."

She slides down my torso. "I didn't. Ask my brothers. They showed up at the club and snuck me back in my papà's house."

"Yeah, right."

"I'm not lying. You want me to call them, and you can ask them what happened that night?"

I roar, "Sure. Why don't I also tell them their sister has me chained to the bed and my cock on lockdown."

Arianna jabs my chest. Her eyes glisten, and her voice cracks, "You shouldn't have allowed her to touch you."

My pulse accelerates, and I raise my voice. "What do you want me to do, Arianna? It happened. It shouldn't have. I'll make sure it never does again, but I didn't want her a few months ago, and I sure as hell don't want her now."

"Why is that?" she fires back.

"Because I have you!" I blurt out.

"Oh. Is that what you told S.O., too? Because I don't see her anywhere around here, and I'm sure she had to mean something to you," Arianna says, and a tear hits my chest.

Confused, I ask, "Who are you talking about?"

She points to my heart. "This, Killian. I'm talking about whatever girl this is."

Stunned, I stare at her.

More tears fall. She quickly wipes them and lowers her voice. "It's bad enough that every time I look at you, I have to think about whoever this girl is you inked to your heart. But I also have all the people raving about your basically naked body online. Excuse me if I don't need your exes rubbed in my face, too."

Swallowing the lump in my throat, I try to put my thoughts together.

She continues, "It's not fair. You took me far away from anyone I know, and you don't have to deal with any of my past. But you expect me to be fine with women you've slept with throwing themselves on you." She turns away and covers her face.

My heart hurts. She has it wrong, but some of it, she has right. I hate what happened tonight. I also loathe what she believes to be true isn't. I softly say, "Arianna, unlock the handcuffs."

Another minute passes, and she keeps crying.

"Arianna—"

She moves off me, grabs the keys from the table, and unlocks me. "Do what you want. I don't even know why I bother to care." She tosses the key for the cage at me and leaves the room.

Shit. I quickly unlock the cage and breathe a sigh of relief. I follow her to the living room. "Arianna—"

"Leave me alone, Killian. I don't want to hear a ton of excuses or lies or whatever it is you think you need to say." She sits down on the couch and wraps the blanket around her.

I scoop her up.

"Killian! Put me down!"

"No. We're married. You sleep in our bed with me," I state, carrying her into the bedroom.

"I'm tired of talking and fighting," she says.

"Good. You're going to be quiet, and I'm going to talk then." I put her back in bed, toss the keys, handcuffs, and cage on the table and tug her into my arms.

She pushes my pecs. "I don't—"

"My brother Sean was murdered a few years ago. That's what the S.O. stands for," I blurt out.

She covers her mouth and freezes.

My chest tightens, and my mouth turns dry. The rage never ends, even though I avenged his death. "Two crime families were involved. The Baileys set him up with the Rossis. The only thing we got back from him was his heart and ring."

Goose bumps break out on her skin. "I'm so sorry."

I swallow the lump in my throat. "Yeah. Me, too. But we also lost his kids. His wife, Bridget, is Tully's daughter. She took the kids to New York and refused to let us see them. She even changed their last name back to O'Connor. When Tully told me I owed him a favor, I negotiated the ability for us to see them once a month. Tully was supposed to bring them to Nolan's wedding and didn't. He claimed until my end of the deal was done, we weren't going to see them."

Arianna presses closer to me. "I-I know Bridget and the kids. I wondered why she wasn't at the wedding at Tully's table."

I'm not sure why I'm surprised, but I am. "You know them?"

She nods. "Yeah. She's older than me, so I didn't know her before she moved to Chicago. I met her when she returned to New York. I knew her husband died, but I didn't know who he was. I had lunch with Bridget a few weeks ago. She wanted me to join a volunteer committee with her. Fiona and Sean, Jr. were with her. I even took a picture with them. Do you want to see it?"

I sniff hard. "Yeah."

She gets her phone and climbs back in bed. She holds it out. "Here."

I stare at my niece and nephew. The grief I feel over the entire situation rises in my throat. Too much time has passed. Years we've missed, we'll never get back. They aren't young kids anymore. They're teenagers. Fiona is fourteen and Sean is sixteen. The only thing I manage to choke out is, "Wow."

Arianna points to Sean. "He's super funny. And confident. He has your personality, doesn't he?"

I shake my head and blink hard. "No. He has my brother's. Everyone loved Sean. He would walk into a room full of people arguing, and within minutes, they'd all be laughing."

She leans into me. "Sounds like you."

I smile, but it's mixed with sadness. "No. He was different." I clear my throat and stare at the photo. "Did they seem happy?"

Arianna nods. "Yeah. Fiona has a boyfriend. She was texting him most of the time. Sean was making fun of her."

I groan. "I wish you wouldn't have told me that."

Arianna softly laughs. She says, "You're allowed to see them now?"

"That's the deal I made with Tully." I point to the phone. "Can I send this to my cell?"

"Sure."

I open her texting app and begin to type Killian and cringe. There are a ton of other guys who start with a K but not me. I program my number under Hot Hubby, send the picture off, then turn to Arianna. "How is it we don't even have each other's phone numbers?"

She puts her hands over her face. "We're the worst married people ever."

"Well, you did just keep me a prisoner in our bedroom with a cock cage around my prized possession."

She starts to laugh, and I put my arm around her. "That thing is going in the garbage."

She stops laughing. "Am I supposed to say I'm sorry?"

For some reason, I think of Father Ercole. "I don't know. Are you seeking forgiveness for it?"

She bites on her lip and sighs.

"Arianna, I didn't know she was going to do that. I'm not interested in her," I repeat, in case she didn't hear it the first dozen times.

"I don't want to worry every time we go anywhere that some girl from your past is going to come up and say stuff to me or try to get you back," she admits.

I pull her on my lap. "I'm not going to lie. I've dated a lot of women."

"Is this a warning I have to deal with it?"

I push her hair behind her ear. "No. I'll have Nora ban Becky and her friends from the pub. But I just don't want you upset if we run into anyone else."

"Do they all come into the pub?" she asks.

"No. Pretty much once I told anyone it was over, they stopped coming in," I admit.

Arianna releases a breath. "Okay."

I pull her down on the bed and reach for the handcuffs. I secure her wrist to the headboard.

"What are you doing?" she nervously asks.

"It's time for me to pay my penance."

21

Arianna

A Week Later

"Malachy and Lennon will go anywhere you do. If I'm not with you, you wait until they give you the go-ahead to enter or exit a building or vehicle," Killian states.

I pretend to yawn.

His eyes turn to slits. "Am I boring you?"

"Yes, you are. I've had security my entire life. I know the drill." I glance over at the two meatheads standing several feet in front of me. They showed up this morning from out of nowhere, and I knew right away they were bodyguards. My papà's men all have dark hair and olive skin, where these two men have fairer skin and lighter hair. That's where the differences end. They're built, have scowls on their faces, and feel dangerous, just like my papà's trusted guards.

"I don't care how much security you've had. We're going over my rules," Killian states.

I roll my eyes. "Okay, baby. And which number are we on?"

His face turns red. "Arianna—"

"Chill out. What else?"

He crosses his arms and studies me. "Don't ever ditch them."

My pulse increases. "Why would you assume—"

"Don't lie to me. I know you've ditched your father's guys plenty of times."

Guilty as charged, I shut my mouth.

"I mean it, Arianna. This isn't New York."

I huff. "I'm sure Chicago is a lot safer than New York."

Killian scrubs his face. "No. It's not. It's just as dangerous, and you know nothing about this city or the threats surrounding us."

"Then fill me in."

He ignores my last comment. "Any other questions before I leave?"

Irritated that I once again know nothing, I swallow down my frustration. "So I can go out while you're gone?" Killian's left me home a few times this week, but I quickly learned his house has O'Malleys watching every angle at all times.

He hesitates then nods. "Yes. Where are you going?"

I huff. "Is this part of the requirement? You have to know everywhere I go?"

"Yeah. You're my wife."

"Okay. Give me the rundown of where you're going. And all the places, don't skip anywhere," I fire back.

Annoyance fills his expression. "Not the same, Arianna."

"It is in my eyes," I claim. Nothing is the same with Killian as my previous life in New York, yet ironically, everything is the same. He's taken the place of my papà and brothers keeping tabs on me. If I knew where he went, I would be okay with it. But I'm kept in the dark, just like before.

His lips twitch. "I'm going to work."

"You think this is funny? It's not."

"Don't get all bent out of shape," Killian orders.

I glance at the bodyguards and rise. "Can you give my husband and me a minute alone, please?"

They nod, and I go into the bedroom. Killian follows, and as soon as the door shuts, I warn, "If you can't tell me where you're going when I have to inform you of my every move, then we're going to have issues."

He arches his eyebrow. "Issues?"

"Yeah, issues."

"Is this a threat?" he calmly asks.

I smirk then use the exact words he used on me before we even met. "I'm an implementer. Don't ever forget that."

He grunts. "Well, since I already tossed the cock cage in the trash and am never letting you handcuff me again, I'd say I'll take my chances."

I glare at him.

He glances at his phone. "I'm going to be late. I'll see you tonight." He steps forward, and I retreat until I'm against the wall.

My pulse beats faster. His entire body towers over my frame, and his loin-burning scent fills me. I stare at his chest until he forces my chin up.

"You didn't tell me where you're going," he says.

"Your meatheads can tell you."

Amusement crosses his face. "Meatheads?"

"Yup."

"Hmm." He drags his finger across my hairline and twirls a lock around his finger. "So that means I don't have to worry about you developing any crushes for your guards."

"Not funny!"

He presses his body against mine. "I like it better when you're happy Arianna and not pissed-off Arianna."

I fire, "Then you should stop being a hypocrite all the time."

He freezes, studying me. "You seem to like calling me a hypocrite."

"Stop acting like I shouldn't know anything. I'm not a child!"

He leans closer to my face. "My job is to protect you. Not involve you in matters or describe details about things that don't concern you."

"Rule number six always seems to lean in your favor. I thought it was supposed to be a two-way street, but it isn't, is it? And it never will be."

His face hardens. "That's not true, Arianna."

"Isn't it?"

"This isn't about trust."

"Seems that way to me."

He sighs. "Fine. If you must know, I'm going to the pub to meet with Liam, Finn, and Declan. After, I'm going to work out to prepare for my next fight. Then I'm going to take care of a bunch of shit I don't want to. And no, I'm not telling you where or what, so don't ask."

I stay silent, happy he gave me something but wishing I could know everything.

He asks, "Now, where are you going today?"

I cave. "The grocery store. Then, I'm not sure. Welcome to my boring life."

He reaches into his pocket and pulls out his wallet. He takes a wad of cash out. "Here."

"I don't need money. I have a credit card."

He snorts. "Which you need to cut up. Your father isn't paying for our groceries."

"It's my trust fund."

"Which daddy paid for, and I'm sure adds to."

"He doesn't—" I freeze. My trust fund is from my mother. I inherited it when she died, but I don't want to get into it with Killian. But in some ways, he's right. I don't even have a bank account or card not tied to my papà or my trust fund. I've never worked. Everything I have is what my mother left me or from my papà.

Killian releases my hair. "I'll call the bank and have a card issued for you."

My face heats. "I...umm..."

"What's wrong?"

"I want to get a job. Do you think anyone will hire me?" I ask, embarrassed but hoping I can work instead of staying at home for the rest of my life.

He smiles. "Sure. What do you want to do?"

I shake my head. "I don't know."

"Okay. Don't stress over it. Let's talk about it tonight."

"Really?" It surprises me he isn't fighting me about it as my papà did. He did say he knows people, but I'm used to years of being told I can't have one.

He nods. "Yes."

"Thanks."

He places his mouth an inch from my lips. His hands slide on my ass. "Are you going to give me a kiss before I leave?"

Flutters fill my stomach. I give him a chaste one.

His warm palms slide in my pants. "You can do better than that."

Tingles run up my spine. I slide my hands around his neck. Our hot tongues urgently flick until my knees weaken.

He presses his body closer. His finger strokes the slit of my ass.

I freeze.

His green flames meet mine. "I think it's time we used some of those toys in your drawer."

My heart races. "Which ones?"

He cockily arches an eyebrow. "Ones you haven't used before."

I stay silent, curious, but not sure if I want to.

He wiggles his eyebrows. "And maybe some you have."

I bite on my lip.

His lips move to my ear. Zings fly straight to my core the moment his breath hits my skin. "I'm your husband, and I'm going to have you in all ways, Arianna. That includes this round little ass of yours you keep teasing me with at all hours of the day and night."

"What if it hurts?" I blurt out, and my cheeks pulse with fire.

He positions his face in front of mine. Confident as always, he asks, "Have I done anything but make you feel good?"

"No," I admit.

"That's right. I know what I'm doing. And once I do it, you're going to beg me for it in the future."

For some reason, my face turns hotter. Is what he's claiming possible?

He winks, chuckles, then releases me. "You're cute when you're worried. I have to go. Have fun shopping." He spins and saunters out of the room.

I stuff the cash he gave me into my wallet and strip to take a shower. I pick up my phone to turn on some music, and my stomach drops from the text message on my screen.

Donato: *We need to talk. Where are you staying in Chicago?*

My mouth turns dry. I almost respond and tell him it's over and to not contact me again but decide it's best not to engage with him. Instead, I block his number, delete the text chain, then step under the hot water.

After my shower, I clean out all the remaining ingredients in the fridge and cabinets that are unhealthy. I throw out the butter, white bread, chips, and an almost-empty package of cookies. The whole milk gets dumped down the drain. Two eggs are in the carton Killian bought a few days ago, and I toss those with everything else. I open the door to the garage then hand the trash bag to Lennon. "Do you mind taking this to the garbage can outside?"

"Sure."

I return to the kitchen. Crumbs are scattered in the pantry, and stains dot the fridge's glass shelves. I spray everything down and wipe it until it looks new then leave for the store.

The grocery isn't far. I let Malachy guide me inside and take my time going through the aisles. I select organic produce, olive oil, almond milk, sprouted bread, spray butter that isn't butter but has the heart-healthy symbol on it, nuts and seeds, several cartons of egg whites, turkey bacon, fish, and lean meat with barely any fat.

When I get to the checkout lane, the cashier smiles. "Three hundred fifty-two dollars and ninety-three cents."

I count out the money, and my gut drops. Killian gave me two hundred and fifty. I put the cash away and hand her my credit card.

We finish the transaction. Malachy and I join Lennon by the front door, and we leave. I get home, and they carry the groceries in. I put everything away then decide to rearrange the entire kitchen.

Killian's spices are mostly expired. I toss the majority of them then wipe out the cabinet and replace the ones that made the cut.

One by one, I remove all items from the cabinets and drawers. I place everything on the counter until there's nothing left inside them. After cleaning each empty area, I decide what should go where.

There is a bottle of spray cleaner for stainless steel, so I work on each appliance until they are clear of fingerprints and look new. I wipe down the counters and sink then step back, admiring my work.

This place needs some color.

I glance around the attached family room and decide it's time for a shopping spree. I'm about to tell the guards I want to leave but realize I don't know where I'm going. I text Selena.

Me: *Do you know where there is a good place to shop for home decorations?*

Selena: *There are several fantastic places. When are you going?*

Me: *I was thinking now.*

Selena: *Want to swing by and pick me up? I'll take you to them.*

Me: *I'd love to. Send me your address.*

She sends it over, and I give it to my driver. It takes ten minutes with traffic to get to her place. I text her again.

Me: *I'm outside your building. Should I come up?*

Selena: *I'm ready, so I'll meet you downstairs.*

Me: *Okay.*

Within two minutes, she gets in the car, along with a bodyguard. He sits in the seat across from us, and after she introduces us, she directs my driver what store to drive to.

"What are you looking for?" she asks.

I shrug. "I'm unsure. Everything in Killian's house is a modern gray, silver, and black theme. The only thing with any color is his O'Malley four-leaf clover sign above the mantle.

Selena's lips twitch. "So you want to accessorize?"

"Yes. It feels super cold right now. I need to warm it up."

"Well, this should be fun!"

"I'm happy you were free to join me."

Excitement fills her face. "Me, too. You caught me at a good time. If I tell you a secret, will you not share it?"

"Sure."

Her smile grows. "I had a doctor's appointment this morning. They estimate I'm seven weeks pregnant."

"Oh, wow! Congratulations!"

"Thanks."

I add, "It seems like everyone is going to be popping out babies."

She nods. "Yeah. I don't want anyone to know I told you. Obrecht and I agreed to tell his mom, Svetlana, first. But we aren't seeing her until tomorrow night for dinner. It feels too far away and I'm too excited about it!"

I zip my lip. "Your secret is safe with me. I'm honored you told me."

"Thanks."

The car parks in front of a building. When the bodyguards deem it clear, we get out. Another bodyguard stands next to the car.

"Kind of overkill, don't you think?" I ask, staring at the four meatheads.

Selena's voice drops. "I'm not going anywhere without mine."

"Okay, you two can stay here," I direct mine.

"No. They come with us," Selena insists.

"But—"

"I was kidnapped in a store just like this. You shouldn't take any risks, Arianna," she blurts out.

Goose bumps pop out on my skin. "Oh my God! Are you okay?"

Her eyes turn glassy. "Yes. It was a while ago. You should never underestimate the threats we have against us. Our husbands trust these men to protect us for a reason. Let's go shop." She turns and trots toward the building.

I catch up and put my hand on her arm. "Hey."

She takes a deep breath and forces a smile. "Sorry. I didn't mean to sound bossy."

"It's okay. I'm glad you're okay."

"I am. Let's forget about it and shop."

"All right."

We step inside, and I glance around, staring at all the colors and extraordinary items.

Selena asks, "This going to work?"

I clap. "This is perfect!"

She selects a cart. Her eyes twinkle. "Do we need one or two?"

I laugh. "We might need a dozen."

"Where do you want to start first? Pillows? Lamps? Pictures? Blankets? Vases?"

"Let's see the pillows."

We spend the next few hours filling two carts full of items. Selena and I have similar tastes, and we spend most of the time laughing. Selena calls Anna. She sends a van to the store. Her guys come in and load it with wall hangings, an entrance table, two rugs, several floor lamps, an oversized chair, and an ottoman. When we finish, Selena comes to the house with me.

She glances around the room.

"See what I mean?" I ask.

She cringes. "Yep. Everything is high quality. Once we accessorize, it won't feel so cold."

"I hope so."

She tilts her head. "Has this been hard? Transitioning from New York?"

I think for a moment then finally reply, "It's better than I thought it would be."

"Are you and Killian getting along?"

I shrug. "Most of the time. Should we pull everything out of the bags?"

"Sure."

We remove everything. The van shows up. Everything gets unloaded into the main room. The men leave, and our bodyguards go into the garage.

Selena turns to me. "If you were going to give yourself a symbol, what would it be?"

"A symbol?"

She points to the O'Malley sign. "Yes. If Killian's is a four-leaf clover, what would yours be?"

I sigh. Everything about my life seems to be exponentially in my face since moving. At least in my papà's house, I took care of him and my brothers. I knew the city well. Plus, I had my volunteer work and family parties to plan. "I don't know."

Selena's face falls. "What's the exasperated sigh for?"

I twist my hands in my lap. It's not something I'm proud of or want the world to know, but something about Selena makes me trust her. "My papà wouldn't let me work. If I'm honest, I'm a bit lost right now. I want to get a job, but I don't even know what I would apply to do. All I did was take care of my family and help plan the monthly parties my papà hosted."

A sympathetic expression fills Selena's face, but I don't feel like she's pitying me. She hesitates then says, "When I immigrated from Greece, I was barely twenty. My ex-husband didn't allow me to do anything. I don't want to get into it all, but if anyone knows how you feel, it's me. Anna was looking for an assistant to help with her design business. I kind of fell into it. Just give yourself a break. You'll figure everything out."

"You work with Anna?"

She beams. "Yeah. I love it, and her."

"No wonder why you have such good taste!"

She laughs. "So do you. Should we figure out where all this goes before Killian comes home?"

"Yeah."

"Do you know where his tools are?"

"No. Let me have one of the guys look in the garage." I text Malachy to search for anything we would need to hang things on the wall.

"I bet one of them can help us, too," Selena says.

"Good call!" I pick up the foiled and lacquered ceramic vase. It has soft blues, greenish-gold, and silver.

"That's an amazing find! I think you should put it here." Selena pats the sofa table.

"Agreed."

I toss the throw blanket across the arm of the couch then add accent pillows to it and the chair.

Malachy comes into the house. He has a level and toolbox. "Need help?"

"Sure!" I motion to the bare wall and touch a painting. "Could you hang this there?"

"Let me call Lennon inside. That's a big one. Also, Darcey from the pub stopped by. She left a case of wine in the garage. Said Nora ordered it for you."

"That was nice of her."

"I'll have Lennon bring it in if you want?"

"Sure."

Lennon comes into the room with the wine, and I put it in the bar area. He helps Malachy hang pictures. Selena and I move the antique blue table to the entryway then add a silver bowl.

"Where do you want the floor lamps?" Selena asks.

I glance around the room then grab one of them. It's silver with glass bulbs from the bottom to right below the white drum shade. I move it to the corner. "This is where I want to create that reading area."

Approval fills her face. "Perfect." She picks up the end of a rug and drags it over.

We unroll it, and more happiness fills me. The center is cream and white with different blues in an abstract border pattern. The oversized white leather chair with tufts and matching ottoman fits the space perfectly. I toss another throw blanket on the chair, add an accent pillow, and have Malachy carry the heavy side table over.

After several more hours, there is nothing left. Selena and I step back and admire our work.

"This looks amazing," she chirps.

My cheeks hurt from my smile. "Agreed. It feels cozy now."

"Okay, well, I better get going. Obrecht and I have dinner plans tonight." She hugs me.

"Thanks for everything. This was fun," I say.

"It was! Thanks for letting me be a part of it."

I walk her to the door, and Killian's driver leaves with her and her bodyguards. I glance at the time and text Killian.

Me: *Are you home soon?*

Killian: *Not for a few more hours.*

Me: *Should I make dinner?*

Killian: *Sure.*

Since my papà had full-time chefs, I haven't cooked a lot. I know how to make basics, but my time in the kitchen is limited. I open the fridge and pull out the halibut then search recipes on my phone, settling on pan-seared halibut with lemon butter sauce. I have everything to make it, except I substitute my spray and olive oil for the butter. I find another recipe for a walnut, raspberry, and spinach salad.

After I make the salad and get all the ingredients prepared for the fish, I open the pantry. I debate but decide on the brown rice and cook it.

I text Killian.

Me: *Can you text me when you're twenty minutes away?*

Killian: *I'm about thirty now.*

Me: *Okay. See you soon.*

I set the table, open a bottle of wine, and put a glass in front of Killian's plate in case he decides to try it again, along with water. I turn on the skillet and cook the fish. I add salad to the bowls then dish out the fish and rice onto plates. I put everything on the table, turn on an indie music channel, and light the new candle on the centerpiece I bought.

For the first time in a while, I feel accomplished. I assess the table and room and decide this could feel like my home.

"Arianna," Killian shouts.

"In here."

He steps out of the hallway and freezes. My flutters erupt as he scans the room. When his eyes meet mine, my gut drops before he gets out, "How much did you spend on all this? And don't tell me you used your papà's card."

22

Killian

ARIANNA'S EYES FILL WITH HURT. "YOU DON'T LIKE IT?"

I ignore her expression. My house looks like a designer showroom, and I no longer recognize it. There's no way she didn't drop a ridiculous amount of money on all these things. The few hundred dollars I gave her didn't buy all this, which means her father bought it all. The last thing I'm going to do is have him supporting us. I firmly state, "It's going back."

"No, it isn't."

"Yes, it is."

She glares at me.

My phone rings. I answer it without taking my eyes off her. "Hello."

Declan's voice hits my ears. "I'm pulling in. Come out."

The hairs on my arms rise. "It's happening?"

"Yeah."

I hang up and look at Arianna. "We'll talk about this when I return."

She scrunches her face. "Where are you going? You just got home."

"I have something I need to take care of." I walk toward the door.

"Killian!"

"I can't talk right now. Don't wait up." Finn and Obrecht planned on picking Judge Peterson up. Declan's call means it went according to their plan. And now we need to go to the garage to make sure they don't kill the judge or Jack Christian before Finn gets the information he thinks they have regarding Brenna's location.

Arianna grabs the back of my bicep. "Don't wait up? Are you kidding me?"

I spin. "I don't have time for this. Stay in the house. You're on lockdown until I get back."

She huffs. "Lockdown? You can't—"

"I can, and I will. And pack this shit up. It's all going back tomorrow." I step out the door and say to Malachy and Lennon, "She's in for the night. Don't let her go anywhere until I return." I beeline to Declan's SUV and get in.

He puts it in reverse and says, "Finn and Obrecht just picked him up."

"We better get there before they do. Who knows how long Obrecht will keep Jack alive. Finn will go apeshit if he kills him too soon," I comment.

Declan puts the blinker on and turns the corner. "If Jack knew anything, Finn would have gotten it out of him by now. Putting him in a room with the judge isn't going to reveal anything new."

"He's so far gone already anyway," I say. Jack's been living in a cage. His body's deteriorated significantly since the night he kidnapped Selena. He's barely sustaining life right now.

Rain pounds the windshield and Declan turns on the wipers. "Hope you and Arianna didn't have dinner plans."

I grunt. "Pretty sure we'd have been fighting all night."

He glances at me in question. "Why?"

Anger flares, and I attempt to contain it. The last thing I need to be is pissed off going into the garage. I relay, "I just got home. I thought I stepped into one of those designer TV shows."

Declan arches his eyebrows. "And this is bad because...?"

I groan. "Think about what you just asked."

"You can't expect her not to put her touch on the place."

I cross my arms. "Putting her touch on the place is one thing. Buying the entire store with daddy's credit card is another. The last thing I'm doing is living off Angelo."

"Yeah, can't say I blame you. When's he coming to Chicago?" Declan asks.

"Arianna spoke with Tristano yesterday. She said end of next week."

"So write Angelo a check, make it clear you didn't know about it, and Arianna won't be using his money anymore," Declan orders, as if it'll solve everything.

"Let's change the subject. Did you hack into the bank server yet?" I ask.

"Working on it. I've got a few more layers to go. But my jitters aren't going away. Plus, we have another issue we need to figure out. It might be related."

The hairs on my neck stand up. "What's that?"

Declan's face hardens. "Another news article just posted about Jack Christian. This one states he's back in town and will be resuming his normal duties starting next week."

I snort. "From inside a fish's belly. Why would anyone report that?"

Declan lowers his voice. "Someone's trying to fuck us."

I claim, "No one knows about this, except our financial advisors."

Declan's eyes darken. "Someone has to know something. Why else would the report have come out? And our advisors make money on our short positions. They wouldn't want the stock to start going back up."

I scrub my face. "If the stock gains momentum on the upswing, we're going to lose our asses."

"It's already up several bucks."

My gut drops. "We need to figure out who's leaking this info. The only other solution is to have Jack's body show up."

"Too risky. Liam and Maksim both aren't going to go for that." Declan pulls into the garage's lot and parks. He shuts off the engine and turns toward me. "When we finish babysitting Finn and Obrecht, I'll hack into the news station's servers. There'll be some sort of trail. Whoever is behind it, we'll have to shut up."

"Add another body to our count," I mutter then open the door and run to the entrance of the garage to escape the rain. Finn lets us inside and locks the door behind us.

"Where's Obrecht?" Declan asks.

Finn's eyes turn to slits. "Jack's barely breathing. I doubt we'll get anything out of him. Obrecht's about to slice him up. If we didn't come tonight, I don't think he'd have lasted until tomorrow."

"Serves the bastard right after what he did to Selena," I remark then go into the only other room in the garage and freeze. I haven't seen Jack in a few weeks. A rope attached to the ceiling is tied around his wrists, stretching his arms as wide as possible. He's on his tip-toes and has lost so much weight, he resembles a skeleton. His hair has turned completely gray. A lot of it has fallen out.

Judge Peterson hangs next to him. Fresh piss pools at his feet. His body shakes, and his breathing is labored.

Obrecht takes the flat end of his blade, places it under Jack's chin, and forces his head up. He orders, "Look at me."

Jack barely opens his eyes. He whispers, "Just kill me."

Obrecht steps closer. He leans into his ear. "You spent years with my wife, the same woman you vowed to love, cherish, and honor. Instead of upholding your promise, you did unspeakable things. There will be no mercy for you. For as long as I can extend your life and keep you in pain, I will."

Finn steps next to the judge, grabs his chin, and jerks it toward Jack. "You want to end up like him?"

The judge swallows hard and closes his eyes.

"For months, we've had him in a cage, just like what he did to Selena. Do you want to join him, or do you prefer a quick death?"

More piss runs down the judge's legs.

Obrecht turns and grunts. "Let him die slowly."

The judge's body convulses, and Finn shouts, "Where is Brenna?"

"I-I-I don't know!" he claims.

"Wrong answer!" Obrecht scolds then takes his knife and slashes it down Jack's forehead, through the middle of his eyeball, and along the remaining skin of his cheek.

A sound comes out of him resembling a wounded animal. Blood seeps out of his face.

Whimpers from the judge fill the air.

"Ah, you didn't like that?" Finn torments him then holds his knife up to his eye.

"Please! Don't!" he screams.

"Tell me where she is!" Finn orders.

"I don't know!"

"Liar!" Finn roars then takes his fist and hammers it into the judge's face.

Blood flies, and a loud crack echoes in the room, followed by the judge's screams.

Obrecht puts the point of the knife on Jack's shoulder. He slowly drags it to the bottom of his torso. Blood surfaces from the knife's path. "You treated my wife like a dirty animal." He slides the metal across his abdomen and moves it toward his other shoulder while Jack whimpers. "The only filthy animal I see is you. And, one by one, I'm going to rip your organs out and feed them to you until you choke on them."

Declan steps next to Obrecht with a staple gun. "I'm going to sew you up as he does it. And every time you think you're going to die, and there's nothing left, we're going to find another piece of your body to extract."

"Please kill me," Jack chokes out.

"Where is Brenna?" Finn demands again.

"I don't know!" the judge blurts out.

"Wrong answer," I say, grab the can of gasoline, and step in front of him.

The judge's eyes widen. "I-I-I—"

I hold the can above his head. I say to Finn, "Get a few slashes in before I pour this on him. Let it seep into his wounds and burn inside and out."

Finn cuts his pecs in a cross, slicing through his nipples, and he screams.

"Last chance. Where is Brenna!" I bark.

Finn grabs the judge's dick and moves the knife closer.

"W-wait! Sh-she was in Philly!"

Finn freezes, and goose bumps break out on my skin. He growls, "Where?"

"I-I don't know."

"Wrong answer," I repeat then pour gasoline over one side of his body.

He shrieks, and another blood-curling sound comes out of Jack, but neither Finn nor I take our attention off the judge.

"Tell me where she is!" Finn screams in his face.

He chokes, "I-I lost her. A year after your sentence. She disappeared."

"Bullshit!" Finn slaps him on the opposite side of the face, where he punched him, and another loud crack fills the air. Blood hits me on the cheek.

The judge sobs. "It's true."

More noises bounce off the concrete from Jack, but I step closer to the judge. "You expect us to believe you knew where she was and let her slip through your fingers?"

"Yes!"

Finn grabs the back of his head with his left hand and yanks so hard, there's a loud snapping noise. He yelps. Tears fall down the judge's face, and his eyes roll. Finn seethes, "Tell me where she is."

"Piece of shit didn't even last fifteen minutes," Obrecht says behind me.

"Doesn't look like the judge made it, either," Declan says.

The judge's body convulses, and his face begins to harden.

"Tell me!" Finn screams, enraged.

"You broke his neck," Declan comments.

Finn continues yelling, over and over, "Tell me where she is, you bastard!"

The judge's face turns a pasty white. His tremors slow. The red in his lips morphs into purple.

"He's dead," Declan says.

"Shit!" Finn growls and tosses his knife on the ground.

"Do you think he was telling the truth?" I ask.

Finn angrily shakes his head. "He was lying, trying to save his ass."

"Maybe he wasn't."

Finn pulls off his shirt and unbuckles his pants. "He was. I've seen that bastard lie too many times to count. I'm showering." He stomps off, naked, and goes into the bathroom.

Adrian and Maksim come into the garage.

"Looks like I missed all the fun," Adrian says and steps in front of Jack's corpse, studying it.

"He was a pussy, just like he's been his entire life," Obrecht seethes then spits on him.

"Where's Finn?" Maksim asks, glancing around the room.

Declan points. "Shower."

Maksim crosses his arms. "You find out anything?"

Declan shifts on his feet. "The judge said Brenna was in Philly for a year then she disappeared."

Maksim's eyes turn to slits. "The judge wouldn't let her out of his sight in order to lose track of her."

"Finn thinks he was lying," I say.

Maksim glances toward the bathroom and takes a deep breath. He points to the dead bodies. "Let's finish this."

We spend the next few hours cleaning up, incinerating the bodies, then disposing of them in Lake Michigan, and finally showering. By the time Declan drops me off, it's close to midnight.

I step into the house, and my stomach growls. The light under the kitchen cabinets is on, so I keep the others off, assuming Arianna is asleep. I make my way to the fridge and open it. An array of color hits me from all the produce. I pull out a plate with foil over it, unwrap it, and pop it in the microwave. I dig through the contents of the fridge, attempting to find a loaf of bread and my butter, but the only thing I see is sprouted bread and fake spray butter.

"What did she do with my butter?" I grumble then open the pantry and freeze. Glass jars with olives, nuts, and seeds sit where my cookies and chips were. Olive oil and zero-calorie spray are where my vegetable oil used to be. Flaxseed and almond flour crackers, brown rice, organic oatmeal, and some sort of wannabe brown sugar stare at me.

I could be in Nolan's house right now.

The microwave dings. I pull the plate out, looking at what's on it for the first time, which is baked fish and brown rice.

I grab a beer out of the fridge, open it, then down half of the bottle. I assess my dinner again, then say out loud, "Jesus, I need to kick this fat complex out of her."

"No, actually, I don't have a fat complex, Mr. Heart Attack in Waiting!" Arianna snaps.

I spin. She's in the corner, on the new chair she bought. Her feet are on the ottoman, and she has a blanket over her. A glass of wine is in her hand. The bottle is on the table next to her.

"Want to tell me what you did with my bread and butter?" I ask. My stomach growls again, and I shove the fish and rice in my mouth.

She mutters something, but it's too low for me to comprehend.

"You might want to speak up," I say then eat several more bites. I wash it down with more beer then repeat, "What did you do with my bread and butter?"

She gets up, leaves the room, and I keep eating. I'm unsure if it's good or if I'm just starving. I finish eating and rinse the plate.

Arianna comes into the room with a big garbage bag.

She drops it in front of me, and it rips. The trash explodes all over the wood floor. "All your heart attack foods are in here. Have at it."

"Are you drunk?" I bark, assessing the mess.

She huffs, and tears fill her eyes. "No. I no longer care." She spins and goes back to her chair then refills her wineglass.

"Get back here and clean this up," I demand.

"Clean it yourself. I did more than my fair share today." She pulls the blanket over her body.

I storm over to her. "This little fit you're having because I'm not cool with daddy furnishing our house is over."

She slams her wineglass on the table. The wine sloshes over the rim and drips onto the wood. "You're such an ass."

"Don't stain the table, or they won't take it back," I reprimand.

She haughtily laughs. "I'm not returning anything."

"Yes, you are!" I insist.

Her golden orbs singe into mine. "No. I'm not."

"Your father's money is no longer an option for you to use."

She jumps up and points toward my face. "You don't know anything about me or where my money comes from."

"Your money? You don't even have a job! How often do you call daddy to put more money in your account?" I sneer.

Her eyes fill with tears. "My trust fund is from my mother. It's money she earned modeling before she met my papà.

Since my brothers are involved in my papà's business, she left it all to me when she died. There are only three things I've ever taken money out of it for. One is charity. Two are the groceries I bought today so I didn't use my papà's card and upset you. The third thing is the furniture I decided to splurge on, which I thought she'd approve of. And do you know why I usually don't spend anything from it?"

My stomach flips, and I stare at Arianna, feeling like I'm about to get my ass handed to me in the ring.

A tear drips down her chin. "My mother only made one withdrawal a year, and it was for charity. So when she died, I decided to keep it for the same thing. But I make two donations. One is for kids with cancer because that was her charity since her sister died when she was a child. The other is for the heart association. Do you have any idea why I chose them?"

I quietly admit, "No."

She wipes her face. "Because my mother died of a heart attack. So, no, Killian, I don't have a fat complex. I was just trying to make sure we don't drop dead at 55 like she did. But do what you want. I don't care anymore." She spins, goes into the bedroom, and slams the door.

Shit. Shit. Shit.

I scrub my face, tired from the day and constantly fighting with Arianna. Most of all, I feel horrible that I never asked her how she got her trust fund and just assumed it was her dad's money. And all the choices she makes regarding food now make sense, which only makes me feel like a bigger ass.

I wipe the new table so the wine doesn't stain it, then clean up all the trash on the kitchen floor. When I go to the bedroom, the door is locked.

I pound on it. "Arianna, let me in."

"Leave me alone, Killian."

"Arianna, let me in my bedroom!"

The door flies open. She laughs through tears and says, "*Your* bedroom. *Your* house. Everything is yours, isn't it? Am I just supposed to be a guest living here?"

I quietly reply, "I never said that."

"Sure, you did. Maybe you just don't hear how you talk."

Crap. I step forward and reach for her. "Arianna—"

She jumps back and yells, "Don't touch me. You don't get to come in here and treat me like dirt and then screw me, or whatever else it is you think you're going to do."

"Arianna—"

Her tears fall faster. "No. For once, shut your mouth, Killian. And listen to me closely. We're finished."

I jerk my head back. "What does that mean?"

She wipes her face and chokes out, "I did what my papà wanted so he wouldn't disown me. But you know what? I have money. I can leave and support myself, and I don't have to rely on you or my papà."

"You're overreacting. I'm sorry—"

"No! You aren't sorry. I'm sick of your sorries. Sleep here, but I'm not sharing *your* bed with you. I'll sleep on *my* chair that *I* own with the blankets and pillows *I* bought. Tomorrow, I'll get all *my* stuff out of here, just like you wanted. And I'll ship all of it to *my* apartment in New York."

My stomach flips. "You have an apartment?"

"No, I don't. But I have the money to get one. So have a nice life—"

I scowl. "Did you forget we're married?"

She shoves past me and says, "Nope. But come tomorrow, I'm filing for divorce."

23

MC

Arianna

All night, I analyzed our situation. The more I thought about how my trust fund came from my mother and the type of woman she was, the more I realized she gave me the entire thing to make sure I was okay. While I don't think she would want me to ostracize myself from my papà and brothers, she also wouldn't want me to be Killian's doormat.

She was independent and strong. Before she met my papà, she had a successful modeling career in New York. Several of her contracts had royalties that paid her for several decades. Since my papà took care of all the bills and never stopped her from buying whatever she wanted, she invested all of it in a trust, with me as the sole beneficiary.

Maybe it's why I was so shocked when my papà told me they had an arranged marriage. I can't imagine her ever doing anything she didn't want to. While my papà ran the household, in my eyes, she always got what she wanted.

My mother would tell me all the time, "Tesora, find what makes you happy and don't stand for anything else."

I was only eighteen, in my final year of high school, when she died. I didn't realize how much control all the men in my life would have. Too many times to count, I've craved the ability to ask her how I'm supposed to do that when everyone else is holding all the cards. Tonight, I finally realized I need to do what it takes to live how I want. And it doesn't involve a husband who doesn't appreciate me or care about me beyond what my body can do for him.

Killian follows me out of the bedroom. "You aren't filing for divorce."

I spin and put my hand on my hip, glaring at him. "It's a free country. I'll do what I please."

"Did you forget the vow you made?" he fumes.

"Did you forget yours?"

"I'm not the one threatening divorce."

I scoff. "No. You just don't understand what your vows mean."

His eyes widen with rage. "Are you kidding me?"

"Fine. Tell me what to have and to hold means."

He crosses his arms, and an arrogant expression appears. "It means your mine, and I'm yours. There's no one else but us in our bed."

I shake my head. "Yep, no idea. Everything is only about sex with you."

"Don't hear any complaints from you when you're screaming my name."

Heat flares in my cheeks. I scold, "Wow! You prove my point so easily."

He grunts. "Okay. If it doesn't mean that, what does it mean?"

"Figure it out. I'm tired. Leave me to sleep in peace. I have a lot to do tomorrow." I pick up the biggest accent pillow I bought, plop down on my chair, then curl up with it and the blanket.

He stands over me, scowling. A cloud moves in the sky, and the living room suddenly fills with moonlight, beaming on Killian's face. In it, he looks like a crazed lunatic.

I close my eyes, wishing I was in his warm bed with him instead of figuring out how I'll secure an apartment in New York, get my things there, and change anything Killian or my papà has control of, like my phone. Tomorrow, I'm cutting up the credit cards my papà issued to me when I was sixteen.

"We aren't going to sleep like this. I already told you rule number eight," he states, as if what he wants is the law and there's no breaking it.

I open my eyes and snap, "That's the thing about creating rules when you have no authority. No one obeys them. And I'm not your measly little subject."

"I never said—"

"Talk to someone who cares, Killian! Why don't you find Becky? I'm sure she'll be more than happy—"

He picks me up and throws me over his shoulder.

I beat on his ass. "Killian! Let me go!"

He holds my legs firmly to his chest. "We're married. Stop having your temper tantrum."

"Stop treating me like I'm your child!"

He goes into the bedroom and leans down. He grabs something out of the drawer then tosses me on the bed. His hands circle my wrists before I can get away, and he pins them to the headboard, securing them with handcuffs.

"Let me go!" I scream, pulling at the metal, but it's no use.

He cages his body over my frame so I can't move. His lips are an inch away, and his hot breath merges with mine. Green flames drill into my eyes. "Let's get something straight. You're *my* wife, Arianna. I made a lifelong commitment to you. And you made one to me."

My voice shakes, and I curse myself for crying. "I'm not your property. Release me!"

He swipes my tears with his thumbs. "I never said you were my property."

"No. You just act like it."

He squeezes his eyes shut for a brief moment. "I'm sorry. I'll work on that."

"Then let me out," I demand.

He pauses, and I think he's going to, but then he shakes his head. "I can't."

"Killian—"

His mouth presses to mine. I try to turn my head, but he holds it firmly to him. I open my mouth to protest, but his tongue slides so fast against mine, I'm left fighting my urges not to return his affection.

I lose, unable to resist the power of his body over mine, just like always. And I hate myself more when I whimper in his mouth, pushing my hips against his growing erection.

He ends our kiss and, with labored breath, stares at me.

I attempt to look away again, but I can't move. He kisses me again and again until my body is burning for more of him. He still has me pinned and mumbles, "Sometimes I get things wrong, Arianna."

More tears fill my eyes then drip to my chin.

He kisses them, and I only cry harder. He softly admits, "Sometimes I'm a dick."

I whisper, "Let me go."

He strokes my hair. "We're O'Malleys. We don't get divorced. We figure our shit out, Arianna."

Marinos don't divorce, either. It would be a massive embarrassment in my family. I'd be the first family member ever not to stay married, but I'm not admitting that nor letting it deter me. "I'm not an O'Malley."

His orbs grow hotter. "You're my wife," he says again, as if I just committed a carnal sin.

I defiantly glare at him, fighting the inner angel that wants to make peace with him and the demon yelling at me to hold my ground. "You don't have a right to keep me tied to this bed."

His face hardens. He rolls off me then rises and goes into the closet.

"Killian!" I shout, but he doesn't answer. I close my eyes, trying not to feel cold from the lack of warmth from his body and fighting my thoughts of wanting him back on top of me.

Time seems to stand still. Blood pounds in my ears, and I yank my wrists but only end up hurting them. I cry out in pain.

Killian comes back into the bedroom, naked.

Jesus, I curse in my head, attempting not to study him but unable to take my eyes off the four-leaf clovers traveling down his V.

"To have and to hold. It's a commitment of love, gentleness, tenderness, and giving—not taking, grabbing, or demanding," he states.

I tear my gaze off his ripped flesh and snarl, "Bravo. Maybe now you can unchain me."

He cockily raises his eyebrows. "If you prefer chains, I'm down."

"This isn't funny!"

He moves to my side of the bed and sits, facing me. "No. It's not. I don't find any humor in my wife demanding divorce."

I sarcastically laugh. "And apparently, you have no idea what the definition of to have and to hold means, even when you Google it!"

He drags his finger down the side of my torso. Against my will, I shudder. Smugness fills his expression. "I think I'm committed to giving."

"Once again, we're back to you and sex."

His finger slides over the slit of my pussy. I fight not to squirm as my insides twist into a quivering mess of lust, anger, and hurt. He taunts, "You don't like all the things I do to you?"

"No," I lie, but my statement comes out weak.

"Hmm. So you don't ever want me to touch you again? And think before you speak, Arianna. This situation with you restrained to my bed can go one of two ways." His finger strokes me, and damn if my legs don't widen.

I blurt out, "There you go again—*your* bed."

He leans over my face, slides his hand under my pajama shorts, and glides through my wet folds. His lips brush mine then curl. "Some habits die hard. *Our* bed."

I take a deep lungful of oxygen, not finding humor in his "bad habits."

"Why don't you tell me what you want, lass? I'm listening."

The lump in my throat becomes thicker. I stay silent, a million thoughts going through my head, along with my lower body pulsing.

"What's going to make you happy, Mrs. O'Malley?" he asks, as if this is a joke.

A heap of emotion floods me. I blurt out the fear I can't escape, "It's never going to be equal between us, is it?" Tears stain the pillow.

His eyes widen, as if he honestly has no clue how much power he has when I have none.

I choke out, "There isn't one decision you let me make. And every time I try to do something nice for you, you don't even notice. All you do is assume who I am or what I'm like. You don't even try to get to know me other than my body."

His eyebrows pinch together. He opens his mouth to speak then shuts it.

I turn away and let the tears flow, which only makes my chest heave. I mumble, "I'm not your play toy, Killian."

He pulls his hand out of my pants and sighs. He slides it under me and turns my chin so I can't avoid him. His arrogance is gone, and he lowers his voice. "I know you aren't. You're my wife. I'll do better."

Every time he says I'm his wife, it creates a more significant pain in my heart. He says those two words as if they alone make me valuable to him, but I'm not. I'm just repayment for his debt. I'll never be anything more to him, and the realization I want to be only stabs me deeper. I shake my head. "You can't do better. You aren't capable."

Shock fills his face. "Why do you think that?"

I close my eyes and try to stop the grief swirling in my chest.

"Arianna, tell me."

I open my eyes. "Forget I said it."

"No. You can't just say that and then stay quiet. Tell me," he demands.

I sniffle. "Fine. You're too self-absorbed. You only consider yourself and what profits you. Even now, you have total control and are only thinking about what benefits you. The truth is, I'm the repayment for your debt. It's the only reason I'm here and the only thing you'll ever see me as. And you don't want to get a divorce, but it has nothing to do with me. You just don't want to piss off Tully or owe him again."

He jerks his head back. His cheeks turn red, and his eyes turn to slits. Several moments pass. The quiet freaks me out, and my heart races. He finally reaches across me to the table, opens the drawer, then unlocks the cuffs. Without a word, he leaves the bedroom.

For several hours, I lie in the bed, waiting for him to come back. I expect him to return and demand something else from me, but he never does. I finally fall asleep, exhausted from fighting and trying to figure out my life. And I'm sad and feel like a failure that my marriage couldn't even last two weeks. I wonder how Killian and I can be so good in bed yet so lousy outside of it.

When I wake up, Killian isn't in the room and the covers haven't been slept on. I'm unsure what I expected or why I'm disappointed. The sinking feeling in my gut returns from the previous night.

I get up, step out of the bedroom, and stop. Breakfast is on the table. Two plates have turkey bacon, egg white omelets, and sprouted toast. A beautiful, fully-bloomed blue orchid sits in the center, which happens to be my favorite flower.

Killian sets two mugs of coffee on the table, taps his hands on his thighs, then spins. He freezes.

Several moments of uncomfortable silence pass. We don't break our gaze. My heart races faster, unsure what to do when he finally steps in front of me. He cups my cheeks and forces me to look at him. "I've never lived with anyone before. No one's even caught my attention enough to get serious about, so I'm not sure how to do all this. And I speak a lot, but I'm shitty with words, and sometimes they get me in trouble."

My pulse beats even faster.

"I'm not letting you divorce me, Arianna. And not because of Tully, nor do I see you as a debt repayment. I said that to piss off Tully and your father."

"Killian—"

He puts his finger over my lips. "I'm not finished."

I take a deep breath.

"I'm not letting you divorce me because you're my wife. I made a vow to you. And if I fuck something up, I'll make it right. But you don't get to quit on me. I don't quit on you, and you don't quit on me. And I'll be damned if you move to New York, so get it out of your head."

I blink hard and stay silent, afraid if I speak, I'm going to say the wrong thing when I suddenly don't know if I should go through with my plan or not.

"We're going to sit down and eat a heart-healthy breakfast, and you're going to tell me all the ways I upset you so I can either stop doing it or tell you why I can't."

I stifle a laugh.

"What's so funny?"

"Heart-healthy?"

He kisses my forehead. "Yeah. But you've gotta bring back the Irish butter. Even Nolan eats butter."

"Nolan?"

"Yeah. My—" He winces. "Sorry, *our* kitchen looks like his right now."

I tilt my head. "And this is a bad thing?"

"I'm not sure. It depends on your cooking skills." He shoots me his cocky grin and winks.

I softly laugh. "I grew up with full-time chefs. I can't guarantee anything."

"Dinner was pretty good last night."

"Yeah?"

He kisses me on the lips. "Yeah. I'm sorry I had to leave and didn't say thanks."

"Where did you go?"

He sighs then spins so his arm is around my waist. He leads me to the table and pulls out the chair. "Eat before it gets cold."

"Killian—"

"I can't tell you, Arianna. Not because I don't trust you. I won't ever tell you anything I think can harm you." He sits next to me.

"So I'm supposed to be in the dark forever? Just like my papà and brothers kept me?"

His face hardens. He turns toward me. "Arianna, what do you think I'm capable of?"

My stomach flips. I've seen the crazed look on Killian's face too many times in the few weeks I've known him. I don't think about it but admit, "My papà has a dungeon under our house. I went into it one time. Men who go there, I don't think they come out alive. I'm pretty sure, whatever my papà or brothers do, you're capable of."

He slowly nods. "Okay. So you know I'm a dangerous man. I did bad shit last night."

"Why?" I ask, unable to stop myself.

He groans then scrubs his face. "Arianna, I'm trying to make you happy, but this isn't something I'll change my mind on. There's nothing else I'll tell you about last night."

I stare at my plate, trying to be okay with not knowing but still wishing I wasn't always in the dark.

"Arianna."

"What?"

"Look at me."

I meet his gaze.

"The details of what I do can only put you in danger. I just told you more than I've ever admitted to anyone. Can you give me some credit?"

I think about what he said and finally cave. "Okay."

Relief fills his face. He slides his arm around my shoulders and leans closer. "I forgot to tell you I like how you decorated the place."

I suspiciously ask, "You do?"

"Mmhmm. Feels like we're in a magazine."

I laugh then say, "The blue orchids are a nice touch."

He wiggles his eyebrows. "Stalked your page. Saw a post where you said they were your favorite."

My heart skips a beat. "Thanks."

He grabs the spray butter and piece of toast. "Want to tell me how this gets on my food?"

"Have you seriously never used spray butter before?"

"That's not butter."

I roll my eyes. "You seem very attached to your butter."

"Not just any butter. Irish butter."

I turn in my chair, pick up a piece of toast, spray it, then put it in front of his mouth. "Try it."

He takes a bite and wrinkles his nose. "My butter needs to come back in the house."

Amused, I huff. "Okay. Fine. What do I get?" I take a bite of the toast and don't understand what he's making such a big deal over. It tastes like butter to me.

He glances around. "Full decorating control."

"I can do anything I want?"

"Yes. And if you want me to remodel something, ask. But don't use your trust. We'll go to the bank today and I'll add you to our accounts."

My stomach flutters. "Our accounts?"

He nods and teases, "Yeah. We're married, remember?"

I test the waters. "Are you giving me a limit on how much I can spend?"

He arches an eyebrow. "Do I need to? Are you going to spend everything I've worked my entire life for? Or do you have a shopping addiction I should know about?"

I relax. "No."

"Okay. Then you'll have full access and I won't put a limit on it."

"Why not?" I ask, still not believing he's going to just add me to his accounts without any restrictions.

"Rule number six. I trust you. You trust me. Remember?"

Feeling like maybe we're getting somewhere, I say, "Okay. Telling me I'm on lockdown needs to stop."

"What do you want me to call it?"

"Nothing. I'm not a prisoner. You can't just tell me when to stay inside."

His face darkens. "When I put you on lockdown, it's to make sure you're safe. There are reasons for it."

"Like what?"

"We've already been through this."

"So I'm supposed to sit at home for an undisclosed amount of time, wondering where you are?" I ask.

"Yeah. Rule number six."

"And we're back to your rules."

"Hey. I just gave you access to all my money and decisions on the house. All I got was my butter," he claims.

"Plus, you still get to keep me in the dark," I grumble.

"Arianna—"

"I don't like not knowing things!"

Killian focuses on the ceiling for several moments then finally looks at me. "What do you want me to say? Do you want me to tell you the details of what I do to men? Is that going to make you feel better? Because I don't want to bring that into our life."

I wonder if I do but suddenly feel a bit foolish. "No. You don't have to tell me."

"So, does that mean we're good for now?"

I ponder some more and finally answer, "Yes."

He scoots his chair back then pulls me onto his lap so I'm straddling him. One of his palms cups my ass, and his other one fists my hair. "Good. One more thing, Mrs. O'Malley."

My pulse increases. "What's that?"

"Rule number ten. We don't ever talk about divorce. If you have a problem with me, scream at me, punch me, put me in another cock cage, but don't ever again say you're divorcing me."

24

Killian

A Few Days Later

THE MAIL FROM YESTERDAY IS SITTING ON THE TABLE. I FLIP through it and open the envelope from the bank, addressed to Arianna Marino. Irritation fills me. "When are you changing your last name?"

We went to the bank several days ago. They wouldn't issue Arianna O'Malley on it since her identification all had Arianna Marino. A few items came with disclosures over the last few days, and every time I ask her if she changed it, she replies she forgot. It's getting old. Everything she needs to make the switch is sitting in a pile on the counter, untouched.

She avoids looking at me. "I will."

"Today," I insist.

She spins. "My papà and brothers will be here in an hour. I'm not doing anything but spending time with them today."

"Why are you making excuses for not changing your name?"

"I'm not," she claims.

I cross my arms. Since our breakfast conversation, things have been good between us, except for this one issue. "You're my wife. Is something wrong with my last name?"

"I said I'll do it, so drop it," she states and walks into the bedroom.

I follow her. "When?"

"When I get to it." She pulls off her top and walks into her closet.

"What is filling your days so much you haven't had time to do this?"

She drops her satin shorts and tosses the clothes into the laundry hamper. Hurt fills her face. "Thanks for acting like I've done nothing."

"Don't put words in my mouth."

"What do you want me to think with that comment?"

I open my mouth then shut it. I've been trying to think before I talk so I don't say stupid stuff that hurts her. Since our last fight and breakfast conversation, we've gotten along perfectly. The last thing I want is to upset her and especially before her family comes into town. She's excited to see them. I don't want to dampen her spirits or have to listen to any threats from her family. I'm related now, and Arianna's family is important to her, just like mine is to me. So I'm hoping to have a good relationship with them and avoid confrontation, not because they scare me, but for Arianna's sake.

She puts her hand on her naked hip and fires, "You told me to research careers. I've made sure you had dinner on the table every night when you got home and also did your laundry. When I wasn't doing that, I've been with you."

Time to do some more penance.

I take two steps forward. She retreats to the wall, and I cage my body against hers. A blush crawls up her cheeks, and she gasps. Every time I see that expression on her face, my dick hardens. All I can do is debate about how I'm going to take her. But she also needs to change her name, and if I need to teach her another lesson, I will.

I press my growing erection against her stomach. I'm only wearing boxers, since we recently got up and just finished breakfast. "This is important to me, Arianna."

She focuses on my chest.

I force her chin up. "You're my wife. You aren't Arianna Marino anymore. You're Arianna O'Malley."

She furrows her eyebrows. "You mean Arianna Marino-O'Malley."

My blood pumps harder in my veins. I sternly reply, "No. There's no more Marino in your name."

"Yes, there is. I'm a Marino first. That's why they have hyphens," she declares.

Air in my lungs becomes stale. "Hyphens are for women who aren't sure about their marriages."

She huffs. "Oh my God. You're such a male chauvinist."

"No, I'm not."

"Yes, you are. Do you even know what year it is?"

I ignore her accusation. "You aren't hyphenating your name."

"Want to make a bet?" she fumes.

I take a deep breath, assessing her, then grab her wrists, pinning them above her head with one hand. Her breath hitches, and I drag my other fingers down the side of her torso. She shudders. I attempt to stifle the exasperation pooling in all my cells but can't. It grows. I engage all my willpower to use my head instead of hurling my initial thoughts at her. In a controlled voice, I state, "Okay. Let's make a wager. If I win, you don't hyphenate."

Her heart pounds hard below mine, or maybe it's my organ beating into her chest. This is important to me. She's my wife and needs to claim me as hers. In my eyes, a hyphen keeps her between her old life and our new one. It makes it easier for her to run back to it the next time things get complicated between us. Things may be better between us, but I'm not naive enough to know she's never going to get pissed at me again. Her previous divorce threat is still gnawing at me.

She finally replies, "Fine. When I win, I hyphenate, and you aren't allowed to bug me about it ever again."

My mouth goes dry at the thought of her winning and having to live the rest of my life with her correspondence and identification screaming at me she's not fully committed to us. I dip my mouth an inch above hers, and it begins to water.

Everything about Arianna seems to make my body react. I've always had a lot of sex. There isn't a day I can remember not wanting it, but it's as if she turned a dial. A constant itch now exists. I can't seem to eliminate the need to know what she's doing, or think about how I want to have her next, or wonder if she's thinking about me. I've stopped myself several times a day from texting or calling her, just so I don't appear desperate or like I'm checking up on her too often.

She arches her eyebrows and challenges, "Do you have something in mind, or should I create the terms?"

One thing I've learned about Arianna is she isn't one to back down if I position my thoughts the right way. I stroke the side of her breast. I take a risk and brush my lips against hers as I speak. "Maybe you should. I don't think you could handle it. You'd break before we got to the airport."

She huffs. "Wow. You just get cockier and cockier, don't you, dear hubby?"

My lips curl against hers. "I'd call it confident."

Her golden flames drill into mine and she smirks. "I think you underestimate me. Unless it has to do with boxing or physically overpowering me like in an arm-wrestling match?"

I grunt. "You think I'd put you in a ring with me or use my strength? That wouldn't be fair now, would it?"

"Well, you do have me pinned against this wall," she mutters.

My cock twitches against her smooth skin. "Sorry, lass, but I didn't hear you tell me to release you." I move my finger over her puckered nipple.

She opens her mouth, and I stick my tongue in it. She flicks in perfect sync with me.

I remind myself she hasn't agreed to any of my terms yet. I retreat and taunt, "I still haven't heard you tell me to let you go."

She avoids responding to my statement. "What's the bet, Killian?"

"You sure you can handle it and don't want to create the rules yourself? You'll need some mental strength," I caution, taking another risk that could backfire.

She steps into my trap, rolls her eyes, then asserts, "Since you're so good at making rules, bring it on."

"You love my rules, don't you?" I tease, but ninety percent of me thinks she does and just won't admit it.

She scoffs. "Don't make me regret giving you the power."

I resist the smile attempting to break out on my face. "Okay. Here's the deal. Whatever I say or want goes."

"And this is different from normal?" she chides.

"Funny."

Annoyance fills her face. "Are you taking away the things you told me I was in charge of?"

"No. You retain full control of those areas of our life."

"So what's the catch?"

I kiss the curve of her neck and mumble in her ear, "There isn't one. You keep all the power you always do. But if you tell me to stop, I win." I lick the back of her lobe. "Or if you beg me to make you come, you lose."

She deeply inhales. "So this is a sex challenge?"

I position my face in front of hers. "Yeah. Do you want to back out? I'll let you."

She defiantly says, "No. But this bet is over at midnight."

"Fine."

"So I have to stay quiet during sex or anytime you touch me?"

"No. You can make any sound you want. I enjoy everything that comes out of your mouth."

She bites her smile.

I continue, "But the moment you tell me to stop or plead for me to make you come, I win, and you drop this hyphen idea of yours."

Nerves pass in her expression. "Are you going to hurt me?"

I twirl a lock of her hair around my fist. "No, lass. I'm not into causing women pain. I'm a giver, remember?"

She stifles a laugh. "Fine. Game on."

"You sure you want to go through with it?"

"Yep. But I need to take a shower and get ready to pick up my papà and brothers. Is that allowed?" She bats her eyelashes.

I give her a chaste kiss then step back. "Sure." I motion for her to go.

She sweetly chirps, "Thanks."

I pat her ass as she passes me, and once she's in the shower, I go through the drawer next to her bed. It's not the first time I looked to see what the girls gave her for wedding gifts. After she imprisoned me in the cock cage, I made sure she couldn't surprise me with anything else.

There's no debate what to take out. I'd bet money my wife will do everything in her power to win. Anything I've been dying to try with her that she's scared to experience, I'm doing tonight, unless she tells me to stop.

And I know what Arianna is thinking. We've got an entire day planned with her family. She assumes I'm underestimating her, but she'll quickly learn her mistake. My wife hasn't discovered the extent of my debauchery. Anything I've done to her in the past is going to be tame compared to today.

I toss the boxes in my drawers, except for the anal beads. I cover them in waterproof lube then step out of my boxers. Arianna's round ass is going to see what it's like to have me inside it today. Right before I take it, she's going to beg me. And right now, I'm horny as fuck, so let the games begin.

I stroll into the bathroom. Hip-hop music you'd listen to at a club comes through the portable speaker on the counter. Arianna's rinsing her hair, and I stroke myself while studying her. Everything about her turns me on, including watching soapy water slide down all her curves. Several times, I wondered if I should thank Tully for requiring me to marry her.

She sings and shakes her ass, as if she's subconsciously taunting me. I step behind her, and she jumps.

"Don't let me stop you. You can grind your ass against my body anytime," I tease.

She glances up at me. "No time for fun and games. We can't be late."

"Are you telling me to stop?" I challenge.

She spins then slides her hands up my chest. In a defiant tone, she replies, "No. But do you want to upset my papà the first minute he steps off the plane?"

I sniff hard. "Your father doesn't scare me. I've told you this a thousand times."

"Yes, you have. But you don't want me to be upset with you all day, do you?" she sweetly asks.

I move her against the wall and pick her up. I enter her in one thrust.

She gasps, and her mouth turns into an O.

I lean into her ear. "See, this is the thing, lass. You shouldn't ever forget who your husband is and what I'm capable of. And all you're going to want to do all day is thank your lucky stars you're married to me."

"Oh?" she breathes and tightens her arms around my shoulders.

I slide my hand with the anal beads under her ass. "You make me harder than fuck. I think about every part of your body and what I want to do to it all day long. And I can get you off fast, or slow, and everything in between. Today, I'm going to show you what it's like to be so distracted by your need for me that you'll know exactly what it's like to be me."

Her pussy clenches my shaft, and she meets my thrusts. A whimper echoes against the tile.

I position the bead on her forbidden zone and press it into her.

"Oh God!" she cries out and digs her nails into my back.

"Relax, lass," I instruct and slow my thrusts. I suck on her collarbone, and when her body returns to its lax state, I push another bead in her.

She moans, and her breath becomes shaky.

I move my face in front of hers. "Want me to stop?" I kiss her, and she slides her tongue against mine.

Her thrusts quicken, and I insert the remainder of the beads in her then mumble, "These stay in all day."

"What?" she asks then steals my lips again.

"Mmhmm." I push my forehead to hers, pounding harder into her, then position my hand over her clit and circle it. "You like it, don't you?"

She doesn't answer. Her cheeks flush a deeper crimson, her hot breath pants into mine, and her warm, tight pussy spasms. "Kill—oh...oh...oh God!" Her body erupts in tremors, and her eyes roll.

I stare intently at her, murmuring, "That's right, lass. All day, you're going to remember how I make you feel and how much you want more of me."

I give her one more orgasm as she comes down then don't even attempt to hold back mine. I come in her like a freight train colliding with a concrete wall.

As the adrenaline slows, I take a moment to regain my breath. I slowly retreat and arrogantly remind her, "You can say stop at any point today."

Her heavy eyes meet mine. "I need to get ready so we aren't late."

I don't move. "I'll let you go. As soon as you admit you liked what I just did to you."

More heat races to her cheeks.

I chuckle. "Why are you embarrassed about this?"

"I'm not," she claims.

I cock an eyebrow.

"Can you let me down now?"

"Not until you admit it."

"Why?"

My heart races. There are so many answers I could give her regarding that question, like the fact I might go insane if I don't take her there soon. Or, she better like it because I don't want it to be the last time. But I only tell her the most important one. "Because if you didn't, I'd pull those beads out of your ass and never attempt anything else like it with you again."

She bites on her lip and stares at me.

"Tell me you liked it, Arianna," I firmly order.

She quietly says, "I liked it."

"Yeah?" I double-check, just to be sure.

She nods. "Yes."

Relief fills me. "Good." I deeply kiss her and mumble, "You better get ready so we aren't late." I release her.

She leaves the shower.

I quickly shampoo, rinse, and dry off. I go to the table by my side of the bed and remove the G-spot vibrator then take it into the bathroom.

Arianna has on a silk robe and is sitting at the vanity, drying her hair. I kneel behind her, wrap my arms around her waist, then slide her knees apart.

She shuts off the dryer, laughs, and turns her head toward me. "I'm not going to be ready if you don't leave me alone."

I kiss her, slide my hand on her thigh, and move her panties to the side. "Lean into me."

"Why?" she asks.

I position the vibrator on her pussy. "Because you aren't leaving the house without this in you."

She glances down then gapes at me.

"What's wrong? Do you want to tell me to stop?" I innocently inquire.

She smirks and leans back. "Fine. Have at it."

I glide it into her then spin her chair so she's facing me.

"Killian, I have—"

I push the button of the vibrator and aggressively flick my tongue on her clit.

"Jesus," she blurts out and grips my head.

Since we don't have a lot of time, I don't waste any. In under a minute, she calls out my name and is quivering on my face.

I turn off the vibrator and shimmy up her torso. She breathes hard, and I put my hands on the counter behind her. "Every second of the day, you're going to crave me. Whenever you think it's impossible, I'm going to surprise you. Before we get home tonight, you're going to beg me to do things that make you blush."

She swallows hard.

I give her a chaste kiss. "There will be no hyphen in your name. You're Mrs. Killian O'Malley. *My* wife. There's no returning to Marino, so accept it." I kiss her one final time and go into the closet. I'm going to win this bet. This morning is just a warm-up. By the end of the night, I'm going to get everything I want. It includes the things that scare her. She will fully commit to me in all ways.

25

Arianna

ON THE RIDE TO THE AIRPORT, I BRIEFLY FORGET THE ANAL beads and vibrator are inside me until Killian straddles my body over him. The moment he kisses me, he turns it on. Unlike the bathroom, this time, he has it on a low setting.

Like most of Killian's kisses, they're carnal bliss he perfectly controls. Every swipe of his tongue has me wanting more of him. It's as if he didn't do all the things he did to me this morning, or we haven't touched in a long time. My skin crackles just like it always does around him. I circle my hips on his lap so my clit is against his hardening erection.

He murmurs in my ear, "You want me to get off that sweet pussy of yours?"

"P—" I almost say please but remember our bet. I curse myself. This is going to be a long day. I should have known better than to let Killian determine the terms of our deal.

He's adamant I change my last name to only his. I never thought I would hyphenate, but something about losing Marino feels like I'm giving up my identity. I barely know who I am now that I left New York. I already feel like I've lost everything but my few personal items. And while Killian and I have made some progress in our relationship, taking the name of a man who doesn't love me and I'm not sure ever will feels wrong. It's the opposite of what everything about his body against mine feels like, and I wonder how we seem to fit so perfectly together. If it were only about our chemistry, this wouldn't be an issue.

It's why I should have never agreed to this bet. I remind myself I need to stay strong and not give him any verbal cues or suggestions. Once midnight hits, I win, and he can't harass me about this subject anymore.

His lips curl, and he circles his thumb on my mound. Tingles intensify everywhere, and I attempt to create more friction between us. He leans into my ear. "Traffic is bad. Why don't I slide down and let you ride my face?"

Excitement perks in my belly, mixing with the heat and adrenaline swirling in my cells. Killian O'Malley's mouth must have been gifted to him by a sex god. When he told me on our wedding night I needed to forget about anything any other man has done to me and that I would be craving him at all hours of the day, he wasn't exaggerating. All he has to do is text me, and my yearning starts all over. He's an itch I can't seem to scratch, and right now, the need is enough to make me want to cave. The memory of what he did earlier while I was getting ready only intensifies my desire.

"You know what, lass?"

My voice cracks. "What?"

He hikes my skirt over my hips, lowers the seat until it's almost flat, and positions his face in front of mine. His hands slide between us. He unbuckles his pants, lifts his hips, then shoves his slacks down. His eyes twinkle. "I need your mouth on me. Turn over. Time for your wifely duties."

I stifle a laugh. "Wifely duties?"

He slips a hand under my shirt and drags a finger down my spine. I shudder, which only makes his lips curl.

"Don't worry. I'm going for husband of the year." He brushes his lips against my ear. "And I know you enjoy your hot pussy on my mouth while my cock is in yours."

It's true and sounds like a good idea to me, but I try not to appear too eager. "How much time do we have?"

"Enough. Now turn over and get your mouth on me, unless you want to say stop?" he challenges.

"Nope." I smile, peck his lips, then flip over so I'm facing his feet. I lick his shaft and lightly suck his cap in the manner I know drives him crazy.

He groans, tugs my body until my pussy is over his face, and licks me at the same speed the vibrator is pulsing.

I moan and circle my hips, hoping he'll go faster, but he tightens his arm over my ass so I can barely move, then returns to taunting me.

I decide two can play at this game. I deep throat him to give him a taste then return to licking him while gripping his shaft and sliding it over him between licks.

"Tease," he mumbles.

I plan on repeating it, but when my mouth goes over him, he takes his hand and fists my hair. He firmly holds me and commands, "Suck."

I don't fight him and open up the back of my throat. He only allows me to have enough leverage to move the length of his cock. The moment I reach his cap, he's pushing me back down.

A rumble rolls through his chest, competing with the vibrations inside my lower body, and something about it only makes me pulse harder. Whenever I give him head, I always wonder if it's better than what Becky used to give him. I hate that I think about her or wonder if he's comparing me to her. But that rumble makes me feel as if I'm winning.

The more I work him over, the more intensely he ravishes me. Instead of only using his tongue, his lips and teeth consume me with an expertise that should be illegal.

If I could beg for my orgasm right now, I would, which makes me grateful his body's in my mouth. I get dizzy from sitting on the edge for so long. The salty taste of his pre-cum hits my tongue, and I suck him harder, wanting more of it and grinding my body into his face as much as possible.

The buzzing from the vibrator never ceases. It's a slow burn of zings, and combined with Killian's mouth, I don't remember ever feeling so needy.

A horn blares in the background and reminds me we're in the SUV. We come to a stop, and I attempt to look up, but Killian pushes me back down then circles one of the beads in my ass. He growls, "We're not finished."

My mouth gapes open, and I arch my back. I had forgotten about the beads after the initial surprise when he inserted them in me. I'm not sure what I expected, but they didn't seem to have a point except to make me feel fuller when we had sex in the shower or right now, as his rotation creates a delicious sensation I've not felt before.

He releases the pressure on my head and sucks me hard while pulling a bead out. His dick flies out of my mouth, and I cry out, "Oh God!"

His fingers massage my scalp, and he returns to lazily flicking his tongue on me. It only serves to make me squirm more.

My body quivers. I slide my lips over his erection again, gripping it with more pressure and keeping my fingers directly under my mouth.

He groans, tightens his fingers on my head, and moves me faster over him. His cock pulses. Right as he comes, he sucks me so hard and pulls the anal beads out of my ass. Adrenaline rushes from my toes to my head so quickly I see stars.

"Fuck, Arianna," he rumbles.

I swallow all of him, not letting up as he continues to manipulate my body into more ecstasy.

When there's nothing left for me to swallow, he releases my hair. His cock falls out of my mouth. My body continues to spasm over him. He rubs his warm palm under my shirt and over my spine.

After a few moments, I catch my breath and reposition myself so I'm straddling his cock backward. He adjusts the chair so he's in an upright position again, then reaches for his pants and pulls out a remote. He clicks it, and the vibrator stops.

Thank God.

He cracks the divider window an inch. "Knox, how far are we?"

"Another ten at least with this traffic."

He doesn't reply, closes the glass, then moves all my hair over one of my shoulders. His lips hit the curve of my neck, and a new humming begins. "I have something new for you."

I turn toward him. "What?"

He gives me a chaste kiss. "Get on your knees and bend over the seat." He nods to the one across from us.

Nervous flutters erupt. I turn to him further. "Why?"

He tilts his head and studies my face. "I'm spending the day preparing you, Arianna."

It's an unnecessary question. He already told me what he wants. I'm not sure what preparing me means, nor did I wake up thinking today would be the day Killian would have me how he keeps insisting he will. Still, I ask, "For what?"

His green flames pin me. "All of you."

I swallow hard, unsure of so many things regarding that scenario. Nothing I do with Killian ever seems tame. Somehow, every touch he gives me is several notches above anything I ever experienced before him. But I've always stayed away from what he wants to do.

His fingers stroke my jawline. "Rule number six. You trust me. I trust you. It involves your body, too."

I open my mouth then shut it.

He leans into my ear. His hot breath seeps into my skin, and I take a deep breath. He questions, "Did you like what I just did to you?"

I don't hesitate. "Yes."

He kisses my neck. "Did I hurt you?"

"No."

He nibbles on my ear, and I whimper. "That's right. I would never harm you, Arianna. Once you fully give yourself to me, you'll understand how good we'll be with no limitations between us."

Hurt, I ask, "You don't think we're good now?"

He positions his face in front of mine and firmly states, "I didn't say that. Don't put words in my mouth."

I stay quiet.

His lips twitch. "We're running out of time. Now, do as I instructed or tell me to stop."

My voice cracks. "You want to do it here?"

He reaches into the console, pulls out a small box, and opens it. The black butt plug one of the girls gave me is in it.

I've been curious about a lot of the things they gifted me. I don't even know why someone would use one, just like I didn't know how good the anal beads were going to feel when he pulled them out of me. Part of me wants to permit Killian to do whatever he wants and not question anything. The other is hesitant as always. I blurt out, "What does it do?"

Amusement crosses Killian's expression. "It's going to prepare you to take me."

I stare at the plug, which is bigger than the beads were.

"Am I putting this in you, or are you going to say stop?" Killian taunts.

He said he wouldn't hurt me, I remind myself. Plus, I'm intrigued since I was wrong about the beads. I thought they would hurt but didn't. I get off his lap and bend over the seat.

A minute passes, and he cracks the divider window again. "Knox, add another ten minutes to our journey." He rolls it back up.

I glance back. "We're going to be late."

He shakes his head and holds up his phone. "No, we aren't. Your father's flight is delayed." He squeezes lube on his finger and rubs it on the plug.

I face the back of the leather seat. My heart picks up speed, and I wonder if I'm worrying about nothing.

Killian's knees touch the outside of mine. His warm frame cages mine, and he commands, "Look at me."

I take a nervous breath and obey. The moment I turn my head, his lips are on mine, his tongue is in my mouth, and his hand is strumming my clit. I moan, pushing my ass against his pelvis.

He pulls away. I close my eyes, and he orders, "Eyes open, lass."

I do what he says.

My confident, cocky, way-too-good-looking-for-his-own-good husband assesses me. "Remember how good it felt when I pulled those beads out?"

My cheeks heat and I nod.

He brushes my lips with his as he speaks. "I'm going to make you feel a hundred times better. I promise. So tell me you want it."

Before I can think, I surprise myself and whisper, "I want it."

His lips curve and his eyes smolder with approval. "Good. Now close your eyes and just enjoy it, lass."

I obey, inhaling the scent of leather and mint, orange blossom, and bourbon vanilla. I expect him to insert the plug inside me, but instead, his lips and breath tease the skin on my ass cheek. His fingers continue to circle my already-sensitive bundle of nerves.

"Killian," I breathe and grip the sides of the seat, on the verge of soaring again.

He groans, puts the end of the plug against my forbidden zone, then lurches back over me. His lips hit my hot cheek. "You make me feel crazy most of the day, Arianna."

I open my eyes. My heart skips a beat.

He stares back at me and admits, "It's driving me nuts. You're mine. I know you are, but I can't stop feeling like you don't know it."

"I-I am yours," I insist, unsure why he would think that.

He slips the plug past my hard ridge.

"Oh..." I breathe, feeling fuller than earlier this morning.

His erection digs into my ass cheek. He slides his tongue in my mouth and hungrily kisses me.

I return his affection and rock on his hand, feeling the adrenaline pool once more.

He surprises me and pulls out the vibrator then enters me in one thrust.

"Killian!" I cry out. The exquisite sensations of his erection gliding against my walls are more intense than usual.

His fingers continue to manipulate my clit, and he pushes his forehead on mine. "I'm your husband, Arianna. From now until forever, you belong to me, an O'Malley. There won't be a hyphen in your name."

"You haven't won," I manage to get out.

"I will. You're Arianna O'Malley," he claims, pounding faster into me.

"I-I...oh God!" I cry out.

His lips hit my ear. He slows his hand. "Who makes you feel good, lass?"

"You!"

"That's right. Who am I to you?"

"My husband," I breathe.

He moves my hair, and his tongue flicks the top of my spine. My whimpers fill the vehicle. He growls, "And what's my name?"

"Killian."

"Killian, what?" he barks.

"O'Malley," I answer. Endorphins ignite and grow until I'm trembling and my eyes roll. Over and over, he thrusts, pounding into my spasming channel, making my head spin with pleasurable chaos.

"Arianna," he groans, and his erection pumps into me like water blasting out of a firehose. His hot breath permeates my neck while he catches his breath. The beating of his heart thumps into my back. He slowly pulls out of me, and I start to move, but he says, "Stay still."

I freeze, and the sound of the console shutting hits my ears.

He takes a wet wipe to my lower body and cleans me up then sits on the seat and pulls me onto his lap. "I'm serious, Arianna. I don't want you hyphenating your name."

The fact he wants the world to know I'm his makes me happy. No matter what has happened or how we got here, the one thing Killian seems to take seriously is our vows. But anger also strikes. I blurt out, "We made a deal. Are you going to harass me all day about this?"

"No. I'm—"

My phone blares out the hip-hop song that serves as my ringtone. I figure it's one of my brothers, reach across the seat and pick it up, then answer without looking, "Hello."

"Why aren't you responding to my messages?" Donato's deep voice accuses.

The blood drains from my face. My insides quiver, and I freeze.

He says, "Arianna, where are you? We need to talk."

I clear my throat and avoid looking at Killian. I firmly state, "No. We have nothing to talk about. Don't call me again."

Killian's body stiffens.

"Arianna—"

Killian grabs the phone and puts it to his ear. His cheeks turn red. He tightens his arm around me and, after a minute, seethes, "If you take one step in Chicago, or anywhere near my wife, you won't live to see the following day. And the next time you think about calling her, don't. If you do, I'll hunt you down and make your death so painful, you'll beg me to end your life. This is the only warning you get." He hangs up and scowls at me. "How long has he been calling you?"

"What? He hasn't. I blocked him after he texted me."

Betrayal fills Killian's expression. "When did he text you?"

"Why are you mad at me? I didn't do anything wrong," I insist.

He snaps, "When, Arianna?"

"Maybe a week ago. I blocked him, though, and didn't respond. What number did he even call me on?"

Killian glances at the screen. His jaw clenches. "It says *Blocked*."

"See, I'm not lying!" I move off his lap.

He deeply exhales. "I didn't say you were lying."

"You pretty much did."

He focuses on the ceiling, then does something on my phone.

My pulse continues to rise. "What are you doing?"

He looks up. In an angry voice, he asks, "Why did you hide this from me?"

"I didn't think about it. I blocked him."

"But you didn't tell me," Killian accuses.

"Stop acting like I cheated on you or something!"

"Jesus, Arianna! He tried to kidnap you in public. What does he have to do for you to inform me he contacted you?"

"Why? So you could go crazy? It happened the day I bought everything to decorate the house."

Killian takes several deep breaths while looking out the window. When he turns toward me, something else is in his eyes I haven't seen before. He tugs me back onto his lap. In a calmer voice, he says, "If he contacts you, I need to know."

I blink back tears. When I was with Donato, I never thought he would hurt me. The last time I saw him at Club D, he proved otherwise. I don't want him contacting me, and I don't want Killian mad at me. I thought I did the right thing by blocking him, but once again, I didn't make the right choice in Killian's eyes.

He holds me to his chest. "Don't cry. I'm sorry I yelled. I don't want anything to happen to you. Promise me you'll tell me if he contacts you again."

I pull it together and look up. "Okay."

Killian studies me for a minute then nods. He tucks a lock of my hair behind my ear. He opens his mouth to speak when his phone rings.

He sighs. "Sorry. I have to take this." He answers, "Declan."

I pick up my purse to pull my mirror out and make sure I look presentable to meet my papà and brothers.

Killian's body stiffens. He fumes, "Tully and I had a deal."

My pulse increases.

The car stops outside the runway. Killian glances out the window then says, "We just got to the airport. I'll call you later about this." He hangs up.

I put my hand on his cheek. "What's going on?"

He slowly meets my gaze. His face hardens. "I wanted to surprise you and take you to New York in a few weeks. I thought we could see your family and Fiona and Sean. But Tully's backtracking on our deal. He said Bridget isn't budging, so we can't see the kids."

My heart skips a beat that he wanted to do something nice for me, but it also hurts. I don't know why Bridget is acting so cruel. "I'm sorry. Is there anything I can do?"

A private plane lands and stops several hundred feet from the SUV. Killian glances at it. "No. Let's go have a good day with your family."

26

Killian

"PAPÀ!" ARIANNA BEAMS.

Angelo picks her up in a hug. "I've missed you, my bambina," he says and kisses her cheek.

I slap her brothers' hands, and they all take turns embracing Arianna.

Angelo hugs me, which takes me by surprise. "Killian, are you taking good care of Arianna?"

"Of course."

He smiles and glances at her. "Good. She looks happy."

Well, I did give her too many orgasms to count this morning during my penance.

I keep my thoughts to myself and nod then lead everyone to the SUVs. Angelo and Tristano get in ours. Dante, Gianni, and Massimo get in the other. A third vehicle is for the extra bodyguards.

"Are you getting to know the city?" Angelo asks Arianna.

"A little bit."

"How was your honeymoon?"

I slide my arm around Arianna. "It was great, wasn't it?"

She doesn't flinch and smiles. "Yep."

"You aren't very tan," Tristano observes.

"Sunscreen and cabanas. How was your trip to Italy?" I ask Angelo, attempting to change the subject.

His face darkens, but it's only momentarily. "Fine. Glad to be back."

Arianna states, "We thought we'd drop you off at the hotel so you could check in and then go to lunch. Are you hungry?"

Angelo waves his hand in the air. "We can check in later. Take us to your house. I want to see where my bambina is living."

I'm proud of my home and what I've earned in my life, but my chest tightens. My house is nothing compared to Angelo's mansion. The thought of the Marinos judging it makes me uneasy. Regardless, I text the other driver and inch the divider glass down. "Knox, change of plans. Go back to my place." I roll the window up.

Arianna's eyes twinkle. "It's nice. Killian even gave me full decorating power, right?"

"Yep. You've done a great job so far, too." I mean it. After the initial issue about where the money came from, I gave Arianna cash to put back in her trust. She has good taste, and I can't say I dislike anything she did.

"Aww, thanks." She bats her lashes.

Tristano pushes the pads of his fingers together. "You going to take us to your gym, Killian?"

I shrug. "I can. I was planning on sneaking away later for my workout with my trainer. Arianna was going to take you shopping on Michigan Avenue during that time."

"He has a fight tomorrow night," Arianna informs them.

Tristano's smile grows. "Well, I guess it's good we decided to stay another night."

"You are?" Arianna asks.

"Yep. We thought we would surprise you."

Arianna claps. "Yay!"

"Sorry, but I'm skipping out on shopping. Okay if I get a workout in, too?" Tristano asks me.

"Sure," I reply.

"Ugh. I suppose Dante, Gianni, and Massimo will skip shopping and go to the gym with you," Arianna whines.

"We're not really into shopping," Tristano points out.

I chuckle and turn to her then wiggle my eyebrows. "I was right." We made a bet when she told me she wanted to take her brothers shopping. I insisted they wouldn't want to do that. Now, she owes me a blowjob.

Arianna slaps my arm with the back of her hand. "Don't be annoying. It's a new city. That's what tourists do."

Tristano groans. "We tell you this every trip."

"You always go with me and buy plenty of things."

"Yeah, because you drag us with you."

"Let them go. You can have me all to yourself. Now, tell me what you've been doing with all your free time," Angelo says.

The blush Arianna always gets when anyone mentions her free time crawls up her neck. Something about it makes me feel like I need to protect her. I tug her closer to me. "She redecorated our house, cleaned out anything that wasn't healthy in the kitchen, and has me on a diet. But I did get my butter back."

"It's not a diet! It's a lifestyle change for your heart," Arianna claims.

Angelo's lips twitch, and he gives me a knowing look. I wonder what's in his kitchen now that Arianna is gone and only in charge of mine.

"Did she make you get a physical?" Tristano asks.

"My appointment is next week. But when my lipid panel comes back normal, I've negotiated my white bread," I inform them.

"She switched you to sprouted, didn't she?" Tristano asks.

"Yep."

"Her nickname is Chef Hitler."

Amused, I grin. "That's appropriate."

Arianna waves her hands between us. "Excuse me! I'm in the car. And please tell me you haven't gone back to eating pasta and bread at every meal." She looks at her father.

He shakes his head. "Nope. Still following your orders."

"And you're working out and getting your massages?"

"Yep."

She sighs as if relieved. I know she worries about this, but it's another reminder how much she agonizes over what happened to her mother.

"Every night, she tries a new recipe and rocks it, so besides my bread and butter, I can't complain. Everything she cooked so far is delicious," I admit.

"What else are you doing all day?" Angelo asks.

She nervously shifts in her seat. "Killian's been showing me around the city. I've gone to yoga and brunch with the girls, too."

"That's nice."

"You've been researching careers," I add.

Angelo's eyes turn to slits. He aims them directly at me. "Careers?"

Way to open my mouth before we even get to the house.

Before I can speak, Arianna frets, "Papà, you know I want to work."

He snaps his head toward her. "And I've told you it's not necessary."

I sit up taller. "Arianna wants a career. There's no reason she can't have one."

Angelo's eyes become daggers. "Marino women don't work. Their husbands provide for them."

"Guess it's good she's an O'Malley then because our women all have jobs. And it isn't about providing for her," I fire back. Arianna's made it clear she wants to work, and I'm not going to stop her if it's important to her.

"She's a Marino first. There are threats, and they don't disappear just because she's in Chicago. We discussed this before you married her."

"Yes, I'm aware, and I'll figure out how to keep her safe. But if she wants a career, she's going to have one," I insist.

"She's not working," Angelo seethes.

"Papà—"

"With all due respect, and I'm not looking to fight your entire visit, but this isn't your decision anymore. I'm Arianna's husband. You entrusted me to marry her and keep her safe. Whatever she decides to do, I'll make sure she's protected at all times," I retort.

The car stops, and I step out, needing air. I reach in for Arianna and pull her into me. Anxiety fills her face.

I kiss her cheek and murmur, "Enjoy your family. Don't worry about this."

"Arianna, show us the house, then I need to speak with Killian alone," Angelo orders.

I internally groan. Arianna nervously glances at me, and I peck her on the lips. "Lead the way."

She takes them inside the house as the other SUV pulls into the driveway. Gianni, Dante, and Massimo get out and join the tour.

It only takes a few moments to show them around. I stay in the kitchen and let Arianna do her thing. When she finishes, Angelo asks, "Where can we talk?"

"Whatever you need to say, do it in front of me," Arianna says.

"This is not for your ears, bambina," Angelo replies.

Arianna opens her mouth, but Tristano interjects. "Show me what you've been researching for careers."

"Tristano!" Angelo reprimands.

"There are many things she could do that wouldn't put her in danger. It's not like when you and mamma got married," Tristano fires back.

Angelo's face hardens. Before he can say anything else, I put my hand on his shoulder. "Let's go talk."

He shoots more daggers at Tristano and follows me into my office. Massimo stays with them. Dante and Gianni join us.

"What's going on?" I ask.

"My daughter is not working."

I groan and cross my arms. "You aren't winning this one. Arianna is bored. She can't sit home all day doing my laundry and making dinner."

"She could get targeted."

"My family deals with threats all the time. I'll keep her safe. Instead of debating this, why don't you tell me where that bastard thug Donato is? He called her before we picked you up," I inform them.

Dante steps closer. He grinds his molars. "What did he want?"

My blood begins to boil, thinking about him maneuvering her through the club, then shoving her into his car. "I didn't keep him on the phone long, but he wanted to know where she was. He said he would come get her."

"Do you think he's in Chicago?" Gianni asks.

Blood slams into my skull. Adrenaline pumps into my veins like it does before I step into the ring. "I'm unsure. The number was blocked, so Declan wouldn't be able to trace it. If he is here, he's not leaving Chicago alive."

Angelo points at me. "This is exactly why it is too dangerous for Arianna to work. He is only one threat that exists."

"What are the others right now?"

"I have enemies all over. We discussed this on the phone before you married her," Angelo reminds me.

"Yes, so do the O'Malleys. It doesn't mean she can't work. And I'm getting tired of reiterating this to you," I snap.

"It is your job to provide for my daughter." Angelo steps closer.

"Stop insulting me. I make plenty of money," I bark.

"Okay, enough." Dante steps between us. "This isn't helping the situation. Killian, when Arianna decides what she wants to do, you run it by us. Together, we'll decide if it's safe enough or not."

Angelo roars, "She isn't—"

"Papà, Tristano is right. There are lots of ways to work nowadays. Arianna has been bored for years. Let her come up with some ideas, and we can steer her in the right direction," Gianni adds.

My initial reaction was to tell Dante no one is deciding anything about Arianna except me, but I hold my tongue. If her brothers can help Angelo be okay with the idea of her working, then I'm all for it. The extra stress on Arianna about her father's approval isn't needed, and I don't want to hear about it the rest of my life.

Angelo clenches his jaw, crosses his arms, and looks out the window.

Gianni quietly says, "We've told you for years Arianna needs something to anchor her. There are things she could safely do."

Angelo spins. He meets my gaze. "I'll consider this. You'll discuss with me what she decides she wants to do before you give her the go-ahead."

I bite my tongue, and instead of reminding him again she's my wife, I agree. "Fine. Now tell me you have some intel on this Donato prick."

His face falls. "All dead ends. We even have his brother and right hand in our custody. They claim to know nothing, and they're either unlike any other men we've ever interrogated, or they don't know anything. Unfortunately, I think it's the latter."

I almost blurt out I want to see their dungeon, but I keep my mouth shut. Instead, I say, "Are they still alive?"

"Yes."

"I'm bringing Arianna to New York in a few weeks. If we haven't gotten anything on Donato by then, I want to talk to them."

Angelo arches an eyebrow. "You think you know how to get information out of men more than we do?"

I sniff hard and arrogantly reply, "Possibly. Guess we'll have to have a little family meeting and see if I can teach you anything."

Dante cracks his neck. "Let the games begin."

I chuckle. "Is there anything else you wanted to discuss? If not, I'm hungry. And since Arianna has me on diet lockdown in our house, I'm ready to eat a real piece of bread."

Angelo's lips twitch. "I'll take it as a sign you two are getting along. She wouldn't worry about it if she didn't care about you."

A tugging on my heart I'm not used to pulls in my chest. I usually avoid women caring about me, since I don't want any commitments from them. For the first time ever, it occurs to me Arianna's feelings for me aren't guaranteed. The notion she doesn't have to care about me makes my gut flip. I don't have any reason to believe she doesn't, but Angelo's comment brings up a topic I never contemplated before.

"Let's go to lunch. I'm starving," Gianni says.

I lead them out of the room, but the nagging feeling doesn't go away. When I step into the family room and see my beautiful wife talking to her brothers with her face lit up, flutters in my gut erupt. I'm not used to physically reacting to women on any level besides with my dick. I'm unsure what to do with this new sentiment, or what it means.

When she looks at me, her face slightly falls, and the anxiety reappears. Another thought pops up in my mind. I don't like her worrying or being anything but happy.

"Good news. As long as you pick a career where I can keep you safe, your father won't have any issues," I announce, knowing it might piss Angelo off but not caring. She hates when she's left in the dark. And all I want to see is her plump lips curve up again.

When she beams at me, the tug in my chest intensifies. I ignore Angelo and hold my hands out to help her off the couch. I even decide I'm not going to eat bread as planned. I'd rather keep the smile on her face. I tug her into me. "Let's go to lunch."

27

MC

Arianna

AFTER LUNCH, KILLIAN TAKES MY BROTHERS TO CHECK INTO the hotel, then to his gym. I walk down Michigan Avenue with my papà. Our bodyguards surround us, but it's nothing new.

My papà places his arm around my shoulder. "I'm glad to see the smile on your face. You seem happy."

My heart skips a beat. I glance at him. I haven't thought about it, but it hits me that most of the time, Killian makes me happy. Before I can even analyze it, I reply, "I am."

Wrinkles form around his eyes. "You and Killian seem to be getting along well."

I can't disagree. "We are."

He tightens his arm around me and kisses the top of my head. "Good. And do you like Chicago so far?"

Before I got here, I wasn't sure what to expect. I assumed it would be horrible, but it's not. I admit, "It isn't New York, but I can't say I don't like it."

"I'm sure you'll learn to love it then. Killian said he's bringing you to New York in a few weeks. I'm glad I'll get to see you again. It's been too quiet without you in the house."

I stop walking. "It's weird not seeing you every day."

He smiles. "Yes. But marriage looks good on you, Arianna. I haven't seen you glow like this since your mamma was alive."

The pang of grief that never leaves flares in my heart. I blurt out, "I think she would like Killian. What do you think?"

His expression momentarily turns sad before he takes a deep breath. "Yes, I do believe she would have."

Something about his admission makes me feel better. I blink hard and return to our stroll. A block away, I inquire, "Killian told you he was bringing me to New York?"

"Yes. Did I ruin a surprise?" he frets.

"No. He told me in the car before we picked you up. I wasn't sure if he was canceling it."

"Why would you think that?"

I gather my thoughts, wondering if I should tell Papà about Bridget and the kids. I hesitate but then realize he might be the only person who could help. I take his arm and say, "Let's get a cup of coffee."

"Instead of shop?" he smirks.

"You don't care about shopping, do you?" I make a mental note to schedule something else for my papà and brothers next time they visit.

His eyes twinkle. "If it makes you happy."

I laugh. "Let's get a coffee." I pull him toward the door, and Malachy opens it for us. He asks what we want, and Papà and I sit at a table while he orders for us. It's not something he usually does, but Killian insisted my guards come with us even though my papà's are here. So there are way too many men protecting us in my eyes. Maybe Malachy feels more useful getting us our drinks.

We take off our coats. Concern fills Papà's face, and he questions, "Tell me why Killian wouldn't bring you to New York."

"Can we keep this between us? I don't know if Killian would want you to know."

"Want me to know what? What has he done?" he frets in a cold voice.

"Nothing. I just...well, it's personal."

He studies me then quietly asks, "What is it, bambina?"

My chest tightens. I confess, "Killian was going to surprise me and thought we could visit his niece and nephew, too. But Bridget won't let him, so I didn't know if he would still bring me."

A deep line forms between his eyebrows. "Why won't Bridget let him see the kids?"

I shift in my seat and don't answer him. It surprises me he doesn't already know this. He and Tully have been good friends for as long as I can remember. I proceed with caution. "Papà, did Tully tell you about the deal Killian made with him when he agreed to marry me?"

"Deal?"

"Yes. Killian said Bridget stopped letting his family see the kids when Sean died. When Tully told Killian he had to marry me, he negotiated that his family could see the kids once a month. Tully called and said Bridget is still insisting they can't see Fiona and Sean Jr. Has Tully never told you about this?"

Papà's face hardens. "No. Are you sure Killian said Tully isn't holding up his end of the deal? That isn't like him."

My stomach twists. "Yes, I'm positive. Can you talk to him? They just want to see the kids. They were close to them before Sean died. I don't know why Bridget is being so cruel. It's not fair to the kids, either."

Malachy sets our cappuccinos down, and my papà taps his fingers on his cup. A few moments pass, and I think he might say he won't help, but he says, "I'll talk to Tully."

Excitement fills me. "You will?"

"Yes. But I've known Tully forever. There must be something Killian isn't telling you for him to go back on his word."

I get defensive. "Killian isn't a liar, Papà."

He holds his hands in the air. "I didn't say that. But there must be more information he didn't tell you."

Hurt creeps into my chest. I stay quiet, wanting to believe Killian didn't withhold information from me, but every man in my life always keeps me in the dark. Something about the possibility Killian might not have told me all the facts about this when it regards his family cuts me deeply.

Papà grabs my hand. In a stern voice, he orders, "Don't jump to conclusions. Let me talk to Tully when I get back to New York and see what the entire situation is."

"Will you tell me if there is something else going on?"

He clenches his jaw.

"Papà! This is my husband. It's a family issue and doesn't have anything to do with my safety! I have a right to know."

Another moment passes. He finally concedes. "All right. If there is nothing I need to worry about regarding your safety, I'll tell you what I learn from my conversation with Tully."

"Do you promise?"

His lips twitch. "Have I ever not kept my word?"

I blow out a frustrated breath. "No. You always keep your word."

He sits back in his chair and releases my hand. "Okay. I'll talk with Tully and let you know what he says unless there are any safety concerns."

"Thank you!"

He takes a sip of his cappuccino. "Now, tell me what you're thinking about for a career."

My nerves jump around my stomach. I'm still shocked Killian got my papà to be open to the idea of me working. "I'm still trying to figure it out, but Gemma suggested I do something with social media since I know how to grow a following. I also thought it would be fun to organize events. I took a test online, and party planning was the top suggestion. Plus, I have a lot of experience since I planned all your parties. I'm going to miss organizing those." A wave of sadness hits me.

He smiles. "Why can't you still plan them?"

"I can?"

"Sure. You have all the contacts. Plus, I was hoping you and Killian would visit during some of them. In fact, why don't I move the party up a week for when you come to town?"

"Would you?" I ask, realizing how much I enjoy creating all the fun things for the kids.

"Sure. And if you still plan my parties, won't that keep you busy enough you won't need to look elsewhere?"

Anger sparks. "Papà, I want to work. Are you trying to con me into helping you because you think I'm going to change my mind?"

His face hardens. "You're a Marino woman. There is no need for you to work."

I roll my eyes. "When are you going to stop being so sexist?"

"I'm not. Your husband should support you. It's how things are in our family."

I shake my head in disgust. "Killian does support me. He even made me put his money back into mamma's trust."

Red fills Papà's cheeks. "Why would you touch your trust?"

I groan and put my hands over my face. *Why did I say that?*

"Arianna!" he barks.

I lock eyes with his. "I went on a shopping spree for the house and didn't tell Killian. When he came home, he added me to all his bank accounts and gave me cash to replace what I spent."

He shakes his head in disapproval. "Your husband should not put you in a situation where you have to touch your trust. If he's not taking care of you properly—"

"My husband does take care of me. And maybe Marinos don't work, but I'm not a Marino anymore. I'm an O'Malley." The moment it comes out of my mouth, my insides quiver. *Did I really just say that?*

My papà's eyes widen. "You'll always be a Marino."

I stand my ground and suddenly wonder why I fought Killian this morning about changing my last name. "That's what you say, but if you wanted me to always be a Marino, then you wouldn't have forced me to get married. I took a vow, and now I'm an O'Malley."

"That doesn't change—"

"I was going to hyphenate my name, but now, I'm not going to," I fire at him, surprising myself when it comes out.

He swallows hard. Tense silence sits between us as his eyes grow colder.

I grip my coffee cup and glance out the window. Pedestrians walk quickly by with their heads down, trying to avoid the snow that is now falling. Cars fill the road, moving slowly. The air looks cold, and I suddenly feel tired of the never-ending battle I'm in to take control of my life.

At least Killian encourages me to work if I want.

I've seen our bank accounts. While it isn't anywhere near what's in my trust, there is plenty to support us. He told me I don't have to get a job unless I want to. And today, he stood up to my papà regarding this issue because he knows it's important to me. So maybe I should embrace being an O'Malley.

My papà lowers his voice. "Your blood is Marino. Don't ever forget it."

"I don't ever remember mamma calling herself a Romano," I point out while feeling guilty about this entire conversation. Yet, something within me shifts. It's as if a curtain gets lifted, and I can see past the darkness. My mamma didn't hyphenate. She always proudly claimed she was a Marino. If Killian will go to bat against my papà and insist I get to do what I want with my life, then why am I fighting him on changing my name?

"She didn't forget who she was," my papà claims.

"Who am I?" I ask.

He furrows his eyebrows. "You're Arianna Marino. My daughter."

I close my eyes and take a deep breath. When I open them, he's blurry from my tears. "Yes. And now I'm Killian O'Malley's wife. Who am I besides those things?"

He takes my hand again. His voice deepens. "You're your mamma's daughter, and you're everything she was but more. You have her beauty, kindness, and heart. And that makes you an amazing woman, my bambina."

I wipe my eyes. Killian's black SUVs pull up to the curb.

Malachy rushes toward us. "Mr. Marino, Arianna, we need to go." He pulls out my chair with me still seated in it. My pulse creeps toward the sky.

"What's wrong?" Papà asks, rising.

"Let's get to the vehicle first." Malachy puts his arm around my back, and before I know it, I'm in the SUV.

Papà gets in, and we take off. He moves the divider window down. "Malachy, what's going on?"

My phone rings, and I answer. "Killian! What's happening?"

"You're safe in the SUV?" he asks in a frantic tone.

"Yes. Why?"

He lets out a breath. "She's safe," he says, then, "Let me talk to your father."

"Tell me what's going on."

"Arianna—"

"Tell me!"

He only hesitates briefly. "That thug is in the city. Now let me speak with your father."

"How do you know—"

"Arianna! Give your father the phone!" he barks.

With a shaking hand, I hand my cell to my papà. He growls, "Where is he?"

The SUV accelerates and goes through a red light. I put my belt on, suddenly afraid of whatever is happening.

My papà seethes, "How did he disappear again?"

My stomach twists. I don't know why Donato won't just forget about me. He had no problem moving on before I got married. Why is he continuing to contact me and try to see me?

"Tell my sons to get their stuff from the hotel and meet at your house." Papà hangs up and hands me the phone.

I gape at him then ask, "What's going on?"

Papà's expression turns so cold, shivers run down my spine. "That thug was outside your house. Killian's security found him lurking around but didn't detain him."

"Why not?" I ask.

His eyes turn to slits. "He shot one of them."

I put my hand on my stomach. "Which one?"

"I don't know. But you're packing a bag and coming back to New York with me."

28

MC

Killian

"ARIANNA!" I SHOUT, GETTING OUT OF THE SUV.

Every ounce of blood I have is pumping furiously through my veins. That thug shot my cousin, Fergal, in the chest. His blood is all over the driveway. The police are outside my house, along with reporters. Yellow tape stretches across my yard.

Liam and Declan are talking with the police chief. Nolan and Finn are at the hospital. The doctors are attempting to remove the bullet lodged in his lung, but I'm not holding my breath. The chances of his survival are slim.

"Arianna!" I holler again, not seeing her anywhere in the chaotic swarm of people.

"Where is she?" Tristano frets, close on my heels with the rest of her brothers.

Declan meets us at the yellow tape.

I ignore the police positioned to stop anyone from crossing it. My heart feels like it may explode out of my chest if I don't see Arianna soon. "Where is she?"

He points down the road. "In the SUV with Angelo." He steps under the tape and leads me toward them.

"How did that bastard come anywhere near my home?" I growl, trotting down the road.

His face hardens. "Tiernan said it happened quickly, but he's too shook up right now. The other guys are all getting questioned by the cops, so we don't have much information yet."

"Not good enough," I growl then see a mix of Marino and O'Malley bodyguards. I jog the rest of the way, open the door, then swallow the lump in my throat when I see Arianna. So much relief fills me, I get dizzy. I pull her into my arms and murmur, "Thank God you're all right."

Angelo's dark scowl meets my eye. I match his sinister glare. After Declan called and said Fergal got shot, Massimo muttered to Dante, "It's time we pay the Abruzzos a visit."

The hairs on my neck stood up. The Abruzzos are the Marinos' archenemies. The two families have been at war for as long as the O'Malleys and Baileys have. I snapped, "What do the Abruzzos have to do with this?"

Massimo stared at me, not answering my question. After an angry exchange, he finally admitted, "Donato is working for them."

So much rage filled me, I had to stop myself from punching each of the Marinos. This isn't information they should have hidden from me. And now I'm staring at Angelo, wanting to rip his head off as well but trying to stay calm so I don't freak Arianna out further. She's trembling in my arms, scared.

Somehow, I find a way to keep my voice calm. I address Angelo, "We need to talk."

"Killian, take the Marinos to my house. There are too many of us to fit into the SUV," Declan orders.

I don't argue. I slide next to Arianna, and Gianni and Dante sit across from us. Declan goes with Massimo and Tristano in the other SUV.

Since he lives close to me, it doesn't take long before we're standing inside his house. I pull Arianna into his bedroom, ignoring her brothers, who all want to talk to her, and cup her cheeks. She's still shaking, and I firmly say, "Everything will be fine. I need to speak privately with the others."

Hurt fills her expression. "He shot Fergal, and I still have to stay in the dark?"

"Listen to me. I need to find out what's going on. Your father and brothers aren't going to speak as freely if you're next to me. You know this."

"Are you going to fill me in when you finish speaking with them? He's coming after me. I think I have a right to know."

My pulse races again at the thought of him even setting his eyes on her. "Let me speak with them. We'll talk after."

"You'll tell me?"

I sigh. "I don't know."

She angrily shakes her head at me.

"Arianna—"

"Why won't he just forget about me?"

I give her a chaste kiss. "I have some ideas why, but let me speak with your family. Stay here." I grab the remote off the dresser. "Watch TV or something."

She puts her hand on her hip and tilts her head, giving me a look of death.

"Do you want me to find out or not?"

She closes her eyes.

I fist her hair and tilt her head back. Her lids flutter open, and I admit, "I think I almost had a heart attack trying to get to you."

Surprise fills her gaze.

"Please. Stay in here so I can have an open conversation with your family. Whatever I can tell you, I will."

"You will?"

"Yes."

Her lips slightly turn up. "Okay. Thank you."

"Now give me a kiss first."

She slides her hands in my hair, draws me to her lips, and urgently flicks her tongue against mine.

I'm unsure which of us deepens the kiss, but my body is soon aching, hardening against her stomach. I retreat and murmur, "I'm going to kill him. If it's the last thing I do, it'll be seeing him take his last breath."

Her eyes widen. "Don't talk about it being the last thing you do."

The uncomfortable feeling in my chest reappears. Her father's words that she must care about me enter my mind. I embrace her one last time and kiss her head. "I'll be back as soon as I can." I leave, and when I'm passing the guest bedroom, I see Declan scowling at his phone. I step inside and shut the door. "What's wrong?"

His face hardens, and the vein near his left eye pops out. It's something that only happens when he's full of rage. In an ice-cold voice, he states, "Another article just came out. It has a picture of Jack working with his staff and claims he's back in the office. The stock price is climbing."

I scrub my face. "That's impossible."

"Yeah. It's obviously from a long time ago. Whoever is doing this needs to get taken out. I've lost too much sleep hacking into servers, yet I'm not finding anything. It's like they've erased their footprint."

"How would they know how to do that?" I ask.

He shifts on his feet and shoves his phone into his pocket. "They're a professional and know what they're doing. Whoever is leaking this doesn't want to be caught."

I cross my arms. "You find anything leading to our advisors?"

"No. All clean...for now."

My stomach tightens. If we cash our positions out now, we'll barely make anything. The stock price going up puts us in a position to lose money.

"We need to sort one issue out at a time. Let's focus on the Marinos," Declan advises.

"Any news on Fergal?"

Declan clenches his jaw. "No. Still in surgery. Anything I should know before we talk to your in-laws?"

A clawing sensation enters my gut. "Donato is working for the Abruzzos."

Declan's vein pulses. He seethes, "And they hid this from you?"

"Yeah."

He shakes his head. "Let's go."

We move to the family room, and I demand, "Which one of you thought it was a great idea not to inform me an Abruzzo was stalking my wife?"

Angelo spins. "We do not make it a habit to discuss our family business."

"It's my wife," I growl.

"We assumed we would find him," Dante states.

Heat flies to my face. My hands turn to fists, and I hold them close to me, struggling not to tear Arianna's family apart. "Wrong answer." I address Angelo. "You let your daughter date an Abruzzo?"

He steps closer. "Keep your voice down. We didn't know he was one. It was clear he was bad news, but we couldn't pinpoint what he was involved in," Angelo declares.

"When did you find out?" Declan asks.

"After we took custody of his brother and right hand."

"That was weeks ago!" I snarl.

"We only got it out of his right hand before we left," Angelo claims.

I step closer. "When were you going to tell me?"

Angelo says nothing.

It adds more fuel to the fire. "You weren't going to tell me?"

"We thought we would find him," he repeats, as if that makes it better.

My hands itch at my sides to strike him then the rest of the Marinos. "It's time we got something straight. Any threats you have against your family are now my business."

"I don't take orders from you. And my family's business—"

"Is now O'Malley business," Declan interjects.

Angelo takes a calculated breath, peering at us.

"We're on the same side or against each other. Take your pick. But Arianna is now an O'Malley. So choose your next answer wisely," I threaten.

Angelo's face turns almost purple. Arianna's brothers step forward, scowling. He rebukes, "Do not ever insinuate you'll turn my daughter against me."

"Your daughter is my wife. If you are not going to give me information so I can better protect her, then—"

"Enough!" Declan scolds. "Killian has no desire to sever your relationship with Arianna. Do you?"

I take a deep breath and admit, "No."

He points to the Marinos. "And you know you fucked up, Angelo. All of you did when you didn't tell Killian that thug was working for the Abruzzos."

They stay quiet.

Declan continues, "We all want to keep Arianna safe. So let's get past this and agree both families are going to keep the other one fully informed of any threats."

Blood pounds between my ears. Angelo finally concedes, "I'll agree."

Relieved, I reply, "Good. Now, tell me, was he dating her to get to you?"

The Marinos' faces all fill with guilt. Angelo admits, "We assume so."

"Why would the Abruzzos cross that line? It's an unspoken rule not to go after the women and children," Declan asks.

Angelo sighs. "It's why we formed a stronger alliance with Tully. Nothing is how it used to be, and everything is blurred. There are no more lines with territories, women, or children. The Abruzzos will stop at nothing to take us down." His phone rings, and he holds up his finger. "Is it booked?"

Uneasiness replaces some of my rage. I glance at Declan.

"We'll be out soon." Angelo hangs up. "The plane is ready to take us back to New York. Where is Arianna?"

"In the bedroom," I state.

"Please get her. I'm taking her back with me until we find that bastard."

Another wave of anger rolls through me. "Excuse me? You can't just take my wife without my permission."

His eyes turn to slits again. "It is safer for her if she's in my home."

"She isn't going to New York. Her home is with me."

He points in my face. "Until he is dead—"

"Killian, you go with them," Declan orders.

I jerk my head toward him. "What? He's in Chicago. We need to find him."

Declan nods. "We will." He points to the Marino brothers. "Two of you stay with us, and two of you go back. Who wants to stay and track this motherfucker?"

They all volunteer.

I object, "It's my—"

"Angelo is right. Arianna is safer in New York at his place right now. You go with your wife. We'll take care of this," Declan states.

I open my mouth to fight him but close it. Arianna's safety comes first. And I'm not letting her go to New York without me.

"Gianni, Tristano, you two stay. Massimo, Dante, you return with us," Angelo orders. He pins his cold gaze on mine. "We need to go now."

I quickly decide Declan is right. I go into the bedroom and shut the door.

Arianna jumps off the bed. Anxiety riddles her face.

"We're going to your father's."

She scrunches her forehead. "Please tell me whatever it is you found out."

I consider everything—the threats against her, my desire to shield her from anything that would cause her any more stress, and the fact she hates being kept in the dark. Ultimately, I decide it's better if she's aware of who is behind this threat against her.

Her voice cracks. "Please."

I sniff hard and put my arms around her. "I'm going to tell you, but I don't want it to frighten you more."

She holds her breath.

In the calmest voice I can muster, I inform her, "Donato is working for the Abruzzo family."

Blood drains from her cheeks. She freezes then swallows hard. "He was with me to get to my family?"

My heart thuds harder against my chest cavity. I hate thinking about her with that thug. The expression on her face is pure pain. I detest everything that is causing it. I want to tell her he was only using her, so it defuses any feelings she could possibly still have for him, but I don't lie. "I'm not sure."

She blinks hard then focuses on the wall.

My phone rings. I answer, "Nolan, is Fergal out of surgery?"

Nolan clears his throat. "No. He didn't make it."

29

Arianna

Killian's face turns white. He shuts his eyes, and a chill runs down my spine. In an emotionless voice, he replies, "I'll tell Declan." He hangs up and stares at the ceiling.

I reach for his cheek, and he slowly meets my gaze. "Is Fergal out of surgery?"

He sniffs hard. "He didn't make it. We need to leave." He puts his arm around my shoulders and leads me to the door.

My gut drops. I cry out, "Wait!"

He freezes and clenches his jaw.

"Are you okay? That's...oh God! I'm sorry. If I hadn't dated Donato, Fergal would still be alive. I-I—"

He puts his finger over my lips. "This isn't your fault, lass. Don't take the blame for what that thug did."

I try to stop my tears from falling, but it's no use. My father and brothers warned me Donato was bad. Why didn't I listen? Fergal was around my age. He didn't deserve to die.

Killian tugs me into his chest. His lips brush the top of my head. "There's nothing we can do about it. Donato will pay for what he's done. The most important thing right now is we get to the airport. It's not safe for you to be in Chicago right now."

I glance up. "You aren't dropping me off and returning without me, are you?"

Something passes in his eyes. "Do you want me to stay with you?"

My stomach quivers. I admit, "Yes."

His lips slightly curve. "Good. I have no plans to leave you in New York on your own."

I take a deep breath of relief. It makes no sense, but the thought of him back in Chicago without me makes me panic.

"We need to go." He leads me into the other room. My father informs me Gianni and Tristano are staying here. I don't ask questions and hug them goodbye, telling them to stay safe. Right before I leave, Declan comes out of his office.

"Arianna, put this on," he instructs.

I glance at the plain gold ring in confusion.

Declan admits, "After Selena got kidnapped, I got a few of these. It has a tracker inside it. Keep it on at all times."

Fear consumes me. It's been so hectic since Killian called, I haven't had time to process the fact that Donato came to Chicago for me. But why?

What does he expect me to do? I'm married and not hiding the fact. I made it clear we were over, in New York.

I shiver, and Killian slides his arm around my shoulder. He takes the ring from Declan and glides it over my left index finger, but it's too big. He removes it and puts it on my middle finger. It fits perfectly. He says, "At least it's gold."

I let out a nervous laugh then say to Declan, "Glad you know my metal preferences."

Declan's vein near his eye pulses. "Don't take it off. I'm sure we won't have to use it, but keep it on as a precaution."

My stomach flips that this is a reality. How could someone I used to have feelings for now be a threat?

Declan hugs me and kisses me on the cheek then says, "See you soon."

"Okay." I force a smile, and the five of us leave. I sit between my papà and Killian. Massimo and Dante are across from us.

"Are we stopping at our house to pack a bag?" I ask.

"No. I'll have clothes and other items brought to you tomorrow," my papà instructs.

"How long will we be in New York?" I ask.

"Until it's safe."

"Meaning?"

Papà stays silent, as do my brothers. I turn to Killian, looking for answers, trying not to explode with anger that they are still trying to keep me in the dark.

He doesn't hesitate and states, "Until Donato is hunted down, slaughtered, and no longer a threat."

"Killian!" Papà reprimands.

Killian tugs me closer to him. His jaw twitches and he shakes his head. "There is no more shielding Arianna. He's coming after her. She's not naive or unable to handle the truth. I'll no longer keep things from her regarding this issue."

His statement shocks me. I hold my breath. No one has ever stood up to my papà the way Killian does. I thought he would always keep me in the dark the same way my family does, but he's not, on this issue.

Deafening silence fills the vehicle. My papà's body stiffens, and he scowls at Killian. My brothers glance between them. I'm not sure what they think, and I don't understand why my father isn't responding to Killian's statement.

I sink into Killian's hard frame but also reach for my papà's hand. I don't want there to be issues between them, but I also want my papà to understand I'm not a child anymore. So I'm torn between the love I have for him and the feelings I have for my husband, which only seem to be growing faster than I anticipated they ever could.

My papà's cold eyes soften when I slide my palm over the back of his hand. "You grow more and more like your mamma every day." The car stops near a private plane sitting on the runway. Papà orders, "Give Arianna and me a moment alone."

Killian hesitantly obeys, as do my brothers. When it's only the two of us, I force down the grief building in my chest about my mamma. I softly ask, "Did you hide everything from her? Is that why you try to keep me in the dark?"

Sadness enters his expression, but his lips curve up. "No. She was as adamant as you are about knowing things."

Surprised by his admission, I inquire, "So you told her everything?"

My father flips his hand so it's on top of mine. "Not everything. But things that pertained to her, she knew about. And some other things."

This new information confuses me further. "Then why do you not do the same with me?"

He studies me, and love appears in his eyes. "Because you're my bambina. My one and only. And your mamma isn't here to tell me that I'm acting too protective."

Emotions overpower me, and I'm unable to hold back the tears in my eyes. "Papà, I'm a grown woman. I won't break if I know things."

He sighs. "My world is full of evil I don't want you to know about or ever experience. It was the same with your mamma. She was my light, just like you. And I don't ever want to diminish your brightness."

I let his words settle and finally disclose, "Killian said something similar. He told me he didn't want to bring that into our life."

Papà nods. "He's right."

I reveal, "I told him I could agree to that, but some things I need to be informed about, like Donato."

Papà's voice turns cold. "He will pay for what he did today and for continuing to come after you."

I blurt out, "I'm sorry I didn't listen to you. Was he only with me to get to you?" The sting of being used pricks my gut.

"Killian told you who he's working for?" he asks.

I nod. "Yes. Was Donato only with me because of something between you and the Abruzzos?" I may not know much about my papà's business, but I'm aware they are our enemy.

He confesses, "I don't know."

I focus on the divider window, kicking myself for not heeding my family's warning. "I'm sorry. I just thought you were trying to control me. I wish you would have trusted me enough to tell me the truth."

He turns my chin toward him. "If I had known he was with the Abruzzos, he'd already be dead. My gut said he was bad news. One thing I'm never wrong about is what kind of a person a man is."

I straighten up. "Am I a bad human being for not wishing any mercy upon him?"

Papà shakes his head. "No. It makes you a Marino. Or maybe a Marino-O'Malley." He winks.

My stomach does another nosedive. I swallow hard. "I-I'm not going to hyphenate my name. This morning, I thought I was, but I don't want to. It's not because I don't want to be a Marino, but—"

He puts his finger over my lips. "You don't have to explain. I didn't expect you to hyphenate. Your mamma didn't, and I wouldn't have liked it if she did. But don't ever forget you're a Marino."

I smile. "I won't."

He hugs me tightly. "I'm sorry for the circumstances, but it'll be nice having you home."

I retreat when he releases me and tease, "I can check the kitchen and make sure you and my brothers aren't lying about what you've been eating."

He chuckles. "I might have let a tub of gelato come into the house."

"Papà!" I reprimand, but if that's the only thing he's been cheating on his healthy diet with, I'm okay with it.

He opens the door. "Come on. Let's go home." He helps me out of the car and leads me into the plane.

I take my seat in the back next to Killian, and the plane soon takes off. Our ride to New York is mostly quiet. From time to time, my brothers murmur things to my papà.

Killian keeps looking at me, but I'm not sure what to make of his expression. Each time he studies me, flutters erupt in my stomach. Heat grows more intense in my cheeks. We say nothing the entire flight, and he keeps his arm around me while kissing my head every now and again. Mint, orange blossom, and bourbon vanilla fill the air, creating calm within me. I spend every second inhaling it deeply.

When we arrive at my father's house, it's as if I never left, aside from my bedroom, which is absent of my personal items. Massimo gave us T-shirts and Killian a pair of shorts, but we don't put them on. The moment my door shuts, Killian pins me against the wall.

He mumbles, "We have under an hour before it's midnight and our bet ends." He puts his lips back on mine, but I pull away.

"You win," I blurt out.

He freezes and arches an eyebrow.

My heart pounds so hard, I wonder if he can hear it. "I'm not going to hyphenate. As soon as we return to Chicago, I'll submit the paperwork for O'Malley."

His breathing deepens. "Why did you change your mind?"

I stroke the side of his head and gather my thoughts. "I...um..." My stomach flips. I'm unsure why I'm nervous, but I am. There are so many feelings I'm unfamiliar with racing around, and I'm not sure what they mean or what to do with them.

He waits and doesn't remove his intense gaze from me.

I swallow hard. "I'm yours. I want everyone to know I'm yours."

The same look he had in the plane appears in his orbs. He fists my hair and leans over my face and professes, "I don't think I've ever felt so scared as when I learned he was so close to finding you."

My lips twitch. "I guess you like me a lot, then."

He slowly licks his lips. His hot breath merges with mine, making my mouth water. "I think it's more than that."

The butterflies dance faster in my gut. I don't speak, only nod. I'm uncertain about what this is I'm feeling toward him but agree it's stronger than what I'm able to express.

His lips press against mine, possessive, passionate, so consuming, I could disappear into it and never come out. We urgently strip each other bare until we're skin to skin, and there's nothing between us. He picks me up and thrusts into me, groaning into my gasping mouth.

I forgot about the plug he inserted in me earlier. The friction against my walls is a tingling sensation of endorphins. He slides his fingers between us and circles my clit. I writhe between him and the door, crying out when adrenaline pools in all my veins. "Killian! Oh God!"

His other hand twists the plug, and he growls in my ear, "I want all of you. Tell me I can have it."

I don't hesitate, no longer worried about anything, trusting him fully to do whatever he pleases with me. "Yes. Take me how you want," I whisper.

He moves his face in front of mine and stops thrusting. "Say it again."

"Take me," I repeat.

Green flames erupt in his eyes. He kisses me with a renewed force, resuming his thrusts, and pulls out the plug.

I moan into his mouth, clutching my arms around his shoulders tighter. He carries me to the couch then sets me down and gets lube out of his pants pocket.

He instructs, "Turn around, lass."

I obey, facing the back of the love seat. He steps so close, his torso is against my spine. He wraps his arm around me and plays with my nipple while sliding his slippery digit past my hard ridge, inching it in and out of me.

I whimper, enjoying all the new sensations.

His lips trail my collarbone before he removes his finger, splays his hand on my spine, and pushes me so my ass is in the air. In a swift thrust, he's in me.

"Killian!" I cry out as a deep, delicious rumble flies out of his mouth.

"Jesus," he mumbles then continues to go deeper until I'm so full, I'm shaking. He bends over so his warm flesh is against mine. Tingles race along my neck under his lips. His cock continues to fill me, giving me something I didn't know existed. "So good, lass. Tell me you love it."

"Yes! Oh...it's...oh God!" I admit as sweat breaks out on my skin.

He drops his hand to my clit, manipulating the bundle of nerves until I'm trembling and gripping the top of the couch so tightly, my knuckles turn white.

"Look at me," he demands.

I turn my head, trying to regain focus.

"My beautiful wife," he states. His lips, tongue, and teeth assault me. He gives me one orgasm after another, never letting me fully come down while increasing the speed of his thrusts.

My body is in a never-ending state of highs. It's gorgeous chaos, annihilating every atom of my existence. Everything he promised me about this experience is true. But that's the thing about Killian O'Malley. Every moment with him is euphoria mixed with greedy bliss you need more of. And it's as if he knows my body better than I do.

"You're mine, Arianna. Mine to have and to hold and do my penance with every goddamn day," he declares.

I still don't understand why he always talks about penance. Whenever I ask him, he says it's between him and the big guy. But there's so much adrenaline surging through my nerves, I couldn't ask him or try to decipher it right now if I tried. Dizziness hits me and I cry out his name again.

He pounds into me harder, pumping his seed deep while burying his face in the curve of my neck, growling, "Fuuuuck."

His flesh presses into my back. I stay lodged between him and the leather couch, listening to our breathing. He slowly pulls out of me and flips me around. His cocky smile erupts on his lips. "Was this my reward for not ordering bread at lunch?"

I laugh.

He wiggles his eyebrows. "It was, wasn't it?"

I pat his cheek. "Maybe. Keep up your good behavior, and I'll let you do it again sometime soon."

30

Killian

It's early in the morning. I left Arianna in bed and just finished a workout. Clothes magically appeared outside her bedroom door. I text my uncle Patrick. I was supposed to fight tonight. While I'm sure my brothers, Liam, or Finn told him to cancel it, I want to make sure. And the itch to hit someone isn't going away since my boxing match won't be taking place. It's only growing stronger.

The two men working for the Abruzzos are in the dungeon somewhere under this house. I'm ready to interrogate them. I need to find Donato before he gets to Arianna. While I'm sure the Marinos are skilled in torture, I don't believe the men know nothing about how to find Donato.

"I want to see them," I demand when Massimo and Dante finish their workout.

Massimo tosses a towel to Dante and me. He says, "You want to shower now or after?"

"After. I plan on needing one when I'm through with them," I state.

Massimo and Dante's lips curl. Dante passes out water and opens the door. "Let's go, then."

We run into Arianna and Angelo in the hallway. Both of them are in workout clothes.

Arianna's smile lights up her face when she sees me. There's a tug on my heart. I palm her ass and give her a chaste kiss. "Morning."

"Morning. You're sweaty," she comments.

I squeeze her cheek and don't miss the way she inhales sharply or that her eyes light up. I tease, "You going to show your father how to pump some iron?"

Angelo grunts. Massimo and Dante chuckle. Arianna grins. "If he hits his calorie burn, I'm giving him an extra piece of toast."

I release her and spin. "Enjoy your workouts. I'm going to hang with your brothers for a bit."

"Where?" she asks.

The Marinos become tight-lipped as always. I almost attempt to cover it up but stop myself before I talk. This is regarding Donato, and I'm not hiding anything from Arianna about it anymore. I study her face and say, "In the dungeon."

She furrows her eyebrows in confusion. "Why?"

I'm not prepared to tell her more than that. Angelo speaks before I can. "It's related to that thug."

We haven't spoken about our altercation on the ride to the airport, and I didn't ask what Arianna and he discussed. While I'm always going to protect her to the best of my ability, I hope Angelo now understands neither of us can keep her in the dark about everything.

Arianna slowly nods then smiles. She pats my shoulder. "Okay. Have fun. Let's go, Papà." She continues into the gym.

I don't tear my eyes away from her or her round ass I happily devoured last night. Staring at it makes my dick twitch. My wife has to be the most gorgeous woman on earth, and there isn't anything I can complain about regarding her body. It makes me wonder how I was happy with all the other women I used to see. Not one of them can hold a candle to Arianna, and it extends past her looks. She's beautiful inside and displays it every second of the day. The more I get to know her, the more I can't imagine ever waking up without her. I once again contemplate thanking Tully for making me marry her.

And it surprises me she didn't ask more questions, but her response only makes my heart swell with pride. She's unfazed by it and seems to understand me more than I could ever hope for. The truth is, I am going to have fun when I step in front of these scumbags. The fact she didn't try to stop or question me further about it deepens my respect for her. The unfamiliar feeling in my heart only expands.

"Ready to show us what you got?" Dante taunts.

I nod. "Lead the way."

We snake through the mansion and go into a sitting room. There's a brown leather couch and two beige armchairs. Blue and yellow accessories add pops of color to the room. It makes me think about Arianna adding her touch to our house. The warmth in my chest expands, and Dante opens a closet.

I don't question anything, and Massimo shuts the door before Dante opens the next one. Blackness fills the small space until Dante turns on his phone's flashlight and presses a code on a panel.

"Pure *The Lion, the Witch, and the Wardrobe*. Is your dungeon in a fantasy forest?" I mutter.

Massimo snorts. "Nope. You might wish it were though."

The wall slides open and a dimly lit staircase comes into view. We descend to the bottom, and the musty smell of decay and bodily fluids flares in my nostrils. The air doesn't move. Rats screech and scurry all over the place. Lantern-type lights are set every ten feet on the walls. Faint moans hit my ears as we pass different cells. The doors are full metal with a twelve-inch-square opening set in the middle.

"Arianna wasn't lying. It is a dungeon," I say, impressed.

Dante cockily smirks. "Welcome to the family." He opens a cell door and motions for me to go inside.

Blood rushes through my veins faster, almost making me dizzy with anticipation. Chains bound the wrists and ankles of the men, stretching them so far out, they're on their toes. One man, who I guess is Donato's brother, Marco, since he looks like him, has a dislocated shoulder. The two thugs slowly look up, as if they barely have the energy to hold up their heads. Scars cover their bodies from what I assume is the Marinos' interrogation methods and possibly rat bites. Different contraptions fill the rest of the space.

"How long have they been here?" I ask.

Massimo steps in front of the one I think is Donato's right hand and presses the flat blade of his pocket knife on his cheek. The man trembles harder, and Massimo heckles, "Not long enough. Tony prefers me over my brother, don't you?"

His eyes shut, and a trickle of piss travels down his thigh.

I step in front of Marco. "Let's try a new scenario. Hold him still," I instruct Dante then take Marco's arm and pop it into place.

He screams and turns his head toward the wall, breathing hard.

I aggressively jerk his chin in front of mine. "New rules. You answer my question, your arm stays intact. You don't, and I'll make sure before I leave, I dislocate both."

His dark eyes fill with hatred, but I don't miss the fear laced within them or the growing realization he can't hide.

"Ah. You know who I am," I state.

His jaw clenches.

My hands itch to throw a punch, but I yank his head back. I put my face so close to him, I can taste his stale breath. I've given up the thought they know where Donato is. He's on the run now. So I move to plan B, which is to find out where he would take Arianna and any possible place he might go to hide. "What's your brother planning on doing with my wife?"

He spits in my face, and it lands on my cheek.

I don't flinch. It's not the first time it's ever happened. The more I torture men and step into my O'Malley roots, the better I get at not reacting. I smile, pat his face, and calmly say, "Ah. You'll have to do more than that to hurt me." I lean into his ear. "But guess what? The only person doing the hurting today will be me. And when I finish, I'm rubbing fruit on your legs and leaving the door open so all the rats can come feast on you."

He sniffs hard, and his body convulses.

"I think Tony's ready for another round on the table, don't you, Dante?" Massimo cheerfully asks.

I step back.

Dante holds Tony's chin. "This time, I'm not stopping until your legs separate from your torso. Then I'm getting the acid out."

Tony breaks. He begins hyperventilating, and a tear slips down his cheek.

Dante taunts, "You don't like that idea?"

Tony squeezes his eyes shut. It's barely audible, but he whispers, "Please."

"Tell me where he'd take my sister," Dante demands.

He stays quiet. The struggle is all over his expression. I almost feel bad for the poor bastard, but the sliver of compassion doesn't last long.

"Tell me," Dante screams in his face, and Tony shakes harder.

I spin and yank Marco's head back and land a right hook on his cheek so hard it cracks, along with several teeth. He screams in pain, and blood spurts on my face and seeps out of his mouth. I demand, "Talk!"

He whimpers but doesn't answer.

Massimo moves to the wall and cranks a circular wheel. The chains tighten. There's already no slack in them. Marco screams as his shoulder pops out of the socket again. The other one is close to doing the same.

"Tony's missing the fun. Give his legs a spin," Dante calls out.

"No!" he begs, but it doesn't stop Massimo.

He moves to another wheel, and when he turns it, the chains around Tony's ankles separate them farther. The cracking of his groin echoes in the air, mixing with his tormented cries.

"Oh. Sorry. Did I not tell you I don't need the table to separate your legs from your torso?" Dante innocently says.

I make a mental note to talk to Liam about upgrading our building and the torture contraptions.

"Again!" Dante booms.

"No! Stop! Please!" Tony weeps.

"Where would he take her?" Dante repeats.

"The-the room under the library."

"What library?"

"Shut up!" Marco orders.

"Not your place to interject," I claim then give him a strong left hook on his opposite cheek.

More blood flies everywhere. Several teeth fall to the ground.

I demand to Massimo, "Again!"

He cranks the wheel, and Marco screams as his other shoulder pops out of the socket.

I grab the acid stick. I know what it is because we have them in our place. It's like a giant bubble wand filled with acid, but a brush comes out when you push a button. I draw a line down Marco's chest, stopping at his belly button and bellow, "What library?"

Marco's wail sounds like a hurt animal. Blisters bubble on his torso.

Dante orders Tony, "Talk, or you're next."

"In the Bronx."

Through Marco's pain, he commands, "Shut up!"

"Another wrong statement!" I take the wand and brush acid over his balls.

"Mother—" he cries out, squeezing his eyes shut and breathing through the opening where his teeth used to be.

I tell Massimo, "Again!"

He cranks the wheel, and Marco's pain-filled sounds echo in the chamber.

"How does he get inside the library?" Dante asks.

Tony seems to get some sort of second wind of loyalty and stays tight-lipped. I step behind him and brush the acid on his spine.

"What the fuck!" he screams.

"Answer!" I boom.

His skin sizzles and blisters form within seconds.

He whimpers, "Raya."

"Tony!" Marco grunts through bloody teeth.

"You're a step away from having your tongue cut out," I warn him then brush a streak of acid down his spine as well.

More terrorized sounds fill the damp air. Massimo orders, "Step back."

Dante and I obey, and he takes a hose and sprays both men's backs, which only creates more loud noises flying out of their mouths.

When Massimo finishes, I yank Tony's head so it rests on my shoulder. "Raya who?"

"I don't know. Sh-she works there," he informs us through tears.

I release him and nod to the Marino brothers. I step in front of both men. "I'm going to check out your information. If you're lying, you'll wish you could experience what we did to you today over the wrath I'll unleash upon you."

The three of us stroll out of the cell, slam the door shut, and return to the staircase. Massimo says, "I'll go to the library and find this Raya woman."

"Want me to go with you?" I ask.

He shakes his head. "Nope. Women don't stand a chance with me, especially a mousy librarian."

Dante points to my face. "You need to clean up before we go upstairs." He leads me to a bathroom. It might as well be another world. It's clean, bright, and free of any rodents. There's a vent circulating fresh air.

I could get used to how the Marinos do things, passes in my mind as I remove my clothes, then diligently scrub my body.

I wrap a towel around my waist then put my clothes in a plastic bag sitting on the shelf. When I finish, Massimo is gone. Dante takes me upstairs. He pats me on the back. "Nice playing with you. I'm going to take a shower."

I grunt and make my way to Arianna's room. I pull joggers and a T-shirt on as Arianna appears.

Her face is red from her workout, and sweat drips down her body. "Everything okay?" she asks, sounding slightly worried.

I give her a chaste kiss. "All good. Should I take my clothes off and jump in the shower with you?"

She laughs. "Normally, yes. But Tully is here. My papà told me to ask you to go to his office if I saw you."

I'm unsure why Tully is here, but I'm glad. If he thinks I'm not going to fight to see Fiona and Sean after we made a deal, he's wrong. I kiss Arianna again. "Okay. I'll see you later." I leave and go into Angelo's office.

Tully rises when he sees me. "Killian. Didn't know you were in town."

"Let's cut the bullshit. We had a deal. You don't get to go back on your word."

He gives me a look like I'm overreacting and he's going to get me to change my mind. He puts his hands in the air. "Just calm down—"

"No. I won't calm down. We had a deal. Once a month, the O'Malleys get to see Fiona and Sean. You're going to stick to it."

He stands straighter. "Bridget said no."

Rage fills me. No one in my family can understand how Bridget could turn on us the way she did when we were all so close. But my respect for her is gone. "I don't care what Bridget wants. Those kids are my blood, and you made a deal with me."

"Pick something else, and I'll give it to you," he says, as if I'm going to just choose something else over seeing my niece and nephew.

"No. You're going to uphold your word."

"Tully, what's going on?" Angelo's voice booms as he walks into the office and shuts the door.

"Nothing. Killian and I are just negotiating," Tully states.

I cross my arms and scowl. "No. We aren't. A deal is a deal."

Angelo steps next to me. "Are you going back on your word, Tully?"

Tully's face hardens. "I can't make Bridget do something she doesn't want to."

Angelo scoffs. "Since when?"

Tully says nothing.

Angelo steps closer. "Why won't Bridget let the O'Malleys see the kids?"

Tully states, "She thinks it's too dangerous."

"Bullshit. You don't have any fewer threats on you than we do," I accuse.

"I agree with Killian. So tell me another reason she would stop the kids from seeing them," Angelo orders.

Tully once again turns silent.

Angelo lowers his voice. "You assured me the O'Malleys weren't in the line of fire as badly as we are when you suggested Killian marry Arianna. Is this not true?"

Trapped, Tully sighs. "It's true. We have more threats."

Angelo keeps his gaze on Tully. "Killian, give Tully and me a few moments, will you?"

I'm not sure what's happening, but I step so close to Tully, my face is level with his. "Before you leave, make sure you're clear I'm not letting you out of this. We will have access to the kids."

Tully clenches his jaw.

I spin and leave the room then pace the hallway for a long time.

The door finally opens, and Tully steps out. "Come over to the house at six for dinner."

I nod, relieved, wishing I didn't have to deal with Tully or Bridget but willing to do anything to spend time with Sean and Fiona.

Tully leaves, and I go into Angelo's office. "I don't know what you said, but thank you."

He turns from the window. His cold eyes meet mine. "You're family now. If you have a problem, it's also mine."

"Likewise," I state and mean it.

He pats my back and says, "Come on. Arianna instructed our chef to make breakfast. I'm sure the spray butter is already on the sprouted toast."

I groan while laughing. "Maybe I can convince her my Irish butter belongs in New York, too."

"Good idea. You can sneak a few pats on mine, then." He leads me into the dining room.

Arianna is already seated, along with Massimo. I take the seat next to her, and she holds a piece of toast up. "Bet you want this."

I bite into it and dramatically say, "Mmm. Nothing beats spray butter."

She laughs, and her eyes light up. "Admit it's growing on you!"

"Nope. I won't ever cheat on my Irish butter." I take another bite, chew, and swallow. I wash it down with some orange juice then say, "Guess who we're having dinner with tonight?"

She bites on her lip. Excitement fills her face, and it hits me she already knows. She still asks, "Who?"

I tilt my head. "Guess."

"Fiona and Sean?" She smiles bigger.

"Yep."

She throws her arm into the air in a victory pose. "Yes!"

I lean into her ear. "Why do I get the feeling you had something to do with this?"

"Who me?" she says in a teasing voice. "Nah. Here, have some food." She puts a bunch of scrambled egg whites on my plate.

The tug in my heart returns. Whatever she did, it definitely influenced the reunion I'm about to have with my niece and nephew. So many thoughts run through my head.

She went to bat for me and, without a doubt, cares about me.

I couldn't have a more amazing wife.

I eat as more pride races through my veins. Watching Arianna beam throughout our meal doesn't get old. The fake butter and bland eggs never tasted so good. And in the back of my mind, I start planning what I'm going to do with her for my daily penance.

31

Arianna

"You look gorgeous," Killian states when I step into the living room. All day, he's had the same look in his eyes I can't decipher. Every time I see it, flutters fill my stomach, and heat creeps up my neck.

"Thanks. Are you nervous about seeing the kids?" I ask.

"I don't get nervous," he claims.

"Never?"

"Nope." He takes my hand and leads me out to the SUV. We get inside, and he slides his arm around me, then brings his face close to mine. "Maybe you should keep this dress in New York for when we visit."

"You don't think I need another one in Chicago?" I tease.

"No. But I think you need to start wearing the ones you have in our closets more often."

"Where to? The pub?"

He strokes my cheek. "Wasn't what I had in mind."

I raise my eyebrows in question.

His expression that's sending my loins into overdrive intensifies. "I've been a bad husband."

I tilt my head. "How so?"

"I haven't taken you on a proper date."

My heart skips a beat. I offer, "We've gone to the pub a lot. And you've shown me around town."

"Not what I was thinking."

"No?"

He shakes his head. "Nope. And I think I have a lot of making up to do. So what do you say we go out tomorrow night on a real date?"

I try to contain my smile. "What does a real date consist of?"

His gaze drifts from my eyes to my lips then back to my orbs. He drags his finger down my arm. "You dress up. I dress up. I take you to a nice restaurant and then a Broadway play. After that, we see where the night takes us."

Surprised, I question, "A Broadway play?"

"Yeah."

"Is that your thing? I didn't take you for a theater guy."

He shrugs. "Not sure if I am. But Massimo said you're into it. And we're in New York, so I think I should take you."

My heart beats faster. I suggest, "We could go somewhere else. There might be a sporting event or something going on."

His face falls. "You don't like the theater?"

"No, I do. But I don't want you to be bored."

He beams. "Good. Tomorrow night I'm taking you to see Chicago."

I laugh. "Chicago?"

He furrows his eyebrows. "What's so funny about Chicago?"

"Did you choose it because of the name?"

"No, although the name is pretty awesome, and it's also about criminals, that isn't why I picked it."

Amused, I state, "Sounds like you've done your research. Why did you decide on that one?"

His expression turns serious. "Massimo said it's your favorite show. Was he right?"

My butterflies get more intense. "Yes."

"Good. I also got a reservation at Francesca's. He said it was your favorite restaurant."

I nod and excitedly affirm, "It is."

Satisfaction crosses Killian's face. "Great. So do you want to go out on a date with me?"

"Mmmm." I pretend to think about it but not for long. "Okay." I kiss him.

He deepens it, stealing my breath like he always does and making me feel as if all he could ever want is me. And I realize it's what I want. Him and me and for him to never get bored with me and look elsewhere.

The car stops outside Tully's house. Instead of getting out, he locks the door.

"What's wrong?" I ask.

He hesitates for a brief moment.

I stroke the side of his head and repeat, "Killian, what's wrong?"

"Nothing is wrong. I wanted to tell you something."

My pulse increases, and I worry. "What is it?"

He pins his serious, green eyes on me. "I'm really glad you're my wife."

My heart skips another beat. Happiness fills me, and I blink hard. "I'm glad you're my husband."

His lips twitch. "Even though your father made you marry me?"

"He didn't. I chose you, remember?" I tease.

His arrogant smile forms. In a playful tone, he states, "That's right, you did, didn't you?"

I nudge him. "Don't get cocky now. You had a chance to get out of it."

His voice changes to solemn. "I'm glad I didn't." He pulls me in for another kiss then admits, "I don't know what you did to make tonight happen, but thank you."

"I'm glad I could help."

He pecks me on the lips one last time then unlocks the door. He gets out and reaches in for me. Once I'm out of the car, he leads me up the walkway. Before we can ring the bell, the door opens.

"Uncle Killian!" Fiona jumps into his arms with tears in her eyes.

He embraces her and strokes her hair. "Hey, Fi. I've missed you."

She cries harder and replies, "I thought I wasn't going to see you ever again."

Killian's jaw clenches. He tightens his hold on her, and anger flares in his face, but it's short-lived.

Sean comes to the entrance and stares at him, shifting uncomfortably on his feet. His face is hardened and he seems to be struggling with what to do.

Killian holds out his arm, and Sean steps forward. He embraces both children for several moments then pulls back. Fiona is still crying, and Sean's eyes glisten. Killian declares, "You're both so grown up."

"Killian. Arianna. Come inside," Tully's voice booms.

We obey, and Killian says, "Fi, Sean, you know Arianna, right?"

They hug me, and Fiona replies, "I can't believe you're married to each other."

Killian slings his arm around my waist. "Small world, huh?"

"Yeah."

"Why don't you take Killian and Arianna to the living room before dinner?" Tully suggests, entering the hallway. "Arianna, how are you?" He kisses me on the cheek.

"Good. You?"

"Same."

We move into the other room. Sean inquires, "Do we get to see everyone else soon?"

Without hesitating, Killian replies, "Yes. They'll be here next month. Nora will bring her baby, Shannon, too."

Fiona gapes. "She has a baby?"

Another wave of displeasure crosses Killian's face, but he hides it well. "Yeah. She looks just like Nora."

"Do you have a picture of her?"

I pull out my phone. "I took some a few days ago. Here." I find the photos and hand the phone to Fiona. Sean glances over her shoulder, and they spend a few moments commenting about Shannon.

Tully comes into the room and goes to the bar. He fills a glass of Barolo and hands it to me. Then he pours two fingers of Macallan for Killian.

"Where is Bridget?" I ask. I still don't understand her choices, but we've always had a good relationship. I'm hoping to keep it.

Tully shifts on his feet. "She's out for the night."

"If only she'd stay out and never come back," Sean mutters.

"Watch your mouth. That's your mother," Killian reprimands.

"Why? She kept us from you and the rest of our family since dad died. She told us you didn't want to see us. If we didn't hear them arguing, we wouldn't have known the truth," Sean vocalizes.

Killian grinds his molars, and he scowls at Tully. "You let them believe this?"

Tully motions to the door. "Let's go have a chat."

"No. Whatever you're going to say, do it in front of us," Sean seethes.

"Careful of your mouth," Tully warns.

"You're just as bad as her." Sean turns to Killian. "Will you take me back to Chicago with you?"

"You aren't leaving New York!" Tully claims.

"Watch me!"

"You're one step away from—"

"From what? Don't threaten me. I'm not one of the goons you boss around."

"Whoa! I know you're pissed off right now, but you can't disrespect your daideó," Killian warns.

Betrayal fills Sean's face. He seethes, "I thought you'd have my back after what they've done to us."

Killian holds out his hands. "I do have your back. Always."

"Do you know they even stole our last name from us?" Sean's face turns redder with anger.

"Sean," Fiona quietly interjects.

He angrily spins on her. "You need to come home, too. Forget about your stupid boyfriend—"

"This is your home!" Tully exclaims.

"No, it's not! We are O'Malleys, not O'Connors! Chicago is where we belong."

"Sean, let's go take a walk," Killian puts his hand on his back and steers him past a glowering Tully.

Tense silence fills the air. I've never seen Sean or Fiona anything but happy. I can only imagine the shock they are in after finding out Bridget lied to them all these years.

Tully quietly leaves the room, which makes me feel relieved.

Fiona's tears fall down her cheeks. Her lips tremble. I slide closer to her and put my arm around her. "Are you okay?"

She looks at me. "Why would my mom lie to us? We-we thought no one wanted us anymore."

I choose my words carefully. "I'm not sure. You'll have to find out from her. But I can assure you, every O'Malley who ever loved you still does."

"I-I don't want to go back to Chicago. I want to see my family, but all my friends are here."

I stroke her hair. "You don't have to. And this is something you need to discuss with your mother. Sean's upset right now. When he cools down, he might see things differently."

She twists her fingers in her lap. "What last name do I use now?"

My heart breaks. Bridget has created so much confusion for her children. I still don't know why or if I'll ever find out the real reason. It's painful to see Fiona and Sean anything but happy. The only thing I can think to offer her is my truth. "Last names are tricky. I just went through this myself. What I learned is you don't stop being an O'Malley or O'Connor, no matter what name you choose."

She turns in her seat to face me. "What name are you going to go by?"

"O'Malley."

"It's strange thinking about you as an O'Malley and not a Marino."

I nod. "Yeah. But I'm still a Marino and always will be."

She tilts her head. "So we're related now?"

I smile. "Yep. You're stuck with me."

Her lips curve up. "Do you like Chicago?"

"I'm still getting to know the city, but yeah, I do."

"Can I come visit if I don't decide to move there?"

My stomach twists. There are so many layers surrounding Fiona and Sean's situation. They're still in high school. They shouldn't even have to think about these topics. "You're always welcome in Chicago. But you need to talk with your mother. I know you and Sean are angry right now, but you only get one mom. She loves you. And she won't want you to move to Chicago."

Fiona looks out the window and quietly says, "It's not fair what she's done."

I sigh, unsure what to say to comfort her and not further destroy her relationship with her mother. I would give anything to have one more minute with my mom. What Bridget did was wrong, but I hope in time, things can settle and Fiona and Sean will find peace with this situation. There isn't any reason they can't be part of both sides of their family.

Killian and Sean come back into the room. I exchange a nervous glance with Killian. He smiles and holds out his hands to Fiona and me. "Time for dinner, and I'm starving. Let's go."

He pulls us up and motions for Sean and Fiona to go first. "Lead the way." They obey, and he wraps his arm around my waist.

I look up, wanting to ask him if Sean is okay. He winks and pecks me on the forehead, guiding me down the hall.

Tully doesn't reappear the rest of the night. It's just the four of us. The mood turns cheerful, and between Killian and Sean's sense of humor, my cheeks hurt from laughing. It's like they were never apart, and I wonder again how Bridget could have denied her children relationships with the O'Malleys. All I see when I look at the three of them is love.

It's late when we leave. The goodbyes tear Fiona up again. Sean's face hardens as it did when we first arrived. Killian puts on a brave face. He orders them to talk to their mom and reminds them they only have one. He also instructs Sean to be respectful to Tully. Then he promises he'll be back next month with their uncles, aunts, and cousin.

When we get in the car, it's bittersweet. I place my hand on his thigh. "Are you okay?"

He licks his lips and nods. "I'm worried about Sean. He's just like his father."

"What do you mean?"

Concern fills Killian's expression. "I told him he needs to stay in New York and finish school. Plus, he's smart and should go to college. If he wants to live in Chicago after, then he can. As much as I want him with us, uprooting him isn't in his best interest. My brother wouldn't have wanted him away from Bridget. But Sean's so angry right now and doesn't have an outlet to release it."

"Maybe you can help him find one?"

His face hardens. "Bridget made him stop boxing when they moved. It's how Sean coped with things. Hell, it's how I do, too."

"Why would she do that?"

He seethes, "The only thing I can think is she tried to erase anything that had to do with Sean."

Another pang of confusion and hurt fill me. A large part of it is the agony I see on my husband's face. I slide onto his lap and caress the side of his head. "Can I do anything to help?"

His palm cradles my ass, and his other hand strokes my thigh. Hot zings oscillate in my core. He voices, "You've already done more for me than I could ever have imagined."

"I only told my father Tully was going back on his word when I asked him to help," I confess.

He stares at me so intensely, I take a deep breath. "I didn't just mean with the kids."

I freeze, racking my brain about what else I've done but unsure what he's referring to.

"I owe you an apology," he declares.

"For what?"

"For calling you a daddy's brat and assuming all sorts of things about you that aren't true."

My lips twitch. "I think I had some misconceptions about you, too."

He takes his phone out of his pocket and holds it out. "I don't have a picture of us. Smile."

I laugh, put my cheek against his, and the light on his camera fills the car.

He shows me the photo. "I forgot to do something important."

"What?"

He swipes the screen then posts it on his social media page. He tags me then types quickly. The caption reads:

I know you're all going to be jealous since she's so smoking hot, but I thought you should meet my forever, Mrs. O'Malley.

#luckiestguyonearth

32

Killian

The Next Night

WHY DID I GET READY SO EARLY?

"Do you have the heat on?" I ask Massimo.

"No."

I remove the sport coat I bought earlier today when Arianna and I went into the city. I'm not a fan of shopping, but I know she is, so I asked her if she wanted to take me on a tourist shopping spree. To my surprise, I enjoyed it. I should have known I would. Something I'm starting to understand about Arianna is anything she's a part of, she puts her best foot forward and makes it fun.

Plus, I snuck into the dressing room in the lingerie store. I held her against the mirror, showed her how much I enjoyed the outfit she had on, and covered her mouth to muffle her cries. The sales lady gave me a knowing look when she caught me stepping out of the room, but I'm sure the commission she made from our hefty purchase made her look the other way.

The same heat I had penetrating me on my wedding day assaults my entire body. I'm one step away from breaking out in a sweat. I remove my shirt. Arianna is getting ready in her room and ordered me to stay out. I announce, "I'm using the shower in Tristano's room."

Massimo arches his eyebrows. "You nervous about going out with Arianna tonight?"

"No. I don't get nervous," I claim then take my clothes upstairs. I remove my pants, underwear, and socks, then step under the cold water.

I stay under the water until I'm shivering from the cold. I towel off, and my phone rings. I glance at the screen and answer, "Declan, any progress?"

His voice sounds irritated. "No. The bastard seems to have disappeared into thin air."

My blood boils, and the chill I felt dissipates. "Not what I wanted to hear."

Declan's next words don't help. "Yeah. Our other issue isn't going away, either. Another article is out, and the stock is almost back to where we placed our orders. Maksim's adding Bogden to the search. I need to work on finding out who's behind this, or we're going to lose our asses."

I stare at the ceiling. Finding Donato is a priority, but we're going to lose too much if Declan doesn't figure this out. "What can I do to help?"

"Unless you acquired my skills, nothing."

I run my hand through my hair. "Let me know if anything pops up that I can do."

"Noted. Bye." He hangs up.

I sigh and take another cold shower. I try to get my mind off our problems so I'm not a sweaty mess for Arianna and my date. When it's close to leaving time, I pick up the long-stemmed red roses I bought earlier for her and knock on her bedroom door. "You ready?"

She opens the door, and my dick betrays me, filling all the room in my slacks until it's straining against the zipper. I don't understand how I can wake up with her every day and spend so much time with her, yet only crave her more. And how does she become more beautiful with each day that passes?

The red dress she chose earlier today hugs her curves perfectly. Her curled hair hangs past her breasts, and her full, red lips torture me the moment I see them.

My skin buzzes, as if she's electricity, and if I go any closer, I might get shocked. Still, I step in front of her and hold out the bouquet. "Wow. You're stunning, lass."

She shyly smiles as a blush creeps into her cheeks. "Thanks. You look great. These are beautiful." She takes the flowers from me.

I cup her cheeks. Kissing her is only going to torment my body more, but I can't resist. I slide my tongue in her mouth, and we might as well be the eye of a hurricane with chaos swirling around us. Nothing exists when I kiss Arianna. It's her body, molding into mine, igniting the need I can't seem to eliminate since I first laid eyes on her. The feeling I can't shake in my chest expands, and I mumble into her mouth, "I love you."

She freezes, and so do I, shocked at what I just said and that it flew out of my mouth before I could even analyze it. Her eyes widen, and she holds her breath.

My heart pounds so violently, it becomes hard to inhale oxygen. Panic fills me. I've never told a woman I love them. Many have said it to me, but I've never responded and always ended things when they said it. Those words always suffocated me. Afraid Arianna now feels how those women made me feel, I blurt out, "Don't say it back. Let's go so we don't miss our reservation." I spin and lead her out of the room before she can read too deeply into it or freak out. With every step down the staircase, I curse myself for my delivery. Surely, I sprang this on her too soon in our relationship. And is it even possible for anyone to love a person without knowing them for years?

By the time we get into the SUV, my mind is spinning out. My palms sweat, and the earlier heat resumes in my body. Tension fills the air inside the vehicle as I struggle with what to say or do. I wipe my hands on my pants.

"Killian?" she softly says.

I take a calculated breath and turn toward her. "I'm sorry. I shouldn't have said it. Let's forget it and have a good night."

She furrows her eyebrows. Hurt laces her voice. "You didn't mean it?"

Do I not love her?

What does love mean?

How do I know?

I can't fathom going back to living without her. Is that love?

Avoiding the answer to her question, I clear my throat and repeat, "I shouldn't have said it. Sorry. I wasn't trying to put you in an uncomfortable situation."

Her expression drops further. "So you didn't mean it?"

I almost lie but stop myself. I broke rule number six once, and I promised her and myself I wouldn't ever again. You can't have trust with lies. I find my courage and decide to let the chips fall where they do. "No. I meant it. I do love you."

She tilts her head. "Then why are you acting so weird?"

"Am I?"

Her lips twitch. "Yeah."

I exhale deeply and confess, "Sorry. I haven't ever said it to anyone before."

Surprise fills her face. "Never?"

I shake my head. "No. But I have plenty of women who have said it to me, so I know I shouldn't have done that to you, and I'm—"

She puts her fingers over my lips. "Killian, stop talking."

I swallow hard and stare at her, wishing the blood would stop pounding between my ears.

She straddles me, putting her face an inch from mine. Golden flames drill into me, as if she can see my very soul. She orders, "Tell me again."

"I love you," I blurt out, and my stomach dives.

She kisses me. It's tender and sweet, and my body wraps around hers without thinking. I slide my hand to her head, keeping her positioned so she can't retreat even though she keeps deepening our kiss.

When she mumbles, "I love you, too," I almost don't hear it.

"What?" I ask then return to her blissful lips.

She ends our kiss and locks eyes with me. "I said I love you, too."

My lips twitch. "You do?"

"Yes."

I'm unsure why hearing her say those three words to me feels so damn good, but adrenaline surges through me like when I'm in the ring and the referee is holding up my arm as the victor in a fight. But no match can compare. Winning Arianna's love is better than a legacy of knockouts. It's the holy grail I didn't know existed.

She assaults my mouth with her tongue, as if it's a weapon, claiming me, ruining any chance I could ever quench my thirst for her. She takes my obsession and drills it so deep in my bones, it's never finding its way out.

When the SUV parks in front of the restaurant, I don't even notice. I'm too intoxicated by my wife's lips, hands, and curvy body. And all these emotions I've not felt before that are making me borderline giddy.

There's a knock on the window, and it pulls me out of my trance. I squeeze her ass, move her off me, then get out and lead her into the restaurant.

The hostess tells us it will be about fifteen minutes and to get a drink at the bar.

"Barolo?" I ask Arianna.

She nods while smiling, lighting me up further. "Sure. I'm going to go to the ladies' room. I'll be right back."

"I'll take you."

She motions to the busy bar. "There's a long line. Get the drinks. We have Ciro for that."

I glance at her father's bodyguard, who was in charge of Arianna's protection before she married me. "Okay." I peck her on the lips and pat her ass.

She leaves, and I stand in line for drinks. It takes several moments until I get to the front. I order her wine and a whiskey. The bartender hands me the glasses, and I pay, then put them on a tall pub table and wait.

An uncomfortable feeling starts to grow in my belly. I glance at my watch. The beeper the hostess gave me vibrates that our booth is ready. I go to the hostess stand, follow her, then put the drinks down. I continue toward the restrooms when a woman's scream fills the air. My walk turns into a run, and when I get to the corridor, Ciro is lying on the ground with blood pooling around his body. Slashes from a knife are in an X shape over his back. A blonde-haired lady is hysterically screaming.

I jump over the corpse and rush into the women's room, screaming, "Arianna!" but she's nowhere. When I get out of the bathroom, I look both ways and see there's another hallway. I run down it then bust through the exit door.

Fresh tracks are in the snow. A black car turns out of the alley, and my heart tears while my gut flips so fast, I get nauseous. I pull my phone out of my pocket and activate the tracer on Arianna's ring. Then I call Angelo.

"Killian?"

"Ciro is dead. That thug took her."

33

Arianna

Hammers slam into my skull. I open my eyes several times, but my lids are heavy. My mouth is so dry, I don't ever remember craving water so badly. I try to move, but my wrists and ankles have something tight on them, and there's no slack.

Nausea fills my belly, but I breathe through it and force my lids to stay open. The room is dark with barely any light. I turn my head and realize I'm lying down on a mattress. Thick, six-inch metal cuffs restrain my wrists.

Chills ricochet in my body, fighting the blood pumping harder through my veins. "Help," I attempt to get out, but my voice is so weak, I barely hear it.

A familiar hand strokes my cheek, and I freeze. Flashbacks of Killian saying he loves me, kissing him in the car, and going to the restroom pop up. I slowly turn and swallow hard.

Donato's dangerous, cold eyes penetrate through the darkness. His face sports a messy beard, unlike his normally trimmed one. His voice cuts through the air, rough and unforgiving. "You've been avoiding me."

My lips tremble, and I consider what to reply, but everything seems as if it might get me hurt. He glides his finger over my lips, and I shudder. I close my eyes, ordering myself not to release the tears on the brink of falling.

He leans closer, and his hot breath hits my cheek. "Did you miss me?"

I look at him and try to keep my voice calm. "Can you unchain me, please?"

His lips curl. "No. I like you better like this."

A new form of horror ignites. The quivering in my belly grows stronger. My voice cracks. "Please."

He drags the tip of his finger through my cleavage. It's something he used to do, and I liked it. Now, it makes my skin crawl, just like every time he speaks. "I was too good to you, Arianna. I played by your rules, but it wasn't exciting enough for you, was it?"

My rules? I don't know what he means.

"Ah, you want to pretend you don't understand me?"

"I don't," I blurt out.

He pulls out a knife and holds it under my chin. A sinister expression appears.

I gasp, trying to sink into the mattress, but there's nowhere to hide.

He repositions it so the sharp edge of the blade faces the ceiling. He slides it under the fabric of my dress and slowly slices through it, tearing several inches. "It's time we played by my rules." He tosses the knife on the ground then lunges over me until he's straddling my body.

I scream as he rips the fabric of my dress until it's no longer covering me, secured only by my arms.

He laughs then says, "If only your father could see you now."

The tears escape. "Is that why you dated me? To hurt my father?"

He leans down to my ear. "Did you think you meant something to me? Hmm?"

His admission hurts. I once again curse myself for not listening to my papà and brothers. All the parts of him I used to be attracted to appear so ugly right now, I'm not sure what I ever saw in him.

More terror erupts when he licks my lobe and murmurs, "But I'm going to enjoy getting my dick reacquainted with all the parts of your body."

"Let me go. Please," I cry out.

He chuckles in my ear, and his hands slide under my body, releasing the clasp of my bra.

"Stop. Please!"

"I'm not—"

The muffled bang explodes in the air, and the door bursts open. Killian comes flying into the room and yanks Donato off me. The next few minutes feel like they happen in slow motion as I watch the horrific scene evolve.

Killian's green eyes glow like an animal who's been caged for weeks and is finally let out. He pummels his fists, over and over, into Donato's face. Blood flies everywhere.

Any punch Donato attempts to make isn't strong enough to faze Killian. The hits landing on Killian's face only seem to add more fire to his rage. Slowly, there's no more fight left in Donato. His face is unrecognizable. Killian grabs his neck and yanks it.

A loud snap echoes in the room. Killian drops Donato's head and stares at him, breathing hard with blood covering his face so much, all I see are his green eyes.

Massimo and Dante run into the room. They attempt to release me but can't. All I can do is focus on Killian.

"Where are the keys?" Massimo shouts.

It seems to snap Killian out of his trance. He reaches into Donato's pocket and pulls them out then tosses them to my brother.

Within seconds, I'm unrestrained. Dante asks, "Arianna, what did he do to you?"

"Nothing." I attempt to move toward Killian.

He barks, "Get her out of here."

"What?" I question, confused and shocked.

"Now!" Killian demands.

Dante picks me up and carries me into the hallway. I don't know where we are, but it reminds me of my father's dungeon.

"Killian!" I cry out and attempt to push out of Dante's arms.

Dante holds me tighter and climbs upstairs. He opens another door, and fresh air hits me. I'm quickly put in my father's SUV. As soon as I'm inside, Dante shuts the door, and the locks go down.

I pound on the window as the SUV drives away. A blanket gets placed over my shoulders, and my papà's voice hits my ears. "Bambina, are you okay?"

I turn and realize he's in the car. "We need to go back. We can't leave them there."

He tugs me into his arms. They're warm and safe. I sink into them, instantly feeling guilty. My husband and brothers are still there. They need to be with me.

My papà says, "They know what they are doing. As soon as they can, they will come home. Arianna, what did he do to you?"

I glance up. "N-nothing."

"Your dress is ripped."

I look at it and shake my head. "Killian...he...he...umm..." I lose it and sob into my papà's chest.

He says nothing, stroking my hair and holding me tight. When we get home, he leads me to my bedroom and takes a bottle of water out of my mini-fridge. He goes into the bathroom and runs a hot bath.

"Where is Killian?" I ask, and new tears run down my cheeks.

He holds my face. In a stern voice, he replies, "Arianna, he will be here when he's finished."

"Doing what? He...he already killed Donato with his bare hands. There's nothing else to do," I insist.

A shadow of darkness moves into his orbs. "There is. When your husband returns, I'll let him answer your questions. Take a bath and drink this bottle of water. I'm calling our doctor to examine you."

"No. I'm fine."

Papà's hand covers my cheek. His eyes soften. "Do you remember him taking you?"

I slowly shake my head.

"You woke up groggy?"

More tears escape, and I nod.

"He drugged you, Arianna. I'm calling the doctor. Take a bath. I'll be in your bedroom if you need anything." He picks up four towels and puts them on the edge of the tub. "Make a pillow out of these." He turns to leave.

I tug on his arm. "Papà!"

He spins.

"Tell me Killian's coming back."

A small smile forms on his lips. "He's coming back. Now take your bath."

I obey. When my father calls out, "The doctor is here," I get out of the tub, dry off, and put my robe on.

Silvio, who's been our family doctor for years and always comes to the house, is sitting on the armchair across from my father. He rises and gives me a hug and kiss on the cheek.

His exam takes about an hour. He asks me tons of questions, draws my blood, and checks all my vitals. When he finishes, he says, "I'll have the blood sample rushed in the lab. My guess is he used chloroform."

Papà's face hardens, and he shakes Silvio's hand. "Thanks for coming."

"No problem. Arianna, drink lots of water and rest. If anything gets worse, let me know."

"Okay. Thank you."

Silvio leaves, and Papà escorts him through the house.

I sit on my bed, and all my worries about Killian come racing back. My papà returns and orders me to go to sleep, insisting Killian is fine.

I don't sleep though. For hours, I pace my room, wondering where he is. When the nighttime begins to turn into the morning light, my door finally opens.

When he walks in, he's freshly showered and wearing gray joggers and a white T-shirt. His face is bruised and slightly swollen. I sob into his chest, relieved like never before.

"Shh. Everything is okay, lass."

I glance up and place my hand on the side of his head. "Are you all right?"

"I'm fine. Are you? Your father said the doctor examined you, and that thug didn't..." He looks at the ceiling and sniffs hard.

"I'm fine. He didn't do anything."

Killian releases a breath, and when his eyes meet mine, they're glistening. "I'm sorry I didn't protect you."

"This isn't your fault!"

He clenches his jaw.

"Killian, what were you doing all night?"

He hesitates then finally says, "Rule number six, Arianna. You trust me, and I trust you."

"Yes. I do. And you can trust me."

"I do trust you. And it's why you aren't going to get upset when I tell you the only thing I'll say is there was stuff that needed to get cleaned up. Anything else could put you in danger." He intensely stares at me.

I freeze then ask, "Clean up, meaning you had to get rid of Donato's body?"

Unspoken words pass through his expression. When it's clear I'm correct, he tilts his head. He slides his finger across my forehead, tucking a lock of my hair behind my ear. "I want a do-over."

"For what?"

"Our date."

I smile. "I think it was going pretty good."

His lips twitch. "I don't strive for good. I come prepared to win."

I laugh. "Yes, you do."

He kisses me then retreats. "I'm starving. Your spray butter toast is sounding pretty good. What do you say we get some breakfast?"

I curl my finger for him to lean down. He does, and I whisper in his ear, "I had Luna pick some Irish butter up at the grocery yesterday."

His eyes sparkle. He palms my ass and declares, "I think you officially just became an O'Malley."

EPILOGUE

Killian

One Month Later

"I MADE A DECISION," ARIANNA DECLARES.

I shut my laptop and push my chair backward then pat the top of the table. "Give it to me."

She sits and says, "I've been overthinking things."

I arch my eyebrows. "What kind of things?"

"About my career."

"Didn't I tell you this last night?"

"Did you?"

I crawl my fingers up her inner thigh. "Yeah. Right before I made you my appetizer on this table."

Heat floods her cheeks, and she crosses her legs. She grabs my chin. "Focus."

I chuckle. "I'm listening. What are you overthinking?"

"Why do I have to pick social media over event planning? Why can't I use my skills I acquired on social media to market my event planning company?" Her face lights up, and the tug in my heart appears.

"See, I told you that you were smart."

"So I should go for it, then?"

"Start your own company?"

A hopeful, excited look fills her face. She bites her lip, wincing. "Is my own company too much without experience?"

"Not at all. You have all the experience you need. Any other skills, you'll learn. I think if it's what you want to do, you should go for it," I tell her.

"Really?"

"Yeah. Stop second-guessing it. Whatever you put your mind to, you'll excel at. And all the volunteer work and parties you planned for your father were preparation for you to win. It's perfect for you." Once I found out all the events Arianna put together for different charities, it was a no-brainer. I've been working on building her confidence so she takes the leap and goes for it. In secret, I've been preparing Angelo so he's nothing but supportive when she finally does feel ready.

She jumps off the table. "Okay. I'm going to do it, then!" She takes a few steps, and I grab her hand and rise.

"Where are you going?" I ask.

"I want to tell Gemma. She said she'd design a logo for me."

I wrap my arms around her. "Okay. When you finish talking to Gemma, pack a bag. I need you to put your business plans on hold for a few weeks."

Worry fills her face. "Why? Where are we going? Is something wrong?"

I try my best to keep a straight face. "Yep."

"What's going on?" she frets.

"I didn't take you on a proper honeymoon. I want a redo."

She freezes, gaping at me.

I chuckle. "You should see your face right now. And I haven't even told you where we're going."

"Where are we going?"

I unfasten a few of the buttons on her shirt and drag my finger across her collarbone. "Somewhere with cabanas, fruity drinks, and beachfront massages."

Excitement fills her voice. "Really?"

I lean down and kiss the curve of her neck. "Mmhmm. Our cabana is private. No one is allowed within fifty feet, except our server when I text him."

She laces her fingers around my neck. "What will we be doing in this cabana?"

I grin. "If memory serves me right, you give a mean massage while talking dirty."

She softly laughs. "Where are we going?"

"Hawaii."

Shock fills her face. "Seriously?"

"Yep."

She claps then kisses me. "I've always wanted to go there!"

"So you said." I glance at my watch. "We leave in two hours."

"Two hours!"

"Yep."

She spins. "On it!"

I follow her into the bedroom and remove our suitcases from the top shelf. It takes me fifteen minutes to pack. Arianna spends almost the entire two hours going back and forth between all her closets.

"You know I'm keeping you naked most of the time," I point out.

"Ha ha! Funny!"

"Who said I was joking?"

She shuts her suitcase and zips it. "All ready!"

"Just in time. Let's go before we miss the flight." I grab both our bags and wheel them to the car. I open the door, and Arianna gets inside the back.

Tiernan opens the trunk. I don't miss the empty look in his eyes, which usually has life in them. It's only been a month since Fergal's death, and Tiernan was the closest with him. I put my hand on his shoulder. "You doing okay?"

"Yep," he says, avoiding me and putting the suitcase in the trunk. "Is it only these two bags?"

"Yeah."

He shuts the trunk and walks to the driver's door.

I follow him. "Hey. Uncle Patrick said you haven't been to the gym."

He spins. "Since when do you keep tabs on me?"

I sigh. Everything about Tiernan right now reminds me of when my father and Sean died. He's pissed off, and I don't blame him. I debate about pushing him but end up ordering, "Get back in the gym. It'll help."

"I'm fine." He gets in the car and slams the door.

Unsure what else to do right now, I slide in next to Arianna. She asks, "He's not doing any better, is he?"

I pull her onto my lap, not wanting her to stress about anything. She feels guilty Fergal died. No matter how much I reiterate it's not her fault, she can't seem to stop taking the blame. "It's just going to take time."

My phone rings, and I glance at it. "Nolan, make it fast. We're on the way to the airport."

"Stop by my house."

"Why?"

"Not over the phone."

My gut dives. "Be there in two." I press the button for the divider glass. "Tiernan, stop at Nolan's first."

He says nothing, turns down the street, and in under a minute, I'm standing on Nolan's doorstep. His face is pale. He says, "Arianna, Gemma's inside."

She glances between us and goes into the house.

"What's going on?" I ask.

Nolan steps outside and shuts the door. He lowers his voice. "I take it you haven't been to Declan's?"

The hairs on my arms rise. "No. Why?"

Nolan crosses his arms. "He found out who's releasing those articles."

I gaze behind me and step closer. "Who is the bastard?"

Nolan sniffs hard. "A woman. He kidnapped her, and he said he's not letting her go."

READ DEVIANT HACKER- FREE ON KINDLE UNLIMITED

SIMONA

A Mafia Underboss Kidnapped Me.

The moment Declan O'Malley laid eyes on me the universe shifted. His inked muscles, seductive confidence, and bad boy vibes lured me to him. He's twice my age. He's experienced.

Now I'm in a dark cell. Bound. Cold. Helpless.

He's determined to turn me into his obedient little captive until I convince him I've told him the truth.

The spark burns hotter, the hunger between us electric.

When he demands I call him daddy, more confusion reigns over me.

I should hate him, instead of wanting to submit.

Yet all I crave is his deviant touch.

READ DEVIANT HACKER- FREE ON KINDLE UNLIMITED

DECLAN

DEVIANT HACKER PROLOGUE

Declan O'Malley

There's no hiding from the truth. It's something I've believed my entire life and still do. Yet the day I stepped into who I really was and embraced my true O'Malley roots, I learned a hard lesson.

My entire life, my moral compass had been a lie. I was a killer and not just any kind. I could extend a man's life until he was begging me to steal his last breath. Every second of torturing him, I got off on. All I could see is the wrong he had done. I became the judge, jury, and executioner.

There was no going back. Once I started, I couldn't stop. The same holds true now. If a man harms my family, there's no limit to what I will do to avenge his wrongdoing.

Rules and boundaries no longer exist. The deeper I sink into my family's issues, the more I only care about making sure our clan is protected. Any enemy we have, we're clear on, and I'm prepared at all times to take them down.

I never lose sleep over it, except for now. For the first time, I don't know who our enemy is.

Several months have passed since an anonymous reporter has been publishing stories about Jack Christian's company. It went public, and we've been implementing the plan Liam and Finn concocted in prison to bankrupt it. We shorted the stock, so we'll make money when the price drops, but whoever this reporter is, they're intentionally trying to destroy everything we've orchestrated.

I've hacked into every server I can to find out who this guy is that is derailing the billions we planned on making. It leads me nowhere. He's a ghost, and night after night he stays hidden.

Every financial news outlet he posts his articles on, I'm tracking. The wall of my office is covered in computer screens with real-time data coming in. All I keep doing is digging, trying to find something to lead me to him.

It always led me to more dead ends—until tonight.

It's around three in the morning. The screen on the wall beeps, and a new article gets uploaded. I trace the location of the guy's IP address.

"Got you!"

I practically run to the wall and peer closer. The location is an apartment building sixteen blocks away. I snap a photo of the location with my phone, and the location disappears.

I have to give this bastard some credit. He knows what he's doing and is a master at covering his tracks. But not this time. I've found him, and he's going to pay for harming my family.

I grab my bag from the garage shelf and get in my SUV.

My heart races the entire time I'm driving. It's pouring down rain, dark, and there is barely any traffic. When I get to the apartment, I switch my tracker on my phone. It'll pinpoint exactly where this guy is from his IP address that I now have.

Blood slams into my skull, and adrenaline pumps harder, racing through my veins. I open my bag and put chloroform on a rag, then shove it in my coat pocket. Whoever this guy is, he's going to die by my hands, but not until I torture every last piece of information he has out of him. I slide my black gloves on and get out of the car.

The apartment complex is in a dangerous neighborhood and rough. The lock to the front door of the building is busted, and I walk right in. There are no security cameras which only makes my job easier.

I climb three flights of stairs. When I get to the unit, I pick the lock. It's cheap and only takes a few seconds. I slowly turn the knob and creep through the apartment.

It's cold as if the heat isn't on. Everything is dark like outside, except for one room that has a green glow. I make sure I don't make a noise and peek past the door frame.

Several computer screens sit on a table. The guy wears a black hoodie. He types quickly. Even from the back of him, I can tell he's smaller than me. I'm not going to have any issue carrying him out of here. I grip the chloroform rag and slide it out of my pocket along with the cloth bag I brought.

I sneak behind him, put the bag over his head, and cover his mouth with the chloroform.

He attempts to struggle but quickly passes out. His laptop is connected to the screens so I yank the cords and shove it in my backpack. Then I remove the dark blanket out of my backpack, wrap it around him, and toss his limp body over my shoulder. I leave the building the same way I came, feeling fortunate it's raining so hard, and this guy doesn't weigh a ton.

I leave him wrapped in the blanket, put him in my back seat, and am back in my garage within a few minutes.

I've never taken anyone I kidnapped to my house before. But I've stewed over this for months.

My assumption is this isn't our typical enemy. Whoever this guy is, he's smart. He knows things about us, or he wouldn't be doing this. Or, someone is paying him, and that's an entire other scenario that may require just as much interrogation. Plus, he might have some skills I don't. If so, he's going to show me before I kill him.

Night after night, I've obsessed over this guy, wanting to know who he is, why he's messing with my family, and who else may be behind this. He's screwed with the wrong person. And I've prepared for this dickhead. I turned a small part of my basement into a cell. I'll keep him alive for months and torture him daily if needed.

I sling him over my shoulder once again and enter my house. I go down the basement steps and into the cell. There's a cheap mattress on the ground and a toilet. I installed restraints in the cement block wall. Nothing else exists.

My pulse continues to increase. I lay him on the mattress, unwrap the blanket, and clasp the cuffs around his thin wrists.

Jesus, does this guy eat?

Maybe he's only a teenager?

My stomach flips at the thought, but then I remind myself he's screwing with my family. I take a deep breath, ready to see who this man is who has the balls to try and fuck the O'Malleys.

I slide the hood off his face and freeze.

Am I seeing things?

My heart beats so fast I clutch it, staring down at a young woman.

Not just any woman.

A lass with the face of an angel. A co-ed who has been in the pub, sitting on my lap, and flirting with me.

She never came back. All these months, I've looked for her, but she's never again appeared.

She's innocent.

She can't be. She has intentionally been sabotaging our family.

She stirs, and a small whimper fills the air. I continue to stare, in a trance, fixated on whoever this creature is in front of me, chained to my wall.

Her blue eyes flutter open. When she fully comes to, she recognizes me, and fear registers all over her face. She tries to move her arms then realizes she's trapped. In a desperate move, she tries to kick me in the balls.

My instincts take over. I lunge on top of her, pinning her further to the mattress and stopping her from having any ability to move her legs.

It's the wrong move. Heat creeps into her porcelain cheeks, the same way it did when I flirted with her in the pub. A lock of her dark hair falls on her face and I force myself not to tuck it behind her ear. Her hot breath merges with mine, and I curse myself for getting a hard-on. She glances at my lips then repins her frightened gaze on me.

I jump off her, race upstairs, and pour three fingers of whiskey, downing it in three mouthfuls.

Jesus. How can it be her?

I should take her to Liam and have him deal with her.

No. She sought me out at the pub. She's not going anywhere until I find out every single thing about her.

I sit down at the computer. For the rest of the night, I watch her through the cameras I installed earlier this past week. It may be dark in the cell, but the system I installed makes it look like the lights are on. Every move she makes I see. I wonder who she is and why she came into my pub. If Finn hadn't killed a man and Liam hadn't come to get Killian and I that night, there's no doubt I would have asked her out. I would have refrained from taking her home that evening until I took her on a nice date first.

Did she even tell me her real name?

Several minutes pass and she looks directly at the camera. Those same damn eyes that got me at the pub register on my screen. I peer closer, mesmerized by her and wondering how I'm going to get the information I need.

She's a woman. I've never hurt any female before.

She's the enemy, I remind myself. But then I think about all the ways I'd get information out of a man. Everything makes me cringe when I consider doing it to her.

By the time morning comes, I'm no less conflicted and there aren't any solutions. My only hope is she'll break easily from the mere suggestion of pain. I avoid thinking about what I'll do if she doesn't.

I'm in over my head. I should call my brothers, Liam, or Finn and have them weigh in on what to do about this situation.

Yet I don't. All I do is continue to stare at my enemy with an angel's face.

ALL IN BOXSET

Three page-turning, interconnected stand-alone romance novels with HEA's!! Get ready to fall in love with the characters. Billionaires. Professional athletes. New York City. Twist, turns, and danger lurking everywhere. The only option for these couples is to go ALL IN...with a little help from their friends. EXTRA STEAM INCLUDED!

Grab it now! READ FREE IN KINDLE UNLIMITED!

CAN I ASK YOU A HUGE FAVOR?

Would you be willing to leave me a review?

I would be forever grateful as one positive review on Amazon is like buying the book a hundred times! Reader support is the lifeblood for Indie authors and provides us the feedback we need to give readers what they want in future stories!

Your positive review means the world to me! So thank you from the bottom of my heart!

CLICK TO REVIEW

MORE BY MAGGIE COLE

Mafia Wars - A Dark Mafia Series (Series Five)

Ruthless Stranger (Maksim's Story) - Book One

Broken Fighter (Boris's Story) - Book Two

Cruel Enforcer (Sergey's Story) - Book Three

Vicious Protector (Adrian's Story) - Book Four

Savage Tracker (Obrecht's Story) - Book Five

Unchosen Ruler (Liam's Story) - Book Six

Perfect Sinner (Nolan's Story) - Book Seven

Brutal Defender (Killian's Story) - Book Eight

Deviant Hacker (Declan's Story) - Book Nine

Relentless Hunter (Finn's Story) - Book Ten

Behind Closed Doors (Series Four - Former Military Now International Rescue Alpha Studs)

Depths of Destruction - Book One

Marks of Rebellion - Book Two

Haze of Obedience - Book Three

Cavern of Silence - Book Four

Stains of Desire - Book Five

Risks of Temptation - Book Six

Together We Stand Series (Series Three - Family Saga)

Kiss of Redemption- Book One

Sins of Justice - Book Two

Acts of Manipulation - Book Three

Web of Betrayal - Book Four

Masks of Devotion - Book Five

Roots of Vengeance - Book Six

It's Complicated Series (Series Two - Chicago Billionaires)

Crossing the Line - Book One

Don't Forget Me - Book Two

Committed to You - Book Three

More Than Paper - Book Four

Sins of the Father - Book Five

Wrapped In Perfection - Book Six

All In Series (Series One - New York Billionaires)

The Rule - Book One

The Secret - Book Two

The Crime - Book Three

The Lie - Book Four

The Trap - Book Five

The Gamble - Book Six

STAND ALONE NOVELLA

JUDGE ME NOT - A Billionaire Single Mom Christmas Novella

ABOUT THE AUTHOR

Amazon Bestselling Author

Maggie Cole is committed to bringing her readers alphalicious book boyfriends. She's been called the "literary master of steamy romance." Her books are full of raw emotion, suspense, and will always keep you wanting more. She is a masterful storyteller of contemporary romance and loves writing about broken people who rise above the ashes.

She lives in Florida near the Gulf of Mexico with her husband, son, and dog. She loves sunshine, wine, and hanging out with friends.

Her current series were written in the order below:

- All In (Stand alones with entwined characters)
- It's Complicated (Stand alones with entwined characters)
- Together We Stand (Brooks Family Saga - read in order)
- Behind Closed Doors (Read in order)
- Mafia Wars (Coming April 1st 2021)

Maggie Cole's Newsletter
Sign up here!

Hang Out with Maggie in Her Reader Group
Maggie Cole's Romance Addicts

Follow for Giveaways
Facebook Maggie Cole

Instagram
@maggiecoleauthor

Tik Tok
https://www.tiktok.com/@authormaggiecole?

Complete Works on Amazon
Follow Maggie's Amazon Author Page

Book Trailers
Follow Maggie on YouTube

Are you a Blogger and want to join my ARC team?
Signup now!

Feedback or suggestions?

Email: authormaggiecole@gmail.com

twitter.com/MaggieColeAuth
instagram.com/maggiecoleauthor
bookbub.com/profile/maggie-cole
amazon.com/Maggie-Cole/e/B07Z2CB4HG

Made in United States
Orlando, FL
17 May 2023

33207379R00274